P9-CRV-019

THE STOLEN JEW

BY JAY NEUGEBOREN

Big Man
Listen Ruben Fontanez
Corky's Brother
Parentheses: An Autobiographical Journey
Sam's Legacy
An Orphan's Tale
The Story of STORY Magazine: A Memoir (as editor)
The Stolen Jew

JAY NEUGEBOREN

THE STOLEN JEW

Holt, Rinehart and Winston *New York*

Published by Holt, Rinehart and Winston, 383 Madison Avenue, New York, New York 10017.
Published simultaneously in Canada by Holt, Rinehart and Winston of Canada, Limited.

Library of Congress Cataloging in Publication Data
Neugeboren, Jay.
The stolen Jew.
I. Title.
PZ4.N484St [PS3564.E844] 813'.54 80–19019
ISBN 0–03–056223–6

Portions of this novel have appeared, in somewhat different form, in The Atlantic Monthly, TriQuarterly, Ploughshares, Present Tense, Confrontation, Shenandoah, *and* National Jewish Monthly.

First Edition

Designer: Joy Chu
Printed in the United States of America
1 3 5 7 9 10 8 6 4 2

FOR JEAN FRANKLIN

The author is grateful to the
John Simon Guggenheim Memorial Foundation
for a fellowship given him while
he was writing this novel.

One
ON A BEACH NEAR HERZLIA
1

Two
THE STOLEN JEW
91

Three
SECRETS
227

Four
HOME
309

ONE

ON A BEACH NEAR HERZLIA

◇ 1 ◇

On the day that his brother Nachman died, Nathan Malkin, a wealthy sixty-four-year-old American, was walking along the beach of a nature sanctuary in Israel. He did not find out about his brother's death until five days later, when he returned to his home in Ein Karem, a small village near Jerusalem, and found the telegram waiting. Nathan's wife, Pauline, had died seven years before, of brain cancer. Their only son, Ira, a professor of physics at Columbia University, had died two years later, from knife wounds received when he came to the aid of an old woman being mugged on a subway train. Nathan knew that the newspaper reports were accurate when they stated that Ira's body lay on the floor of the IRT downtown local in a pool of blood all the way from the 116th Street stop to 23rd Street before help was summoned. The assailant was never found. The woman whom Ira saved, senile at the time, was still alive at the age of ninety-one, in the Jewish Nursing Home of Far Rockaway. Every year, just before Rosh Hashanah, Nathan received greeting cards from each of her two daughters.

Nathan had been drawn to the nature sanctuary not by its beauty, which meant little to him, but by the fact that a young American woman, Gail Rubin, had, several weeks before, on a morning in March, walked on the beach there, near Herzlia, searching for wildlife to photograph. That she should discover instead, a writer for *The Jerusalem Post* had written, Arab terrorists who had landed secretly; that they should question her and decide she would be dangerous to them if allowed to live; and that the events from that moment on, in Israel and then in Lebanon, had become ever bloodier—thirty-seven dead and eighty-two wounded, the worst civilian atrocities in Israel's history—was, the writer had concluded, one of those ironies that tax human understanding. Nathan did not agree. He found no ironies in the situation, nothing that taxed his understanding of life.

But the story stayed with him, irritated him. Gail Rubin's cameras, the newspapers noted, were found in the sand, next to her body, and that fact took hold of Nathan's imagination. Well, he said to himself. If they left the cameras, then they were not muggers, were they? Nobody could call them muggers. But after he had put away the newspaper, he found that he could not stop thinking about the young American woman walking on the beach at dawn; he could not stop seeing a picture in his head, as if it had been printed in the newspaper: a close-up of half-buried black-and-silver cameras, of unmoving white sand, and of a black shoulder strap resting across the smooth tanned skin of the young woman's ankle.

He was also aware, at once, that he was thinking of things he did not want to think about, of things he had been able, for the most part since his arrival in Israel, to put out of mind: of Ira, and of Ira's death; of Pauline, and of her gruesome last months; and, worst of all, of the years that lay in wait for him. Nathan's own father, despite a life plagued with unhappiness and failure, had died in his sleep at the age of seventy-nine; his mother, a vain woman who complained daily of the suffering life brought to her, had passed away peacefully, while ironing, a year and a half later, at the age of seventy-seven. Nathan himself was, as always, in excellent health. He had never smoked. He was not a drinker. He ate only because he had to. Only four months before, in Jerusalem, his doctor had told him with admiration that he had the heart and lungs and circulation of a man of forty. He might then, he realized, live for another twenty or thirty years.

The thought was for Nathan as depressing as it was inspiring. He had little interest in living. But to bow his head and bend his back before the tragedies life brought—before that force he referred to, in his mind, as the Maker of the Universe—was, in his own private decalogue, the most forbidden of acts. When he awoke each morning and knew that he was still in the world, he felt for an instant the same acute bitterness he had felt in the moment in which he had learned of Ira's death; to submit or surrender, then, he felt, would somehow lend too much reality to evil and to chance; it would bring dishonor to the lives of his wife and son. It was as if, he often thought, he had decided to stay alive precisely because life was senseless, precisely because he had such a distaste for it; it was as if he had determined to live on for as long as he could merely to spite the Maker of the Universe.

To this end, and until the day upon which he read of Gail Rubin's death, his life in Ein Karem suited him. There, though surrounded by Jews—though living in the midst of a people whose lives, without exception, had been touched with extraordinary loss (after the Yom Kippur War, he read, one out of every three Israelis personally knew a soldier who had been killed)—he knew nobody, he had made no friends. The village of Ein Karem, made up of ancient Arab houses whose stone walls were several feet thick, was stunningly beautiful, as no other in Israel, yet he was indifferent to this beauty. He liked the village because, in it, he was left alone. He ate, he gardened, he swam, he took long walks, he watched television, he listened to music, and he read. On Tuesdays and Thursdays he took the bus into Jerusalem, where he worked as a volunteer for the United Israel Appeal, doing clerical work. In the bureau to which, at his request, he had been assigned, he helped process forms relating to the immigration of Jews from the Soviet Union. He was asleep by 9:30 each night and his sleep was deep and easy, a continuing proof to him that against Nathan Malkin the Maker of the Universe would not, for some time yet, emerge victorious.

In this way, and until the day upon which eleven Arab terrorists came ashore in rubber rafts near Kibbutz Maagen Mikhael and murdered Gail Rubin, the years passed as he wished them to pass. After that day, however, his peace disturbed, the good life he believed he had found in Israel seemed gone. When a few weeks went by and Nathan saw that he could not get the young woman out of his mind—that the picture, and the thoughts stimulated by the picture, would not go away—he decided to visit the place where she had been struck down. Then, he told himself, he would believe it. For the strange part of his obsession, he had come to realize, was that he was not able to accept the fact of Gail Rubin's death.

Whenever he saw the photo in his head—of the half-buried cameras, and the sand, and her skin—he found that he was seeing himself also, walking along the same beach, searching for her; and when, within this picture, he looked closely into his own eyes, he saw that he was hoping the newspapers had somehow erred—he was hoping to see the young woman coming toward him from an opposite direction, barefoot and smiling, her sandals in one hand, her cameras slung over her shoulder;

and whenever he imagined this scene, he would recall that five years before, in the first instant in which the news had been given to him, he had believed fully in the fact of his own son's death.

It was almost, he had often thought since, as if he had foreseen that death. No news, in such a life, could surprise him. He had nodded in a way that signified he was learning nothing new; and in that first instant, he recalled, he had known what his decision would be: he had seen himself selling out his interest to his partners; he had seen himself boarding the airplane; he had seen himself inside the darkened plane, high above the endless oceans; he had seen himself going through customs; he had seen himself—a stranger in a strange land—walking through the streets of a small village in Israel.

He had gone to the city morgue and identified his son; he had sat all night with the body while members of the *Chevra Kedisha* chanted prayers; he had let the rabbi slit the collar of his suit with a razor; he had recited *Kaddish* and shoveled earth onto the pine box that was lowered into the ground, alongside the clean gray stone that, a year before, had been installed to mark his wife's grave. He had sat *shiva* for a week and had received condolences. He had listened to words and to weeping and to wailing. There is a word for a child who loses a parent, the rabbi had eulogized, and a word for a husband who loses a wife, and for a wife who loses a husband. But there is no word, so terrible is the loss, for a parent who loses a child. Nathan was unmoved by the rabbi's words. In his heart he felt only coldness and rage.

When he announced his decision, nobody opposed him. They understood the strength of his will. Within two days of getting up from *shiva*, he and his partners—they were manufacturers of women's coats—and their lawyers had worked out an agreement that assured him of enough money to last him the rest of his life. Nothing required him to live on in America, the land of his father's dreams, the land to which his father had come with his young bride almost seventy years before. When Nathan Malkin flew out from Kennedy Airport, five weeks after Ira's death, he took with him only clothing and books; he felt that he was leaving nothing behind, and that he would never return.

WHEN NATHAN CAME BACK TO HIS HOME IN EIN KAREM AND FOUND THE telegram from his sister-in-law Rachel waiting, informing him of his brother's death, and when he realized that the funeral had already taken place, and that his only brother was gone and in the ground, something in him gave way. He relented. As he held the telegram in his hands and looked at the bare stone walls that were his home, he remembered the first time he had ever seen his brother. He remembered opening the door to his own bedroom in Brooklyn and seeing his mother there, sitting in the middle of the small room, holding the blue woolen blanket within which his new brother lay. He remembered how beautiful his mother looked, with sunlight streaming in upon her from the side window. He remembered staring at the motes of dust that floated lightly toward Nachman. He remembered watching Nachman suckling at his mother's breast. *Come to me,* his mother had said, in a voice so gentle he had not recognized it, and she had reached out to him with her free hand. He remembered the softness of his brother's skin.

He did not telephone or send a telegram. Instead, he took the bus to Ben-Gurion Airport and bought a ticket on the first available plane going to New York. He wondered, during the flight, if he would have come home had he not gone to the nature sanctuary; for had he received the telegram in time to have been there for Nachman's funeral, he did not believe he would have come. He also found within himself a great desire to telephone Gail Rubin's parents, who lived in New York, and he tried to imagine what he might say to them: that he felt for them? that he had visited the spot upon which their daughter had died? that he knew, from the newspapers, that Gail was a shy and introverted young woman who lived alone with two dogs, and one cat? that he knew she was planning to return to New York to help celebrate her father's seventy-fifth birthday?

Awake on the plane, while others around him slept, he imagined Gail Rubin's parents inviting him for dinner. He imagined himself telling them of his life in Israel, and of the deaths of his own wife and son. He imagined them showing him scrapbooks, containing photographs of their daughter, and clippings from the many photographic essays she had published in magazines. And then he imagined silence. He imagined that they would have nothing to say to each other, and that he would be sorry he had come. He concluded that there was nothing he could do for them, except to cause them more pain.

In the semidarkness of the airplane's interior he recalled his mother's voice, mocking him from behind, as he sat at his desk, writing. *Another Tolstoy!* she had sneered. *Another Tolstoy.* He did not turn around. *No Momma,* Nachman had said then. *Nathan will be greater than Tolstoy!* Their mother had laughed then, and pressed Nachman to her bosom.

She had praised him for being so full of love for his brother. Another Tolstoy, Nathan thought. When Tolstoy's own brother Dmitry died, the brother to whom he had felt most close, Tolstoy refused to go to the funeral. Instead, he dressed and went out to a reception, and then to the theater. Dmitry the pure, Nathan thought—not so unlike his famous brother—visiting prisons and fasting and caring for the sick. Abstinence had been his great pleasure. Dmitry the pure, Nathan thought—propped up on pillows in a foul garret, spitting blood into a handkerchief, drinking tea brewed for him by Masha, the prostitute he had purchased from a brothel, the only woman he had ever known. Nachman would have been amused by the comparison, Nathan knew. *Another Tolstoy,* he heard Nachman say. *Didn't I tell you?* He could see Nachman smiling up at him, from the grave.

THE TAXI DRIVER LET HIM OUT IN HIS OLD BROOKLYN NEIGHBORHOOD, AT the corner of Nostrand Avenue and Linden Boulevard. Nathan took his suitcase and paid the driver. The driver looked at the suitcase and warned Nathan to be careful. The neighborhood was dangerous. Nathan nodded and walked away. He crossed the street. The red-brick apartment houses along both sides of Linden Boulevard looked the same to him—solid and imposing—but Nostrand Avenue, where he had walked with his brother only a few years before, seemed like a war-ravaged street. The windows of shops were smashed or boarded up, refuse was strewn everywhere, the streets and sidewalks were torn up, broken, scarred. It looked worse to him than streets in Israeli cities looked after terrorist bombings.

Nathan watched an elderly black man stuff his garbage into a mailbox. He watched two teen-age girls run across the street, portable radios swinging at their sides. Several black men and women, brightly colored bandannas on their heads, sat on the steps in front of Rachel's building, staring ahead sleepily. Nathan entered the lobby, and inhaled the odors of urine and rotting garbage. Nachman had been a fool, he decided. He could have moved. As part of the settlement, Nathan had arranged for his partners to give Nachman a good job—to sell Nachman's music store for him—but Nachman had, as always, been too proud to accept the gift.

"Hey man, shine your shoes?"

A thin dark-skinned boy of thirteen or fourteen, one eye red and swollen, stood next to Nathan. Nathan started up the stairs.

"Your shoes real dirty, man."

"Go away."

"Hey man, don't be a fag-ass—"

The boy snatched at Nathan's suitcase, but Nathan's grip was like iron. He lifted the suitcase and slammed it against the boy's head so that the boy fell down the stairs.

"Go away," Nathan said.

"You're dead, man," the boy called. "My brother gone to fix you good. You'll see. He gone to fix you up good—"

"Go away," Nathan said, and he continued up the stairs, to the third-floor landing.

He knocked on Rachel's door and entered. He walked down the long dark corridor. Everything seemed the same as it had been five years before. The warm rich fragrances—of food, of furniture, of old rugs, he supposed—reminded him of the house in which he and Nachman had grown up, a few blocks away. The living room was crowded with people, and despite the fact that they were there on a *shiva* call—to console Rachel, to pay their respects—the atmosphere seemed festive: people were laughing and chattering and eating; the light seemed excessively bright; the colors—bowls of fruit, boxes of candy, handsome clothing—were intensely vivid. A white sheet was draped over the mirror behind the couch. The piano was covered with two old army blankets. In a glass on the windowsill, a *yahrzeit* candle flickered. Nathan stood in the doorway, holding his suitcase. Nathan's two sisters—Rivka and Leah—were there, he saw, as were their husbands. Rivka and Leah lived in Florida now. Nathan had no desire to see his sisters; he had no desire to comfort them or to be comforted by them. He felt very warm, and he took a step backward, into the darkness of the hallway. He heard a faint roaring inside his head, as if he were pressing seashells against his ears.

Rachel sat in front of the couch on a wooden bench, holding the hand of her son, Michael. Michael's wife, Ruth, sat next to them. Ah, Nathan thought. Michael! My talented and wonderful Michael! My lovely Ruth! Michael was a psychiatrist. He had not, Nathan told himself, thinking of Nachman's hospitalizations, been afraid to succeed where his own father had failed. He was wearing sneakers. Rachel wore slippers. Nathan had to give Michael credit. Michael had always been strong—stronger than Ira. Rachel laughed, and she touched Michael's cheek gently, with the backs of her fingers. Ruth smiled, and when she did Nathan thought of Gail Rubin. He wished, suddenly, that he and Michael were alone so that he could tell Michael everything he knew about Gail Rubin. Rachel looked up, toward Nathan, but she did not seem to realize who he was.

"I'm here," Nathan said, and when he spoke he felt childish, as if he were a little boy.

Then Rachel stood, and gasped. "*Nathan!*"

She came to him at once and embraced him, and he found that he was returning her embrace and, as she wept upon his shoulder, as her warm wet cheek pressed against his own, that tears began to well in his own eyes. He heard his sisters' voices and knew that their hands were touching him also, but it hardly mattered. They could do what they wanted. It was all the same to him.

"I'm sorry," he said to her. "I'm very sorry, Rachel. So many years." The room was silent. Now Nathan heard nothing but the sound of Rachel's sobbing and of his own voice, trying to soothe her. His sisters left him alone. "I came as soon as I could. I was away when the telegram arrived, staying in a kibbutz near Herzlia for a few days, or—"

"Shh," she said, putting a finger to her lips. "You don't have to explain. Shh . . ."

LATER, WHEN ALL THE FRIENDS AND RELATIVES WERE GONE AND HE WAS alone in the guest bedroom, the room that had been Michael's when he was a boy, Nathan realized how comfortable he felt in Rachel's apartment. When, to the question of where he was going to stay, Rachel had replied that he would, of course, stay with her, he had been surprised to find that he had not wanted to object. He had looked to Michael for approval, and Michael had smiled in a way that made Nathan feel that it was all right to say yes. Harvey, Rivka's husband, had wagged a finger at him then—everybody was in a cheerful mood once again—and asked him if he had come all the way from the Holy Land to claim his bride. Nathan was puzzled at first, and Harvey, a know-it-all accountant whom Nathan had always despised, explained that it was a biblical law—that the brother of a dead man must, if unmarried, marry the widow. It was called a levirate marriage, and Harvey, in his unctuous manner, began explaining to the room some of the reasons the rabbis gave for this ancient law: to avert the calamity of a family line becoming extinct, to prevent a man's name from perishing and his property going to others. Nathan listened carefully. Harvey reminded Nathan of his own Uncle Harry —the husband of his mother's sister Zlata—whom he had hated when he was a boy.

Michael, seeing how embarrassed his mother was, tried to change the subject by asking Nathan about his life in Israel, about his work, but

Harvey only laughed and told Michael not to protect everybody so much, that he was only teasing, why should everybody get so upset? "The law does not apply to Rachel," Nathan said then. "If you will look carefully into Deuteronomy, you will note that the law applies only to the widow of a brother who has died childless."

"My brother the rabbi," Rivka commented, and she laughed in a way that made Nathan feel very cold.

Nathan sat on the edge of the bed, in his brown cotton pajamas. The Comanche Indians had the same law, Harvey had continued, so what, he wanted to know, did it all prove? Nathan pushed Harvey's voice from his mind and thought of his son, Ira—his brilliant and sweet Ira—measuring the sun. Before his death, Ira was performing experiments that had to do with measuring the size of the sun, with determining the degree to which the sun departed from being a perfect sphere. It was somewhat flat at the top and the bottom—like an orange, Ira said. If his hypothesis were correct, and his figures turned out the way he thought they would, Nathan recalled Ira saying, then a portion of Einstein's general theory of relativity would have to be called into question. Well, Nathan thought. My son measured the sun. My son measured the sun.

He lay down and covered himself, and he thought of his son's face—eager and intense, like the face of a young boy—trying to explain things, showing Nathan, at his office in Mudd Hall, the precision instruments he had been designing—and when Nathan remembered the instruments he thought also of Gail Rubin's cameras. Gail Rubin was thirty-nine. Had Ira lived, he would now be forty. Ira had never married. Gail Rubin had never married. If I call Gail Rubin's parents, he thought, perhaps something can still be arranged. Why not?

He closed his eyes and chided himself for his bitterness. His bitterness—what good could it do? He heard no roaring sound inside his head now. He put Gail Rubin out of mind and thought instead of Hanoch Tel-Oren, an American who had once served in the U.S. Navy. Hanoch too had come to Israel from America. On the same day that Gail Rubin was wandering along the beach in Maagen Mikhael, Hanoch and his family were driving south from Haifa. Hanoch and his wife, who played first and second flute with the Israel Philharmonic Orchestra, had seven children. While Gail Rubin lay dead in the sand, one of Hanoch's sons, Imri, a fourteen-year-old boy who, the newspapers reported, was a good basketball player and played clarinet in the Jerusalem youth orchestra, was killed in his father's car by a terrorist bullet. Nathan found that he felt more for the father than for the son. The father's hand had been shot off. He could never play the flute again, and Nathan wondered what, if he could no longer make music, he would do for the rest of his life. Be a listener? A grandfather?

"Tell me," Leah had asked, when they were alone for a moment in the kitchen. "You don't have to answer me, but I was hoping for it ever since you left, Nathan—that maybe, all by yourself in Israel, that maybe you might find the time to write again. But if you don't want to tell me—"

"I'm not writing again," Nathan had said; then, seeing the hurt look in Leah's eyes, he had touched her arm with his fingers, and added, "But I've been reading a lot. I still like to read. I read more now than I ever did."

Nathan sighed. Rachel's friends and family—and even his own sisters—had, he realized, been truly happy to see him. Nobody seemed to hold it against him that Nachman had died and that he was still alive. It was so unlike Leah—shy and fearful Leah—to dare to mention his book, or to ask him about his writing. Why? If Rivka had asked him—if any of the others had mentioned *The Stolen Jew*—he would not have been surprised. But nobody else had. Instead they had asked him questions about Israel—about the Yom Kippur War, about hotels in Jerusalem and Tel Aviv and Haifa, about the exchange rate and terrorist attacks and the black market. He told them what he knew—about Ein Karem, of the work he did for the United Israel Appeal. Michael smiled. He would be going to Moscow in a few months, he informed Nathan—to try to make contact with Jews there, and in Leningrad. He was working for the National Conference on Soviet Jewry. Nathan leaned toward Michael, eager to hear more. Is it true? he had asked.

"Sure it's true, Uncle Nat," Ruth said. She bent close to him, and whispered into his ear: "Michael wants to be a hero."

Then she stood and left the room. Rachel told Michael to go after her, but he refused. He told Nathan that he was thinking of spending a year in Israel, after his return from Russia. He was making arrangements to work at Hadassah Hospital. Nathan told Michael that, when he took walks along the paths that led from Ein Karem, he could see Hadassah Hospital on one of the mountains that overlooked his village.

Was I a good father? He saw himself sitting in the living room, surrounded by voices and noise, and he saw how much he had wanted to ask Michael this question. *Was I a good father to Ira?* He saw Michael smiling down at him and in Michael's smile he sensed an invitation:

perhaps, if there were still enough time, he might talk with Michael—he might be able to give Michael all the memories and stories he had carried with him from Israel. Michael was a good listener. Like Nachman. Nachman had been a good listener too. Nathan remembered sitting up in bed with Nachman, telling him stories. He thought that he could still see the beautiful light in Nachman's pale blue eyes whenever Nathan read sections of *The Stolen Jew* aloud. In Michael's chosen profession, Nathan supposed, listening was an asset. What good had it ever done Nachman?

Nathan wanted to ask Michael about Ira. Michael and Ira had been close when they were boys. Michael had, during Nachman's frequent breakdowns, come to live with Nathan. Michael and Ira had played ball together. They had gone to the movies together. They had played chess and checkers and cards together. They had stayed up late at night, in Ira's room, talking and laughing. Remembering such facts pleased Nathan.

Outside the window, a bottle broke on the pavement. Nathan listened to the sounds of sirens and cars, to screaming Spanish voices and crying children. He did not mind. He felt strangely at peace. In the morning he would speak to Rachel about moving away, to a safe neighborhood; he and Michael would arrange it. He looked forward to being with Michael again. The apartment itself was quiet. Nathan dozed. He awoke to the sound of something breaking—a glass, a dish—and he knew that the sound did not come from outside. He hurried to the kitchen, without his slippers or robe. Pieces of a large plate lay shattered on the linoleum. Rachel was crying. Nathan saw blood. He felt faint, not when he saw the blood, but when he looked at the pieces of broken blue-and-white china.

"Here," he said to her. "Come here. Show me."

Rachel pulled her bathrobe close and Nathan watched the blood dripping along her finger. "You should suck the blood," he said, but Rachel could do nothing but stand there, head bent, and weep.

"Please—"

"Oh Nathan," she said. "What will I do? Tell me. You were always the strong one. Tell me. What will I do now, without him?"

"You should suck the blood," he said.

"What will I do?" she asked again. A drop of blood fell to the linoleum, but she did not notice. "Oh Nathan . . ."

"Here," he said. "Give me."

She held her hand forward and he took the cut finger into his mouth. He sucked the blood and it tasted sweet to him. He pressed his thumb against the cut, then placed her thumb where his had been. "Press hard," he said. "And hold the finger up, above the level of your heart. Where are the Band-Aids?"

"In the bathroom," she said. "In the medicine chest."

"Stay here," he said. "Don't go away."

"Where would I go?" she asked, and laughed easily. "Oh Nathan," she said, and her voice sounded normal again, affectionate. She lifted her finger above her shoulder. "Like this?"

"Like that."

He went to the bathroom and returned with the tin box of Band-Aids and a tube of antiseptic cream. He held her hand while she washed the cut under the kitchen faucet; then he applied the cream and put on the Band-Aid. She sat on a kitchen chair and watched while, on his hands and knees, he swept up the pieces of the plate. She warned him to be careful. When he was done sweeping, she showed him where the vacuum cleaner was and he vacuumed the floor.

"There's something on my mind," he said, when he was done. "Come. There's something I want to talk to you about."

They sat in the living room, and as he looked into her face—at her tired eyes, her gray-brown hair, her soft cheeks—and as he remembered how faint and helpless he'd felt, staring at the pieces of the broken plate, he felt weary suddenly of holding back, he felt as if he wanted to tell Rachel all that was in his heart. But he did not know how to begin.

"You looked so frightened before," she said, encouraging him. "When you first came into the kitchen. As if—"

He nodded. "Listen," he said. "I'm glad you noticed. But Nachman must have told you, no? About when we were children—how our father would break plates?"

She smiled and shook her head. "No."

Nathan shrugged. He wanted to tell her what he was remembering, but what if she didn't believe the story? What if she mocked him for telling it? "It's probably nothing important."

"Tell me anyway, all right? I'd like to hear." She looked away. "Nachman would rarely talk about what things were like when you two were boys together. He was so much in awe of you, Nathan. So much. He kept talking of us going to Israel, to visit you, but I knew he never would. He couldn't get his courage up. Michael tried and tried to get him to talk—I gave up long ago." She smiled. "In his way Nachman was really worse than you. He kept everything to himself. He gave very little."

Nathan nodded. "He was always weak," he said. "That's true."

"Yes," Rachel said, moving closer to Nathan. "But his weakness drew me to him, Nathan—didn't you know that?"

"It's an old story," he said, but he did not look at Rachel.

"I remember, even at our wedding, how I kept looking at you—the great success, the firstborn, the *macher*, the big brother—and I wondered if I was going to regret settling for Nachman, and what I answered myself, even while I stood under the *chupah*, was that I wanted to marry somebody who would not come through every crisis in life with flying colors."

Nathan nodded. "Yes," he said.

"Nachman was never there when I needed him." She shrugged and looked down at her hands. "I suppose I wanted to marry somebody who needed me."

"Nachman needed you," Nathan said, and he moved closer to Rachel, as if moving close to her might stop her words. He was afraid that she might want to talk about other things, that she might become too tired to hear the things he wanted to tell her. "But listen—I wanted to tell you about what I remembered before. Will you listen? If Nachman already told you, maybe you would let me tell you anyway. I want to talk to you, Rachel. Tomorrow I'll find another place to stay. I'm thinking I'd rather be with Michael. I won't bother you anymore, but now—"

She touched his hand. "It's all right. I want to listen."

Nathan spoke quickly. "All right," he said. "This is the way it happened. I must have been ten years old and Nachman was three and we slept in the same bed then, in the apartment on Winthrop Street, where Michael and Ruth live now. We were very close when we were boys—we were very affectionate with each other. Did you know that? I liked to hold hands with him whenever we took walks, and we would even kiss each other on the lips when Momma wasn't near, and give each other our secrets." Nathan stopped. He was afraid to look at Rachel, afraid he might see doubt in her eyes. He talked rapidly, trying to tell her what he saw, trying to make sure that everything he said gave her an exact picture of how things had been. "Momma and Poppa were always fighting then. But you know that. In the Old Country, Poppa had been looked up to by others, he had been a carrier-of-heavy-loads, and Momma used to tell us often that when she married him he was the handsomest of men, and that when he carried loads on his back—boxes of shoes tied to large wooden planks, machinery for the factories, breads and fruits and books and clothing—others stopped to stare in admiration.

But when they came across the ocean to America something changed and he became sick and the doctors didn't know what it was exactly, and he lost his strength and Momma never forgave him. She said he had become weak in order to hurt her."

"Oh Nathan—!"

"You shouldn't interrupt," he said sharply. For an instant he wondered why he was telling the story to Rachel instead of to Michael. If he gave the story away to Rachel, what story would he be able to bring to Michael? "Momma worked in a zipper factory when she could, and she would ride the trolley all the way from Brooklyn over the bridge into Manhattan, and sometimes, to save a nickel, she would walk all the way home and with that nickel buy some chocolates for Nachman and me. She would always tell us what she had done to be able to buy the chocolates and she used to mock Poppa in front of us and say that he had had to ride home from work because he didn't have her strength. She was right. Who can explain? All I know is, Poppa got weaker and she got stronger, and even on *Shabbos* she would yell at him that he should go out and try to find an extra job, that she didn't have enough money to feed us, that Nachman and I would become sick and weak like him. It was terrible, Rachel. Once he was a handsome and strong man! She would cry out to us. Oh you should have seen him! He was so handsome and strong! But in America, look at him."

Nathan stopped. I was in Israel yesterday, he thought, and now I'm here. He nodded to himself. He would be able to tell Michael about all the books he had been reading during his years in Israel—about all the things he had learned, all the things that he and Ira might have been able to talk about had Ira lived. He had made an effort to know the world that Ira's mind understood. He would have been able to ask Ira questions —about Einstein's theories, about the sun and the moon and the stars, about quarks and angular momentum and red shifts and black holes. He would have been able to ask Ira questions about particles and antiparticles, about matter and antimatter, and he would have been able to take pleasure from listening to Ira's explanations. Ira had been three years older than Michael. Ira had often kept Michael entertained for hours with made-up stories. Ira had been a very imaginative child.

"Are you all right?" Rachel asked. "You look very tired, Nathan. Would you like a glass of water?"

"I'm all right," Nathan replied, and he fixed his mind upon the story he wanted to tell. "Yes. In Jerusalem last year they had an exhibit of photographs and I saw a photo of a man and it said he was a carrier-of-heavy-loads in Vilna. He did not look very strong to me, even though he carried an enormous board on his back, piled high with bolts of cloth. He looked pale and frightened and weak, despite his smile, which was, beneath his burden, forced. Momma had a sister, my Aunt Zlata—"

"I remember Aunt Zlata."

"—and her first husband died of tuberculosis and she remarried an American man, a German Jew—my Uncle Harry—who was very successful, and Momma used to envy her terribly. There wasn't a day that passed that she didn't tell Poppa how beautiful her sister Zlata's house was—how beautiful Zlata's new couch was, how beautiful Zlata's new stove was, how beautiful Zlata's new coat was, how beautiful Zlata's new carpeting was. But who knows, Rachel? Who can figure."

"I didn't like Zlata," Rachel said.

"I did," Nathan said. "I liked Zlata but I hated Harry. Once he made Poppa cry, when Poppa asked for money," Nathan looked up. He wanted to smile. "Poppa was a pious man, and he loved to read. Did you know that? It was what he loved more than anything in the world. *Zimzum*. Did Nachman ever tell you about *zimzum*? How Poppa believed in *zimzum* and loved to be with his *landsleit* in *shul* and pray with them and sing with them and study with them on *Shabbos* afternoons and argue with them? Did Nachman ever tell you?"

"No."

"It's all right," Nathan said. He recalled explaining *zimzum* to Ira, and he remembered how proud he had felt to tell Ira that the story of *zimzum* had come from Poppa—from Ira's grandfather. Ira wrote a report on *zimzum* for Hebrew School; Nathan wished that he still had the report, that he could look at Ira's handwriting. "Poppa loved to read. He was against the Chassidim—they were fanatics, he said—but one of their beliefs, he admitted, had merit. If God was already everything, he would ask me, then how did He create the world? Where was there space for anything else, if He was already everything and everywhere? I would shrug, and give no answer, and then Poppa would smile and close his eyes with satisfaction, and I would love him more than ever." Nathan smiled, for the first time. "He knew something that I did not know."

Nathan felt as if his mind were suddenly a large room that had been flooded with light. The affinities seemed so obvious to him—between his father's theory and Ira's theory—but he was afraid to offer them to

Rachel. They would require too much explanation. He was surprised, in fact, that Ira had never mentioned it. Why? If the big blast theory of the universe was true, as Ira had explained it to him, and if the universe was infinite in the first minute of its creation, and if it was infinite now, how could it, at the same time, also be an expanding universe? Could Ira have answered that question, or would Ira have smiled back and praised Nathan for having thought to ask it?

"The chemistry of the sea is very similar to the chemistry of blood," Nathan said.

"*What?*"

"The chemistry of the sea is very similar to the chemistry of blood," Nathan said. "It's something I learned from a book."

Rachel put her hand on his. "My finger is all right. I'm certain the bleeding has stopped—but you look so pale. Are you sure you want to continue? We can talk in the morning. You must be exhausted."

"How did He produce and create this world, Poppa would ask," Nathan continued. "Like a man who gathers in and holds his breath, would be Poppa's answer—and he would take a deep breath then and I would look at him as if . . . as if . . ." Nathan turned up the palms of his hands and tried to smile. "Poppa was a sweet man, you know, and he was happiest, I think, when he talked to us about *zimzum*, about God's contracting into Himself. Nachman and I would walk around the house sometimes, and we would breathe in and see who could hold his breath longest—it was one thing Nachman could sometimes beat me at—and we would try to imagine what it had been like, when God had decided to create the world. Like a man who gathers in and contracts his breath, so that the smaller might contain the larger, Poppa declared, so did God contract His light into a hand's breadth, according to His own measure, and the world was left in darkness, and in that darkness did He cut boulders and hew rocks.

"By drawing into Himself, Poppa taught us, He made it possible for something that was *not* Him to exist. Do you see? The story fascinated us—no matter how many times he told it—but if Momma caught him talking to us about *zimzum*, or showing us things in his books, she would tell us to go outside and play and to stop wasting our time, and she would rail at Poppa for teaching us things that would make us grow up to be failures the way he was a failure. What good were words when we didn't have enough food to eat. But do you see, Rachel, how what Poppa taught to me and what I gave to Ira—do you see that maybe Ira's mind for science came from Poppa?"

"I don't understand such things," Rachel said. "Michael has ideas too." She shrugged. "But I like listening to you talk. I always did, Nathan. I always liked to listen to you tell stories."

"That's not the point," Nathan said. "But all right. Listen. All this we took for granted—the fights, Poppa's weakness, the way he drew into himself and became quiet, the way he snapped at us most of the time if we asked questions, the way Momma suffered and then made him as miserable as she claimed she was—and what I realize now is that it seemed so natural that they treat each other the way they did that I never questioned it or thought it bothered me. It was the way we lived. If I imagined anything back then, I imagined that life was the same in the homes of all my friends in the neighborhood, of all poor Jews. But I don't believe I imagined things like that then."

Nathan looked toward the window, where the glow from the *yahrzeit* lamp cast soft orange shadows on the wall. He looked at the shape of the piano, under the khaki blankets, and he tried to hear the sound of Nachman playing his violin, he tried to recall how happy he had been to hear Nachman playing. Einstein loved the violin, Nathan recalled. Tolstoy, who could not weep for the loss of those dearest to him, would weep whenever he heard music. "So," Nathan said, softly. "What did I remember before, Rachel? I remembered how we woke one night, Nachman and I, because we heard screaming and crying and the sound of something breaking. We walked out of our bedroom and we held hands—Nachman was very frightened—and we looked into the kitchen, and what was Poppa doing? Poppa was taking dishes out of the cabinet above the stove and he was lifting them, one at a time, and he was smashing them on the counter. Momma looked terrified—I'd never seen her frightened before—and she kept one hand across her mouth all the while that Poppa broke the dishes and screamed at her. 'What do you want from me?' he kept yelling. 'What is it you want from me? Tell me what you want from me, all right? What is it you want from me?' And each time he asked her the question he would smash another dish."

Rachel had covered her mouth with her right hand. "I liked your father," she said, lowering her hand and reaching toward Nathan. "He was very kind to me. I liked it, whenever Nachman was in the hospital, for him to sit with me and to say nothing. When you call him a sweet man, I know what you mean."

"What do I mean?" Nathan asked, but he continued before Rachel could answer. "When Momma saw us standing there her face changed and—I see it very clearly—she was truly happy, as happy and triumphant as I'd ever seen her. She opened her arms and called to us to come to her. I tried to hold on to Nachman's hand but he broke away and ran to Momma and they embraced and she began weeping. 'This is my precious one! This is my love child! This is my darling one!' she cried, and she kissed him everywhere. 'This is my precious one, who loves me! This is my sweet child, who cares!' I did not move, Rachel, I can assure you. I did not move. Nor did I look at Poppa, though I could see that he had covered his face with his hands, in shame. I stared instead at the broken dishes, the pieces lying everywhere, and as I did, and as Momma called out to me to come to her, something inside me went cold. Very cold, Rachel. So cold that . . ."

Nathan stopped and pressed the palm of his right hand against his chest. He looked at Rachel and her face was, for an instant, blurred. In his ears he heard the sound of the sea again. He saw black spots, flickering outward. He felt Rachel drawing closer to him and he put out his hand, as if to stop her. "I'm all right," he said. "Don't worry about me. But listen. Listen to what it was like." The words came now in a rush, and as they did he felt the pressure on his chest diminish, and he could see Michael's handsome face, smiling down at him. "Because what I didn't feel then, maybe I was feeling when I saw you standing there—you looked frozen to me—standing there with the broken dish on the floor. Michael is the expert. He could tell you about what I did feel and what I did not feel." Nathan could see his mother, holding Nachman close to her. He saw that his father would not look at him, and he recalled how much he had wanted to touch his father, to comfort him, and how scared he had been to try. He recalled his mother's voice, mocking him, and how he had hardened himself against it. "How can I know what I felt then, Rachel? Momma told me that she always knew I was cold and that Nachman really loved her. Nachman was her good son. Nachman cared for her and Nachman understood her suffering and Nachman had a warm heart and I was a cold fish. A cold fish, Rachel! She called me a cold fish and she was so proud to use such a phrase, such an American way of speaking."

Nathan shrugged, his eyes closed. "Well, I suppose what I decided then was that I shouldn't prove her wrong. I was cold. I was very cold. How could I deny it? Coldness was my strength." He looked at Rachel and tried to think of where he had been, only one day before. He tried to remember what he had felt like in his home in Ein Karem, when he had found her telegram. He tried to remember what he had felt like there, through all the years before, when there had been no words. "But what I can feel now," he said, "when I see how small and frightened we were—what boys—is how much I wanted to run across the room and snatch Nachman from her arms. Except that he loved it there so much. And I wasn't brave enough."

Nathan rubbed his forehead. He wondered what his voice sounded like to Rachel. "Maybe Michael can explain it all when you talk to him. I felt a little bit faint before, when I saw the dish. You've had enough sorrow. Why do I burden you with so many words? But once I started—" He put up a hand again, to stop her from replying. "But listen. When we went back to bed that night, Nachman and I, we didn't touch each other. I remember that. Things were different afterwards, I think. I think things were different after that."

Nathan rubbed his eyes. "Maybe I'm making more of it than was there. I don't know. Who can tell?" He sat back and felt the full measure of his exhaustion. Was he really in America? He sighed. "Poppa," he said softly. "Oh Poppa, you were the one who carried heavy loads, but I never saw it." He rested. He wondered if, in Michael's presence, he would be required to tell the story all over again, and if, afterward, Michael and Rachel would compare the different versions—would talk about what he had added and what he had left out. But what had he lost, by talking? In his mind he looked for the room full of light, but he found that everything was gray and dim. He let himself rest. He let his mind drift. He saw a long tunnel, with flecks of white spiraling toward the far end. When he opened his eyes it surprised him to see that Rachel was still there, sitting next to him. He smiled weakly. "I'm not very used to talking so much," he said. "You don't have to believe what I say. But I loved Nachman. I did love Nachman. We were brothers. I wanted you to know that. I think that's the reason I told you the story. Would you believe, after all these years, that I can still remember how soft his skin felt whenever I would hold him next to me in bed?"

"Nachman was a sweet man—like your father," Rachel said. "And like you."

Nathan laughed. "Like me? Don't make jokes, Rachel. Momma was right. I was cold and hard, always. Even with Ira. Even now. It's just that I remembered what happened that night and I wanted to tell you."

"You haven't asked me how he died."

"Somebody said a heart attack."

Rachel smiled, but her lips quivered. She looked down. "Nachman took pills. Michael got a doctor from Kings County—they went to medical school together—to come and sign the certificate, but Nachman took pills. I think he may even have telephoned Michael and warned him, so that I could be sure to collect the insurance. Michael won't say yet, but I think—"

Nathan stood above her. "He had no *right*!" he declared, angrily. "He had no right!"

Rachel smiled up at him. "But this was one thing you couldn't stop him from—or Michael either—no matter how strong you were, don't you see?"

Nathan looked at his bare feet, on the carpeting. "He could have been a partner. He could have gotten a good price for the store. I arranged it before I left. But he was always—"

"Oh Nathan," Rachel said. "You arranged it. *You* arranged it." She waved a hand at him, exasperated, and stood, as if to leave. "It was just like you, he said, to arrange his life. Don't you see what you did to him?"

Nathan shook his head. "I did nothing, Rachel. I've thought about this often. People get what they want in life. I did nothing to him, my whole life. What did I ever stop him from becoming? Nachman stopped himself. He didn't have to—" Nathan shook his head again. "I did nothing. We should both go to sleep. It's late. In the morning I'll go to Michael's house."

"What were you going to say?" she asked. She came closer to him, one hand on the belt of her bathrobe, and Nathan found himself stepping back. He didn't want her to be too close to him. He licked perspiration from his lower lip, and he remembered the times, before she married Nachman, that he and Rachel had walked along the boardwalk together, at Coney Island; he imagined that she was remembering those times also; he imagined that she was willing, if necessary, to use his memories of those times against him. There was something about her tired eyes, her full lips, her pale cheeks that made him want to push her away. He could recall, vaguely, the sweet odors of wet wool. He could see them running through the rain together, to the subway station. "What were you going to say before?" she asked. "What didn't Nachman have to do?"

"It doesn't matter."

"Tell me. Please—"

"Nothing. Just that he didn't have to go to Momma, that's all. To let her hold him that way so he could gloat at me." Nathan shrugged. "It doesn't matter. He got what he wanted and I got what I wanted. The thought was in my head, from the story I told you, that he could have stayed with me and not gone to her, but he wanted to be sick and weak, he wanted to fail, he wanted—"

"And you wanted your mother to hold you too," Rachel said. She sighed. "You were only a child. How could you not have wanted it?"

He said nothing. What he wanted now was to close his eyes; what he wanted was to be back in Ein Karem. He wanted the moment he was living in to disappear. He thought of things he could say to Rachel —words and explanations that could carry him through the moment— but he decided that the best thing was to let her have her way, to let her think she understood him. He had made a mistake, coming back. He had made a mistake, staying with her. He had made a mistake, to talk so much, to tell her such a story.

"I'm worried about Michael," Rachel said.

Nathan nodded. "I'll speak with him."

"Michael's not as strong as you think. These things take their toll. Nachman was his father, after all."

"I said that I would speak with him."

Nathan stood there, in the middle of the living room, as if waiting to be excused. He saw the picture in his head again, of Gail Rubin lying on the sand—of the cameras, the shoulder strap, her skin—and he wished that he had never read about her. If he had not read about her, he would not have returned to America. He thought of Ira, measuring the sun, and calculating the size of the universe, and trying to decide if it was expanding or contracting, if it was finite or infinite, and he decided that he was fooling himself, that, had Ira lived on, he himself would never have read the books he'd read, about science, and that they would not have talked together the way he sometimes imagined they might have. They would not have understood one another. They would not have drawn close, one to the other.

He breathed out and looked at Rachel. "Listen," he began, but he stopped when he saw that the belt of her robe had slipped, and that her robe had opened. His eyes widened, as if in horror. He leaned his head forward and stared at the pale and withered flesh he saw beneath her robe, at the waist. Rachel looked down and moved quickly, to pull the robe to, but before she could, Nathan let out a moan, more sorrowful than any he had ever heard. He could hardly breathe. He reached under her robe and touched her soft skin with his fingers, and then he moved his arms around her and clutched her body to his as if he would never let go. And when he caught his breath finally and stopped heaving, still he held to her, and he wept freely, for the first time, and he did not try to tell her what he was feeling. He did not try to think of all that he had, across a lifetime, forbidden himself to think and to feel, of all that—the thought would not be denied—if she would accept him, and if there were enough time, he might still be willing to tell her.

◇ 2 ◇

NATHAN WANTED TO BE ABLE TO LEAVE THE APARTMENT BEFORE RACHEL awoke, but when, early in the morning, he entered the living room, it was already filled with men. They were walking back and forth, chanting and mumbling in Hebrew, and Nathan wondered, at first, how it was that they did not bump into one another. He saw Harvey, and he saw Raymond—Leah's husband—and he recognized a few of the other men: old friends of Nachman, from the neighborhood. Michael stood at the far end of the room, facing the window, leading the men in their morning prayers. All the men wore *talises* and *tephillin*—white prayer shawls around their shoulders, black straps wound around their bare left arms, black boxes set upon their foreheads. Long black straps trailed down their backs, from under their *yarmulkes*.

A short man, standing next to Michael, banged on a table for silence. "*Kaddish*," he announced.

Michael began intoning the Mourner's *Kaddish*. His voice was strong, his back was straight. "*Yis-gadal vi-yis-kadash sh'mai rabah* . . ."

Harvey touched Nathan's arm, as if to offer his sympathy. Nathan did not respond. He could see himself looking into Ira's grave—looking down at earthen walls, at the pine casket. He looked up and saw the cemetery in Queens, the endless horizon of gravestones. In Israel, he recalled, when the Yom Kippur War had begun, rabbis had gone around and consecrated all the public parks, in case they were needed for burial grounds. Nathan remembered the rabbi at Ira's funeral placing a prayer book before him, on the lectern, and pointing to the words. They stood under a green-and-white canopy. Nathan saw himself pushing the book away, angrily, and reciting the *Kaddish* from memory.

Nachman had not been there. The only funeral I ever want to attend is my own, Nachman had often joked. Well, Nathan thought, Nachman had his wish. Nathan did not want to recite the *Kaddish* now, because he saw that the men were looking at him, to see if he would. But he recited it anyway. That would be easier, he decided. He would not have to make explanations afterward. He recited the words along with Michael, and he watched some of the old men whisper to one another. *The brother!* he imagined them saying. *That's the brother who came from Israel.*

Though the room was quiet, the man next to Michael banged on the table again. He named the day of the week in Hebrew, and announced that afternoon services would take place at the synagogue, at 4:45. The men chanted the prayers to themselves, with moving lips. A Jew must move his lips when he prays silently, Nathan recalled his father teaching him, so that others will be certain he is praying. We can know a man's heart only by his actions. Nachman had been in the hospital on the day of their father's funeral. He had tried to come. Harvey and Rivka had gone to the hospital to pick him up, and he had walked from the hospital to their car, carrying his little orange satchel. He had opened the car door, and then he had closed it; he had turned and walked back to the hospital. *When I was saying Kaddish, I thought of you*, Nathan told him that evening.

The men were unwinding the straps from their arms, placing the black boxes inside old velvet and cloth bags. Some of them came to Nathan and shook his hand. They offered their condolences by closing their eyes and shrugging their shoulders. They were neighbors, they had known Nachman for many years, they were sorry. Nachman had seemed so happy. He had looked so well. He had always had a joke ready. Who could tell when it was time?

Nathan looked at them closely. They seemed incredibly old to him, like the men he remembered seeing at his father's *shul*, when he was a boy. He looked at Michael, across the room, and Michael waved to him. Michael was so much taller than all the others. Michael was folding his *talis*. Why do you want to go to Russia? Nathan heard himself ask. Why do you look so happy? He thought of the Jews and writers in Russia who never left their apartments without satchels, in case they should be picked up by the secret police. In their satchels they kept what they wanted to take with them into prison or exile: writing paper, books, photos, pens, candy bars. He saw Nachman in his hospital room, unpacking his satchel. *I was proud of you,* he said to Nachman. *When I heard. I was proud that you tried to come to the funeral.* Nachman nodded, without turning around. *But Nachman,* their mother said then. *Nachman my love! We were all expecting you.* Nathan had not been angry with her. Nothing she did surprised him. She was a very old woman by then.

"I'm your cousin Andy," one man said, smiling up at Nathan. "I used to drive you to the country every summer. Do you remember me?"

"I remember you," Nathan said.

"It's been a long time." The man wheezed. "I remember you when you were a boy." He turned to the others. "I knew Nathan when he was a boy," he announced, proudly. "I'm eighty-seven years old now," he told Nathan. "I have a pacemaker that keeps me going. It's wonderful."

Nathan turned and looked behind him, and he felt his heart lurch. Rachel was standing there, at the entrance to the living room, and she was smiling at him. "Come, everybody," she said. "We fixed something. You must be hungry—"

Rachel was standing in the same spot in which Nathan had stood the night before, when he announced his arrival. She looked well rested, happy. The old men pushed by Nathan, toward the dining room. Rachel's cheeks were not pale, and this surprised Nathan. When she smiled she seemed much younger to him than she had seemed the night before. She was still a beautiful woman. Nathan looked toward Michael and he wondered what, given what had happened, he was now required to do. All this letting go, he wanted to say. All this talking, all this telling and sharing the things that lay in one's heart—what good did it ever do? In the end they always took away everything.

"Come," Rachel said. "Come, Nathan. You should eat something. The trip must—"

"I'm sorry," he said. "I'm very sorry, Rachel."

She laughed. "For what?" she asked, and she touched his hand. He drew it back, as if stung.

"I'm sorry," he said again. "It was a mistake."

Michael bent down and kissed Nathan on the forehead. "Good morning, Uncle Nat," he said. He put his arm around Nathan's shoulder and Nathan did not pull away.

"I forgot about the *minyan*," Nathan said to Michael. "I'm sorry."

"I'm glad you're here," Michael said. He kissed his mother on the cheek. "We all are."

"I didn't bring a *talis* or my *tephillin*," Nathan said. "I was in too much of a hurry."

"Don't worry about it."

"Nachman had an extra set of *tephillin*," Rachel said. "If you want me to get them . . ." Nathan looked at Rachel, remembering what his father and his son had looked like in their caskets, with their *talises* around their necks; their *tephillin* bags had been lodged beside them, he supposed, where he could not see them. The rabbis had urged him to come away; they had explained that the Jewish custom was not to look at the deceased after death—that you were supposed to remember what the person had been like when the person was alive. But Nathan had done what he wanted. He had wanted to look at them for as long as possible. Each time, after the funeral service, for his father and for Pauline and for Ira, he had waited until all the relatives and guests were in their cars, to go to the cemetery, and then he had stood by the casket, before it was closed, and stared.

"Why do you want to go to Russia?" he asked Michael.

"It's a long story," Michael said. "But come. Mother's right. We should eat—and then we'll talk, okay?" He pressed Nathan to him. "I'm very happy you're here." His eyes were moist. His father died, Nathan thought for the first time. Nachman was his father, and he died less than a week ago. "I'm sorry for the reason, right? But it means a lot to me that you came. You and me, Uncle Nat . . ."

Nathan tried to decide if Rachel had already spoken with Michael. Michael was holding him too tightly. Perhaps Rachel was right to worry about him. But Nathan didn't have the time. He needed to be alone, he told himself, so that he could sort things out, so that he could figure out why it was he had acted so foolishly the night before. What he had done, he decided, and what he had felt, had had nothing to do with Rachel. She had, simply, been there. But he needed time. He was more confused than he wanted to be. He did not want to mislead Rachel in any way.

The old man who had stood next to Michael was now standing on the couch, in his socks, his arms stretched high. He was pulling the sheet away from the mirror. Was the week of mourning over already? Nathan tried to calculate the number of days that had passed—he tried to account for the change in time, from Israel to America—but he could not figure out the difference. Some scientists, he had read, believed that the edge of this universe was the boundary between positive and negative time. Would Ira have agreed?

"Well," Harvey said, gesturing to the mirror. "You got here in time, didn't you?"

Nathan said nothing. He let Harvey's voice roll past him and wondered if Gail Rubin had bought her plane ticket for her trip to New York before she had gone to Kibbutz Maagen Mikhael. The newspapers had not mentioned finding a ticket inside the purse that lay beside her cameras. Raymond patted Nathan on the back affectionately. Nathan tried to smile at him. He had never disliked Raymond. For forty-three years Raymond had been a shoe salesman in a store on Flatbush Avenue. That was quite a feat, Nachman had joked when Raymond retired. Nathan smiled. He would ask Rachel if he could go into her room later, so that he could look through things that Nachman had left behind. He missed Nachman.

"It's hard to believe, isn't it?" Raymond said. "I keep expecting to see him here—I keep expecting him to just walk in like nothing had happened, if you know what I mean."

"No," Nathan said. "I don't."

Raymond swallowed. "We'll be going back to Florida tonight," he said. "They put us on a midnight flight. We'll all go together, with Rivka and Harvey." Nathan was surprised that Raymond was talking so much. He could not recall ever having had a conversation with Raymond. "Leah wanted us to fly in separate planes, just in case—she always makes the children fly in separate planes when they come to visit us, did you know that?"

"I didn't know that," Nathan said.

"I'm sorry," Raymond said. "I should have told you. Most of the time I give in—especially for the grandchildren. I mean, look at it this way—if, God forbid, there should be a crash, how would I feel afterwards that all of them were gone at once and that Leah had warned me? But for this time, I put my foot down."

"Good for you, Raymond," Harvey said.

Nathan looked at his reflection in the mirror, behind the couch, and he was surprised at how young he looked: how strong and healthy and well tanned. Even alongside Michael. He would ask Michael about a place to swim. He liked to swim every day. But was swimming forbidden during the first thirty days of mourning? There were different rules for each period, he recalled: for the first seven days, and for the first thirty days, and for the first year. There were different rules for wives and for sons and for brothers.

"Come on," Michael said, and Nathan let himself be led into the dining room. He realized that he had not yet asked Michael about his children. Neither had he seen them. And where was Ruth? The old men moved aside so that he could reach the table. He heard Rivka's voice, scolding Leah for having put too much hot water into the coffee. The man who had removed the sheet from the mirror told Nathan to come to the synagogue on Sunday morning, to pick out the spot for Nachman's memorial plaque. He gave Nathan prices. He told him that, on the board outside the sanctuary, there were only a few places left. There was already a new board upstairs, next to the balcony, but this man had saved places on the board near the sanctuary for the old-time members. The man had known Nathan's and Nachman's father. He had studied Talmud on *Shabbos* afternoons in Michael's house, with Nathan's father. Nathan stared at the man's mouth. The man looked at Nathan's feet and clucked his tongue. Nathan should not, as a mourner, have been wearing shoes. But then too, Nathan was not supposed to have recited *Kaddish*, since the son was there to do it.

See? he heard Nachman say. *Even my famous brother gets off on the wrong foot sometimes.*

Ah Nachman, Nathan thought. Nachman. Where are you? He could see Nachman grin back; he could see Nachman standing at the corner of Church and Nostrand avenues, playing his violin. Nathan stood across the street watching—worried that Rivka might come by. Afterward, with Nachman, he counted the nickels and pennies.

Your nephew is a real *shul mensch*, the man stated, with pride. How many young men were there in today's world who could still *daven* the *amid* for the morning *minyan*? Michael came to *shul* every Friday night and every Saturday morning. All the other boys Michael's age were leaving Brooklyn and marrying *shiksas* and joining *shuls* where they sat without *yarmulkes* and listened to organs.

The old man shook Nathan's hand. His grip was surprisingly strong. "Your brother was a wonderful man," he said. "He came to *shul* every week—whenever he could. My name is Menachem Katz. Ask for Menachem Katz when you come on Sunday. Everybody in the *shul* knows me." Then he laughed, in a way that irritated Nathan. "I remember you too, you know, from before you were rich and famous."

WHEN THE MEN WHO HAD COME FOR THE MORNING PRAYERS WERE GONE, and only the family was left, Nathan went into the bedroom, put his pajamas in his suitcase, and closed it. He had forgotten to bring his toilet articles. He walked to the bathroom. The mirror on the medicine chest, above the sink, was soaped up. Nathan took a towel and wiped the soap away. During the week of mourning, he recalled, one was supposed to be defended against vanity—one's mind was not supposed to dwell on one's self, on one's own image. Nathan found Nachman's razor and shaving cream in the medicine chest. He started to shave, very carefully. He saw Nachman's face staring back at him.

So tell me. How are you?

I'm here.

Nachman smiled.

Nathan finished shaving and washed his face. He cleaned Nachman's razor and returned it to the medicine chest. He went back to the bedroom, took his suitcase, and walked down the corridor to the living room. Everyone was there—Rachel and Michael; Leah, Rivka, Harvey, and Raymond—and they were all smiling at him. *Why?* Harvey asked him where he was going, with his suitcase. Back to Israel, Nathan thought of saying, but he realized that he did not have a ticket. Rivka asked if he wanted to go with them to the cemetery, to see where Nachman was buried.

"No," Nathan said. He spoke to Michael: "Are you leaving soon? I'd like to stay with you, if you have room. If Ruth doesn't mind—"

Rachel and Michael exchanged glances that made Nathan feel there was something they knew that he did not know. "Sure, Uncle Nat," Michael said. "If that's what you want."

"Listen," Harvey began. "You shouldn't be so sensitive about what I said last night. Rachel needs somebody to be with her. She—"

"It has nothing to do with what you said," Nathan stated.

"I'll be all right," Rachel said.

"The trouble with you, Nat," Harvey said, "is that you don't have a sense of humor."

"I have a very highly developed sense of humor," Nathan said. "It's just that very few things in life make me laugh."

"Look—maybe you'll come down and visit us in Florida," Rivka said. "We have plenty of room. We put in an air conditioner on the back patio."

Nathan said nothing. He was sorry he had said anything at all to

Harvey. He was aware of the others, staring at him. He would have preferred it, he knew, had Nachman been there. Despite everything, and even in the worst times, they had had a way of talking to one another that pleased Nathan. They had had their routines.

So how are you feeling?

Not so well.

Not so well?

In the last two weeks I spent over a hundred dollars on doctors.

A hundred dollars! But that's terrible, Nathan. In the Old Country you could have been sick for a year for a hundred dollars.

Maybe Nachman had been right. Maybe, years before, everything would have worked out for the best if they'd gone into vaudeville together.

"So tell me," Harvey asked. "Now that you're in Israel—I'm interested—are you still collecting things? I imagine the opportunities there are terrific."

"I sold my collection before I left," Nathan replied. "You should remember that."

"I forgot," Harvey said, and he tapped himself on the forehead.

"He sold it to strangers," Rivka said, to Rachel and Leah. "It was just like him. Believe me, if he really loved me, he'd have done otherwise."

"I sold my collection to Jews," Nathan said. He did not move. He wished for a moment that he could have had Nachman's tongue—the license Nachman had always taken, when talking with Rivka.

I could love you if you were dead.

Michael stood. "We can leave whenever you want." He touched his mother's cheek. "It's over."

"It's over," she said, and she kissed the back of his hand. Then she stood and Michael held her and she wept, very easily and softly, against his chest. Michael stroked her hair. Nathan thought of the objects he had bought, and saved, and sold—the silver spice boxes, the brass *menorahs*, the coins, the *Shabbos* lamps and the Torah breastplates and the finials and the framed maps and the *kiddush* cups and the *Seder* plates—and he wondered how it was that pieces of wood and metal and paper could have meant so much to him. He wondered how it was that he could have spent so many hours and so many years studying objects and deciding on which ones he wanted to own, and which ones he didn't.

"Michael's been very good to me," Rachel said.

"Michael's a good boy," Raymond said. "I always said so."

"Ira was a good boy too," Rivka said. "Don't you remember how he used to take a taxi downtown to the hospital every day to see Pauline?"

"Do you miss them?" Leah asked. "In Israel, do you ever miss any of the things you sold?"

"No," Nathan said.

Rivka laughed. "I don't believe you—not for a minute."

"I agree with Rivka," Harvey said.

"But I have a new hobby," Nathan found himself saying then. The room was silent. Nathan imagined Nachman, sitting in the corner, delighted—urging Nathan to continue, to say what had occurred to him. "What I've decided to do is to collect the family secrets. I've decided to go to each member of the family and to ask for a secret—for something you've never told anybody else."

"He's crazier than Nachman," Rivka said, waving a hand. "I always said so. Only they let him walk around." She wagged her finger at Nathan. "You don't fool me, you know, with all your schemes—you don't fool me at all." Nathan looked at Leah, and he saw that her face had become very pale. He was sorry that he had upset her. He turned to Rivka. "If you have something in your life that you're especially ashamed of—something you've never told anybody else—that's the kind of thing that would interest me."

"Wise guy," Harvey said.

"But he's just teasing you," Rachel said. "Can't you see that?" She sat next to Rivka. Nathan kept his eyes on Leah. He wanted to take her in his arms and comfort her, but he stayed where he was.

"No," Nathan said. "I mean what I say. I'm not teasing."

"He's always been a troublemaker," Harvey said. "From the first day I ever met him, I said to Rivka that she was right, that he was a born troublemaker."

"Last year, in her Judaic studies course at Brandeis, my Barbara said that they used your book," Leah offered. "She called long-distance to tell us, she was so proud."

"It's true," Raymond said.

"The book is full of errors," Nathan said. He turned to Michael. "Come."

Michael kissed his aunts good-bye. Nathan turned, without saying good-bye, and walked to the door. He did not want to talk about his book, or answer any questions. So many years, Nachman, he thought. So many years. Nachman smiled back and said nothing. Nathan stepped out onto the landing and set his suitcase down. He remembered the dark-skinned boy from the day before. Michael closed the door behind them. "Is there an elevator?" Nathan asked. "I think I'm tired."

Then Michael burst into laughter. He picked his uncle up and twirled him around. "Did you see their faces?" he asked. "Oh Uncle Nat—did you see Rivka's face when you asked her for her secret?"

"Put me down," Nathan said. He had forgotten just how powerful Michael was. He did not like being held this way, with his feet dangling in the air.

Michael embraced Nathan, hugging him tightly. "But did you see the way Rivka froze? Did you?"

Michael set Nathan down. Nathan looked up into Michael's face and realized that Michael had not shaved for a week. He wanted to touch Michael's cheek—to smooth down the soft dark hairs that had begun to curl—but he held back. "Then you really like it?" he asked. "You really think it's a good idea?"

THEY WALKED ALONG NOSTRAND AVENUE, SIDE BY SIDE, AND NATHAN LET Michael carry the suitcase for him. He felt safe beside Michael, as if, he thought, he were walking through the Arab section of Jerusalem with an armed Israeli soldier by his side. He did not look behind to see if the boy who had tried to steal his suitcase was following. He did not worry about the sounds of sirens or about the men he saw lying in doorways or about the blacks who passed them.

He asked Michael about Ruth and the children and Michael sighed and told Nathan that Ruth and the children were living on Long Island, in a house they had rented. He and Ruth were separated, and had been for almost a year.

"I'm sorry," Nathan said.

"Better a good divorce than a bad marriage," Michael said. "I guess."

"No," Nathan said.

A bad wife is worse than death, Nachman had said. Death only comes once.

Michael shrugged. He set the suitcase down. "Don't worry about me, okay?" he said. He leaned down and stared hard into Nathan's eyes. "Whatever Mother said to you—don't worry about me, okay? Promise me that." He closed his eyes and spoke as if reciting words he had memorized. "I'm not my father, and what my father did—"

"I'll speak with Ruth," Nathan said. "She should take you back in."

Michael shook his head. "Let it go, okay? For a while—until after Russia."

Michael picked up the suitcase and began walking again. He crossed the street, and Nathan followed him. He wondered if Michael's trip to Russia had anything to do with *The Stolen Jew*; Michael had loved *The Stolen Jew* almost as much as Nachman had. He remembered what Ruth had said, about Michael wanting to be a hero, but he said nothing. He would give Michael time. They walked along Parkside Avenue. Michael told Nathan that of course he missed the children and Ruth, but that in a way the time he'd been spending alone in the old house, during the past year, had been the most wonderful period of his life. Ruth wanted him to sell the house. She refused to live in Brooklyn anymore, and though Michael could understand her feelings and her fears, he refused to move. The house meant too much to him. His father and Nathan had grown up there. He would not just abandon it.

"You could sell it," Nathan said. "I wouldn't mind."

They stopped when they came to Rogers Avenue. A mailman was going door to door, accompanied by a policeman. Michael pointed. "Social Security day," he said. And then, "But the thing of it is that the house is so full of memories, Uncle Nat—all the things you've told me and my father told me . . . and I guess what I'm afraid of is that if the house is gone, then the memories will go with it."

Nathan nodded.

"Do you understand?"

"I understand," Nathan said. "But it's not so."

Michael laughed. "Don't you think I know that?" He sighed. "But I need a little time, that's all. Come on—" He pointed to the schoolyard where, behind the wire fence, some black men were playing basketball. "I'll show you one of the things I can't leave behind—that perpetual adolescence Ruth says I'm wedded to."

Michael walked through the gates of the schoolyard and waved to some of the ballplayers. When they waved back and began calling to him, Michael beamed, and Nathan saw the color rise in his neck and cheeks. Michael set down Nathan's suitcase and shook hands with some of the players. They slapped his palms and he slapped theirs. They were obviously delighted to see him.

"My man!" they exclaimed. "Oh my man Michael—how you been?"

"Good," Michael said. "Good. Real good."

"Where you been?"

"Hey Michael babe," one of the players called, from the court. "What looks good?"

"You, Jimmy. You look good."

A player patted him on the stomach. "When you ready to sell, man, you let me know."

They kidded him about his beard, about his wife, about the color of his skin. They pointed to his feet, and asked where he'd bought the swift running shoes. On the court, the game resumed. One or two of the players were taller than Michael, but none was more broadly built. Michael had been a great athlete in high school and college, at Erasmus and at Columbia. He had played ball for two years after college, wandering around Europe with a professional team from Antibes. He had met Ruth in Europe, when, during her junior year abroad, she attended a game. He had even been drafted by a professional basketball team, although he had told Nathan that he'd been smart enough to know his limits. He had not even gone to tryout camp. Nathan had no interest in sports; still, he had been proud. He had gone to games with Nachman and Ira. He had felt very happy whenever Michael would leave his teammates and come to him, wherever he sat.

"This is my uncle," Michael said, one arm around Nathan's shoulder.

The players nodded to Nathan. Nathan listened to Michael give him their names: Walt, Moses, Cicero, Truck, Jimmy, Ben, Olen. On the court, a skinny black boy, shirtless, darted through a crowd, and suddenly the ball was rising above hands and falling softly through the net. There was cheering. The game was over.

"You want nexts with me?"

"What else?" Michael asked. He slipped out of his jacket and handed it to Nathan. He winked. He looked at his sneakers. "It's been eight days since I've touched a ball."

"Where you been, man?" a tall black player asked. He seemed older than some of the others.

"His old man died, stupid—didn't you hear what we said before?"

The black player turned and swung his fist at the other black. "I didn't know, all right? You get off my ass, Moses—" He turned to Michael. "Real sorry, man. That's heavy."

Michael nodded. "It's heavy."

"I remember when my old man went. Tore me up, you know?"

Michael nodded. "I know."

The player shrugged, and grabbed Michael's shoulder, squeezing hard. The others were silent. They looked down at the concrete. They shuffled their feet, as if embarrassed. Michael put out his hands. "Hey—aren't I entitled to some warm-ups?"

Nathan ducked, thinking the ball that was suddenly zooming toward his face would hit him, but Michael caught it and moved away, bouncing the ball twice and then gliding through the air and slamming the ball down through the hoop. The other players moaned their approval. "He's real mean," one of them said. "Don't he look mean today?"

"That what death do to you sometimes."

"That Mike, he means to be mean."

Nathan moved back, to the fence, carrying his suitcase. Michael shot the ball several times, then came to Nathan. He was breathing easily. He took off his shirt. There were a few gray curls among the dark ones on his chest. "Is it okay?" he asked. "I mean if I play one game. It won't take long—" He glanced behind, so the others would hear. "Easy pickings today."

"Big mouth," one of the players said. "He still got the big mouth."

"Big *white* mouth," another player said, and they all laughed. "Big *fucking* white mouth."

"Hairy face too."

"I don't mind," Nathan said. "Play if you want. I always liked to watch you play."

Michael moved the suitcase next to the fence. "You guys make sure no one takes my uncle's suitcase, okay?"

"Hey, what you mean? Nobody round here ever got ripped off, Michael—you know that."

They all laughed. "Let your uncle sit on it. That way he be sure."

Nathan sat down on the suitcase and, to his surprise, his action made them laugh. He tried to smile. "You go ahead and play," he said. "It's all right."

Michael went out on the court. Nathan folded Michael's jacket across his lap and set his shirt on top of it. The game started and the ball went to Michael at once, in the far corner of the court. Michael rose in the air even before the ball seemed to be there, and sent it in a long high arc toward the basket. It fell through the net without touching the rim and the others whistled. Michael beamed and moved back toward the center of the court. He seemed very happy. He had always been happy when he was in motion, Nathan recalled. He had always seemed happy when he was in his schoolyard, playing ball. Why should Ruth want to take him away, to make him leave?

To either side of Nathan, the players waited their turns, their backs resting against the wire fence. Michael and Ira had gone to school here, from kindergarten to eighth grade. They had played on these courts as children. They had lined up, holding hands with their friends, somewhere within these high wire fences. Nathan looked at the building—Public School 92. Ira and Michael had learned to read and to write and to count inside the old red-brick building. The building, which was deteriorating now, had been new when they were children.

The blacks did not seem interested in Nathan. They laughed and teased one another, and they shouted at Michael. Michael moved around the court like an enormous bear, yet he was as graceful in his movements as any of the blacks. He shouted back at them, returning their taunts, and they seemed to love him for his cleverness.

"You still shrinkin' heads, man?"

"Why—yours too big?"

Nathan saw black heads and black arms and black shoulders and black muscles. The game seemed very rough. He wondered how it was that Michael survived, struggling with them for the ball in the crowd of bodies that surged under the basket. They seemed much younger than Michael. They pushed him and shoved him and chopped at him with big hands.

Nathan wanted to tell Michael about what had happened the night before. He wanted Michael to explain to him why it was he had done what he had done. Michael leapt high in the air and snatched the ball from the backboard. Nathan could not understand how Michael was able to rise from the ground to such a height. Ira, who studied the motions of the sun and the moon and the stars, who understood the miracles of gravity and light, maybe Ira would have been able to explain Michael's abilities. Michael fell. Nathan stood. The sound of Michael's body hitting the ground was dull and awful. *But if I should marry Rachel, then Michael will be my son.*

Nathan moved toward the court, but Michael was already standing and brushing himself off. He did not look toward Nathan. "Come on, come on," he called, hands open. The game continued at once. Nathan sat down on his suitcase, feeling weak. Was that what he himself wanted, after all? Was that what he had been after all along? The man who was guarding Michael tried to slap the ball from Michael's hands. Michael tempted him, holding the ball toward him briefly, and then—Nathan could not tell exactly how it had happened—the ball had slipped between the defender's legs, Michael was behind the man, the ball in his hands. Then he was directly under the basket, leaping through air, his body diagonal to the ground, slicing between a narrow space that separated the black players, twisting his body at the last possible second, moving upward with almost miraculous ease, and plunging the ball down into the hoop, backward, over his head.

"Oooo-eeee!" the players moaned. "Oooo-eeee! That man must have black blood in him."

"I told you he real mean today."

"You're bad, Michael. You're real bad."

Michael pointed a finger at the man defending him. "Shrunk your head good," he said. "Real good."

Nathan blinked. He watched the black man—the players called him Ben—set his jaw. Ben was two or three inches taller than Michael. His eyes were bloodshot. He looked to either side. His friends now mocked him for the way in which Michael had gotten the best of him. Ben breathed in deeply, as if to fill himself with needed pride. "Come on," he said to Michael. "You come again."

"Any time," Michael said. "My pleasure."

Nathan could hear Rivka's voice: *You always wanted what your brother had. That's all. You always wanted whatever it was you couldn't have.* Was it so?

Michael began to move toward the basket and Ben stood in his way, arms and legs spread wide. Michael tried to shoot the ball, but Nathan saw the black man's enormous hand rise up and shove the ball back down. "Stuffed you!"

Michael clapped his hands. Nathan was very warm. Nathan remembered Rivka saying, the night before, how fortunate they all were that Nachman had not died during a heat wave. The others had talked of the time the city's gravediggers had gone on strike, of the photo in the newspaper—of a Chassidic Jew, a diamond merchant, who had been found trussed and rotting in a trunk. Nathan watched Michael and remembered that Ira had, even when he was in college, kept a scrapbook full of clippings about Michael. Ira had been a good athlete also, but never as good as Michael. Who was? Michael had been good at all things—at anything he tried. Nathan remembered the routine Nachman and Michael had often gone through.

My mother tells me I can be anything at all when I grow up.

Then what is it you want to be, darling?

I don't know.

But of course you do. You want to be anything at all—that way you can never be any one thing, yes?

Nathan saw Nachman's smile. He saw him kiss Michael on the forehead. Surely Rachel would have thought of what I've thought of, he told himself. That if I offer to marry her and she accepts, then I would become Michael's stepfather. He listened to the sound of men jumping on concrete, to the slapping of skin against skin. The black boys seemed like ballet dancers to Nathan, the way they leapt and glided and soared. *That came from me.* He remembered Nachman pointing to Michael, on the court at Columbia University, and saying those words to another man, a neighbor from Brooklyn whose son was also a student at Columbia. *That came from me.*

Shh, Nathan wanted to say. It's all right, Nachman. Michael's all right.

"His old man really die?"

"What?" Nathan asked.

A young black boy with a purple kerchief on his head, like a pirate's, and a pearl earring set in the lobe of his left ear, was speaking. "I said if his old man really died?"

"Yes," Nathan said. "His father died. We were brothers."

The boy stubbed out a cigarette with the heel of his sneaker, but he showed no reaction. There was a good deal of shoving and pushing and grunting going on under the basket, and Nathan was frightened for Michael. He could not, for several seconds, find him. Then the players moved apart and Nathan saw the black man called Ben, his back to the basket, and Michael hunched over him, from behind. Ben jabbed an elbow backward suddenly, into Michael's stomach. Then, as Michael backed off, Ben turned and let the ball trail off his fingers. It rolled around the rim and fell in.

"Foul," one of the players on Michael's team yelled. "Hey man—foul—our ball. We got the ball."

"You call anything?" Ben said to Michael.

Michael was bent over, hands on thighs, trying to get his breath back. He shook his head sideways.

"See?" Ben said to the others. "If the man get fouled he gone to call it."

He smiled and Nathan saw light flash from a golden tooth. "Ain't that right, Mike?"

"Play the ball and shut your mouth," Michael said. He stood up and breathed in deeply. His body was wet with perspiration.

"Oh man," Ben said to the others, laughing. "Now Mike the Kike really starting to—"

Nathan did not hear the end of the sentence. Even while Michael was grabbing Ben somewhere near the neck and lifting him from the ground and carrying him forward with amazing force, toward the fence, Nathan was rising. A black boy grabbed Nathan by the arm. He was a head taller than Nathan. "It's theirs," he said. Michael slammed Ben against the fence with a ferocity that made Nathan's chest hurt. Nathan tried to get his arm free, but he could not.

"Give 'em room," he heard. "Let's give 'em room."

The other players did not jump on Michael. Nathan was very frightened. He moved forward now, pulling the black man with him. He heard a hissing sound that he knew came from Michael. He saw Ben's arms around Michael's shoulders, the hands clawing. Michael's face and neck were red. He saw Michael's right arm smash down, and he saw Ben's head snap back, his dark arms go limp. Michael pressed Ben against the fence, his large hand spread in the middle of the black man's glistening chest, as if holding him up. Some of the players were urging Ben to fight back, but they did so without enthusiasm. Nathan saw now that blood was pouring from Ben's nose. His head hung limply. He shook his head, to clear it. Michael backed off; then, still enraged, he turned back to Ben. He jabbed him with a finger, lifted him and slammed him once more against the wire fencing. He grabbed him by the chin and held him there, as if to get his attention.

"Maybe you haven't heard," Michael said, breathing hard. "But Jews don't take crap anymore."

Nathan wrenched his arm free, and walked to Michael. He grabbed him by the arm. Michael swung loose, almost knocking Nathan to the ground, and moved toward Ben again. "Enough," Nathan shouted. "Enough, Michael!"

"I think he broke his nose. What you think?"

"Your nose broke, Ben?"

Michael turned to the others, fists clenched, as if he were ready to take them all on. Some of them smiled and showed Michael their open hands, their light-skinned palms. "Hey man, you made your point. Let's play the game."

Ben was bent over now, bleeding into a handkerchief. The boy with the purple kerchief was trying to help him, but Ben kept pushing him away.

"Maybe we better get you to emergency at Kings County."

"Oh yeah. If it not broken yet, they finish the job."

"I'm sorry," Michael said to Nathan, between breaths. "I'm sorry. All right?"

Ben lay down on the concrete, with his head back, resting on somebody's sweatshirt. His body seemed even longer lying down than it had standing up.

"Anybody else want to say something about—" Michael broke off. His chest, heaving in and out, was flecked with blood. Nathan stared into Michael's face, at the curly black hair, the blazing eyes, the vein that pulsed visibly in the middle of his forehead. He thought of Einstein's brain, in a bottle, on a shelf of a laboratory in Wichita, Kansas. He thought of Pauline's head, wrapped in bandages, of her thin body, like a refugee's, under the sheets. He looked at the black faces all around him, and it occurred to him, for the first time, to try to imagine that a face like one of these might have belonged to the man who had put a knife into Ira's stomach.

Ben stood up. His friends talked to him, told him to shake Michael's hand, asked if he felt well enough to continue. One of them said that Michael was a doctor. Michael nodded. "Sure," he said. "That's me." He moved forward. He touched Ben's nose with his fingers, along either side, very professionally. "No break," he said. He turned and walked back to the court. He had not shaken Ben's hand. "But get some ice on it."

One of the blacks put an arm around Michael's shoulder. "Hey—you best to lie down and rest, Mike," he said. "Your blood shooting up in your head too much."

Michael pulled away. "Anyone else got anything to say about Jews?" he demanded.

Nobody spoke. "Good," Michael said. He picked up his shirt and wiped himself with it, along his shoulders and neck and under his arms. He looked at Nathan and seemed to see him for the first time. His eyes showed puzzlement. "My uncle came home last night from Israel," he said then.

"No shit."

"Come on," Michael said to Nathan. Nathan picked up his suitcase. Michael began to walk toward the gate.

One of the blacks stopped him, a hand on his arm. "Hey listen," he said. "Ben just got—you know—I mean, we happy for you when the Jews kick them Arabs' asses, Mike. Ain't that so?"

The others murmured that it was so. "You so stupid, Ben," one of the blacks said. "His old man just died a week ago, didn't you even hear?"

"Ben sure picked the wrong day to start with Michael."

"Fuck off," Ben said, and he sniffed in.

Michael said nothing. He took the suitcase from Nathan's hand and began to walk away again. Nathan followed. Michael stopped at the gate, as if he had reconsidered. He turned and waved. "See you guys around," he called. Then he left the schoolyard. They walked along the street, saying nothing.

"Hey—wait a minute."

The black player named Cicero was calling to them. Michael waited. When Cicero spoke to Michael now, he spoke very correctly, Nathan noticed. Like an educated white man. His speech was not at all slurred. "It's about my sister," he said.

Michael nodded.

"Could you see her again, Michael?"

"Does she want to see me?"

Cicero shrugged and looked down. "Who knows what she wants? She just sits around all the time, saying nothing. It's been four days this time. My mother wants to put her in the hospital again, but I said to give me a chance with her." Nathan could hear the pleading in the boy's voice. "I've been coming down here every day—I left work, I used my sick-time—hoping I'd see you. I called you at home a few times. I'm sorry. I didn't know about your father."

"So?" Michael demanded.

"Okay. If I bring her, will you speak with her? You're the only doctor she trusts."

"Maybe," Michael said.

"Please? If I bring her tomorrow, will you just speak to her? I'm scared if she goes back into the hospital. I mean—"

Michael nodded. "I know what you mean," he said. He licked perspiration from his lips. "Tell her I said I'd like to see her, but that I'd like her to call me first."

"Okay." Cicero hung his head. "But what if she won't call?"

"I think she'll call."

"She just sits in her chair and won't say *nothing,* Michael! It scares the shit out of me."

"Is she eating?"

"If we tell her to. But I don't know if she sleeps or not. She just—"

"I've got to go," Michael said, cutting Cicero off. "But don't bring her. Do you understand? If you bring her without her calling me first, I won't see her."

Michael picked up the suitcase. "I'm real sorry for what Ben said," Cicero said. He whistled. "I never saw a man move the way you moved when he—"

"Save it," Michael said, and he turned and walked down the street.

◇ 3 ◇

ONCE, ALMOST FIFTY YEARS EARLIER, WHEN THE ROOMS WERE ALL occupied, Nathan remembered, he had dreamt of writing seven different books at the same time, one in each room of the house. Every morning, he had thought, he would start in one room and work on that room's story for an hour or so. Then he would leave that room and go into the next, and work on the next room's story. The idea had been returning to him, ever since he had begun living in the house again with Michael, and he realized that it appealed to him even more now than it had when he was young. If, when he returned home from *shul* each morning, after the *minyan*, he worked on each book for an hour, and took an hour off for lunch . . .

Nathan stood in the middle of the living room and turned around slowly, in a circle. From the room, doors led to the four other rooms—the three bedrooms and the kitchen—and to the foyer. Upstairs were two small rooms. Rivka and Harvey had lived in the larger of these rooms when they were first married. The other room had been used for storage, and for guests. When Nathan was twenty-one years old he had converted it into an office for himself, with a desk and bookcases and a wooden chair and two stand-up lamps and a cot, and he had lived in it while he was writing *The Stolen Jew.*

The Stolen Jew. Michael had, on their first evening together in the house, shown Nathan the Russian edition, which had been published three years before. The book had been a great success in the Soviet Union. Nathan told Michael that he had, in Israel, already seen the book, that he knew there were rubles waiting for him in Moscow, should he ever go there. *The Stolen Jew* told the story of Noah, a young Jewish boy in mid-nineteenth-century Russia, saved from the cantonist *gzeyra*, the dread twenty-five years' service in the tsar's army, by being replaced by another boy, Mendel. Mendel is kidnapped by the Kehilla—the Jewish Council of Elders—and sent off in Noah's place. Mendel keeps himself alive by nurturing a dream of vengeance throughout his years of service and eventually he follows Noah to America, where Noah has become a famous virtuoso violinist, and he murders him. Nathan attributed the book's success to the fact that it was perceived by the Russians as being not only anti-tsarist, but anti-Zionist. It was a book in which Jews preyed upon Jews. It was a book in which Jews committed violence against other Jews. It was a book in which Jews sent off other Jews to die.

Nathan picked up the book and ran his fingertips across the gray cloth binding. There was something about seeing his name written in Cyrillic letters, in an alphabet he could not understand, that pleased him. Michael had been studying Russian for almost two years, and he had been proud to show his knowledge to his uncle. He had read the title page and the first paragraph aloud, in Russian, and the mysterious sounds had seemed beautiful to Nathan. Michael wanted Nathan to go to Russia with him. He was already in correspondence with Mischa Gronsky, the Russian translator and editor of Nathan's book, and Gronsky was very excited about the possibility of a visit by Nathan. Gronsky said that, before its official publication, Soviet Jews had copied the book and passed it to one another secretly.

Why was Michael going to Russia? He was going to Russia, he explained, in order to smuggle goods and information in and out, to and from Jewish dissidents and refuseniks. Refuseniks? Nathan despised the term. Why were they called refuseniks when it was the government that was refusing them? Why was it that people named them with a word that, like beatnik or all-rightnik, seemed to belittle them? Nathan shook his head. The world was ever the same. Nothing changed.

Nathan asked Michael about the dangers of his trip to Russia, but Michael laughed and said there were no dangers. The KGB was well aware of everything the dissidents and refuseniks did, of the many ways foreigners had of smuggling information and manuscripts and goods in and out. They watched and they waited, and they took action when they wanted to. They had files on everybody. Give us a man, they said, and we'll make a case. They had little desire to hassle American citizens, and the terror they wrought upon their own citizens was, in recent years, Michael claimed, more psychological than physical.

Nathan did not believe Michael. He had read books by Mandelstam and Sinyavsky and Solzhenitsyn. He did not believe either Michael's reasons or his facts. He trusted the Russians as little as he trusted Michael's judgment. Ruth was right. Michael was still a child. He was certain, in Russia, to do something foolish. Being there—meeting those men and women and children whom he wanted to save and could not—would surely drive him to do something rash. Nathan could see Michael, slamming the tall black man against the fence.

Coded messages and secret police and smuggling and espionage—these were glamorous notions, but Russia itself was dull. The lives of the people Michael wanted to save were dull. Nathan had met them and had worked on their cases. They were able to leave Russia when the Russians decided to let them leave, and not before, no matter the actions of all the Michaels in the world. And if Michael acted rashly and was arrested and never heard from again? Who, with influence, would care? Who, with power, could do anything for him?

"You," Michael had replied, his eyes bright. "You can, Uncle Nat. You can come with me and protect me from myself. You can make sure I stay in line and keep to the script."

The telephone rang. It would be Rachel again, Nathan knew, inviting him to come and have lunch with her, to come with Michael for supper. Nathan let the phone ring. Michael was at work. Nathan was alone in the empty house. Perhaps, he thought, smiling to himself, since there was not enough time left for him to write seven different books, he could instead write one story about a man who *wanted* to write seven books at the same time, in seven different rooms. But how, he wondered—and the same question had occurred to him years before, when the idea first tempted him—how would he ever be able to make all the stories seem to be part of one story?

Publishers had written to Nathan through the years, asking him if he was working on a new book. Libraries and collectors were interested in his manuscripts—in the early drafts to *The Stolen Jew*. And Michael had been urging Nathan to write again, to set down his memories, so that they would not be lost.

"Like the family secrets?" Nathan had asked.

Michael had laughed. "When I was a boy," he had said then, "I used to imagine that you were twins. Did you know that? What I couldn't figure out, though, was how a man who was so successful in business—so hard—could, at the same time, have once been the author of a book that had so much feeling in it, and what I used to imagine was that the family was keeping the secret from me, but that someday before you died your twin brother would show up at our house and we'd find out that this other Uncle Nathan had really accomplished all kinds of wonderful things in his life, had written dozens of beautiful books, since the time when he'd been a boy and had run off and forsaken the family."

Nathan sat in his father's red easy chair and thought of the nights when he had tiptoed upstairs after the rest of the family was asleep, and sat at the desk in the room next to the room where Harvey and Rivka were already living, and had written *The Stolen Jew*. He remembered balancing his old Underwood typewriter on top of a stack of towels, to muffle its sound. He remembered, most of all, how still the house was, and how good it felt to be conjuring up voices and stories where nothing had existed before—voices and stories that, once they were down on paper, neither his mother nor his sisters would ever be able to take away from him. He remembered Nachman's smile, when he and Nachman would sit in bed together and Nathan would read aloud from the drafts of the chapters he was working on.

"Why did you stop?" Michael had asked. "I always used to be afraid to ask you. Why didn't you ever write anything else?"

"I decided to make money," Nathan answered. The sentence was there, in his head, just as it had been over forty years before. "I decided to make money. Nachman was in a state hospital, and he had chewed his tongue up so that it was swollen to twice its size. He was in a back ward with—" Nathan stopped. "—Do you really want to know?"

"I want to know."

"He was in what everybody called then the snake pit. A back ward at Creedmoor State Hospital, with cretins and maniacs. With old men who sat all day in their own piss and shit. I tried to get him into better hospitals—private hospitals. I wrote letters, telling the hospitals his story—telling them of his talent, of what he had been like before. They wrote back and thanked me for my moving letters. They told me how much it would cost a year for them to treat Nachman in these hospitals with beautiful lawns and private rooms. They told me they were very sorry but there were no scholarship patients."

Nathan closed his eyes. The living room seemed very cold. It worried him that Michael yearned so for Nathan's memories—that they seemed so precious to him. *I decided to make money.*

I didn't know. You should have told me.

Is that you, Nachman?

Yes.

I missed you.

You should have told me. I didn't know.

Why? So you could have held that against me too? All I did for you! Don't play games with me, Nachman. You didn't know!

I didn't know—but I suspected. Listen. Sometimes, when Michael was away at work, I used to come over and sit there the way you're sitting, Nathan, in Poppa's chair, and I used to think about all the things we did together. Rachel used to telephone me also—and I used to not answer. Just like you. Sometimes I'd make believe you were here with me instead of in Israel—this was near the end—and we'd have very nice conversations together.

Why did you do it, Nachman?

You don't know?

I don't know.

And everybody always thought you were so smart!

Don't play games with me. You did it to hurt me, didn't you? To get even. To show me how much I hurt you.

Such theories, Nathan, you'll excuse me—but such theories you should take to Michael's office. Maybe you could lie down on his couch for a while, for a few sessions. He'd give you a discount, I'm sure, for family.

You had no right.

And you had no wrong? Listen, Nathan, Michael's right—maybe it would help if you would start writing again. Now that I'm gone, who else is left to give all the memories to Michael, and to his children?

Rachel is worried about Michael.

It keeps her occupied. And you? Who's worried about you?

Not to worry.

Nachman laughed. It's what Poppa always said—not to worry. But listen, darling, what I did I did for my own reasons. It had nothing to do with you, believe me. Nachman paused and cocked his head to one side.

You weren't thinking of joining me maybe, were you? Because if you were, I was going to tell you that you should wait awhile. Like Poppa used to say, your health comes first, you can always hang yourself later.

No noose is good noose.

Ah, Nachman said. That's very good, Nathan.

Nathan looked at the bookcase, against the far wall, in which a few of his father's books—those he had brought with him to America—were lined up, on the top shelf.

I want your opinion, though. Tell me what you think. I was thinking of writing again—of maybe making some notes for Michael, about Poppa, about the way Poppa loved books and would sit with us every Shabbos, from Pesach to Rosh Hashanah, studying tbe Pirkay Avos—and then I was remembering my idea for writing seven books in seven rooms and it made me feel very frightened.

I'm sorry.

Don't interrupt me. I was remembering how the idea would sometimes frighten me so much that I couldn't write anything—how it used to make me think I was crazy the way you were, only nobody knew it. I never told you that, did I? I used to be afraid that if I wrote again—seven books in one book or one in seven—nobody would understand what I was doing, and—Nachman?

Silence.

Nathan opened his eyes. Although it was still morning, outside the sky was black, and the living room was dusk and chilly. There was no stove to light, Nathan realized. Had the phone been ringing again?

The ringing's in your ears. It's very hard for you to be with me without getting angry, like always. Ah Nathan, don't you see what the trouble is? That even when you imagine me and conjure me up, you don't really trust me.

Maybe.

You invent me so you can become angry with me, that's all. So you can have an enemy.

Nathan stared into the darkened room and he remembered the time a guest had stayed with them for the Sabbath. When the guest left he took the family's silver candlesticks with him. Nathan's father did not get angry, and Nathan could hear him, the next Friday evening, when others were furious, explaining to them that the *oyrech*—the guest in the community, the stranger—was an honored man according to Jewish law.

Nathan saw himself sitting on the carpet, with Nachman and his sisters, his chin in his hands, listening to his father tell them all the legend—of how the rabbis said that on every Sabbath eve God sent the prophet Elijah, dressed as a needy stranger, to visit the Jews and to observe the ways in which they were fulfilling His commandments.

Nathan looked around. He could hear the sound of men laughing. *I have gone through the Talmud three times!* a young man declared, proudly.

Ah, but how much of the Talmud has gone through you? his father replied.

How generous and warmhearted and clever his father had been! How the other men, during those early years, had hung upon his words and his sayings and his smile. And how hard Nathan had tried, after things changed, after the men stopped coming to their house, to reach his father—to find that generosity and warmth and sparkle again. He brought him jokes and he tried to discuss Talmud with him and he tried to be affectionate with him. He worked hard in school and brought home prizes, hoping to make his father proud by his successes. All the while he was writing *The Stolen Jew* he would imagine how happy his father was going to be when he would one day read the story and know that his son had understood the sorrow of his life—when he would one day hold the book in his hands and know, by the dedication, just how much his son did love him.

When he first opened the book that Nathan presented to him, and read the dedication, Nathan's father had, in fact, broken down and wept like a child. The two men had held one another tightly, and Nathan recalled how happy he was in that moment—how he'd laughed through his own tears, and caressed the back of his father's head, telling him over and over again that it was all right, that he understood, that there was nothing to be ashamed of, that he wanted nothing more from life than to be able to give his father such a gift.

But in the days and months and years that followed, his father was unable to talk with Nathan about the book itself, and to all of Nathan's other gestures, before and after, his father hardly reacted. He remained unhappy and distant and silent. He seemed to want, most of all, to be left alone, and the only times he showed any feelings were when, in his presence, anyone else in the family would—after visits to Nachman in the hospital—try to talk about that situation. Then Nathan's father would erupt in wild anger, screaming at everybody to shut up and hold their tongues—that there was nothing to be done, and nothing to be said. *This is it and this is it!* he would cry out.

This is it and this is it. Michael was right. Nathan did wish he could go back somehow—that he could do what he wasn't sure he'd ever done: let his father know that he'd understood his hurt, that he'd loved him despite everything.

Love is sweet, Poppa used to say. *But tastes best with bread.*

Nathan sighed. He didn't expect Nachman to talk with him. He wished, though, that Michael were at home. He wished that he and Michael could be together for a long time. He didn't want Michael to leave—to go to Russia. He was frightened for him. He had enjoyed the few days he'd spent with Michael. He had enjoyed walking to and from *shul* with him each morning and afternoon, so that Michael could say *Kaddish*. He had enjoyed sharing his meals with Michael in the evening, and listening to Michael tell him about his work. He had enjoyed going for a swim with Michael each night, at the synagogue pool. He enjoyed Michael's childishness and extravagance. Michael loved to laugh. Perhaps, if he shared it with him, Michael would understand and would like the idea Nathan had, of writing seven books in seven rooms. Perhaps he could convince Michael not to go to Russia. Perhaps the stories would help. He had never told anyone in the world about them.

NATHAN SLEPT FOR A WHILE. WHEN HE OPENED HIS EYES HE FOUND HIMSELF recalling a moment during which, in the same room, he had once watched Leah braid Rivka's hair. It was a rainy afternoon and the family was sitting there together, listening to Nachman play the violin. The moment was an extraordinarily peaceful one, and he recalled envying his sisters—envying the tenderness they were able to show one another in such an ordinary and physical way. He gave himself up to the feeling now, and found that the mixture of peace and envy soothed him. He closed his eyes and imagined that Nachman was playing one of the sweet Beethoven romances their father had loved.

He remembered sitting there after school, while Rivka painted Nachman's toes and fingers with nail polish. When she was done she brought Nachman a mirror and held his hand and she taught him to apply lipstick to his lips. Nathan cringed. He remembered how his mother, instead of becoming angry, had, when she came home from work, lifted Nachman up and kissed him on the lips and hugged him and told him how beautiful he looked. She called him Norman then—she said she wanted him to have an American name. She and Rivka and Leah called him Norman. He and Poppa called him Nachman.

Nathan felt his body tighten, against the cold. He saw Rachel's face, her gaze intent, as she listened to him tell the story. Rachel had always called his brother Nachman. Did he want to share his stories with her? Was he willing to trust her? One afternoon, when his sisters were away, he went into their room and put lipstick on his own lips, lightly, to see what it felt like. The waxiness and sweet-smelling taste had disgusted him. He'd felt very frightened—oppressed, breathless, panicked—and he could recall the ferocity with which, using a wet washcloth, he'd rubbed the sticky substance from his mouth.

How full the house was with memories! How easily Nathan could, now, recall what he had seen and felt! How much he wished he could share his memories with somebody—with Michael or with Rachel or with Nachman or with Ira. Or even with Pauline. Poor Pauline. He should never have married her. He had given her very little. But she had been very undemanding. She had reminded him of Leah. Nathan wondered if, instead of writing seven books in seven rooms, what he should really do with the time he had left was simply to wander from room to room and sit in each one and wait there until he was able to remember all the things that he had, in the course of his lifetime, forgotten. He smiled. Michael would like that idea, he knew.

He drifted off again, into sleep, and when the telephone rang this time he walked to the kitchen and answered it.

"Are you all right?" Rachel's voice was high-pitched, unnatural.

"I'm all right. I was sleeping."

Rachel began to cry. "Oh Nathan. I'm just so frightened, I—"

"What do you want?"

"It's not what you think," she said. "It's not—" Her voice dropped, to a whisper. "I tried to get Michael first, but he was in conferences and they couldn't reach him. I didn't want to bother you, believe me, but who else *is* there?"

"What do you want?"

"All right. Listen." She was still whispering. "Before, when I was cleaning up, there was suddenly somebody at the window—a black boy on the fire escape, and—"

"I'll be right there. I'll come."

"No, wait a minute. I'll be all right, I'm sure. I didn't want to bother you. I just—"

"If you don't want me to come, then why did you call?"

"Because I was frightened." She breathed out, heavily. He could see her hand, on the belt of her robe. "But I feel better now, just having you to talk to. Stay on the phone with me, all right? You don't even have to talk. I'll do all the talking for us. I know the boy, you see—I know his mother. He lives in the building. So he won't—"

"Is one of his eyes very red and swollen?" Nathan asked. "Does it seem larger than the other one?"

"Why yes," Rachel said. "His name is Manuel. The eye is from when he was born—but how did—?"

"I'll come."

"Really, Nathan—you're sweet, but there's no need. When I—" She stopped. "There's somebody at the door. Wait a minute, please. All right?"

"Be careful. Don't open it unless—"

But Rachel was gone. Nathan heard her set the receiver down on the table. Nathan looked up, at the kitchen window. Across the alleyway, in the private house in which his friend Shmuel Levy had lived—Shmuel, who used to drop water bombs from the roof of the synagogue; Shmuel, who at the age of twenty-nine was killed in a forest somewhere in Belgium—he saw a young Puerto Rican girl with long black hair. She was undressing. Nathan looked down, and fixed his eyes upon the potato bin, under the window.

"It's all right," Rachel said. "Michael's here. It was Michael." She was sniffling.

"Michael? But—"

"Oh Nathan, you will forgive me, won't you? I was afraid that if I told you Michael was on his way, you wouldn't come or stay on the line with me, and I was afraid because it takes him so long to get here, and sometimes . . ."

"It's okay, Uncle Nat," Michael said. He had taken the phone from his mother. "She's a little upset, that's all. But look—I do need to get back to the clinic. Could you come and stay with her for a while?"

"I'll come."

"Take your time. She's very upset and she's insisting that I tell you not to come—but let me be with her for a while, and then you call for a taxi and come over." Michael laughed. "She's feeling very guilty about having tricked you. She says to tell you she's sorry."

"It's all right," Nathan said.

"It's progress," Michael said.

Michael told him not to rush, then left the phone for a few seconds. When he returned he told Nathan that he had changed his mind; he would telephone his clinic and, if others could cover for him, he would stay with his mother and then Nathan could come whenever he wanted and the three of them could have dinner together. It was the first day since Nachman's death, Michael explained, during which Rachel had had no visitors and had had to be alone in the apartment.

Nathan turned on the gas, so that he could make himself a cup of tea. He sat at the kitchen table, feeling cold and dazed. He looked at the window, and he saw that where the Puerto Rican girl had been, a large, fat man, much older than the girl, was now pulling the window shade down. Nathan had not yet mentioned Gail Rubin to Michael. He wondered what Michael would make of the story—of how her death had disturbed him, of his having gone to the beach, of the things he had imagined.

The door of the potato bin, which had always been black, was now painted in yellow enamel, like the walls of the kitchen. Nathan had been proud, when he was a child, to be able to open the heavy iron door so that he could bring his mother the potatoes or onions or carrots that she asked for. The door had been too heavy for Nachman. Nathan remembered thinking that the builder of the house must have been a very clever man, to have thought to leave that square opening in the wall under the window, so that his mother would have a cool place in which to store her vegetables. He remembered how, before sleep, he would sometimes imagine escaping from the house with Nachman, if thieves came, by crawling through the potato bin. He had imagined them shrinking themselves and hanging on to the edge above the sidewalk outside, their feet dangling, like Lilliputians. He saw the iron door open slowly, he heard it creak. He saw two points of light—eyes sparkling with mischief—and then he saw his own young face, peering out from inside the dark box.

He thought of the times the room would be filled with his father's friends and he imagined now that he was watching himself dance around the room, as if he were one of the old men who'd danced there years before, when, on *Shabbos*, the men of the community had gathered between the afternoon and evening prayers, for *shaleshudes*: to study Torah, to sing, to argue, to dance—and to eat their meal of herring and onions and chick-peas and *challah*.

It was a picture he wanted to remember to give to Michael. He saw himself—an old man imitating old men—hopping now on one foot, and now on the other, while he let his cheek rest upon his open palm. He closed his eyes and hummed one of the melodies he'd listened to when he was a boy. Then, he recalled, he had sat under the table with Nachman, tying the laces of one man's shoes to those of another.

How he wished that Michael could have known him as a boy! How he wished that Michael could have been there with them, under the table, that first time! He saw Nachman sitting cross-legged next to him, his hand pressed against his mouth to keep from screaming with delight. Above them, the men's singing filled the room, and when the men started to move back, to dance, Nathan and Nachman darted out from under the table and ran from the room. At the doorway to their bedroom they stopped and heard, to their surprise, the rich sound of their father's laughter.

Their father, he recalled, had never told on them to their mother. But why not? Why was it that their father had not become angry with them for such pranks? Nathan had often wondered if his father had, as a boy, been mischievous in a similar way. Once, he and Nachman had managed to tie the shoes of six men to one another.

Was it possible that Rachel had invented the story, of the boy at the window, merely to get Nathan to be with her? He was surprised. It was not the kind of act he expected of her. He wondered what she was telling Michael about now, while they were alone together, waiting for him. He looked toward the sink. He saw Rachel's brown eyes—so trusting—as she allowed him to bandage her finger. He saw the pieces of the broken dish on the floor. The breaking of the vessels. He had not explained to Rachel about the breaking of the vessels, about *kelippot*. Well, he thought. There will be time.

Nathan walked upstairs and sat in his writing room. Except for a bed and a dresser and a stack of wire hangers and some posters of nursery-rhyme characters, the room was bare. Ruth must have taken everything else with her, for the children. He pulled down the window shade and lay on the bed. There were so many memories he wished he could give to Michael, and he didn't believe there would ever be enough time. Maybe if he began writing, and if he began talking with Michael of what he wrote, maybe then—maybe if Michael and Nathan did go to Russia and could spend their days traveling from village to village, maybe then Nathan and Michael would be able to feel free to talk for as long as they wanted about their childhoods. Maybe then Nathan would be able to talk at last about those times when he and Nachman would go to their Uncle Harry's apartment and sleep outside, on the fire escape. Maybe then they would be able to talk about that hot summer night in August of 1925, when Nathan was eleven and Nachman was only four . . .

Nathan went to the closet and found a blanket. He took off his shoes and lay down again, under the blanket. Maybe if there were enough time, he thought, he would be able to tell Michael, in detail—if he could, ever, truly remember the details—of the night Nachman had slept with him on the fire escape and had fallen over the edge and landed on his head.

Nathan could hear the sound of the subway trains going by, on the elevated platform next to his Uncle Harry's building. He could remember when he spent nights wondering if a train, coming around the curve toward Throop Avenue, would ever continue in a straight line and soar through space, above the street and sidewalk, crashing into the side of his uncle's building. Again, as he had more than fifty years before, he imagined the trains heading west from Brooklyn, toward wide horizons and noiseless cities. It was the very sound of the trains, he thought, that had, after Nachman's fall, caused him to run away from home. He had imagined the trains steaming silently through beautiful cornfields and across lush green valleys. The red of the grass seemed to him to be blotting the prairies with wine stains. The wheatfields stretched before him—rippled by a gentle wind—like the ocean itself. He imagined himself coming to new cities where families of wealthy Jews took him in and taught him trades and nurtured the hope that, when he came of age, he would want to marry their beautiful daughters . . .

He stayed away for less than a week, and got no farther than Newark. He lived on peanuts and raisins and halvah and chocolate bars, and he spent most of his time riding the subways from one end of the city to the other, changing trains only when he thought a conductor was becoming suspicious of him. At night he slept in parks, and on trains, and in subway stations. Tired and hungry and humiliated, he returned home on a Friday evening, for *Shabbos*, to find that Nachman was still in the hospital. His mother accused him, again, as she had in the first instant—even while she was clutching his brother, bleeding, from the pavement—of having dropped Nachman over the side.

I was richer than Uncle Harry, Nathan thought. I became wealthier than any of the families of Jews that I was capable of imagining then. Did I drop Nachman over the side? He shivered. Even now, so many years later, he did not know if his mother was right or wrong. She told the story so often during his childhood—and Rivka had picked up where she left off—that on some days he found that he believed he had dropped Nachman from the fire escape, and on other days he believed that he had not. As for Nachman, he had always pretended to be proud of his great fall. He claimed to remember it fully, to have seen his entire life pass before him—and though he'd often told Nathan not to worry about it, he had never, Nathan knew, really confirmed or denied the truth of their mother's accusation.

"You should write again," Michael had said to him. "Nobody tells stories the way you do. You have a great talent, Uncle Nat."

"Don't be so free with advice. Don't be a doctor."

Michael had laughed. "If I was talking as a doctor—given my trade—I wouldn't be telling you what to do. I'd be letting you decide for yourself."

Nathan remembered how good he'd felt when, in the middle of the night, or toward morning, he would wake Nachman and carry him from the crib to his own bed. Whenever he wanted to conjure up the love he'd felt for Nachman, he thought of those nights. Did he still feel guilt for what had happened so many years before? He did not think so. He had gone ahead and led his own life. He had, despite Nachman's illness and failures, been a great success. But he did wish that he could know the truth of what had happened; he did wish that he could determine whether or not his mother's story was true.

He looked up and imagined that his father was in the doorway, smiling at the two of them as they lay curled together under the covers. Nachman held the pillow. He held Nachman. Nathan had never, despite many women, touched skin that was softer than his brother's skin. But his father, so pleased to see his sons together in one another's arms, made the mistake of calling Nathan's mother. *No! No!* Nathan had cried to him, silently. When she came she accused Nathan of disturbing his brother's sleep. Nathan had taken Nachman from the crib out of meanness and jealousy. *He has a desire to hurt. I know the boy, believe me. I know him well.*

Nathan looked down. He felt very drowsy. He coughed. He could see Nachman hiding under their bed, dressed in a blouse, skirt, and high heels. He smiled. He could hear Rivka, yelling about the police and about her friends and about the clothing she never got back. In her dresser drawers, where her clothing had been, she would find chocolate bars and balls of string and paper clips. And Nachman—beautiful talented Nachman! beautiful Nachman with the golden curls!—he could see Nachman roaming the neighborhood, playing his violin on street corners and in candy stores, dressed like a gypsy in Rivka's clothes. The pennies people tossed at his feet he would bring home to his mother, hoping to save her from unhappiness and poverty.

When Nathan opened his eyes, he saw Michael's face, and he heard Michael speaking to him very calmly and deliberately, asking him if he was all right. Nathan nodded. He felt terribly sleepy. He let Michael lift him from the bed and carry him to the open window. He followed Michael's instructions and took deep breaths. He listened to Michael, who was trying to reassure Rachel. He let Michael carry him downstairs. He liked being held by Michael. He smiled. Rachel's face, at the bottom of the stairs, was very pale, and he wondered why she seemed so frightened. Michael told her that there was no danger; then she started to weep, her face in her hands. Had she broken another dish? He should explain to her about the breaking of the vessels—about how his father had regarded the Kabbalist's theory of *kelippot* as nonsense. He wanted to reach out and touch her hair, to reassure her, but he felt too sleepy to speak, or to move.

He felt very happy in Michael's arms. It made him feel good to see them, and to listen to them talking about him. It made him feel good that they were so worried and concerned. They told him what had happened—that they had called and gotten no answer, that it was getting later and later, that they had been worried, that they had come and found the door unlocked and the gas on. Nathan nodded and smiled. *Did I do that?* he wanted to ask.

Rachel wiped her eyes and apologized. Michael asked Nathan to stop grinning, but this only made Nathan grin more broadly. The sensation —of being half-asleep and half-awake, of having no need to speak—was pleasant. Michael was cursing Nathan and Rachel was trying to calm Michael down. Nathan closed his eyes and rested his head against the pillows, on the couch. He imagined that he was upstairs, in his writing room, and that Nachman was playing to him on his violin, through the door.

Nathan saw himself opening the door. He could hear the sound of Rivka's voice and his mother's voice. They were screaming at Leah, who had burnt some pudding. Where was Poppa? If Poppa wasn't there, they chose Leah.

Is it helping? Nachman asked. I'm trying to play loud enough to drown out their voices, but soft enough to inspire you.

Nathan returned to his desk. He left the door open. Nachman entered and played. Nathan began writing and then looked up, at Nachman.

You're a very good muse, he said.

Michael was lifting Nathan, roughly, and dragging him to the front door. "Breathe, God damn you!" he said. "Breathe in some air, do you hear? And don't fall asleep on me again!"

Nathan inhaled. I'm sorry, he wanted to say. I'm sorry you found me that way. I didn't want to upset you again. He felt as if he were falling through warm water. But why are you so angry? he wanted to ask. It had nothing to do with you, darling. Don't you know that? He looked over Michael's shoulder and saw Rachel, her hands clasped, her face white. He smiled at her. Her mouth was open, but she did not speak.

"Why did you do it?" Michael demanded. He held Nathan by the shoulders and shook him. Rachel pleaded with Michael and reminded him of his temper. Michael ignored her. "Stop giving me that shit-eating grin and tell me! Do you hear? *Why did you do it?*"

Nathan kept smiling. He watched himself at the desk, writing. He moved closer and peered over his own shoulder; he saw that he was making changes on a page of *The Stolen Jew*—that he was rewriting it, even though it had already been published. "It was an accident," Rachel said. "Please, Michael—don't get yourself so worked up. He forgot, he was upset. It was an accident."

"There are no accidents," Michael said. He lifted Nathan, under the arms, and walked him back and forth across the front porch. "Now breathe in, damn you. Breathe!"

Nathan took deep breaths. "Like this?" he asked.

"Like that."

Nathan smiled. "You're a good boy," he said. "Raymond was right. You're a good boy, Michael. You're a very good boy."

Michael's dark face seemed to glow with anger, and Nathan thought that Michael might hit him. "God damn you, Uncle Nat," Michael said, his voice low. "Just God damn you. What in hell is the matter with you to—?"

"Shh," Rachel said. "It won't help anything to yell, Michael."

"Maybe," Nathan offered weakly, "we should call a doctor."

"I *am* a doctor!" Michael said, and he dragged Nathan down the front steps to the sidewalk. "A lot of good it does any of us . . ." Nathan wanted to laugh, to explain to Michael that he had been making a joke, to impress upon Michael the fact that, even now, despite Harvey's words, he did possess a sense of humor. He could tell that others were watching him. He was pleased that they had come. He wondered if the young Puerto Rican girl were there. He thought of her yellow skin, of its smoothness. He wondered if Cicero's sister had seen Michael, or if she were still sitting in her chair, looking down at the street. He held himself, arms crossed, for warmth, and when he felt the skin of his own forearms, he thought of Nachman's skin, when they would cuddle in bed together.

That was the room I would have chosen, Nachman said.

Then it happened in Michael's house? Nobody said.

When death makes a visit, it likes to come back soon, while it still remembers the way.

Of course. I forgot.

You forgot? Don't make me laugh, Nathan.

"What he do, man?"

"Left the gas on."

"Hey Mike—you want some oxygen?"

"You've got oxygen?"

"For my old man's heart. We keep a tank next to his bed."

"Get it," Michael said.

Michael carried Nathan back into the house. There were many others in the room, Nathan knew, and he was grateful, for he imagined that they were warming the room with their bodies. They followed him to the kitchen and Nathan opened his eyes and stared at the stove. He smiled. "Did I do that?" he asked Michael. "Did I really do it?"

"You did it," Michael said. Then, "Sure. Mental illness isn't inherited, right? It just tends to run in families."

"Very good," Nathan said. "That's what your father, he should rest in peace, used to say. But it's very nice of you to remember a saying like that at a time like this."

"I give up," Michael said, exasperated.

"He's not himself," Rachel said. "Shh . . ."

Do I sound like Nachman? Nathan let himself be lifted by the elbow and led to the living room. He saw the oxygen tank, like a deep-sea diver's, and he felt his body stiffen. "It's all right," he said, trying to pull away. "I'm all right."

"Like hell you are."

Nathan saw Michael turn and knock something from a boy's hand. "What are you—crazy?"

Others cursed the boy for starting to light a cigarette. "I forgot," the boy said. "Lay off. He put the fucking gas on, not me."

Nathan felt warm and sleepy again, the way he remembered feeling when he was a boy, at Passover, and had drunk too much wine. He smiled at the crowd. He watched Michael adjust valves. He could not remember the last time he had felt so good, so relaxed. He sat in his father's red easy chair and let Michael place the oxygen cone over his mouth and nose. He breathed in.

"That's one lucky man," somebody said.

"You said it."

"His brother died less than two weeks ago," Rachel offered. "He's been terribly upset. I really think he just forgot, you know. He was . . ."

"Now take deep slow breaths," Michael said. "Do you hear me?"

Nathan nodded.

"He looks much better already," Rachel said. "I'm so relieved. But when we found him upstairs, I just—"

"Must of been you I heard scream. Didn't I tell you I heard a woman scream, and you said no. Dumb-ass!"

"But my son knew what to do. He's a doctor." Nathan heard people talking about the color in his cheeks, about how old he looked. Rachel was holding his hand and he did not withdraw it. How many years ago was it that they had walked along the boardwalk together? Nathan tried to remember the taste of the salty air. He tried to remember the odor of wet wool—of Rachel's sweater and skirt, when they had become drenched from the rain. He remembered kissing her and how wonderful her lips tasted, with the rain and the salt on them.

"He your father, Michael?"

"You shut up. His father died. Didn't you hear before?"

Rachel was talking about Nachman's death—he had been here, in the house, waiting for Michael to come home from work, when he had passed away. She said that Nathan had flown in from Israel—that was why his skin was so brown—but had arrived too late for the funeral.

Nathan pressed Rachel's hand. He could tell that Michael was annoyed by his mother's talking. He wanted to tell Michael to relax—that it was all right for Rachel to tell them anything she wanted. He breathed in, slowly and deeply. He felt less drowsy. To be born and to die in the same house, he wanted to say to Michael. How many, these days in America, have such an opportunity?

He saw Nachman nod, in agreement.

"Luther says he wants to ask you something, Michael."

"Sure."

"It's nothing."

"Go on and ask."

"Is it true—some guys said so in school—that when you Jews die you get buried standing up?"

The boy's mother slapped him. Rachel tried to interfere—she withdrew her hand from Nathan's—but the mother hit the boy again. "Stop smiling and breathe," Michael said sharply.

"I'm breathing," Nathan said, pushing the oxygen away. His voice was stronger. He felt a wave of anger begin to rise within him, where drowsiness had been. "I'm breathing, can't you tell?"

◇ 4 ◇

NATHAN SAT IN THE BACK SEAT OF MICHAEL'S CAR, HIS HEAD RESTING against the side window. Outside, the skies were a deep black. Nathan watched for flashes of lightning. Rachel sat next to him, and she said nothing. In the silence, Nathan imagined that it was snowing—he had not seen snow for over five years—and that Michael's car was the only car on the highway, cruising along between enormous white drifts of snow, through lower Brooklyn and across the Brooklyn-Queens Expressway. He imagined that he was watching the snow collect on the bridge cables, that he was watching the ice floes below, on the river. The snowdrifts seemed higher than the car windows. They protected him.

He imagined that he was back in Michael's house and that Michael was in the cellar, shoveling more coal into the furnace. Michael made him tea and wrapped him in his bathrobe. He saw men—the scene was from a book, but the book was not his own—tunneling through snow, from house to barn, and then warming themselves among the heavy cows. He looked toward Rachel. Her eyes were closed, her lips parted.

"Your mother's sleeping," he said.

"Good."

"I'm sorry, Michael. It was a mistake—I was going to make some tea and then I went upstairs, to where I used to do my writing, and I forgot."

"It's all right."

"But I had a dream. Can I tell you about it?"

"I'm not in my office."

"I thought that maybe, for relatives, you made exceptions."

"Okay. Tell me about it."

The car skidded slightly to the left. The rain fell more heavily, drumming loudly against the roof of the car. The lightning seemed very close. Nathan leaned forward, so that Michael would hear him. He told him that in his dream a large man had been chasing him through the rooms of his house with a long stick. Michael was with Nathan and Nathan had his arm around Michael, protecting him, and trying to explain to Michael that the stick was not a present—a fishing rod or baseball bat or bow and arrow, as Michael thought.

"You looked very sweet," Nathan said. "You were very trusting."

"I was trusting."

"But I warned you that we had to escape, so I showed you the secret door—you were the first one I ever showed it to—and we opened it and ran through it along a narrow passageway, and then I showed you the house I had that was inside my father's house. It was very beautiful."

Michael turned slightly, and when he spoke his voice was gentle. "Go on—"

Nathan shrugged. "I don't know what it means, but in the dream—I can see this now—you were a young boy but you looked just like me when I was a young boy, and when I showed you the room we'd escaped into, I said to you—my voice was very clear—'Here is my childhood!' "

Michael nodded. Rachel opened her eyes and smiled. She touched Nathan's hand. "I like it very much," she said. "You always had a wonderful imagination, Nathan—"

He shook his head. "I didn't imagine it," he said. "I dreamt it." He sat back. He had not intended for Rachel to hear. He had thought he was sharing his dream only with Michael. Had Ira been in the dream?

"Go on," Michael said. "I'd like to hear the rest."

Nathan nodded. The strange thing about the dream—the part that didn't seem to him to make sense—was that the house within the house was, when they had entered it through the narrow passageway, somehow larger than the house itself. What did it mean? It was the secret place Nathan came to when he was a boy, and nobody else knew it was there. The rooms were peaceful, with soft blue carpeting and lovely stuffed easy chairs covered in wine-red velvets, and with large windows that let in streams of sunlight. Within the dream, Nathan said, he had understood its significance and had explained it all to Michael.

"Yes?" Michael said.

Nathan shrugged. "When I first woke—it was before you got there—I could remember everything I've told you, but I fell back to sleep and now I can't remember what it was exactly that I told you its meaning was."

"That's what Michael's for," Rachel said. "He's very brilliant at things like this. He'll tell you what it means."

"What does it mean?"

"What do you think it means?" Michael asked.

Nathan laughed.

See? he heard Nachman say. Didn't my son choose a good profession for a nice Jewish boy? He answers questions with questions.

So tell me, Nachman—how are you?

How should I be?

Nathan let his head rest against the car's window. He looked at the back of Michael's head, and he could see the men sweating while they shoveled their way through snow, from the barn to the hog house. The thatch roof had fallen in there, from the weight of snow. Nathan breathed out, and he watched his breath fog the car window. He saw a cloud of steam rise from the hogs. The top pigs came off alive and squealing. At the bottom, wet and black and warm and smoking, twelve hogs lay dead.

"I'm glad you told me about your dream," Michael said. His head bobbed. "It's a good dream, Uncle Nat."

"Should I save it?"

Michael laughed, for the first time since he'd found Nathan upstairs. "Sure," he said. "You could start a collection."

Rachel touched Nathan's hand. "See?" she whispered.

WHEN THEY ARRIVED AT RUTH'S HOUSE, IN ROSLYN, LONG ISLAND, RUTH was surprised to see them. The radio said that the entire Northeast was receiving the tail end of a hurricane and had warned people to stay off the roads. The children were frightened of the thunder and lightning. Nathan watched Michael kiss Ruth. They held to each other as if they were still in love. Nathan kissed Ruth. She smelled of lilacs. She told him how happy she was to see him, and she took his hand and led him downstairs, to the family room. Michael was gone. The house seemed very lived-in, as if Ruth had been there for years.

Ruth handed Nathan a towel, to wipe the rain from his hair. Where was Rachel?

"I didn't know about you and Michael," Nathan said. "I'm sorry."

Ruth smiled. "Me too," she said.

"I told Michael already—you should live together. The way young people marry and unmarry again these days is a disease. Why? They have desires? They want to fulfill themselves? There are things in life more important than self-fulfillment."

"I agree."

"Then why—?"

Michael came into the room, a walkie-talkie to his ear. He handed Nathan a second walkie-talkie. "The kids are upstairs," he said. "So this is what we'll do. I'll make believe I can't find them and then you'll—" He stopped. "Hey—you've never seen the two boys, have you?"

"No."

"Christ!" Michael exclaimed. "So much time, Uncle Nat. So much time . . ."

"I'd like to meet them," Nathan said. Michael sat on the arm of Ruth's chair. He let one hand caress the back of her neck. She leaned against him and closed her eyes. She was, as ever, stunningly beautiful. Nathan recalled the first time he'd met her, when Michael had come home from Europe and brought her to his office in Manhattan. He remembered that she had, by smiling at him, been able to make him smile. He'd always felt easy in her presence. He'd taken them out to lunch and her quietness had not bothered him. Michael had talked enough for all of them. Two days later she'd come to his office by herself, in a pale blue shirtwaist dress, bringing him a box of cookies she'd baked—to thank him for lunch.

Later, she'd given him a copy of *My Ántonia*, which she said was her favorite book. Nathan nodded. The scene he had been remembering—of the snowstorm—had come from one of Willa Cather's books. He had never read anything by Willa Cather before he met Ruth. She had wanted him to understand about all those things she had a hard time talking about. She was not, she told him, a word-clever woman. Nathan had read the books, and had loved them—their spareness, their simplicity, their severity. *Some memories are realities, and are better than anything that can ever happen to one again.* The line had come from *My Ántonia*, and Nathan had, through the years, often repeated it to himself.

Rachel came into the room, a drink in her hands. "You sent me photos," Nathan said. "I have photos of the boys, in Ein Karem. I left them there."

Ruth nodded. Her golden hair—the color of honey—brushed past Michael's hand. Nathan saw his father, on the eve of Rosh Hashanah, spreading honey on *challah*—for a sweet year. "Did Michael tell you what happened?" Rachel asked Ruth. "Because it was only an accident, I'm certain."

"I was there," Michael said, and he turned and left, without looking toward Nathan.

"What happened?" Ruth asked.

"I left the gas on," Nathan said. "They found me."

Ruth's eyes showed alarm. "*And—?*"

"That's all," Nathan said. "They found me upstairs. I was sleeping."

"But what did Michael say—what did he think?"

"You know Michael," Rachel said, sighing. "He got angry and he yelled a lot, but he stayed in control and took care of things beautifully."

"He gave me oxygen. I feel all right now."

Rachel sat next to Ruth and took her hands. "Oh Ruth—while he's gone for a minute, tell me—is there a chance? Please? What do you think?"

"No chance," Ruth said. Her voice was dry.

"But I thought that with his father gone—I hoped—and the two of you together so much—going through the funeral with each other, and—"

Nathan heard sound coming from his walkie-talkie. "This is Michael M. calling in. Do you hear me? Please respond."

Nathan lifted the walkie-talkie. "Hello?" he said.

"Identify yourself. This is Michael M. Over and out."

"That's Michael," Ruth said, and she rolled her eyes, the way she had the night Nathan had arrived from Israel. *Michael wants to be a hero.*

"Michael wants me to go to Russia with him," Nathan said. "He says he needs to have somebody along who can protect him from himself."

"Makes sense," Ruth said, and she stood and walked away. "Six months ago he said he was going to go back to Europe, to play basketball again—in Italy, for Milan. He said his jump shot is still good enough."

"I didn't know," Rachel said.

Ruth opened a pack of cigarettes and lit one. "I offered to go with him to Russia, did you know that? Did he tell you that?"

"No."

"But he won't let me. Too dangerous, he says. And do you know what?"

"What?" Rachel asked.

"I don't believe him." Ruth drew in on her cigarette, and though she did it very naturally, Nathan realized that he had never before seen her smoke.

"This is Michael M. Do you read me, Nathan M.? Please respond."

Nathan sighed. "I read you," he replied. "I read you like a book."

Ruth smiled.

"Good. Receiving background static from your command post. Sounds familiar. Nothing new to report here. Need to refuel."

Nathan could hear the children giggling through the static, somewhere near Michael. Ruth stood with her forehead pressed against a sliding glass door that led to a backyard. Before their engagement, she had been, briefly, one of Michael's patients. Nathan had been surprised. He had never thought of Ruth as being a woman with problems. She had always seemed very calm and stable to him. She and Michael had always seemed very good for one another. Before she had children, she had been a guidance counselor. Before that, he recalled—at college—she had, despite her shyness, been an actress. She had always seemed to Nathan a very beautiful and capable woman. That she had come from the Midwest, from Indiana, had made her seem especially attractive to him. When he first met her, he had thought of her in the same way that he had, previously, thought of those noiseless cities and wide horizons into which trains from Brooklyn would, peacefully, disappear. In her presence, he had felt the calmness that he had previously believed his imagined cornfields and valleys and prairies contained. He had been pleased that Michael had chosen her, had found something of what he himself had, as a young man, yearned for.

Michael was in the room, across from Ruth, pouring himself some bourbon. Ruth turned to him. "When are you going to stop?" she asked, softly.

"When I grow up," he answered. He raised his glass, toward Nathan. "*L'chayim*," he said. "If you know what I mean."

He walked to Ruth and tried to put his arm around her shoulder, but she pulled away, angrily. "Finish your game and let the children get to sleep," she said. "They have school tomorrow."

"But aren't you even going to let Nathan meet them?" Rachel asked. "I think it would reassure them. Given Nachman's death, and then the funeral, and the two of you separating, and now us here, with Nathan—don't you think—?"

"We know all about it, Mother," Michael said. He clicked on his walkie-talkie. Nathan heard the children's voices. "I hear every word you're saying," Michael told them.

"See?" a girl's voice said. "Didn't I tell you to stop?"

"Miriam?" Nathan asked.

"Miriam," Rachel said. "She's such a young lady, Nathan!"

"Poppa! Poppa!" a boy yelled. "It's me! It's me!"

"Hi," Michael said. His voice was easy and gentle. He covered the mouthpiece of his walkie-talkie and spoke to Nathan. "That's Aaron —wait till you meet him. He's terrific."

"Hey, Poppa! Poppa!" Aaron called. "Listen—"

"I'm listening."

"They call him Poppa?" Nathan looked around, surprised.

"They call him Poppa," Ruth said. "He's always insisted. He said—"

"Shh," Michael said, and he spoke into his machine. "Please repeat. I repeat. Please repeat. Not reading you. Over and out."

"—that if you go to Russia and leave us here with Momma we're going to kill the baby," Aaron said.

"No we won't," Miriam said, sighing. "We'll just run away with him."

"Kill!" Aaron shouted. "*Kill! Kill! Kill!*"

"Oh Aaron, you're such a dummy," Miriam said.

"You're a bigger dummy." Nathan heard a baby scream. Miriam told Aaron to leave Eli alone. Michael laughed and flipped a switch. "This is Michael M. calling for an immediate cease-fire. Leave Eli alone, okay? I'm ready to negotiate if you are. Over and out."

"Poppa, do you know what?" Aaron asked.

"What?"

"Someday when I grow up and be a poppa and you're the child and you're bad, I'm gonna spank you too."

Michael laughed. "Sure," he said. "But just leave your brother alone now, okay? Lay off till I get there."

"I was wondering," Nathan said to Rachel, "if you've had a chance to think of anything."

"To think of what?"

"Of a secret you could give me. Something you've never told anybody else—"

Rachel blushed. "*Nathan!*"

"Now would be a good time to remember," Nathan said. "While you're still upset by what Nachman did, by his loss."

"Stop!" Rachel said, her voice cold. "Stop being this way."

"Tell me," Nathan said to Michael. "You're a smart boy. What's the answer? Why did he kill himself? Why is it that people commit suicide?"

"You're interested?" Michael tilted his head to one side.

"I'm interested."

"I'd love to give you an answer," Michael said, "only the problem is that I've never been able to interview anyone who succeeded, if you get what I mean." He set his glass down. "In my line of work the only people I get to interview are the failures."

Nathan nodded. "I see what you mean," he said.

"Stop it," Rachel said. "Just stop it. The two of you . . ."

"Shh," Michael said, and he put his ear to the walkie-talkie again. Nathan stared out the window, into the darkness. He listened to the thunder and the wind and the rain. He remembered walking across Brooklyn Bridge, with Rivka, the two of them carrying a bucket of coal. It was raining. He was crying. Rivka was stronger than he was. She carried the bucket most of the way, scolding him all the while. In the morning Leah was born. Michael told the children that he and their Uncle Nathan were coming upstairs to make an offer. Nathan had come all the way from Israel, to negotiate a settlement. Miriam seemed impressed, but she said that the offer would have to be fair.

Ruth was next to Nathan. Nathan found himself standing at the window, looking for flashes of lightning. "Hey listen," she said, and she leaned against him. Her eyes were half-closed. She let cigarette smoke trail from her lips. "If you're really looking for secrets, you've come to the right girl."

"Did Michael tell you?" Nathan asked. He smiled at her. "I decided I would collect the family secrets, so that they wouldn't be lost before we all die."

"That's a swell idea," Ruth said, in a mock tough-woman's voice. "I like it a hell of a lot, Uncle Nat. Believe me. Can I call you Uncle Nat?"

"Stop," Michael said. "The kids are waiting."

"Hold it a minute, big boy," she said to Michael. She touched Nathan's ear with her fingertip. "Since you're in this secret business, I've got a really terrific one for you about your son, Ira. Terrific. Do you think you can take it?"

Nathan heard his heart pound. He inhaled quickly, and heard the sound of wheezing, from his chest. "He was only making jokes," Rachel said, to Ruth. "To annoy Harvey, after Harvey suggested that—"

"*Enough!*" Michael shouted. "God damn you, Ruth. *Enough!*"

Michael grabbed Ruth roughly, above the elbow. Nathan watched Michael's thick fingers press against Ruth's flesh. Ruth smiled up at Michael. "Well, well," she said. "So the big man of peace gets violent now and then, doesn't he?"

"Just cut it out. There's no need to bring anyone else into this. Get your rocks off some other way, okay?"

"Could you tell me how you feel about my telling secrets to others, Mr. Malkin?" she said to Michael, her voice sweet and solicitous. "You seem to be somewhat upset. Perhaps you'd like to talk about it . . ."

Ruth laughed in Michael's face, then walked from the room. The children were shouting—they were tired of waiting, they were thirsty, they were going to run away if Michael and Nathan did not come to them immediately. Michael breathed out. "Come on," he said to Nathan. Then, "Suicide is the last way dead people have to take revenge upon the living. Okay?"

Nathan followed Michael up the stairs and down a hallway. Despite Michael's skepticism, Nathan was convinced, now, that in leaving the gas on he had been more forgetful than willful. Moses Mendelssohn, Nathan recalled, had given the definitive refutation of suicide for a Jew. To commit suicide was to commit a crime against both nature and reason. A man who did not allow his life to proceed to its natural end thrust himself into a condition different from the one for which he was destined. Nathan smiled, pleased that he could recall Mendelssohn's logic. Nachman would agree, Nathan knew, that Nathan would never have taken such a step into the dark. To prefer death to life, death would have to appear, beforehand, to be preferable. *He's too selfish.* The annihilation of consciousness, Mendelssohn maintained—and Nathan thought, as he had in Israel, of all the years that lay in wait for him—would never appear better to a man than the smallest morsel of reality, however terrible. Nathan could not recall the rest of Mendelssohn's reasoning, but he thought of telling what he remembered to Michael, of explaining it to him, so that Michael could use the theory for some of his patients.

See? Nachman said. I finally succeeded at something.

And I failed.

You shouldn't feel bad, darling. We can't be good at everything, after all.

Nathan looked down from a narrow balcony that joined one side of the house to the other. Below, the foyer floor was spotted with wet footprints. Michael whispered to Nathan to follow him. Nathan kept his hand on the iron railing. Could the children fall through the openings? Nathan passed a bedroom and saw stuffed animals on a bed, a yellow-and-red dump truck on the floor. He thought of the poet Mandelstam—the great Mandelstam—at the end of his life, in a forced labor camp near Vladivostok. Mandelstam sat cross-legged in the loft of a barracks, reciting his poems to a band of criminals. He was small and thin, like an undernourished child. He would not eat the awful and meager food they gave him in the camp because he believed the food was poisoned. He was not afraid, though. Of that Nathan was certain. Mandelstam knew no fear. He was beyond fear. The criminals honored him and protected him from the other prisoners. Mandelstam recited his poems, which he had long before committed to heart, by candlelight.

Nathan felt water on his forehead. He looked up.

"The roof is leaking," he said. "You should fix it."

For years Mandelstam had lived without hope. When one no longer has hope, Mandelstam's wife had written, then one no longer has fear.

"About going to Russia . . ." Nathan began.

"Shh," Michael said again, and he pointed. Nathan looked in at the three children. He gasped at their beauty. A desk blocked the doorway. The desk opening, for the chair, was stuffed with blankets and pillows. Toys and boxes and books and dresser drawers were piled behind the desk, and a golden-haired boy with blue eyes—Aaron—stood a few feet behind, an enormous grin on his face, a water pistol in each hand. Miriam sat on the floor, next to Aaron's feet, the baby Eli in her arms, and she was cooing to him and telling him that their father was a mean man.

He means to be mean, Nathan thought, and he moved forward, so that he could be nearer to the children. The sight of them there, next to one another behind their barricade, melted him. Did they look like Michael when he had been a boy? Like Nachman? Like Ruth? Nathan saw his mother, with Nachman in her arms, the first time. "Oh Michael," he said, and the words that came into his head—*I'm so happy you found me in the room*—did not come out. "Just look!"

"Don't fire," Michael said, and Aaron squirted one of his water pistols and hit Michael on the cheek.

Eli whimpered. "It's all right, sweetie," Miriam said to him. "It's all right. Poppa won't take you away to Russia with him. We won't let him. You just rest now. You rest." Her voice was sure and loving—and it had a calming effect on Nathan, and, he saw, on Aaron too. Aaron sat down next to Miriam, set his pistols on the floor, and put his thumb into his mouth. "You're tired, aren't you, little Eli?" Miriam said to the baby. "You're so tired." She rocked him gently and began to hum. Nathan imagined that Ruth had looked just like Miriam, when Ruth was a girl. He saw Ruth sitting within a clearing in a wheatfield, brushing her long hair.

He peered over the barricade. "I'm your Uncle Nathan," he said.

Aaron stopped sucking his thumb. "Hi Uncle Nathan," he said.

They're my grandchildren, Nachman said.

They're beautiful, Nachman. You can be proud.

But you don't have any grandchildren, Nathan.

I know that.

And you never will. Not even if you marry Rachel. That's what I wanted you to understand.

"Listen," Nathan said to Michael. "I have an idea." He tapped on the side of his walkie-talkie. "When I die, maybe you can see that they put one of these machines into the box with me, along with my *talis* and *tephillin*. That way we could still keep in touch when we wanted to."

Michael did not laugh. Nathan wondered if Michael would have laughed had Nachman said the same thing. Nathan had watched funerals in Ein Karem. They did not use coffins in Ein Karem. The bodies were wrapped in shrouds and covered with earth.

"You should go to Russia with him," Ruth said. "Since he asked you to. You two were made for each other—"

Nathan turned. "I didn't know you were listening."

"Listen," Michael said, to the children. "This is the deal, okay? I sell the house in Brooklyn and go to Russia with Uncle Nathan, and—"

"You'd sell it?" Ruth exclaimed. "Do you really mean it?"

"Shh," Michael said. "Just listen. I sell the house and go to Russia and when Nathan and I get settled there, we send for Mommy and you kids. How's that sound?"

"I knew it." Ruth sighed.

Michael glanced at Ruth and winked at Miriam. The baby started to suck its thumb, and Miriam removed the thumb gently and gave the baby her own finger to nibble on. "That's a no-no," she said. "You're going to have to be a big boy now, for when Poppa is gone."

"No-no," the baby repeated.

"I didn't know it could speak," Nathan said.

"Do you know what, Poppa?" Aaron asked.

"What?"

"I love you."

"Don't say it *now*," Miriam whispered to him.

"But I *want* to."

"When he's sitting there alone like that," Nathan said to Michael, "your Aaron reminds me of myself when I was a little boy."

"I'm not alone and I'm not the little boy," Aaron said, but without anger. "Eli's the little boy. I'm four." Aaron made a fist and then opened his thumb and three fingers, one at a time, counting.

"Is it a deal?" Michael asked. He sat on Miriam's desk. She looked down, at the baby. "Listen," Michael said. "If not Russia, it can be someplace else—anywhere except Long Island, okay? All I'm trying to do is to figure out a way that we can all be together until you three are grown up, got it?"

Miriam nodded. She saw her father wink at her again and she tried to keep from smiling. She looked toward Ruth, briefly. "Can we go to Florida if we want, where Aunt Rivka is?"

"No," Michael said. "Florida's out too."

"How about France?"

"France is okay."

"I studied about France in school. We had a unit."

"Your momma and I met in France."

"I know *that*," Miriam said.

Nathan saw Aaron's eyes start to close. Nathan stepped back and stood beside Ruth. He thought of his head, resting against the car window. He wasn't used to being with so many people. It confused him. Things had been simpler in Ein Karem. He wasn't used to talking so much or to listening so much. And when he awoke, some mornings, in Michael's house, he realized, he had forgotten to be bitter—he had forgotten to remember about what had happened to Pauline and to Ira. Miriam's cheek was next to Eli's. Nathan heard Rachel calling from below, and telling them about another leak she had found. Nathan could smell what he guessed was a full diaper. He looked at Ruth, but her face was impassive. "Okay?" Michael was asking. "Is it a deal then?"

NATHAN HEARD SOUNDS BELOW, IN THE KITCHEN. HE HEARD MICHAEL'S voice. His own room was dark. In the hallway there was a light, so that the children could see their way to the bathroom should they awaken. Nathan thought of Tolstoy, in his grandmother's room when he was a child, listening to the old man Leo Stepanovich tell stories. Stepanovich was blind. He ate from a bowl of scraps. Prince Volkonsky, Tolstoy's grandfather, had purchased Stepanovich because of his gifts as a storyteller. Each night, Tolstoy and his brothers and sisters took turns sleeping in the room with their grandmother, watching her heavy body, robed in white, lean back against the pillows, her head rigid in a white nightcap, as if, Tolstoy had thought, she were looking down upon the world from a throne of snow. Stepanovich mixed Russian folklore with tales from *Scheherezade*, and Tolstoy lay there and listened, terrified and enchanted. *Once there was a powerful king who had an only son . . .*

The house was wonderfully still. Outside, no rain was falling. Nathan saw Michael on the roof, during the storm, hammering at the base of the chimney, where the flashing had come loose. He saw Michael hanging on to the ledge and dropping to the grass. He saw lightning split the black sky. *Do you command me to proceed?* Stepanovich would ask, and Tolstoy's grandmother, without kindness, would command him to proceed. Nathan closed his eyes, as if he were the boy in the room with his grandmother. He listened to the blind storyteller. *I understand loss. My name is Tsvi Toporofsky and I am an old man now, living by myself in . . .*

Nathan heard the sound of dishes. He heard a woman's voice. He was not sure which room Rachel was sleeping in. *Another Tolstoy! Ha! If he keeps at it long enough in that room, he'll wind up in the hospital too.* When he was a young man his mother had often predicted that he would, because of his writing, wind up in a mental hospital with Nachman, but it had never occurred to Nathan that what she said had had anything to do with his decision to stop writing. If anything, he had always believed that her voice had only served to make him more determined—to persevere, to finish his book, to never have the life Nachman had.

Momma helped us in different ways. It's what I always said. Look at it this way, Nathan. If you'd wound up with my life, would I have wound up with yours?

No.

So you can see that things worked out for the best. Oh Nathan—you shouldn't be so serious. You shouldn't be so hard on yourself—that's all I'm trying to say. I really don't understand you. For all those years, when we were boys, I looked up to you and tried to be like you, and now, when I'm gone, now is when you decide to imitate something I did. Why?

It was an accident.

I agree with Michael, and I should know. There are no accidents.

Did I ever tell you that when you were in the hospital and I was upstairs, trying to finish the book, I left the door open one day and Momma glared in at me, with her arms folded, and promised me that if I stayed where I was, writing, I'd wind up with you?

But she only wanted us to be together, Nathan. She knew how much we missed each other.

Don't always make jokes. Answer the question, please. Did I ever tell you about it?

Silence.

Nathan sighed and pulled the covers closer, to his chin. He listened to the sounds below, in the kitchen. He heard Michael laughing. He saw himself meeting Rachel downstairs, in the family room. He saw himself explaining to her about the breaking of the vessels—about *kelippot* —about the belief that all the evil in the world had originated when the vessels which held God's light proved too weak to contain it, and so broke, shattered, and fell. Nathan could hear his father's voice. In the shattering, his father explained, and from the shards that resulted when the vessels were hurled down, came the dark forces—the *sitra ahra*—of the world. From this shattering had come all things material and evil.

It had not occurred to Nathan, that first night, to speak with Rachel of *kelippot*. He had never mentioned it to Ira, and he wondered now how this mystical theory would have corresponded to theories Ira understood concerning the origin of the universe. When he was a boy, Ira had loved stories. He had had favorite authors: Robert Louis Stevenson and Jules Verne and Rafael Sabatini and Charles Dickens and H. G. Wells. He had loved to have Nathan read to him. He had loved the story of *zimzum* as much as Nathan and Nachman had.

The rabbis say that God created the world because he loved stories.

I know. Poppa taught us that.

You remember then? It wasn't just my imagination?

It wasn't just your imagination.

But Poppa didn't believe in kelippot. He only taught us about kelippot so he could show us what nonsense it was.

Of course. The hidden life of God didn't interest Poppa—he was never a theosophist. You're a lot like him in that way, Nathan. You've never been interested in things you couldn't see or touch. It was what was always different about us.

Was that why he had gone to Maagen Mikhael? Nathan saw the empty beach again. He saw the sand and the sea. He saw himself walking there and trying to remember what he had felt five years before, when he had first heard the news about Ira. He had, he realized now, wondered when he was on the beach near Herzlia about Ira. Had they told him the truth? In the months preceding his death, Ira had seemed especially depressed. He had never, since childhood, been a cheerful boy. He had never been like Michael. Nathan recalled listening to Ira, sometime shortly after Pauline's death, tell him that he had already passed the age by which most mathematicians and physicists had made their great discoveries. Einstein had presented his four great papers—including the two that introduced his special theory of relativity—when he was twenty-six. Newton had, by the age of twenty-four, invented differential and integral calculus, explained the spectral nature of sunlight, and put forth his universal theory of gravitation. I'll be forty soon, Ira had said; he had gestured to his instruments and notebooks. The rest of his life would be little more than figuring and calculating and measuring. Drudgery and bookkeeping.

Nathan wondered, for the first time, if Michael and Ruth had, concerning Ira's death, gone to elaborate pains in order to fool him and protect him. But he had seen the body, he reminded himself. He had talked with the police. He received New Year's cards each Rosh Hashanah. "Ira always knew he was brilliant," Michael said afterward. "But he used to tell me that he was afraid he didn't have enough imagination to go along with his brilliance."

Perhaps, Nathan thought, I should have given Ira more of Poppa's stories. Perhaps . . . Nathan nodded, to himself. He was surprised at the ease with which he could, now, hear his father's words. According to the Kabbalah, his father said, the destruction of the early worlds that God created was not itself anarchic or chaotic, but followed its own internal laws. Not all the shattered light descended. Some of it made its way back to its source, to *Ein Sof*—the Infinite. Then too, those vessels that were struck by the sparks of God's own light began, in the moment of their shattering, to reconstruct themselves. For the light that struck them and shattered them remained captured within the shards of the broken vessels, and this light became the source of their restoration, a process that began in the very instant that followed the original disaster.

In Israel, Nathan had read *The First Three Minutes,* a book that explained to him what scientists believed concerning the origin of the universe. The book spoke of the unfathomably intense light and heat that, filling all of time and space, was the universe in those first seconds following the moment of creation. About the moment of creation itself, scientists were in disagreement. Were we the end product of the first and only universe, exploded seventeen billion years ago in a way that no one yet understood, or were we a universe reborn from the death of an earlier universe? Were we living within one phase of an endlessly recurring cycle of creation and expansion and destruction? Or were we, perhaps, living inside what scientists called a black hole—those collapsed stars whose density was so great that their light could never escape? Nathan thought of the inside of the potato bin. He wished that Ira could have been with him in Israel when he was reading the book. He wished that he could have talked with Ira about black holes and neutron stars, about the light of photons and about the light of the *Sefirot,* those ten holy numbers that the Kabbalists believed denoted God's attributes. From these numbers all of creation emanated—that pure and endless light that filled and overflowed God's vessels. Nathan wished that Ira could have been there, watching, when Poppa scoffed at the Chassidim and the Kabbalists, who even believed that *zimzum*—the wondrous *zimzum*—represented a kind of primordial breakage within God Himself.

But such a theory, Nathan's father would point out, proud in his reasoning, required the belief that God created the world not out of His goodness and His will, but out of His imperfection—which, since God was perfect, was an impossibility. Nathan saw his father's smile—the thin slanted lips, the chipped yellow teeth. He saw himself, as a boy, leaning against his father's arm, following the path his father's finger traced as it passed under the sentences and around words, as it pointed out the sayings and the theories, in the Torah and the Talmud and the other books—some written in Yiddish, some in Russian—that further refuted the nonsense of the Kabbalists and the theosophists.

Nathan got out of bed. He had always been hard on Ira. He had always demanded that Ira do well, and Ira had never disappointed him. Ira had done well in public school and in Hebrew School. He had won a scholarship to college. He had won fellowships and had earned his doctorate and had become a professor at Columbia. He had published papers and attended conferences. But he had never married or had children. He had rarely, during his last years, smiled. Nathan saw that now. He walked from his room and looked down, from the balcony. What did Michael think? There were lights on in the kitchen and, beyond that, in the family room. Nathan wished, still, as he had when he was a child, that he could know all that his father had known about Talmud and Torah. He wished that he could have read and understood all his father's books. He wished that he could know all that Ira had known about the universe and all that Michael knew about the brain. He even wished he could know what Nachman had known, to have been able to make such beautiful sounds from such a small box of wood.

Once, he had wanted to know everything. He had, when he was a boy of nine or ten, spent many days trying to figure out how many books, and which books, he would have to read and understand in order to know everything there was to know. He had believed that there would be enough time, if only one could choose the right books. He smiled. Was that why he had first decided to write fiction? It was, when he thought of it now, such an unlikely choice—to have wanted to make up stories. But when, as a boy, he read stories and novels, he recalled, he had been transported in ways that astonished him, and he had wondered about the invisible authors, like Gods, who had created the books. They had, by inventing stories, seemed to know more even than the rabbis. How could they have known so much about what lay in the hearts of so many different people? How could they have understood everything that other human beings had experienced and felt, in so many different times and places? *God created the world because He loved stories.*

Nathan started down the stairs. Nachman was wrong. By writing, Nathan knew, he had not merely done the opposite of what his mother wished. For though she had mocked him for writing, she had always urged him to study. She had laughed at her own husband for his books and his reading, but she had always urged Nathan to study, and he had drawn strength from her demands. *You must know everything!* she had screamed at him, even while she beat at him with her fists. *You must know everything!*

They were in the kitchen. In the living room his father was begging Uncle Harry to lend him money. But Harry mocked his father. Nathan stood in the doorway, watching as his father begged Harry to lend him money, to give him a chance to prove that he could earn a living. An old printer, to whom Nathan's father made deliveries, would sell him his shop for five hundred dollars. Harry and Zlata—his mother's sister—sat there in their fancy clothes and they laughed. His father was on his knees. Him earn a living? They would be throwing their money away! It was safer to give the money to Nathan's mother, as they had been doing, than to let Nathan's father have it. Nathan stared. Why was his father down on the carpet, like a beggar? Why did he allow them to laugh at him in such a way? *Why?* His mother pulled him by the ear, into the kitchen. While she screamed at him, his father, on the other side of the wall, wept. "You must know everything!" she screamed. "Do you hear me? You must know everything. Study so that you will know everything and have everything—wealth and fame and success! Study so that the whole world will fall at your feet and grovel before you. Are you listening? Everything, Nathan! Do not trust anyone. Do not have friends. Do not lend anyone money. Do not give away your heart. Everyone must envy you."

Nathan looked into the kitchen. It was empty. *I decided to make money,* he thought. *Not to save Nachman, but so that I would not be like him, or like Poppa.* He thought of Rachel, and of how young she still looked. He imagined Michael smiling up at him—like Aaron—from under the kitchen table, in Brooklyn. Sweet Michael! Michael wanted so much for Nathan to give him stories of what things were like when Nathan and Nachman were boys. But there was something too intense about Michael's desire, and so Nathan worried about Michael in the way, he knew, that Michael worried about all that he had missed. Well. Nathan believed that Michael was right to worry. A memory of something you wanted to do and never did do was more powerful than anything you ever could do. Nathan believed that. Nothing they did now—even if Nathan should come to write seven books, or if Nathan should render for Michael every moment of what had passed in Michael's house before Michael lived in it—nothing could ever replace what they had not done when they were young. But Nathan feared that Michael did not know that. Rachel was right to worry.

Nathan walked down, from the foyer to the family room. Michael and Ruth were sitting on the couch together, Ruth's head resting on Michael's shoulder. He could tell that Ruth had been crying.

"I couldn't sleep," he said. "I saw the light on."

Ruth sat up straight. "I didn't hear you—" she began.

Michael pulled her back to him. "It's all right," he said, softly. "It's legal. We're still married."

"Oh stop," she said, and pulled away. "Would you like some tea? The water's still hot."

"I'm sorry."

"Don't be," Michael said. He stood and walked to the kitchen. Ruth and Nathan followed. Michael made tea for Nathan. Ruth asked him if he was sleeping well, if he needed anything. Nathan said he had been sleeping very peacefully. He told them how beautiful their children were. He told them that he had been frightened, earlier, when Michael had gone up on the roof.

"But I didn't," Michael said.

"You didn't?"

"You were dreaming again," Michael said.

Nathan sipped his tea. "Maybe," he said.

Ruth smiled at him and reached across the table, to take his hand. "It's nice, though—that you were frightened for him."

"Yes," Michael said.

"Maybe it means that I feel I should go to Russia with you, to protect you."

Ruth rolled her eyes. "Maybe," Michael said.

"He won't commit himself to much, off-hours," Ruth said.

Nathan saw Nachman smiling at him. Who knows? Nachman said. Maybe if you're dreaming here, you're awake somewhere else.

It's a thought.

Listen, Nathan. What's real, anyway? Maybe we only exist because we think we exist. Maybe we're both sleeping here, but we're both awake somewhere else.

Then each of us could have two lives.

At least. And maybe in one of them I could have yours and in another you could have mine.

No.

Had he hurt Nachman's feelings? Nathan put his hand out, palm up. "Sometimes," he said. "Sometimes I think that there's a little room inside me too, right here—" he pointed to a spot above and slightly to the left of his heart "—in which I've been keeping the real Nathan locked up all these years. I was thinking of writing again today—of what you said about twins—but I was afraid to unlock the door."

"What's inside?" Ruth asked.

Nathan smiled. He looked at his chest. "It's a little bit open now," he said. "Can you tell?"

"I can tell," Ruth said.

"And there's a tiny old man in there, who looks just like me, only smaller, and he also looks like me when I was a little boy," Nathan said. He looked up and smiled. Michael and Ruth smiled back at him. Nathan shrugged. "He's crazy, if you want my opinion—a real madman—but I like to take him out once in a while and let him dance around on my palm and fill my head up with the stories he's been saving over his lifetime. You wouldn't believe the ideas he has sometimes—the things he'd love to do, if he could."

"But he *can*," Michael said, with force, and Nathan stopped smiling.

Ruth spoke: "When I was a girl, whenever I got angry with Mother and couldn't tell her about something, I used to stand in front of the mirror in my bedroom—it was on the inside of my closet—and I'd watch myself cry." She laughed to herself, easily. "Sometimes I'd line up my dolls behind me, leaning them against books and shoes, so they could watch my performance too."

"Yes?" Michael said.

Ruth looked down. "It's what I thought of—the picture of a little me, in the mirror—when Nathan was talking just before . . ."

Michael kissed Ruth on the cheek. He reached out and put his hand on Nathan's shoulder. "Hey listen," he said. "As long as we're talking this way—it's been a while since we've been together like this—can I tell you something I've been wanting to tell you?"

"You're asking permission?" Ruth said.

Michael touched her cheek with the back of his hand. "No," he said. He looked at Nathan.

"Should we wake Rachel?" Nathan asked. "She'll be upset if she misses anything. She likes stories."

"Let her sleep," Michael said.

Nathan nodded. He was puzzled. "Why is it I feel so much freer at times like this?" he asked. "It's always been this way—when I first wake up in the middle of the night, or if—"

Ruth looked to Michael. "It's probably that you haven't had time to put your defenses on," Michael said. "But listen," he went on quickly, "I wanted to tell you about why I first decided to go to Russia, all right? The real reason."

Nathan realized that his palm was still stretched out across the table, toward his niece and nephew. He watched himself there, and when he leaned down slightly and the little old man, his hand cupped over his mouth, whispered his idea to him—about how to make even more money from *The Stolen Jew*—Nathan smiled. He withdrew his hand and lifted his cup. It was almost empty. Ruth poured more tea for all of them.

"About eight months ago," Michael began, "a Russian Jew turned up at the clinic. His name was Lazer Kominsky. He was about my age, maybe a year or two younger, and he was almost as tall as I am. He came with his wife and his mother. They were both worried about him. I liked Lazer." Michael smiled, and turned to Ruth. "Yes, I do my best to help all my patients, but there are some I like more than others, and I liked Lazer. I liked him a lot."

Nathan wanted to interrupt Michael, to tell him his idea—not that he would write something new, but that he would begin to rewrite *The Stolen Jew*. He had always been good at making money. That was his great talent.

"Although Lazer said it wasn't so, and that they were worried about nothing, his wife and mother claimed that he had, several times, tried to kill himself. Once by falling asleep in his car, with the motor running, and once—" Michael did not look toward Nathan "—by leaving the gas on in the house when the others were gone. Lazer denied that it was so, but he agreed to see me several times. Anything, he said, that would make his wife and mother leave him alone.

"We got along well. As I said, I liked him—and, more than that, I admired him. I started to study some Russian—basic words, to make him feel more comfortable, to show him that I was making an effort too—and he supplemented our sessions with clippings that he said his wife and mother insisted he bring to me. They were news items and profiles, placed by the synagogue that had sponsored their immigration, about his coming to America. Local Synagogue Welcomes Soviet Family—that kind of thing. Lazer had been incarcerated in camps and prisons for over eleven years, with time out for a few stays in what the Russians call psychiatric hospitals."

Nathan looked at Michael and decided not to interrupt. "Let's not go into what they're like, okay?" Michael said. Nathan nodded. He saw Nachman, in Creedmoor State Hospital, wrapped in a straitjacket. He saw himself staring at Nachman while he held Michael's hand. Michael was eleven or twelve years old, not yet Bar Mitzvah. Michael's eyes were wide with fright and misery. Why had Rachel insisted that Michael come to see his father like this? *Why?* She claimed then that his imagination would invent worse terrors than reality ever could—the unknown, she said, was always worse than the known—but Nathan had not agreed. Life always turned out to be worse than people imagined it could be.

"He'd been arrested, originally, under the famous Article Fifty-eight that they get everybody under—for alleged counterrevolutionary activities. In his case it meant that he was arrested for passing out Zionist literature. He demanded the right to live in a Jewish state. He was a Jew the way a Ukrainian was a Ukrainian and a Georgian was a Georgian. He demanded the right to live in a Jewish state. He was sent away for three years. When he was released, he applied for an exit visa, to emigrate to Israel, and he was, for this, immediately dismissed from his job as a carpenter in a furniture factory. They confiscated his identity papers and—within a month—arrested him again, for having no job. This they called 'parasitism.' They sent him to a forced labor camp. I'll spare you all the details—he was beaten, tortured, interrogated, told that his family had betrayed him, was asked to betray close friends, was driven half-mad. In addition, he lost four of his toes from frostbite. He complained and wrote letters—had them smuggled out. For this letter-writing, he was sent to a psychiatric hospital—the first of several stays—where, as nearly as I can make out, they used him for the testing of new drugs, most probably dissociative anesthetics such as the ketamines, and, for sure, MDA and DMT—amphetamines and tryptamines that induce severe states of regression, micropsia, and macropsia."

"Translate," Ruth said.

"Regression. And a feeling that the world is shrinking—that it's expanding." Michael stared at Nathan. Nathan wondered if Michael was remembering the same visit to Nachman. He wondered if they could look hard enough into one another's eyes so that they would be able to will pictures and memories there. "But okay," Michael said. "All that is standard, right? If you live in that awful country—that drab hell—and you speak out, those are the chances you take and the things that happen, right?" Michael leaned back and laughed. "But Lazer—I'll give you one anecdote so you can see why I was drawn to him, why I liked him—lacked a certain dullness that even the bravest of the dissidents usually possess. Lazer had flair, okay? When he went on trial for his Zionist activities, he showed up in court garbed in *yarmulke*, *talis*, and *tephillin*. It said so in one of the newspaper articles he brought to me. He spoke to me of his act. It was so, he admitted, and then, smiling sheepishly, he confided something to me that he'd never told anyone else. He had, he was ashamed to say, wrapped the *tephillin* straps on the wrong arm—the right instead of the left—and he found this very funny. It made him laugh a lot." Michael imitated a man with a Russian accent:

" 'But Michael, excuse me, please, and tell to me—who was to know the difference?' " Michael did not smile. "There were, of course, no Jews in the courtroom—if there were any at all—who were old enough—who had survived—and who remembered the proper way to put on *tephillin*. All right.

"What fascinated me about him, though, as the months went by—he saw me for one week short of six months—was the ease with which he could describe for me his life in Soviet prisons, camps, and hospitals. He had no trouble whatsoever in describing in gross detail the most extraordinary tortures, both physical and psychological. He had no trouble whatsoever in describing for me the intricate and not so intricate ways in which his friends and fellow inmates were mutilated and destroyed, mentally, spiritually, and physically. And yet—and here's what first made me suspect that his wife and mother were right to be concerned, because for a while I guess I was taken in by Lazer—for a while I guess I identified with him too much and thought that what worried them was nothing less than his bravery, his extraordinary willingness to take risks—and yet this is what fascinated me and worried me: he could never describe for me anything about what his life was like *before* the camps and prisons.

"Whenever I would ask him about his childhood, or about his mother and father and brothers and sisters—whenever I would ask, in the most tentative way, if something he'd said, or something I'd said, reminded him in any way of something from his childhood, he would, with great calmness, begin to tell me about some *other* experience from a camp or prison or hospital that he was reminded of. For a while I felt he was right to do this—that what had happened in those places was so awful—and in ordinary ways, mind you—for it was the dullness and *meanness* of his day-to-day life that seemed most horrifying—that I didn't see the pattern."

Michael paused, and drank some tea. Ruth looked at him. "I wish you'd told me," she said.

"When?" Michael asked sharply. "On visiting days?"

Ruth raised her shoulders slightly. "That was up to you," she said. "You could have—"

Michael waved away her words. "But wait," he went on. "I did—from the newspaper articles, and from interviews with his wife and mother, begin to piece together some things about his background. His father had been a very wealthy man before the war. He had owned a large furniture factory in Vilna, and when—this would have been in the early spring of 1941—the Russians occupied Vilna, before the Germans overran it, his father was arrested and shipped to Siberia—for his capitalist crimes. His father spent the war in a camp there, and was thus saved, by the Communists whom he hated, from the Nazi concentration camps. After the war he remarried—a non-Jewish woman—and was rehabilitated, as the Russians say, and with his skills rose again and became the foreman of a furniture factory in Leningrad. He had five children, of whom Lazer was the third, and the only boy.

"The father, it seems, requested and was given permission to travel to Lithuania, and to Israel. He searched the family's history. All his relatives—his mother and father and wife, his two children by his first marriage, his four brothers and two sisters, and every aunt, uncle, niece, nephew, and cousin—had been murdered by the Germans, most of them by the *Einsatzgruppen* in the summer of '41, the rest in the death camps. Lazer's father returned to Leningrad with photocopies of documents he had obtained in Israel, at Yad Vashem. He read them constantly. When he was not reading them he kept them locked in a special safe. When Lazer was eleven years old, his father went berserk one day at the factory—he deliberately destroyed expensive equipment, he killed a guard whom he accused of having murdered Jews, by throwing the man into a giant wood-chipping machine—and then he went to his office, locked the door, and shot himself."

"My God!" Ruth exclaimed.

"No," Michael said quickly, correcting her. "*Our* God." Nathan leaned forward. He thought of the way in which Michael had spoken with Cicero, outside the schoolyard. He remembered, after Ira's death, noting his own disappointment with Einstein. Einstein had believed that, though God may have been subtle, He was not malicious. Nathan was pleased to hear Michael talk like this. "I asked Lazer about his father's death," Michael continued, "and he confirmed what I had already learned. But he added nothing. His father had survived the Nazi death camps as, I suggested to him, he himself had later survived the Soviet labor camps—but when I asked him to react to this statement, when I asked him to tell me something about his father, when I asked him if he could remember him—when I asked him if, for starters, he would simply tell me what the man had looked like, he would not, or could not, respond. He gave nothing. Every defense in the book came to his rescue then—denial, displacement, sublimation, intellectualization, rationalization—you name it, he used it. He could go on forever about the camps. He could, even in his halting English, and with wonderful Russian expletives thrown in, express every feeling he'd ever had while there, and recall every experience, and tell me everything he felt about these memories and feelings . . . but he could not and would not remember his childhood."

Michael stopped. Nathan thought of reaching his hand out to him, of patting him on the shoulder, but he didn't. All stories had endings. "And then, Michael?" he asked smiling. "And then what happened?"

"And then one day he didn't show up. I called his home. They thought he was with me. I told them to check in his room. They checked. They found him there as I'd expected they would. He was dead."

"How?" Nathan asked.

"Sleeping pills," Michael said. He flashed a false smile. "I had prescribed them. He'd saved them up."

Like secrets? Nathan thought of asking. But he said nothing.

"But why should his story make you want to go to *Russia*?" Ruth asked. "It's a terrible story, Michael—but I don't understand what—"

Michael smashed his fist against the tabletop with such force that Nathan's teacup fell to its side. Michael stood. "You wouldn't, would you!" he said. He leaned down, his fists pressed against the table, and spoke, enunciating his words with painful deliberateness, as if speaking to a disobedient child. "I-have-to-go-because-they-are-Jews-and-I-am-a-Jew. I-have-to-go-because-there-are-other-Jews-like-Lazer-Kominsky-there-and-I-want-to-get-them-out-before-it's-too-late."

Ruth looked up at Michael. When she spoke, her voice was hard. "Why? So they can kill themselves too?"

Michael drew back his hand, as if to hit her. "Don't!" Nathan cried. He grabbed Michael's forearm. "Don't, Michael. Please—"

Michael pushed Nathan's hand away. He glared down at Ruth with such rage that, when Nathan looked into Michael's eyes, he was reminded of only one other person: Nachman. "The camps have nothing to do with why he couldn't remember his childhood," Ruth said to Michael. "You should know that better than anyone. He couldn't remember his childhood because there's something in it that must have been even more painful than what happened to him later. He couldn't—

"All right," Ruth said. She closed her eyes and shook her head, as if agreeing with him, as if submitting. "All right."

"I don't understand," Nathan said.

Michael's eyes darted to the side. Nathan looked to the doorway also. He thought of Rachel, in the back seat of the car, pretending to sleep. Michael inhaled deeply and sat down. "Do you want to understand?" he asked.

"I think so," Nathan said. "Yes."

"All right," Michael said. He rubbed both his eyes, starting at the inside corners with index fingers, then smoothing downward, along his cheeks, with his hands. It was a gesture Nachman had frequently made—a gesture their father had made, when he sat in his red easy chair. "Lazer wasn't free because he was still imprisoned by certain fears that he carried with him from childhood," Michael said. "Exactly what they were I can only speculate on. They were probably much the same as those fears you and I live with, Uncle Nat. Since, however, he could not recall them, or talk about them in any way, he could not deprive them of their power over him. You and I can, more or less—all right? But . . ."

Michael's eyes seemed to glaze over for a second. He turned to Ruth. She nodded, encouraging him to go on. "All right," Michael said. "Lazer wasn't *free* to remember, don't you see? What happened was simply this: Vilna, Auschwitz, Siberia, the prisons, the trials, the camps, the hospitals—Lazer had spent so much of his life surviving these things that he had no energy left with which to survive his childhood."

Michael exhaled. He rubbed his forehead. "I'm tired," he said. "What time is it?"

Ruth glanced up at the kitchen clock. "Ten to four."

"We should get some sleep," Michael said.

"Do you miss your father?" Nathan asked. "You rarely talk of him."

"I miss my father," Michael said.

Nathan felt that he understood most of what Michael said—he knew that he wanted to understand—yet he was still worried. "You're not like your father in that way," he offered. He thought of Michael, on the roof, in the midst of the storm. "What I mean is, seeing you—what you've become—nobody would ever confuse you for him."

Michael leaned toward Nathan, as if to hear better. "Confuse—?" he asked.

Nathan felt weak. He felt, for the first time, that Michael was observing him professionally, that Michael was judging his words. Nathan tried to speak more firmly, with more conviction. "You're everything he never was," Nathan said. "That's all I mean."

Michael smiled. "The way you were?" he asked, and then, before

Nathan could reply, Michael stood again, put his arm around Ruth, and spoke: "Let's all sleep, okay? I'm glad you found us down here, Uncle Nat. And I'm glad I found you upstairs, right?"

"*The Professor's House*," Ruth said. "I was thinking of it before."

"Michael is a professor too?" Nathan asked.

"No," Ruth said. "*The Professor's House*—by Willa Cather. The book. I gave it to you to read once, do you remember? He leaves the gas on too."

"I liked it," Nathan said. "The professor wrote history." He nodded. "I've always liked stories about men who know things."

Ruth closed her eyes briefly, as if to recall a passage she had once memorized. " 'When he's alone in his house, resting upstairs, the storm blows the stove out and the window shut. The long anticipated coincidence has occurred. All he has to do is open the window, but instead he lies on the cot and wonders how far a man is required to exert himself against accident.' "

"Yes," Nathan said.

" 'He lies on the cot and wonders how such a case would be decided under English law. He hasn't lifted a finger against himself—is he required, though, to lift it *for* himself?' "

She kissed him on the cheek. "Good night, Uncle Nat."

"Good night," Michael said.

TWO

THE STOLEN JEW

◇ 5 ◇

NATHAN PLACED THE MANUSCRIPT ON TOP OF THE STOVE, BETWEEN THE gas burners. From a saucer he took a damp tea bag and pressed it against a corner of the first page with the palm of his hand. He turned several pages, past the opening fragment, until he came to the section about Noah's first New York recital. In the manuscript he was now preparing, he had decided to have the two sections follow one another. He opened the tea bag and sprinkled tea leaves along the margins.

It's a very Jewish book.

And why is it a very Jewish book?

It's a very Jewish book because—take these fragments, for example—the pattern is what I would call mosaic.

Nachman groaned. Oh Nathan!

And the little touches I'm adding—things that have to do with ultimate matters—those I'm putting in for what I call cosmic relief.

Nathan told himself to save these jokes for Michael. He smiled. Michael had loved his idea—had even, from his clinic in downtown Brooklyn, brought home two reams of old yellowed paper that had been stored there. Nathan sat at the kitchen table. He looked at his book, and at the blank yellow pages. Nobody loved and honored literature as the Russians did, he knew. Even their awful leaders had a boundless, almost superstitious respect for poetry. "Why do you complain?" Mandelstam used to ask his wife. "Poetry is respected in this country—people are killed for it. There is no place on earth where more people are killed for it." How wonderful it would be, then, Nathan thought, to screw the Russians.

The Russians loved manuscripts. In the thirties, under Stalin, many writers had kept themselves alive by selling their manuscripts to collectors. The same officials who refused to publish their manuscripts would often buy them privately. Now, when their authors were in the ground, the books and poems and stories were published. Now, in the Soviet Union, cowards rushed forth to rehabilitate and praise those whose deaths they had not even mourned. If they knew—Babel and Tsvetayeva and Gumilev and Mandelstam and the others—would they smile? How the Russians loved, again and again, to rewrite their own history. But exactly how much effort, Nathan wondered, was required for intelligent men and women to believe in each new version of the same event?

Well, Nathan thought. He could rewrite history too. And in so doing, he saw, he would also be saved from having to write new stories. He had been right, and Michael would see that now. Perhaps someday he might consider writing something new—Michael was urging him to turn Lazer Kominsky's story into a book; Michael believed that, with his knowledge of Russia, Nathan was the perfect man for the job—but for now, Nathan had insisted, the best thing for him to do was to rewrite the one story he had once written.

Nobody, Nathan claimed, would be interested in new stories by an old man. Nobody would want to believe that a writer who had not written for almost fifty years could write again, could simply open a door inside himself and let what had been locked away for so long come forth, as bright and wild and original as it had ever been. Who would ever believe that the stories he'd kept inside him for so many years would have improved from their long rest, would really have matured with age?

So what Nathan had decided to do—and his idea pleased him as much as the writing itself did—was to cash in on his small measure of fame, and on the success of his book in Russia. He knew about cashing in on things, he said. Collectors would pay more, he believed, for old manuscripts by a writer such as himself, than magazines and publishers would ever pay him for new stories and new books.

What Nathan decided to do, then, was to invent his one book, *The Stolen Jew*, all over again—making up new versions that Michael could then offer to the Russians as if they were early drafts for the book that had appeared when Nathan had been a young man. Nathan told Michael to write to Gronsky, the translator, and to tell him what he would be bringing. Gronsky could line up buyers. There was only one condition: no Jewish dissidents or refuseniks would be allowed to purchase his manuscripts. The money obtained from the sale of the manuscripts would go to help them—to buy food and books and medicines, to purchase exit visas. The money obtained from the sale of the manuscripts would, Nathan hoped, help the Lazer Kominskys who were still alive.

The idea of rewriting history—his story!—appealed to Nathan. He could not, he knew, change large things with his writing. He could not free Russians. He could not bring Lazer Kominsky back from the dead. He could not give life to Mandelstam or to Babel or to Tsvetayeva or to Mayakovsky or to the others. He could not, in things more private, give life to those people he himself had known and loved. He could not bring back his father or his brother or his wife or his son. He could not give to them the happiness they had never had. But he could rewrite the story he had once written, and thereby exact on their behalf, as it were, a small measure of revenge. He knew about revenge in the same way that he knew about making money. He could rewrite the story he had once written—he could, at last, *use* its success for others instead of for himself—and thereby let those who were still alive, and those whom he still loved, see in what ways he loved them, and in what ways he asked their forgiveness, and in what ways he still hoped to be able to give to them.

Nathan enjoyed his work. It was work he understood. He made small changes and large changes; he invented preliminary notes and lists; he deleted chapters and he forged variant endings; he added new material and new characters—all of which, his buyers were to understand, had never wound up in the original version. He went to stationery stores and rummaged in back rooms to find the oldest paper he could; he used old ink and old fountain pens; he baked his manuscripts in the oven and wet them down with tea bags and kept them in the refrigerator; he slept with them under his pillow.

Nathan was happy. His days were full in a way they had not been since a time before both Pauline and Ira had died, when he had, sixty and seventy hours a week, worked at his office on West Thirty-eighth Street, managing the business—Distinctive Women's Wear—that had made him his fortune.

Even to think of the noise in that office, and of the factory that adjoined it, and of the street below, irritated Nathan. In Ein Karem, in the three small rooms of his stone house there, he had become accustomed to the lack of sound. For most of his life, in the garment center, he had assumed that he had thrived on the constant noise and motion. But now, in Michael's house, as in Ein Karem, he was surprised to find that he loved silence. When he was growing up, he had always been afraid of silence. When there was silence, he knew, anger was sure to follow. Silence was hostility. If conversation lagged at a meal, even for a split second, he'd always rushed to fill the empty space. The house had been so full of words all the time, of words and chattering and yelling and fighting—everybody telling everybody else what to do, everybody reporting to everybody else on what they'd done, everybody minding everybody else's business, everybody giving warnings and threats and guarantees and ultimatums—that when he had, upon occasion, arriving home from school, opened the front door and heard nothing at all, he had at once assumed that the others were dead.

His heart would stop then, and he would stand just inside the front door and imagine that his mother and sisters were lying on the kitchen floor, blood flowing around them, knives and cleavers and ice picks in abundance, kosher salt sprinkled everywhere. He would tiptoe through the rooms, from one to the other—eager, fearful—never calm until he was certain that he was, in fact, alone. When he was older he'd taught himself to call out *It's me—I'm home!* the instant the sound of his opening the door did not produce other sounds.

Nathan saw himself sitting in the living room, watching his father sleep. He had always enjoyed watching his father sleep. *A father may be envious of anyone except his own son.* Nathan heard his father's voice, teaching him the rabbinic saying. His father—how his mother hated him for the ability—was able to fall asleep in his chair whenever he wanted to. He could simply sit, close his eyes, and—no matter what had been happening—he would fall asleep at once. Nathan took the manuscript from the stove and sat at the kitchen table. He would add his father's saying—he would give it to Tsvi. He turned pages, looking for the right place. *The rabbis say that a man may be envious of anyone except his own son, and yet . . .*

In saving the old woman, Nathan wondered, had Ira been trying to emulate Michael? Ira had done so well in school that it had rarely occurred to Nathan that Ira might have been envious of others, of Michael.

The Russian edition of Nathan's book lay on the table, next to the

American edition. He opened it, to the title page. From a folder, he took three title pages, which he had typed upstairs the day before. Now, on one of them, he carefully copied out, in black ink, the title and his own name, from the Russian. These copies, he decided, he would sell at a premium. And in the manuscript itself—Michael could show him where the words corresponded to one another—he could, here and there, write Russian words in the margin.

Later, when he was done with his morning's work, he would have lunch with Rachel, and they would walk together, in Prospect Park. Nathan leaned down over the table, pen in hand. He read from his manuscript, making corrections as he went along.

THE STOLEN JEW

a novel by Nathan Malkin

Everything is foreseen, yet freedom of choice is granted; in mercy is the world judged; and everything is according to the preponderance of works.

—*Pirkay Avos*

LOSS!

1.

I understand loss. My name is Tsvi Toporofsky and I am an old man now, living by myself in the great city of New York, and waiting, happily, for the day of my death, when I shall be joined with those I loved. But I was a young man once, with hopes and dreams and a heart that overflowed with happiness! Let me tell you my tale, then, dear friends, of how I came from Russia to the United States of America, with my wife and my darling son, Noah, and of how I came to lose everything.

I was born in the village of Burshtyn, in the year 1818, of parents who had come to Russia from Galicia earlier in the century, I know not the year. My earliest memory is of two events which occurred within the same week: my grandfather's death and burial, and the birth of my brother, less than three years younger than myself—a brother who never made the journey to America. Of nine children born to my mother, six died in infancy.

I can see Momma holding the newborn Noah at her breast. A shaft of light comes in through the window of our bedroom and I am standing in the doorway. I have heard such screaming and cursing all through the night that when my father tells me that I may go into the bedroom, I am frightened and I try to flee from the house. But he grabs me by the arm, roughly, and he sets me down in the doorway. And now I am standing there and I can see Momma holding the newborn child at her breast! She is looking up at me, and—how my heart fills, the transformation is so magical—I see that her face is relaxed in a way I have never before seen it. Oh how beautiful she is! How I love her!

"This is your brother Noah," she tells me, but my eyes are transfixed upon the motes of dust which filter across her chest. I stare at Momma's breastbone, flat now, like pale satin. Where, I wonder, have all her screams and her pain gone to? The baby is so tiny next to her swollen breast that I fear it cannot be alive. "Come—don't be afraid," she says to me, and I move forward and touch my brother's skin. It is the softest thing in the world.

My mother touches me so tenderly then that I begin crying, and, without letting Noah loosen his grasp upon her nipple, she hoists me to her lap, and, from her other breast, she lets me drink of her warm sweet milk. Noah's face is turned sideways, his eyes steadfastly fixed upon mine, yet without malice. I look to the doorway, but my father is gone.

Yes, dear friends, I can see myself standing in the doorway as I stood there on that day, and suddenly—and this is what I recall above all, so dreadful was the feeling that coursed through me—I am my mother's eyes, looking at me and seeing in my frail young body everything I have been, am, and will become, even unto the final hour of my life!

My grandfather's body, three days later, was laid upon our kitchen table, and my father, a member of our community's *Chevra Kedisha*—the Holy Brotherhood—as my grandfather had been before him, helped wash the body and prepare it for burial. While men wailed funeral chants all night long, beside the body, my brother Noah cried with a startling pain, as if the spirit of death had entered his soul.

He spurned my mother's breast then, and I tried to enter her eyes again, so that she would not see his mouth, but her eyes were frantic with hatred and anger, and her body, when I went to her to be touched again, was rigid like the wooden board upon which I slept. Even when her nipple was in his mouth he would not suckle. During the night I would lie awake and listen to him gurgle—it was as if Lilith were playing with him—but my mother did not wake to slap him and chase Lilith away, as was the custom.

When Noah died, before the end of his first year, and was laid in the ground next to my grandfather, my mother said wicked things, for which my father beat her.

My grandfather's body, fat and pink, his stomach hairless, looked, upon the kitchen table, like nothing so much as the body of a pig, one like those I would see in the slaughterhouses of the Gentiles. How I loved to steal into their farmyards to watch them stab the neck and singe the fine hair! And how I loved—there is no denying it—to watch my mother weep and tear her hair when she remembered her dead children.

2.

The rabbis say that a man may be envious of anyone except his own son, and yet I see now that when my Noah performed, my heart hungered to be inside him. I longed to feel what he was feeling, to know what it was like to hear the music he heard, from within—to hear a voice that could tell those precious fingers where to place themselves. They say that sons live their lives in fear and rebellion, seeking to surpass their fathers without losing their fathers' love, yet my life has taught me differently, and so you read here the story of a man who brought about his son's ruin by desiring to steal his son's childhood.

Even now, at the end of my days, I long to know what was in my son's heart that enabled him to touch the hearts of others, and mine so especially. Mr. Davidov, for whose theaters in New York I moved props and scenery and costumes, offered to give my Noah his chance. Noah thanked me politely, and kissed my hands. I was moved by his gesture, and I put my hands upon his head and gave him my blessing, something I had not done for years, but something I had done, with love, every Friday evening when he was a child—asking that the Lord bless him as he had, in former times, blessed Ephraim and Menasseh.

When I had finished, Noah told me that he would, now that his chance had come, do more than merely perform music—but he would tell me no more. He set about inventing his own act, an act he would not reveal to me before the day upon which I first saw him perform in America. My wife made for him a black silk vest with a white silk blouse whose puffed sleeves would billow as he played. I sat at the side of the theater, in Mr. Davidov's box, ashamed of my own vulgar appearance, for I believed that everyone in the audience could look at me and know that I was little more than a *grauber yung*.

I believed, despite the outward signs of his gratitude, that my son despised me, for being the object of others' scorn. At home, and especially in the presence of his mother, he treated me with respect, but away from home he would mock my halting English and mimic my Yiddish, a language he willed himself to forget. My bent back was a burden to him, my old clothes were his shame, my hooked nose his curse. On the few occasions that we traveled together, here in America, if he saw ladies and gentlemen approach, he would separate from me and cross to the other side of the street. And what did I, in my wisdom, do, even while I was remembering those precious times when he had traveled with me in our wagon, curled against my side, on the roads that led to and from Burshtyn? I encouraged him to be an American! I stopped talking to him in Yiddish. I admired his sparkling blue eyes and his straight nose. I did not remind him of the journeys we had made together in the Old Country, and of how he had loved to be with me, to listen to my stories. I never asked to know his American friends, or that he go to *shul*, or that he observe the Sabbath, or that he study Torah. It had become enough, for me, to hear him, in his room, practicing his music. That alone gave comfort to my soul—for in his music, I believed, his true heart lived.

There was forgiveness and love in his music. When he played, then did his heart speak directly to his fingers! And I believed that they would sustain his true self until that time when he would come to know me again, and to understand that no matter how much he wished not to seem a Jew, and the son of a Jew, the world would never let him forget who, in truth, he was. The glories of his heritage he would have to discover for himself. The secret of his salvation—from twenty-five years' service in the tsar's army, and from Russia—would be his in due time. But never did I believe that, because of what I had done for him, I wanted to own him.

He was not yet sixteen years old, yet he looked no more than twelve, a fact that Mr. Davidov said was greatly in his favor. In addition, said Mr. Davidov, the public believed that the gift of playing the fiddle had been given to the Jews at Sinai, and so, in my son's chosen profession, his race was also his fortune. Noah looked directly at me when he bowed to the audience, and I longed to flee from the theater. Yet his clear blue eyes fixed me to my seat. I sat there and I imagined his mother coming to his bed in the night and whispering to him the secret I had so far forsworn to tell. Yet which was the dream, I wondered—her coming, or my imagining that she had come? I felt, in the warmth of the theater, that I was going mad, for as Noah nodded to his pianist I thought suddenly and only of the other boy—the boy I had paid the Kehilla to kidnap and send off in my Noah's place—and in my head that boy had the narrowed eyes of a half-starved wolf.

I felt that he could see us across oceans, here in America, and that his eyes could devour the look that passed between myself and my son! That was when my heart leapt as never before—that was when I felt that I wanted to enclose Noah's heart within my own, to protect it!

But when Noah placed the golden-hued instrument under his chin and began playing, my desire to protect was transformed into a desire to possess. I saw the eyes of the other boy, somewhere in Russia, and he was eating by himself beside a fire that had been kindled in the snow. And then I shut that boy's eyes out of my mind and I gave myself up to the magic of Noah's music, to the mysterious gift given him to create such sweetness and sadness.

But then did my great pain reveal itself to me—*I would never know what he knew!* . . . And now that my Noah is dead, the knowledge that was in his heart and in his fingers is gone with him. It can be bequeathed to no one. How I longed to know how he could know just where to place his fingers along that narrow bough of wood that bore no markings. *More!* When the long sweet notes drifted into the air between us, I wanted to be the very notes themselves.

What did he play that night long ago in New York? The famous "Devil's

Trill," by Tartini, and I have come, dear friends, remembering that night and that music, to believe that the devil who played to Tartini in a dream, inspiring him, and tempting him with the languorous beauty of the painful drawn-out opening, and those fluttering trills which beckon afterward—that this devil was then playing not in Noah's dream but in my own, and was poisoning the well of my love.

Noah played only the first movement. Then he astonished me. He set his violin down upon the piano and announced that he wanted to tell a story. His music had spoken to him as ever I had dreamt it would! He looked at me and said that the story was one that I—his father—had told to him, a story that my father had told to me. The story took place in Russia, he said, and he apologized for not remembering his Russian and Yiddish well enough to render it as I had rendered it for him. How I admired the beautiful English he spoke: He recited the story with feelings I had not believed he could contain, and in the midst of his recitation he would stop, pick up his violin, and play from other movements of the sonata—furious double and triple notes, heartbreakingly falling melodies—and even when he came to weep as he played, I saw that he had never before loved playing itself as deeply as he did on that night. He was playing for me.

The story was "The Casket and the Jewels," and Noah acted out all the parts. I do not, of course, know what he felt while he performed. That is eternally denied me. He wept and he lamented and he got down on bended knee and he walked from one side of the stage to the other. His voice was a voice of anguish and suffering, and then it was soft, like a woman's. And how much was felt, and how much was feigned, I could only imagine.

The story begins in the village of Burshtyn, in Russia, where the two small sons of a rabbi are dying. The wife of the rabbi sits by their bedside, alone, describing their last moments for us. When the rabbi comes home at night, he asks why his two sons were not in school that day, and instead of answering, the wife tells him that she has a problem that only he, in his wisdom, has the answer to.

A friend has loaned her some jewels and now the friend wants them back. What should she do? The rabbi answers that, of course, she must return the jewels at once. The wife kisses his hands and leads him to the bedroom, where she shows him the bodies of their two sons. "These are the jewels," she says, "and God has asked for their return!"

Then Noah played once more, even while everyone could see the tears streaming down his rouged face. Was I the only one in the theater with dry eyes? For whom was he weeping? If I could have entered his heart, and put on his knowledge with his feeling, would I have foreseen his final fate at that very instant? Was that why my own heart refused to melt?

Or was I only angered because he had taken the story my father had given to me, and had given it away to strangers? While the audience wept and Noah played, my mind—betrayed and confused—opened yet again to the picture of the other boy, that boy who would one day, as a man, come across the ocean also and, having kept himself alive with the dream of the moment in which he did finally live, revenge himself against my son. I saw him riding across the frozen tundra, spurring his horse with abandon, a shimmering sword raised high in his right hand. He was handsomer than my Noah! The horse's mouth foamed, yet the boy's face, without sweat, was like the earth: solid and frozen and pale. His blue eyes were as deep and furious as the raging ocean. A silver medallion—the Star of David—glistened against his chest, blinding me.

I never told my Noah of what I saw on the day his life changed and his public career, here in America, began. Nor did I ever, even until this moment, truly stop coveting his life.

NATHAN PLACED THE MANUSCRIPT ON TOP OF THE STOVE AGAIN, AND HE smiled. What surprised him each time he looked at the words he had written so many years before was that they seemed to contain so much feeling. He had never thought of himself as having been a man with feeling. Nachman had been the son who possessed feeling. Nachman had been the son who possessed imagination. Nathan had been cold and hard and persistent. That was why, even in his writing, he had succeeded wherever Nachman had failed.

Nathan arranged the papers on the kitchen table and put them into folders. He took the folders with him to the living room. He sat in his father's easy chair, and he realized that he was no longer certain, when he added or subtracted items from the manuscript, that he was doing so for the first time. A true mosaic, he told himself, was made by shattering the original picture—and then putting it together again. Were these new first drafts so dissimilar to the real first drafts he had written once upon a time? Perhaps not. So many years, he thought. So many years. He rubbed his eyes with his index fingers. He was tired.

He thought of Mandelstam's wife, the extraordinary Nadezhda, still alive in a small apartment somewhere in Moscow. He thought of how, fearing the destruction of all her husband's poetry and prose, she had, during the reign of Stalin, set herself the task of memorizing her husband's works. While he was in a labor camp, and after he had died or been murdered, and while she was working in a clothing factory, she repeated his poems and stories to herself, hour after hour and day after day and year after year, one following the other—and when she came to the end of all his work, she would return to the beginning, so as never to forget. Although she forced his poems into the homes of friends brave enough to hide them, in her memorizing them, she knew, lay the only hope, the only certain way, unless she too should die, of ensuring that his works would not perish. But how many works by how many other writers had not been set to heart by those who survived? The great Russian writers—Babel and Mandelstam and Tsvetayeva and Gumilev and Sinyavsky and Solzhenitsyn and Esenin and Khlebnikov and Brodsky and Blok and Markish and Mayakovsky and Meyerhold and Pilniak and Mikhoels and Livshitz . . . the names went on and on, an endless trail of death and exile, of suicide and murder. So many lives lost, Nathan thought. So many books that would never live again.

So many years. It's what you said when you first saw Rachel.

I'd forgotten.

But I like your idea, Nathan—what you're doing with the book. It's the kind of idea I might have come up with, if I'd had your talent.

Michael said the same thing—that it was the kind of thing you might have thought of. You always liked to fool people.

Publish or perish, that's the way I always put it. You published and I perished. But in Russia, the writers get to have it both ways, don't they?

First they perish, and then they publish. Is that what you mean?

Exactly. Listen, Nathan. Do you remember the story of the little old Jewish man selling ice cream to the goyim, with a sign on his ice-cream cart that says I DON'T SELL TO JEWS?

Of course. And one day his friend wanders into the gentile neighborhood and sees the sign and all the goyim buying the ice cream and he starts ranting and railing. And the little old Jewish man keeps shushing him and telling him to go away.

And when all the goyim are gone and the man screams again and says it's true what people say, that there's no anti-Semite worse than a Jew, the little old Jewish man shushes him again, looks around, and then whispers—

Listen, have you tasted *my ice cream?*

Poppa liked that joke, Nathan, didn't he? I never understood why when I was a boy. But it's good to fool people sometimes. I think it's very nice that you're going to fool the experts. Perish and publish. I like it. And in the meantime, you and I can have fun playing with the changes and trying to figure out why things are different now.

Why, the scholars will ask, did I leave out the image of Tsvi suckling at his mother's breast, in the final version?

And why did you add the paragraph about his mother saying wicked things and his father beating her? That's what I would ask, if I were a scholar.

"For in his music, I believed, his true heart lived." I had forgotten that I wrote that. I had forgotten that I used to wonder, sometimes, what you thought of my writing it.

Listen, Nathan, what I came to tell you was that I'm sorry you told Michael about these conversations we've been having. I was hoping it could be something we kept between ourselves, just the two of us. I was hoping you'd let me add things to your collection—some things I'd never told anybody else. And do you know what I decided to call them?

What did you decide to call them?

Grave secrets.

Nathan smiled. That's very good, Nachman. Grave secrets. I like that. Do you know what Michael calls you?

What does Michael call me?

He calls you my observing ego.

Michael can call me whatever he wants. It's his right. We don't live in Russia, after all.

Not yet.

You have a point, Nathan. But listen, the part that interested me most—I saw that you left it the way it was—was when you said that Tsvi says that he was the only one who didn't cry. I found that very interesting, given your own life.

I didn't cry when Pauline died. I didn't cry when Ira died.

That's what I mean.

But when you died, and when Rachel held me . . .

Nathan put the Russian edition of his book on the top shelf of Michael's bookcase, next to the other Jewish books. The boxes of letters were gone—the brown and orange boxes that had been so precious to Nathan's father. There were errors in the other chapters—errors of fact that Nathan could, with the knowledge of Russian history he had gained through the years, now correct. He had, secretly, been ashamed of them, though nobody had ever pointed them out. He wondered if he had, for these errors, been attacked in Russian reviews?

He took out one of his father's books and opened it. The title page was blotted with stains, but the Hebrew letters were legible. That was another story he wanted to remember to give to Michael and to Ruth. Had Nachman ever spoken to Rachel about it? Nachman had been so young—not yet five. Had he even remembered? Nathan saw Nachman, standing in the rain, between the hedges, clutching the soup greens and carrots in his hands.

Nathan put the book back—it was a *mahzor*, for Rosh Hashanah—and sat. He closed his eyes. He did not mind remembering. He did not mind hearing those voices he had not heard for so many years. Why wait? Although he and Rachel had not talked about that first night again, he could tell that she knew now that he no longer felt ashamed of the way he had acted. He did not believe that he would ever again feel the way he had felt then—but neither did he believe that he would hurt anyone, himself or Rachel or Michael, by telling them of the things that he was hearing and remembering. Michael, he knew, would urge him to write his memories down. Michael would try to persuade him by praising his storytelling powers. Well. First he would finish the early drafts to *The Stolen Jew*. Then he would go and collect the family secrets. Then—he hadn't told this to Michael yet, but he had made his decision—he would go to Russia with Michael.

But he would go to Russia only if Michael agreed that he would, upon returning, live with Ruth and the children again, for a set period of time. After that Nathan would consider himself and Rachel and their future. And when all these tasks were accomplished, maybe then he would think about writing something new. Maybe then he would consider Michael's suggestions. There were many things he still had to do. There were many books he still wanted to read. Most of his father's books were gone, but the books he himself had bought—the great multivolume sets on Jewish history and ideas by Dubnow and Wolfson and Baron and Graetz—were there, across from him in Michael's bookcase, mixed now with the works of Freud and Jung and Sullivan and Winnicott and Kernberg, and with those by others of whom Nathan had never heard.

When he first bought those multivolume sets, he had planned to read through them all. Through all of Dubnow and Wolfson and Baron and Graetz. But in America he had never had the time. He had worked too many hours. He had not taken the books to Israel; he had left them with Nachman and with Michael. In Israel, however, he had borrowed single volumes from the library at Hebrew University, and he had read in them. He had read enough to know of the errors he had made in his own book. Was there enough time to read through the sixteen volumes that Baron had spent his lifetime writing? *A Social and Religious History of the Jews*. Nathan had read Dubnow's three-volume *History of the Jews in Russia and Poland, from the Earliest Times until the Present Day*, but what of Dubnow's many other works? Nathan stared at the half-shelf of his father's books. They were all that remained, and he would never know enough Hebrew to understand them. Still, it comforted him to be in the same room with the books. He closed his eyes. Poppa's books, he thought. How Poppa loved his books.

HIS FATHER'S SMALL LIBRARY OF BOOKS HAD BEEN HIS JOY, AND WHEN Nathan was eight years old he was first permitted, on the day before Passover, to help his father air them and dust them, so that his father could be certain they were completely free of leaven. They set up benches and chairs in the backyard behind the house, and they placed long boards on them. Then Nathan went back inside and crawled under the table in the living room—the special dark mahogany table that was used only for Rosh Hashanah and Passover—and, from the shelves that were hidden behind the table, he took down the books, carried them out two or three at a time into the sunlight, and gave them to his father. His father smiled at him and placed the books, one by one, on the boards, and opened them. When the shelves were empty, his father gave Nathan a goose feather, and Nathan carefully dusted the sides and backs of the books. Then they sat together and watched the wind leaf through the pages; Nathan liked being close to his father then, because his father seemed very happy. His father said that the wind itself was like a brilliant scholar who could glance through many books in only a few hours, and yet possess within his mind and heart forever after what it took ordinary men years to acquire.

When the sun began to set, they brought the books inside, and Nathan crawled under the table again and put them back, in the order in which he'd taken them out. He was always proud—from the time he could crawl, from his earliest memory—to be able to fetch his father's books for him, to be able to tell the difference between the various bindings and titles. Often, when his father was with friends, in *shul* or at work, he would tell them how brilliant Nathan was—how, when he would ask for his *Siddur*, before Nathan was even a year old, Nathan would crawl under the table, and from all the books on the three long shelves, know which book was the *Siddur*, and bring it to his father. And when his father would ask for other books—for his *Shulchan Orech* or his *Tanya* or his *Pirkay Avos* or his *Gittin*—Nathan would, by signs known only to him, by size and markings and scratches and colorings and fragrance and stains, know which they were and bring them to his father. Before the age of three—before he had learned to read all his Hebrew letters—he knew every book in his father's library, and could return them to their proper places.

Poppa's books, he would say to his father, smiling. Poppa's books. He loved his poppa's books, and the times he spent with his father, listening to him explain where he had obtained each of them, and what was in them, and why he had placed them where he had, were the most wonderful hours of his childhood. They were times he could be close to his father—times they could talk with each other, times Nathan could savor the words of a man who rarely spoke.

The bookcase of early childhood, Mandelstam had written, is a man's companion for life. Nathan could still remember the exact order of his father's bookcase. He remembered the large two-volume *Siddur* that had belonged to his grandfather—square books that were full of wine stains on the pages that contained the Passover *Haggadah*, and spotted with tears where the Rosh Hashanah *Amida* appeared. They stood at the head of the first shelf, followed by the various *mahzors* and *Haggadahs* and single volumes and tractates from Talmud sets that his father had collected. Alongside these books was the smaller *Kitzur Sheloh*, a classic of Ashkenazi mysticism that his grandfather had adored, and then the book Nathan had loved especially—a thin dark blue volume called *The Book of the Angel Raziel*, which, his father confided, was guaranteed forever to save their home from fire. When, then, Nathan would see the wonderful black pictures of angels and golems and beasts and bearded prophets leap into the air, he would always be terrified that, while the book was in the backyard, the house itself, unprotected, might catch fire. He always brought *The Angel Raziel* back inside first, and the following morning, when his father would burn the bread crumbs and goose feather and wooden spoon in the bright flames of the cellar furnace, Nathan would, with closed lips, silently bless its magical powers.

Nathan loved too the large *Gemorra* that his father would, in his bathrobe on Saturday mornings, read before going to *shul;* he loved a small eighteenth-century *Haggadah* with marvelous etchings of the ten plagues; and he loved to open the two orange-and-brown boxes from the bottom shelf, the boxes his father had forbidden him to open. In these boxes were the letters that had broken the heart of his father's grandfather Pinchas—letters from Pinchas's son, a son who had been a victim of the cantonist *gzeyra*, a son who had been forced to leave the *shtetl* and to serve for twenty-five years in the tsar's army. Nathan loved to untie the strings that held the letters together, and to try to make out words and phrases. The letters were written in Yiddish, in an almost indecipherably small script, and even when Nathan could, with a magnifying glass borrowed from his stamp collection, make out some individual letters or words, there remained, mostly, multitudes of words and phrases he did not know, and felt he never would know.

Often, sitting cross-legged under the table when nobody else was near, and looking at the frail tissue-thin pages—at brownish blots that he believed were bloodstains—Nathan would try to imagine what this young man's life had been like. He had been sent off to the army at the age of twelve, and Nathan would, after inventing gruesome and heroic encounters for him, find himself trying to imagine also what it was the boy's father had felt during all those years he did not see him. When he would imagine what this invisible man felt—there were no photos —Nathan would also, of course, begin to think of his own father. He could recall this now. He would begin to wonder what feelings lay in his father's heart, and he would ache with the desire to share his own imaginings with him, to have his father read to him from the letters, to have his father tell him stories, to have the two of them talk to one another as he dreamt a father and son should.

But his father would say little about the letters, except to declare with anger that someday when he was ready—*When I'm ready I'll be ready!* he would shout, the few times Nathan dared to question him—he was going to have the letters printed, so that Jews in America would not forget what their lives had been like before. The truth was that it amazed Nathan, and thrilled him, to have had his father shout at him in this way, for as Nathan grew older his father rarely spoke to him with passion of any kind.

But before Nathan was old enough to try to decipher the contents of these letters, and before his father became so sullen and withdrawn, so silent and irritable, Nathan loved to have his father tell him about the books, and he loved most of all to have his father tell him about those works on the special half-shelf next to the reference books—the *Zecher Rav* and *Mishpat Ha-Urim* and *Seder Ha-Dorot*—the books and pamphlets written by men his father had known personally. Many of these books his father had brought with him from the Old Country—from the *shtetl* of Burshtyn, in which he was born—and when his father would hand Nathan one he would often tell the story of the time the author himself had first come and presented his father with the book, and of how many of the rabbis would bring the books and pamphlets to him wrapped lovingly, as was the custom, in freshly laundered handkerchiefs.

The picture of these unknown men, all of whom were dead by the time Nathan was born, haunted him, and one Friday when he was seven years old—it was just after the birth of his brother, Nachman—and while his mother and sisters were in the kitchen, preparing the Sabbath meal, Nathan went into his mother's room, and then into the room that Rivka and Leah shared, and he took all their handkerchiefs from their dresser drawers. Then he crawled under the living-room table and spent the afternoon wrapping as many of his father's books—the smaller and thinner ones first—as there were handkerchiefs. When his father arrived home from work, Nathan met him at the door with one of the books and then drew his father with him, by the hand, to the living room, and showed him the others, all neatly stacked under the table. His father smiled with moist eyes, and he pressed Nathan to his chest. But Nathan's mother and sisters were furious, and his mother chastised him and beat him about the legs with a wooden spoon, and she screamed at his father, as she often did in those years, for filling Nathan's head with his useless knowledge and his vain dreams.

Why had Momma screamed in this way? She had screamed for the same reason that she had, in the first place, made Nathan's father hide his books against the wall behind the mahogany table. In the Old Country,

Nathan's father had been a learned and honored man. He had been a carrier-of-heavy-loads, and Nathan's mother often spoke to him and to Rivka and to Leah of how handsome he had been, of how all the other young women had envied her when, at the age of sixteen, her marriage to him was arranged. Although their father was only twenty years old at the time, he was already looked up to for his brilliance by many of the older men of the community. In the disputation of Talmud, only the Burshtyn Rebbe and Reb Zalman, the ritual slaughterer, knew more, and some believed that, had his family allowed him to give up his work and to devote himself solely to the study of Torah, he could have become a truly great scholar. In this opinion, his father told him with sad eyes, the Burshtyn Rebbe concurred.

But there was no Torah without bread, his father said. There was no Torah without bread. His family was too poor—even when the Burshtyn Rebbe offered to raise enough money to send his father to the Yeshiva in Minsk—to allow him to leave. His family needed the money his strong arms and back brought to them. The Burshtyn Rebbe and the Yeshiva at Minsk might support him in his studies, but, with him gone, who would feed his widowed mother and his younger brothers and sisters? And what of his new bride? So Nathan's father continued to work, and to study when there was time left over, and when life grew worse for all Jews, after the Passover pogrom of 1903 in Kishinev, and after the more bloody pogroms of 1905, in Kishinev and Odessa and Bialystok and Kiev and many small villages, he and his wife and his wife's younger sisters, Zlata and Chava, took what possessions they could and left Burshtyn and crossed the ocean and came to America.

In America everything changed. Zlata married and her husband died of tuberculosis. Nathan's father grew ill during the third winter—first his lungs, then his heart—and he lay in bed for fourteen straight months. He did not die. But when he rose from his bed, their mother would later tell them, he was an old man. Zlata, when her year of mourning was over, soon met and married another man, Nathan's Uncle Harry, who was a manufacturer of interlinings, and she moved out of the house. Harry and Zlata gave their mother money and bought for her the small house on Winthrop Street. Chava married also—Nathan's Uncle Jack, a dentist —and Chava and Jack moved away, to Chicago, where they had five children. Nathan never met Chava.

Nathan's sister Rivka was born during the first winter in America. Nathan was born ten months after that. Leah was born twenty months later, during the first year of his father's recovery; then—five years after that—an accident, Nathan learned, from their arguments—his brother, Nachman, was born, and afterward his mother was different. She looked, suddenly, as old and as tired as his father. Before Nachman was born, she had seemed to Nathan to be a beautiful woman, and he always noticed that she never looked in mirrors. But after Nachman was born, the left side of her face fell, the skin hung loosely in flaps about her chin, her eyelid drooped permanently, and she began to look at herself in mirrors all the time.

She began, more frequently, to curse Nathan's father for his failure to make money, and to hold up to him the example of Nathan's Uncle Harry. When his father returned from *shul* in the morning, before setting out to work, she would ask him how much his friends paid him for the knowledge he dispensed to them. Such a brain! she would cry out. And see what he uses it for! He did not love her, she would claim—to him, on *Shabbos*, and to her children the rest of the week, when he was away—and the proof was the fact that he had afflicted her with poverty when he possessed the brains to have given her a life even better than that of her sisters. On *Shabbos* she would nag him to go out and find an extra job instead of going to *shul*. All day he sits and he studies and he prays and he rocks back and forth, she would mock, and what does it bring us except misery!

She came also to talk to Nathan about his someday becoming a dentist or a doctor or a lawyer, and whenever she caught him with one of his father's books in his hands, she would snatch it from him and throw it under the table. Did Nathan want to end up with his father's life? Did he want someday to visit such unhappiness upon a bride of Israel? Poppa was a poor book-peddler, and not even a book-peddler. He did not write the books or make the books or even sell the books. He merely carried small packages of them from one factory to another. And he was so slow and weak, and became so lost on the way, in his precious discussions, that a water-bearer, the most lowly of trades in the *shtetl*, would, she claimed, have earned more than he did.

Nathan could not argue against her, even when, for a month or two at a time, his father's strength would return, and the house would fill up with his father's friends—but he did grow hard and cold. When she would finish one of her harangues and try to kiss Nathan, he would draw back and stiffen. He would not return her kisses or her caresses. He wanted to refuse her her wishes. He wanted to protect his father from her words. He would make himself rigid and he would think of those times, fewer and fewer with the years, when his father would talk to him about his books, or take Nathan with him to visit the warm buildings in which books were being made. While his mother railed, Nathan would clamp his jaw shut and fix his mind upon pictures of himself being lifted up in his father's arms so that he could smell the pots of glue and see the white sheets, like miracles, coming off the black metal presses with words on them. He would close his eyes tight and fix his mind upon pictures of his father's proud eyes, when he would show Nathan off to his friends by having Nathan read to them in Hebrew. He would think of his father, in the backyard—the most peaceful and beautiful picture of all—bending over the benches, a faint smile on his lips, while he opened his books to the wind.

Nathan had been named for one of his father's brothers—Na-tan ben Tsvi—his father's youngest brother who, left behind in Burshtyn, had died of pneumonia at the age of twelve. Nathan's father had always believed that it was his fault that his youngest brother had died—that, had he been able to earn enough money to send to Burshtyn for the other Nathan, the boy would have come to America and would have been treated in an American hospital and would have survived. Nathan's father named Nachman after his own grandfather—Nachman ben Chaim—but their mother refused to call him by this name. She wanted her sons to be Americans. She called him Norman, and she made Rivka and Leah call him Norman, and Nathan was astonished, and pleased, that in this one thing his father had the courage to defy her. He continued to call his younger son Nachman, and Nathan did the same, despite, in her presence, being hit upon the ear each time he did. Nathan's mother also stopped talking to them in Yiddish. Only to herself or to the walls—when she was railing against his father, or bemoaning her fate—did she sometimes lapse into Yiddish.

Nachman seemed happy either way. He loved to sit on his mother's lap and to accept her kisses and caresses, while she spoke to him in her broken English and called him Norman—and he loved to have their father and Nathan speak to him in Yiddish when their mother was not near, and call him Nachman. Unlike Nathan, Nachman was both a sickly and a happy child—frequently ill, but always smiling, always affectionate toward his mother and sisters, always accepting their attentions and their food and their gifts when he was bedridden, always trying to please them by helping them to clean and cook, by bringing them gifts, by playing for them, by singing for them, by doing whatever they asked him to.

But Nachman must have loved their father as much as he loved their mother, Nathan knew, and he must, even, have been jealous of Nathan—of the fact that their father could sometimes share his books and his knowledge with Nathan in a way he never did with him. For though Nachman would sometimes bring books to his father, or lay them on his father's bed so that they would be there when he returned home from work, their father, as if acknowledging his wife's dominion over Nachman, never remembered to ask Nachman to fetch him a book.

One day, three weeks after Passover—Nathan was eleven and Nachman was now past four—Nathan returned home from school to find that Nachman had set up the benches in the backyard by himself, and that he was taking all the books from the living-room shelves and, one by one, was stacking them on the boards. The two boxes were open, and the small bundles of letters were lined up neatly along the board nearest the house. Nathan smiled at his brother. Nachman beamed back at him, his eyes glistening, and told Nathan that their mother had given him permission at last to do for Poppa what Nathan did for Poppa. Their mother stood on the steps, her arms crossed. "It's only a game," she said.

Nathan looked up at the sky, which was black with clouds. "But it's going to rain!" he cried. He pointed. "Look—"

Their mother shrugged. "It's only a game he's playing. You had a chance. He should have his chance too. Just because you're the oldest—"

Nathan stood there, their mother watching, while Nachman skipped around the benches, happily dusting the books with a goose feather, and crying out with joy each time he believed he had found a crumb or a piece of dust. When he found some bits of cracker—Nathan suspected their mother had placed them there, to please him—he brought them to her and she kissed his face all over and told him how proud his father would be when he came home from work.

And Nachman was so good, she went on—so *grown-up*—that she also wanted to let him, for the first time, go on an errand for her. He had done a good job and had finished with the books. Now she would give him a nickel and a note and he would go to Mr. Krichmar's fruit-and-vegetable store and get her some carrots and soup greens. Nachman smiled at Nathan and put the nickel into his pocket, with the note from their mother.

"But what if it rains?" Nathan asked.

Their mother blew air through her lips and waved a hand at Nathan. "He'll go for me," she said, smiling at Nachman.

Nathan put his arm around his brother's soft shoulders. He pointed to the sky, to the fast-moving clouds. "Bring the books back in first," Nathan whispered. "In case it rains. Bring the books in first. I'll help—"

But their mother pulled Nachman from Nathan and pushed him toward the street. "Go now. Momma needs to start supper. Go now, darling. I'll watch the books. Go for me, my sweetheart."

Nachman's eyes blinked. Their mother pushed him again, through the opening in the hedges, and she kissed him and whispered to him how much she loved him for being so grown-up. Nachman looked back at Nathan, his eyes wide, and left. Their mother turned and Nathan thought she would go into the house, so that he could start to bring the books in, but instead she came near to Nathan and stopped between two of the benches, as if standing guard.

She said nothing and Nathan could find no words. He felt ill—dizzy and weak and nauseated. He placed his own school books under one of the chairs, and he waited. A minute later he felt the first drop on his forehead. "But they're Poppa's books!" he pleaded. The sky was black. He heard thunder. "He'll be angry with Nachman. He'll lose everything! We must—"

Nathan started grabbing the books and stacking them against his stomach, to run with them. His mother shook her wooden spoon at him. "Then let him be angry. Let Norman learn now. Let him learn, do you hear me?"

The rain was falling on Nathan's face and hands and spotting the covers of the books. He looked around, hoping he would see his father—hoping he would find somebody else in the yard who could help him. "Please—" he cried. "It's raining. Can't you see?"

His mother did not seem to hear him, or even to be talking to him. "What did books ever get for us? Look at Harry—look at Jack. Look at the way people look up to them. Do they set their books out before Passover?" Her left eye closed all the way. "Ha!" she cried.

Nathan started to run toward the house with the books, and she moved at last, blocking his way with her broad body. Nathan tried to get by her, and she began hitting at the books and knocking them from his arms with her wooden spoon. "Norman put the books out—you shouldn't take away from him!" she yelled. "You shouldn't be a bully to him. Norman put them out!"

Nathan tried to pick up the books, and when he bent over she beat him upon the back and the neck. The rain was pouring down and, in his mouth, it tasted salty. He looked behind him. The benches and boards were darkened with water. The shower was splashing against the books and he could see the droplets springing back into the air, in tiny explosions. Two bundles of letters had fallen to the ground. He ran past his mother, to the porch, dropped the books he still held in his arms, and grabbed a blanket. He ran back out and threw the blanket over the letters. He started to grab more books and his mother chased him now—cursing and yelling at him—and for an instant he stopped and let her beat against him with her spoon and her fist, so that he could be certain he was not dreaming. Her blows hardly hurt. He started moving again, as fast as he could, and she continued to chase him and to shriek at him—her head lifted to the skies. Norman would not turn out like his father, but Nathan would, she cried. She saw that now! Poppa would have knocked down a Cossack for her when he was young, but now he could not even lift a sack of flour! Her mother and sisters had been raped while wealthy Jews traded their jewels for freedom! Nathan watched rainwater slide down her chin. She tore at her hair. He found another blanket, but while he was spreading that over a line of books, his mother was howling in pain and lifting the first blanket. The letters were drenched. His mother howled the way he remembered her howling on the night his brother, Nachman, was born.

Thunder crashed and broke the skies, closer to them, and Nathan covered his head, afraid that the limb of a tree would fall upon him. His clothes were soaked through. He stood and looked at the books, and he knew that all hope was gone. His mother saw him stop. She was no longer howling. Her body sagged. Nachman came running through the hedges, carrying carrots and soup greens in his two tiny hands. He ran straight to their mother and she lifted him and hugged him. "My precious Norman. My darling. My *bubeleh*," she cooed to him, forgetting, in her agony, and speaking in Yiddish. "My darling Norman. My love child. My sweetness. It's not your fault, don't you see? It's not your fault, my precious."

Nachman burst into tears. Nathan wanted to go to him—to snatch him from his mother's arms—but even while she covered Nachman's pale face with kisses, she glared at Nathan so coldly that he dared not move. He covered the books again, with the wet blankets, and picked up those books that had fallen upon the dirt and the grass. The letters were heavy with mud and water. "Did your poppa ever tell you not to take his books out?" she was saying in Nachman's ear. "Did he tell you not to bring them back in? Did he let you help him air the books at Passover or did only your brother? Come with me, *bubeleh*. Come, darling—"

She carried him into the house. Nathan came in after them, with as many books as he could carry, but his mother did not pay attention to him. She was changing Nachman into dry clothes, by the kitchen stove. She was covering his wet face with kisses. They were all drenched, to the skin. The books were dripping. Nathan brought them all in anyway, through the rain. He wiped them with newspapers and rags. When their mother left the bedroom, he went to Nachman. Nachman was under the covers, shivering. His lips were blue. His eyes were closed. "Don't tell Poppa on me, all right, Nathan?" he said, and Nathan swore to him that he would not.

He took off his wet clothes and dried himself with a towel his mother had used for Nachman. He put on dry clothes. In the kitchen their mother was singing to herself, in Yiddish. When their father came home and saw what had happened—when she told him over her shoulder, triumph in her eyes, that Nachman was only trying to do for him what Nathan had done for him, that he only wanted to please his father and that he shouldn't scold him—his father's thin body went straight and Nathan saw a look of fire in his eyes that he had never seen before. He stayed in the kitchen with them and they did not shoo him away. He saw his father's shoulders spread and he saw his mouth grow stiff and hard, and he thought that he knew, for an instant, the kind of man his father must have been before his mother had married him.

But then his father collapsed onto a chair, and he put his face onto his arm and he wept. Still, Nathan's mother would not comfort him, and Nathan stayed where he was, not wanting to go to his father until she went to him first. When his mother looked at Nathan she did not seem angry anymore. Nathan saw nothing in her eyes, neither unhappiness nor misery.

His father looked up at her and sniffled. "Well," he said to her. "So you have what you want at last, don't you?" She stared at him, without bitterness. "No money could ever buy for you what you have received today," he went on. "You are a wealthy woman at last. You are a wealthy woman at last."

Nathan went to his father then and he threw his arms around his neck. "I tried!" he cried out. "I tried, Poppa. I tried to stop Nachman. I tried to take in the books. I tried but the rain came too fast."

His father stood, without hugging Nathan. Nathan clung to his neck. "I tried, Poppa!" Nathan cried out. "I tried! Please *believe* me! I tried!"

His father grabbed Nathan's hands, behind his neck, and tore them apart. His hands were very strong. Then he slapped Nathan's face, hard. Nathan fell down on the kitchen floor and looked up, into his father's face. His mother warned his father to leave Nachman alone, but he did not seem to hear her, or to remember that Nathan was on the floor beneath him. When he left the room Nathan let go and burst into tears, kicking and thrashing about on the floor. His mother tried to pick him up, and at first he accepted her embrace and let her hold him close to her warm, soft body. But then he grew hard again and he started pounding at her chest with all of his might, until he was free. He ran from the kitchen. He passed his father, who was sitting on the floor of the living room, the wet books and letters around him. He ran into his bedroom and slammed the door, and he found Nachman hiding under the bed, pressed close to the wall. He crawled under and lay next to him, and he held Nachman's trembling body close to his own.

◊ 6 ◊

"RIVKA AND LEAH WANT ME TO COME TO FLORIDA."

"Yes?"

"I thought I should tell you."

"You told me before."

Rachel sighed. "Oh Nathan," she said. "Please don't be this way. Please don't make me . . ."

Her voice trailed off. They sat together, on a bench in Prospect Park, across from the lake. A policeman, on horseback, stopped in front of them. He tipped his hat and warned them to be careful, to call for help should anyone molest them.

Rachel smiled at the policeman. She stood and stroked the horse's neck. She told the policeman that she had ridden horses in Prospect Park when she was a young woman, and along Ocean Parkway and Eastern Parkway too, when there had been bridle paths there. The policeman smiled at her. His horse seemed enormous to Nathan—tall and wide and strong. Nathan wondered if the policeman needed to stand on a box or ladder in order to mount. Rachel asked the policeman questions about his horse, and while they talked Nathan thought of himself in Ruth's kitchen, telling her and Michael about the little man who could emerge and dance upon his palm. He saw himself, sitting on the grass, reading the story of Tom Thumb to Nachman. Nachman was four years old. Nathan was eleven.

Rachel sat next to Nathan again. She took his arm. The policeman waved and left. "Look, Nathan," Rachel said. "I was never one to use subtle wiles. Let me be frank, all right? I've enjoyed being with you these past few weeks. I think you've enjoyed being with me. You yourself said I should leave Brooklyn, that I shouldn't live alone."

"You've lived alone before," Nathan said. "Whenever Nachman was hospitalized."

"It's not the same thing," Rachel said. Her brown eyes were fixed upon his own in a way that made Nathan think of Michael. "I'm not as young as I was. The neighborhood is different. My friends are gone."

Nathan shrugged. "You seem to have all the answers already," he said.

"Except for yours—" She withdrew her arm from his. "What I'm trying to say is this—and you do make it difficult for me—but before I decide about Florida, I thought I should ask you what, as they say, your intentions are."

Nathan nodded. "Yes," he said. "I was wondering about that myself."

Rachel smiled. Nathan looked at her. When she smiled her gums showed slightly, the way Michael's did when he smiled. Her lips, like Michael's, were soft and full. "The first time I ever saw you you were on a horse," he said. "Do you remember?"

"Of course I remember."

"Why don't we walk," Nathan said.

They walked, arm in arm. Rachel's face seemed very dark to him. He recalled the black velvet riding cap she had worn, and how, looking up at her that first time, he had decided that he wanted her.

"You've been very sweet with Michael," she offered. "You've been very good to him."

"It's easy to be good to somebody else's son."

She squeezed his arm. "Don't," she said. "Don't be so hard on yourself. What's past is past, Nathan."

"No," he said. "What's past is never past. I suppose I don't agree with you."

"Michael says you've been writing again. I'm glad."

"Why not?" Nathan said.

They walked over a narrow footbridge. Nathan watched ducks, dipping their heads into the water. Nathan stopped. Rachel rested her head against his shoulder. "I do love you, Nathan," she said. "I always have. But you know that."

Nathan nodded.

"Do you mind if I talk to you this way?" she asked, and then, before he could reply, she went on. "But even if you said yes, it wouldn't stop me. Why stand on ceremonies at our age? After all that's happened."

"Why stand on ceremonies," Nathan said.

"You're not angry with me?"

"No," he said. "I'm not angry. But I need time. That's all. I need some time."

She laughed. "You sound like Michael. It's what he keeps saying."

"I wanted to pull you down from your horse."

She lifted her head. "What?" she asked. "I don't understand—"

"The first time I saw you—I wanted to pull you down from your horse. The way you looked at me." He shrugged. "It's what I remembered just now, seeing what you looked like that first time."

"I was what we called in those days a saucy young woman."

"Don't be clever," Nathan snapped.

Rachel walked away from him. Nathan followed. Black women, wheeling baby carriages, passed them and nodded hello. Nathan recalled walking beside his mother as she and his Aunt Zlata wheeled their carriages, side by side, through the park. Every *Shabbos*, and on the Jewish holidays—Passover, Rosh Hashanah, Sukkos, Yom Kippur—the park had been filled with well-dressed Jews, wheeling carriages, walking with their families.

"I'm sorry," Nathan said. He thought of the beach near Herzlia, of the stillness there, at dawn. He imagined the rubber rafts with their deadly crews, bobbing innocently in the water.

She took his arm again. Her cheeks were flushed. "I took a chance back then—but you knew that, didn't you? I took a chance that when you heard about me and Nachman you'd be afraid to lose me." She brushed her hair from her forehead. "I lost."

"I lost also," Nathan said.

She stopped and placed herself directly in front of him. "Please, Nathan," she said, holding both his arms, and when she spoke, the passion in her voice reminded Nathan of the passion in Michael's voice, when he was speaking of Lazer Kominsky. "Let's not make the same mistake twice, all right? We can be good for one another. I know it. I'm not supposed to say things like this, Nathan, but I know it's so. We could be happy together if we'd let ourselves."

"It's too soon," Nathan said. She let go of his arms, but she did not look away. "It's too soon," he repeated. He stopped looking at her face.

Her gaze was too intense. He watched three tall young black boys walking toward them, and he took his hands from his pockets, to be ready. They passed by. Nathan sat. Rachel sat next to him. She said nothing. Nathan could recall the exact way she had looked, sitting upon her horse. Her eyes had flashed at him from what seemed a great height. He could recall how she had played with him, her head cocked to one side, her scarlet lips pursing and then parting, to reveal her beautiful smile. It was *Shabbos*. Did the Bible, she asked, say anything about not riding horses on *Shabbos*? Why didn't he rent a horse and ride beside her? Was he afraid?

German Jews! his friend Irving had said. *They think they own God too. They'll find out different someday . . .*

How many Jewish girls in those days rode on horseback? How many Jewish girls would have flirted the way she flirted? What Jewish girl that he knew would have dared to question the Sabbath? He had glared at her. He had wanted to pull her down from her horse, to shake her, to lecture her, to dirty her fancy clothes, to teach her a lesson. He had desired her. He had desired her more than any woman—Jewish or Gentile—he had, until then, ever known.

"It's too soon," he repeated. "The thirty days are just over. Nachman is still, as they say, warm in the ground."

"So?" she asked, and in her voice he heard that hard sound he had heard so many years before, when she had defied her father by continuing to see him. She had loved defying her father—at times he had sensed that she loved being with Nathan more because it angered her father than because she loved Nathan.

"You haven't changed, have you," Nathan said. "You're still used to thinking that anything in life you want you can have."

"And you're different?"

"No."

She sighed. "Oh Nathan, please—*please* let's not go through this all again. Please let's not get into a battle of wills all over again—because we'll both lose if we do. Don't you see that? We have so little time."

"Was marrying Nachman worse than marrying me?" he asked. "I mean—for your father. Would it have made him less angry if you'd married a poor writer than a poor madman?"

"Stop," she said. "You don't have to be so hard anymore, Nathan. I thought you had changed—that his death had freed you somehow. That first night, hasn't it . . . ?" She closed her eyes. "No. I'm sorry. I didn't want to use that against you," she said.

Hard? Nathan thought of asking. Hard? He wanted to speak out, aloud, and contradict her; he wanted to tell her that he had never wanted to be hard, but that conditions had made him hard. He wanted to tell her that maybe he would never have been soft even if he had had another life than the one he'd had. He wanted to speak out and tell her that he hadn't chosen to be the kind of man he had become. But if you take even a vine and cut it back again and again, he wanted to say, it will grow hard, like a tree.

"Nachman had his own sweetness," she was saying. "I did love him, Nathan. He was very charming when he was well. He was kind. He was very good to me. He knew how to make me laugh. We cared for each other."

"But your father hated me more because . . ."

"You know that neither of us ever told Michael—about before. About us."

"Why not?"

"There seemed no need. Michael was always angry enough as it was. It was hard on him, that his father was gone so much and that—"

"—And that he stayed with an uncle who was so unlike his father?"

"I'll leave the theories to you and Michael," she said. "You seem to be the experts."

"Your father hated me more because he knew he could not bend my will to his," Nathan declared. "You married Nachman so that you could have it both ways, Rachel. You could rebel against your father—yet you didn't have to lose him. You chose a man who could not and never would replace your father. When Nachman broke again you went to your father's house. And he took you in the way—"

Nathan stopped. "Yes?" Rachel asked.

"The way my Uncle Harry used to give my mother money, I suppose. That was what I was going to say." He looked up. "What does it matter now?"

"Nathan?"

"Yes?"

"You're very smart when you talk about these things—you always were. It was why, even when you didn't think so, you were able to write your book." She bit her lower lip. "But I agree with Ruth. You're just like Michael in the way you use your insights—your understanding of why it is we feel the way we do—in order to distance yourself from people. You're so like Michael in the way . . ."

Nathan looked out across the lawns of the park. He saw himself and Nachman, hand in hand, walking over the low rolling hills, and disappearing. When he was in high school he would often take Nachman for walks with him in the park because he found that having Nachman with him allowed him to meet pretty young women. They seemed less afraid of a young man with a beautiful golden-haired young brother than they were of a young man alone. Nachman charmed them. He won them.

Nathan smiled, but he did not tell Rachel what he was remembering. Rachel's father had been a doctor. She attended a private school. She took lessons in all things—riding, dancing, tennis, piano, elocution. She was unlike the Jewish girls from his own school and neighborhood, and it had occurred to him, even then, that in trying to win her and to possess her, he was also trying to win and possess the wealth and power of the world from which she came. Well, he thought. He had gotten what he wanted. Rachel had gotten what she wanted. They were like one another in this way. She had married Nachman to teach Nathan a lesson. He sighed. Maybe he always wanted what he didn't and couldn't have simply because he couldn't have it. And now that he could, again, have her . . .

"Rivka and Harvey have an apartment for me—they put down a deposit so that I shouldn't lose it."

Nathan blinked. "What?" he asked.

"Rivka and Harvey put down a deposit for me, on an apartment. I told them I hadn't asked them to do it. It was their choice."

"It was their choice," Nathan said. "You're right."

"I won't push you," she said. "I told them I needed time. All right? Come. We should go. Ruth and Michael and the children are coming for supper. But don't be afraid of me, Nathan, all right?"

They walked back, in the direction from which they'd come. Nathan looked out across the lake and imagined that he and Rachel and Ruth and Michael and their children were living together in a park like Prospect Park. It was the twenty-first century and the park had been declared a special preserve for endangered species. As the last relics of the twelve tribes of Israel, they lived and camped and prayed there, among Bengal tigers and whooping cranes and snow leopards and bald eagles and California condors and giant pandas. Nathan smiled. Rachel's arm was in his and he covered her hand with his own. He saw himself filling his days by being the family's emissary to the park's management—trying to get them to let into the preserve, before it was too late, one of each vanishing Jewish type: a *shlemiel*, a *shlimazel*, a *yenta*, a *grauber yung*, a *baleboss*, a Talmud *chacham*, a *kvetch*, a *Chassid*, a *shnorrer*, a *momzer*, a *klutz*, a *nebish* . . .

Nathan thought of sharing the list with Nachman, and of how the two of them would laugh together. They could add to it infinitely. It would be a list with no beginning and no end. Rachel spoke of Michael, of how she worried about him. He took too many chances, at home and at work. He needed to be with Ruth, to have Ruth take care of him. There was no reason for them to live apart, no reason for Michael to go to Russia, no reason for him to live on in Brooklyn. Nathan thought of Michael's rooms. He thought of Nachman, hiding under the bed. He thought of his own words, on the old yellow paper. He thought of telling Rachel about his idea for writing seven books at once. He thought of what these seven books might be about, and he wondered, as he had so many years before, if one of them would be a story that contained all the others, and if this story might somehow turn out to be the story of his own life.

He wanted to tell Rachel that he was writing his book all over again, not merely to fool the Russians, but so that he could give the new sections to the people he loved, as gifts. He had thought about this. "Loss!" had been for Nachman. "Star of David!" would be for his father. "Kehilla" would be for Michael. And "Noah's Song"—when he could bring himself to rewrite that section—would be for Rachel. But he said nothing, for he was afraid that if he told her about what he was doing, she might find it foolish.

STAR OF DAVID!

Horses! Horses! Horses! They rear up all around me and I slash at their legs with the side of my saber. The family crouches behind me. I hold the boy against my side with my left arm. His sister clutches at my leg and weeps inconsolably. I hear wailing and crackling. I see fire leaping around us in a ring that extends for miles, far beyond the circle of horses. I smell the horses' rankness and feel their warm sweat-laden bodies. Their flanks are enormous. I fear being crushed.

Their veined eyes are crazed with fright. Their enormous lips unfold and they bare their teeth at me. Steam rises from their bodies into the freezing air. They heave and rush about and I shout at them to go back. Their masters have little control over them. Suddenly I slip and I am underneath the swollen belly of a horse and I see that the belly is smeared with blood. With my saber I jab at its thighs and chop at its forefeet. It moves off and I can breathe again. A riderless horse now rises at my left, its shaggy hooves thrashing the air, and I bury the boy beneath me, my body pressed down upon his, and I pray. I glance up and see that the horse's hollow hooves are clotted with mud and snow and dead grass. The horse whinnies and its hooves strike at the snow beside my boots, but miraculously I am not touched.

Do I dream? The horses are taller than the houses. They are wider than the night. I long to slit their bellies and plunge my cold hands in, deep into the steaming blood and entrails. There would I find comfort! In my heart I know the frenzy the Tartars and Cossacks feel when the wild tarpan horses steal their stores of hay and entice away their mares. I have seen them kill entire herds of these small-boned and beautiful creatures. I have seen them feast and drink afterward. There is nothing I have not seen.

Now the Jews are leaving Kiev—expelled at midnight by order of the tsar—and I, in my old soldier's uniform, am among them, a traitor to the army I served for so many years. When the fires began I took my uniform out of the chest next to my bed and I fled from the city, to stand with a cavalry regiment on a small hillside and to watch the lines of weeping Jews, with their nags and their barrows, their broken-down droshkies and their packs, setting westward from the city in the middle of the night. They trudged through snow, wailing and chanting like madmen. The soldiers raced their horses at them now and again, and swung their swords, but more to keep warm than for the pleasures of cruelty. Beside me was a magnificent Cossack racer, its harness showy and complicated: breast-pieces with black tassels, supple crupper straps studded with colored stones, silver-plated snaffle bridle. The Cossack wore a jacket cut out of a blue carpet, with an embroidered lily in the middle of the back. His sweaty forelock was plastered down over his left eye, which had been gouged out. I held back and watched. The sky was bright with fire and falling snowflakes. The night was windless. My own horse was strong and well rested.

I watched the exodus and it fulfilled my every hope! Jewish backs were bent and Jewish eyes were frightened. At last! How I had hated their devil's eyes! How I had loathed the black pools in those eyes, those pools deep with schemes and lies and tricks! When I approached in my uniform, they stared at me with such fear—with such frank servility and submissiveness—that I longed to pierce those dark eyes with my dagger, to stab through the veil of fear and suffering to the flesh beneath.

I watched children riding on the backs of their fathers, old men sitting in the snow and pleading for mercy, young men beating their own fathers with whips and branches to make them rise and go on. Yet all the while I felt nothing but scorn for them. They were dirty and verminous, vile and odorous, a curse on mankind! Wherever they went they carried with them their plagues and diseases, their books and their lies. How I relished their anguish. Their eyes were phlegm-drenched, their noses large and red and dripping, the men's beards tangled with grease and crumbs and scabs, the women's and children's scalps encrusted with sores. The chosen people, I laughed to myself. The chosen people! They were the ones who chose to be different! They were the ones who declared themselves the anointed of God. Then let them now reap the grim harvest!

Even the rich Jews were bent over, and this satisfied me most of all. What will you do with all your money now? I asked. Tell me that. What will you do with your walls of books and your silk clothing and your gilt-edged furniture and your chests of coins? Now at last you will be real Jews too—now you will feel what I have felt forever. Now you will suffer the way my father suffered and my mother suffered, and the way their fathers and mothers suffered before them. Now you will pay for their suffering! Except, I thought, that you will not be as strong and cunning as I have been, and you will not know how to survive your suffering. You will wander as wandering Jews have always wandered, but, set loose in the wilds of Mother Russia, you will not, like me, know how to find and kill animals where no animals can be seen, or to keep warm when you have no heated home, or to stave off disease when you have no doctors.

I saw a family of wealthy Jews walking among a mass of poor Jews. The poor Jews made way for them. The father walked in front, his body almost erect. He wore a hat of gleaming black lamb's wool, a coat with a fur collar. He wore precious eyeglasses, rimmed in gold, and he carried nothing except a single book in a gloved hand. His wife, in black silk and fox furs, walked three steps behind him, and behind her there walked a man and a woman—perhaps a daughter and son, perhaps a husband and wife —carrying bundles in their arms. There were smaller children behind them, dressed luxuriantly, like dwarf merchants, and there were servants behind them, pushing barrows and pulling wagons of clothing and furniture and food.

A soldier charged at them, his saber slicing circles in the air above his head. But the Jew did not bow down. His wife knelt, her hands upon the back of her neck. The children huddled together and screamed. The soldier taunted the Jew but did not kill him. Why not? He took the Jew's hat and then he leaned down from his horse and tore the Jew's coat from him. The Jew gave him money and rings. The wife gave the soldier silver candlesticks, a golden *menorah*. The servants foraged frantically in the wagons, finding more gifts—jewelry and silver and spice boxes and pots and silk and dresses and food and coins.

When the soldier returned to our lines, laden down with his spoils, we laughed and cheered him. He carried a woman's undergarment on the tip of his sword. In his ear was a gold coin. But the rich Jew walked on, bareheaded through the snow, as if he were too proud to even glance back at us and acknowledge what had occurred. How I loathed him then! And how I envied his riches and his family and his pride! I watched him fade into the white landscape, a crown of snow upon his bare head, and I cursed his soul. I thought of the old joke my father had told to me when I was a child, a joke I had repeated to my fellow soldiers many times through the years, but which I dared not repeat now. If a rich Jew should ever want to know how he can live forever and gain immortality, my father said, you must tell him that the secret is to come and settle in our town. Then, before he spoke again, my father would pause and his eyes would twinkle. No rich Jew ever died here, he would say.

Soon word was given that the bulk of the Jews were gone from Kiev and that the soldiers had permission to return. I returned with them. Their bloodcurdling screams of joy brought comfort to my soul. I raced my horse with theirs, even as they cut through the long lines of Jews, knocking them down and trampling upon their rag-covered bodies. I pulled up my horse once, when I was stopped by an old woman, rising from a snowdrift as if she had been living in it. "Bread!" she cried to me, her empty hands trembling in the air. "Children!" she cried. "Bread and children! Bread! Bread! Bread and children!" But what were her losses to me? Her eyes were crazed, her lips seemed to be exploding in small boils. I was furious with her. I dipped my saber down and cut through the snow, to frozen earth. I dislodged some and I flung it at her so that her mouth was filled with it—then my lungs surged with marvelous warmth, and I raced on to the city. Was I dreaming, even then? Had she been there? Was there anyone to whom I could turn to ask if I had seen and done what I thought I had seen and done? My heart filled with a terrible joy. "To the city!" I cried. To sack and burn the houses of the rich moneylenders! To take pleasure from strange women! To avenge myself yet once more for what was done to me so many years ago . . .

Yet even as I rode on amidst the thunder of other horses, I knew in my soul that it satisfied me but little to pillage and loot the homes of wealthy Jews, or to take my bestial pleasures from their wives and daughters. I had satisfied myself in these ways before, and I knew how deeply I had come to loathe myself for doing so. And yet I knew also that without these opportunities—meager as they seemed to me—to satisfy the rages and desires within me, I would never have survived at all. For these acts of vengeance were tastes to me of the feast to come—they kept my Dream of Vengeance alive—that Dream which spurred me on, that Dream and Hope which were lodged forever in my breast and which sustained me when all else failed. For I had learned this, during all the years that had passed since that dread day when I had been stolen from my village by Jews and sent off to serve in the tsar's army: that the actual taking of revenge for what had been done to me only served to fill up the wells of my bitterness.

In the city the soldiers and the police were beating the Jews with unmerciful cruelty, torturing them without cleverness. I saw a Cossack cut out the tongues of three old men, then sheathe his sword in red velvet. I saw a soldier club an aged woman into the snow and drag her into a doorway and lift her black skirts. I saw a man with blood spilling from a hole in his eye. I heard mothers wailing for lost children. I saw a woman appear at a window high above me and tear patches of hair from her head before she shrieked and tumbled to the ground. But I did not hear her fall. I saw a man try to run past soldiers, a Torah in his arms, but the Torah was ripped from him, and the gold and silver ornaments were ripped from the Torah. Jews scurried like rats, trying to flee, trying still to load themselves with possessions. I could smell the fragrant rich odors of burning flesh. My heart was full.

I abandoned my own horse and left it in my blacksmith's shop, directly outside the Jewish quarter. Then I made my way toward their homes —toward the homes of the wealthy Jews, those whose horses I had shoed, whose droshkies I had repaired, whose iron gates I had built. I knew them well. I knew the favors they could buy, from the police and from the army and from the government. And I knew in which houses lived the members of the Kehilla. Here, as in the village in which I had been born, they were the worms who, in their vanity, believed themselves to be the chosen of the chosen—the most beautiful of God's creatures. But now, their houses in flames, though they would crawl upon their bellies, they were not even cunning serpents. What will befall all Jews, I thought, remembering the old saying, will befall each Jew! Forever and forever and forever! No longer would they prey upon poor Jews, no longer would they live without fear! Their feast was done and I would have my way with them!

But most of their houses were already deserted and in ruins. The soldiers and police had been there before me. I had stayed too long outside the city. Still, I took my pleasures—I smashed windows and goblets, I slashed at furniture and walls, I searched for hidden treasures in floors and ceilings. I drank and grew dizzy. I threw my arms around the shoulders of my fellow soldiers and I kissed them with abandon. We poured marvelous curses upon the Jews. May they wander forever in the snow with the howling of wolves in their ears! May their feet and hands freeze and may we be there, in our mercy, to pour boiling water upon their toes and fingers! May the mothers live to see their daughters violated by the horses of Turks!

Then I heard the screams of a solitary wealthy Jew, who had not yet fled, and my heart thrilled as I rushed through the door of his house. But three policemen were already there, laughing raucously. The room had been ravaged, books torn apart, sofas slit open, crystal smashed. Against a wall I saw the back of another policeman, bent over. Underneath him a boy with startled and pained eyes stared to the side, in horror. He was half-dressed. I followed the boy's eyes and I saw that the other policemen were forcing the mother to watch this unnatural act, a knife at her throat. My dull senses were suddenly on fire, and it was not the screaming in the room that had enflamed them, and awakened me.

Rather, it was the sound of gentle breathing that made me turn. An old man sat against a wall, abandoned by the policemen. His daughter lay next to him, her eyes covered with her forearm, in shame. She clutched at her legs, but I saw no blood. The old man stared across the room, his eyes wide and blind—and when I looked into them and he did not look back, it was as if, in the deep pools of those eyes, I could suddenly see myself, and my own father's suffering, when I had been taken from him.

I had seen men couple with other men before. I had seen men kill other men and violate small children. I had seen men in the most abominable acts of degradation. I had seen them perform with animals. I had seen men torn apart by wolves, and I had, in the coldest winters, not even turned my eyes away when starving men sustained themselves by the only means possible, when all help was gone and their comrades lay dead and frozen beside them. There was nothing I had not seen during the many years since I was first stolen from my father's house and taken by the Kehilla, and sent away to serve for twenty-five years in the tsar's army.

And suddenly I was that little boy again—the boy who had once been his father's Hope and Dream. All had been sacrificed so that I might study and become a man of learning, for in me, my father believed, God had planted a special gift. I was my father's jewel. Unlike him, and unlike my brothers and sisters, who were good and hardworking Jews, I had been chosen by God, my father believed, to serve Him with my mind. My father dreamt of seeing me sit one day in the synagogue along the Eastern wall, with the other honored and learned men of the community. He dreamt of seeing me sit at the right hand of our Rebbe, studying Talmud. How cruel his dreams! How vain his hopes! But how wonderful his clear brown eyes when he heard me read and called my brothers and sisters to hear me. Worship was the highest expression of love, he had been taught, and study was the highest form of worship! He held my hands, and touched my fingers gently, and he told me that they would always remain pale and fine, like a scholar's —never rough and broken like his own. Never would I be an *amoretz* like himself! Never! Never . . .

How proud his eyes when the Rebbe of Burshtyn came to our meager dwelling one evening to tell my father that yes, there was a special quality that God had put into my soul that made it incumbent upon the Rebbe to take me as his pupil, without fees. My father counted the Rebbe's words as if they were pearls. The Rebbe praised my father for having borne me into the world and for having protected me until that day. Jews, he said, were like unto a vine of which grapes represent the scholars and the leaves the simple folk. I hung upon his words and they made their way into my heart so that, through all the years, I never forgot them. The leaves of the vine had two important tasks—they were essential to the growth of the vine, and they protected the grapes—and therefore, they were of greater importance, since the power of the protector was always greater than the power of the protected. In the same way, he went on, as the rabbis had taught, it was better to love than to be beloved . . .

How beautiful my father's eyes when he listened to the Rebbe's words—his eyes were, I thought, the color of the soft earthen bottom of the clearest lake. How full and rich and complete his life would have been, had he carried the Rebbe's praise to the grave! How happy he was to sacrifice all so that I might study. Torah was the most precious of wares, he would often say, and a Jew must sell all else to have those wares.

And so I began to fulfill my father's hopes and dreams—I learned to read and to pray, and when I began the study of *chumash* my father bought for me a new suit and I was covered with a *talis* and my mother and sisters showered candy and nuts upon me. But I never even began that real study with which the Rebbe tempted me so lovingly—the study of Talmud. For it was while I was walking from my home to his house one morning only a few months after his visit to our house that I was suddenly set upon by three men, who told me that the Rebbe was ill and that they had been sent to take me to the doctor's dwelling, where the Rebbe was waiting to receive me so that he could, should he die, give me his blessing. Their treachery was boundless, and I followed them without suspicion, for my heart was open in those days.

But then were my father's eyes made blind and his heart cut in two by their evildoing! For they led me straightaway out of our village and to a hovel, wherein I was bound hand and foot, and mocked by my kidnappers. They are Jews too . . . they are Jews too, I kept thinking, while they taunted me with terrible stories of the life I would lead in the service of the army of Tsar Nicholas the First. But even their cruel visions turned out to be nothing compared to the life I did come to live. Their imaginations were as meager as their souls.

They counted their money in front of my eyes, and the name they uttered was that of Toporofsky. They were fearless and shameless but I told myself even at that very moment that they were only servants doing the master's bidding. I had heard before of boys like myself being snatched by the *khappers*—kidnapped and substituted for the sons of the wealthy, whenever the cantonist *gzeyra*—the evil order—chanced to fall upon a wealthy family. I knew also that Toporofsky had only one son, the *shayne* Noah, as he was known in our village—a boy who was already studying with the Rebbe when I had come to him, and who was as fair as he was brilliant. I was never able to deny it—I had wanted him for a friend. My beloved Noah—my beautiful talented Noah! I had singled him out as the boy I would have desired to have had as my own brother.

But my tender feelings toward Noah were short-lived. Feeling more the hurt my father would soon feel—that helpless rage at not being able to reach me and to bring me back, that passionate loathing he would surely come to direct against himself for my loss—my heart, rather than breaking in two as I believed my father's would, filled with bitterness. I vowed, even as I lay on an earthen floor in a hovel in the woods, that someday I would make the father of Noah suffer as he had made my father suffer. If I could not escape from my fate—and my father with me—yet would I do everything I could to see that I shared that fate with the Jew who had been its instrument.

All this I remembered—and more—as I stood in a strange Jew's house in Kiev, and saw a father sit by, helpless and dumb, as his son—a boy the age, I imagined, that I was when I had been stolen—became the object of a degrading spectacle that would soon become a memory more hated than life itself. God had promised Abraham that one day His Jewish People would be as plentiful as the stars in the heavens and the grains of sand in the sea, yet surely life had shown that it was the bitterness that was forever being held in store for us that was so plentiful. And tasting a portion of that bitterness yet again, I also realized something strange, and for the first time—the discovery stunned me, as if I had been struck an actual blow—that surely, by now, my father was dead and buried, and that he and I had never, in all the years that had passed, seen one another again.

For when my service of twenty-five years was done I had chosen not to return to my village, feeling that to see the animal I had become would have been more painful to my father than to have seen that I was alive. Better to live with a scarred heart, I reasoned, than to make that heart tear again. But I did not fool myself. I knew, even when I made my cowardly decision, that there was something I feared even more than seeing my father again—that if I had returned and we had embraced and he had come to know all that had happened to me during the years we were apart, he might have forgiven me—and I might have come to forgive myself—and that if this had happened, I would have lost the desire to avenge myself, and with it the very dream that I had come to believe was the essence of my being—my true self—and the sustenance of my life.

Almost forty years had passed since the day I did not arrive at the Rebbe's house, and listening now to this other father's quiet breathing, and thinking that my own father had already died—never having seen me or touched me or known me as a grown man—I realized also that I was the age he must have been when he had last seen me, and that I had not, with my seed, borne children who would live after me.

He had died without having seen my face again, and imagining in my mind's eye his hungry eyes staring at me from his deathbed—his eyes searching for me, and longing to give me his blessing—my heart broke at last. I tore at my hair and I screamed so lustily and with such desperation that the policeman turned to me as if I were the very Angel of Death. In his eyes he already knew—but he did not have a chance. I pulled his head backward by the hair and I slit his throat from one side to the other, in a dark and beautiful crescent of blood. Then, still howling, I made for the others—but they saw my eyes and what I had done, and they fled.

I could not utter a single word. My mouth opened but my tongue was swollen and mute. I turned away so that the family could endure their shame without my eyes upon them. I heard the father weeping now. I looked back. The father was down upon his knees before the boy and they were embracing. I wondered how he could have touched his son so soon, without revulsion, and then I wondered how I could be so low and loathsome as to doubt the strength of a father's love. I was frightened, as the policemen had had cause to be frightened. I stepped toward the family and they moved back from me and I saw in their faces that they were now wondering if I was going to set upon them next.

I felt as if my life's blood were pouring out of my heart and running in rivulets across my hairy chest, flowing through the cloth of my cursed uniform, drenching it and weighting me down. I felt that they might die of fright if I could not find words with which to save them. I breathed upon them and then I spoke. "I too am a Jew!" I declared, but I could say no more. The girl fell forward and clutched at my leg, uncovering her eyes. The father bowed his head, and, still on his knees, he began to give me his blessing.

I stopped him and I spread my arms and they came to me. I would be their protector! I showed them the door, and made signs to them with my hand and with my knife. They understood. We would go out into the streets and make our way, with other Jews, past soldiers and horses and burning buildings, and I would save them. I felt delirious. I bent over the policeman and I removed the jacket of his uniform, so as to cover his face, and when I did I found—may God forgive me as He will surely never forgive him! —that against his bloodstained undergarments he too wore the silver Star of David.

◇ 7 ◇

NATHAN HELD ELI IN HIS ARMS. AARON PUT THE BLACK BARREL OF HIS plastic gun against Eli's forehead, and pulled the trigger. "Bam!" he said. Nathan smiled. He reached out to Aaron with his free hand, but Aaron turned away and ran from the room. Rachel was ladling soup into bowls.

"I'll take him now," Ruth said. "I'll nurse him and then he'll sleep for a while."

Ruth took the baby from Nathan's arms, but as she turned to leave the room, Michael entered, holding an envelope in his hand, waving it in the air. Aaron came in with him. "This is the surprise," Michael announced. "What you've all been waiting for, right?"

Aaron and Miriam jumped up, trying to snatch the envelope from Michael's hands. "Please, Poppa! Please—!"

"Hold on!" he said. "Hold on. Get in your seats first, and then I'll tell you."

They sat down at the table. "You stay too," Michael said to Ruth. He bent down and nuzzled Eli. "He's happy. He'll wait."

"Haven't we had enough games?" Ruth asked sharply.

Michael tried to touch Ruth's hair, but she pulled away. "You're wrong," he said. "You're wrong about what you're thinking."

"How do you know what I'm thinking?" she said. "You're not in my head, Michael. Don't you understand that? Maybe in your office, you—"

"Oh my God," Miriam sighed. "Here they go again."

"How long are you gonna fight this time?" Aaron asked wearily. "We want our surprise *now*. We—"

Rachel laughed. "Just stay for a minute," she urged Ruth. "Let the children have their surprise."

"And let Michael have his way again, right?"

"Wrong," Michael said. He opened the envelope and took out two airplane tickets. "Tell them, Uncle Nat. Tell Ruth first—"

Nathan smiled at Ruth. "I'm going with him," Nathan said. "There's a ticket for each of us. I'm going with him and I promise you that I'll bring him back. And when I do—"

"Hooray!" Aaron shouted. "Hooray!"

"Shh," Miriam said. "You're interrupting."

"And when I do, Michael will come to live with you and the children."

Rachel stood, her hand to her chest. "Is it true?"

Ruth's eyes narrowed. "He can live with me now," she said. "He doesn't have to get to Long Island by way of Russia." She forced a smile. "But it's easier for him to live with you, don't you see, Uncle Nat? And if there were beds in the schoolyard, he wouldn't even need you—"

"I'm selling the house," Michael said, softly.

Ruth's eyes widened, Nathan saw, and tears formed in them at once. "What?" she asked. She moved toward Michael, pressing Eli closer to her bosom.

"When we come back from Russia I'm going to sell the house so that I can move to Long Island and live with all of you again."

Aaron and Miriam clapped their hands.

"But why?" Ruth asked. She turned to Nathan.

"I drive a hard bargain," Nathan said. "I always did. In business I was considered a very hard man."

Miriam and Aaron were jumping up and down, tugging at Michael's arms, shouting "Hooray! Hooray! Poppa's coming home!" Ruth set Eli down gently, in his playpen. Then she put her arms around Michael's neck and they embraced. Aaron and Miriam hugged their parents' legs.

"Why is Momma crying?" Aaron asked.

Rachel looked at Nathan, smiling, her eyes moist.

"I'm sorry," Ruth said. "Really, Michael."

"I forgot all about it," Michael said. His eyes were closed, and he rubbed his chin against Ruth's hair. He spoke softly. "Honestly. I never wanted to know. What's past is past. I can't forgive you because there's no need for forgiveness. Whatever you—"

Ruth's head snapped back, as if she had been slapped. "What are you talking about?" she asked, and she looked around, at the others. "I only meant that I'm sorry I didn't give you a chance before, to tell us the surprise. But you thought—" Her nostrils flared. "Oh my God, Michael. You are such a child sometimes . . ."

Michael looked at Ruth. Ruth stared at Nathan, her mouth open, her eyes wide. There was a look of fear in her eyes that made Nathan want to take her in his arms, that made him want to shove Michael away, so that he could hold Ruth close to him and protect her. Eli started crying. Ruth bent down, picked him up, and walked from the room.

"Why is Momma so angry?" Aaron asked.

"Sometimes Momma likes to be angry," Michael said.

"But not as much as you do," Aaron said.

Michael raised his hand and Nathan saw Aaron flinch. "Don't!" he said. "Please, Michael—"

Michael glared at Nathan. "Terrific," Michael said. "This is really terrific."

"Go to her," Rachel said.

Michael's body relaxed. He smiled. He kissed his mother on the cheek. "You know what?" he asked.

"What?"

"That's a good idea. I'll go to her."

Michael left the room. Rachel told the children to get in their seats, to eat their supper. Then they would still have some time left to play together before they had to go back to Long Island. Aaron asked her how late it would be when he got to sleep, and when she told him it might be ten o'clock, he grinned broadly. Nathan buttered bread for Miriam and Aaron. He looked toward the bedroom, where Michael and Ruth were, and he wondered what items he would find when he looked in Nachman's dresser, and in the cartons Rachel said were in the closet, waiting for him.

"Is he really going to come and live with us?" Miriam asked. "For good?"

"Yes," Nathan said. "He is. He promised."

"But first he has to go to Russia, right?" Aaron asked.

"But first he has to go to Russia," Nathan said.

Rachel sighed. "If you want my opinion," she said, "Michael should work on trying to save his own marriage before he tries to save the Jews of Russia."

Nathan sipped water. He tried to think of words he could use to defend Michael—of the things Michael had said to him and to Ruth about Lazer Kominsky's life and death—but he found that he was too upset to speak. He heard Michael's voice, and he was afraid for a moment that Michael was yelling at Ruth, that they were fighting again. Then he heard the sound of Ruth's laughter. He looked at Miriam and Aaron, but they did not seem to be paying attention to the sounds that came from the bedroom.

"The baby's fast asleep," Ruth said when she came back into the room. She buttoned the top button of her blouse. "What a sweet child he is."

She leaned down next to Nathan and pressed her warm cheek against his. "I'm sorry, Uncle Nat," she said. Nathan nodded. "I'm glad you drove such a hard bargain, though, right?"

"The man I was doing business with didn't resist much," he said.

"I know," she whispered. She swallowed, and he could tell that she was holding back tears. "I wish Ira were here, that's all. That's what I'm sorry about. I never told you how much, Uncle Nat. I couldn't back then, and I'm sorry. I was thinking of him before, when the children were jumping up and down so happily. It was his face that was in my head then, when I looked at you, did you know that? Oh Uncle Nat—I do wish that he could have lived to—"

Nathan turned himself around, in his chair, so that he could hold Ruth, so that he could let her cry against his shoulder. The children sat perfectly still. "It's all right," Nathan said, stroking the back of Ruth's head. "It's all right."

"THE HOUSE SEEMS VERY EMPTY, WITHOUT RUTH AND THE CHILDREN. Doesn't it?"

Nathan nodded. He watched Rachel take off her coat. He thought of saying that he was filling the house with his stories. Couldn't she tell? "I wish you had telephoned first," he said instead.

Her eyes moved from side to side, as if, Nathan thought, she were noting the changes, the items that were missing, that Ruth had taken with her. "The landlord didn't give me any notice—he wanted to show some people around and I didn't want to be there. A nice young black couple. Schoolteachers."

"Then you're leaving? It's definite?"

She did not look at him. "Shall I make us some tea?" she asked.

"Where am I going?" Nathan asked.

He followed her into the kitchen. To Russia, he thought. But why? His manuscripts and books were spread out on the table. "I'd like to read something you've written," she said, touching a folder. She looked around, approvingly. "You and Michael keep house together very well, I see."

"What do you want, Rachel?"

"What do I want?"

"What do you want from me? Why did you come here and disturb me while I was working?"

"I told you—the landlord was there, I needed to get out—where else should I go?"

Nathan shook his head. "No," he said. "I don't believe you. You wanted to let me know that you've decided to move. That's why you came."

She put a kettle on the stove. "Maybe," she said. "You know everything, I suppose. As always. Where can I hide from you?"

"I asked you to give me time," Nathan said. "I need a little time."

"And I asked you not to go to Russia with Michael." She smiled, bitterly. "Michael was such a child the other night—showing us the plane tickets and the brochures, as if—"

"It's only a short trip. It's not for pleasure. We'll be back."

Rachel took down cups and saucers from a cabinet above the stove. "Michael's mission, yes?" She sighed. "I know all about it . . ." Nathan wanted to say something to her, but could find no words. Hadn't Michael made a promise? Nathan looked down at his manuscripts. He was very angry with her for coming. He was angry with her for saying what she said about Michael. He was angry that she was in the kitchen, looking at his manuscripts, seeing how he worked. He wanted her to go. "Come," she said. "Leave your papers. We can sit in the living room."

"What do you want from me, Rachel?" he asked again, softly.

She took out two spoons from a drawer. She cocked her head to one side and smiled. "Your heart," she whispered.

Nathan turned his back to her and faced the window. "Don't fool with me," he said. "Don't play games."

She placed her hands on his shoulders, from behind. "I'm not," she said. "Oh Nathan, please—"

He felt his body tense. He realized that he wanted to turn and to hit her. He wanted to slap her face and shake her and scream at her. But he restrained himself. He clenched his fists and breathed in, through his nostrils. He did not want her to know how much she angered him. He stepped forward, bent down, and opened the door to the potato bin. He took out the chapter he had placed there the day before and he set it on the table. "Here," he said. "You can read this section. It's an old one. Most of it will be familiar to you." He stacked his books.

"Thank you," she said. Her voice was gentle. "But that's not why I came. Really."

"I said you could read it."

She sighed. "Look Nathan—I'll leave if you want me to." She waited for a second, but he said nothing. "I know I should have called first—of course—but if I'd called—the truth—wouldn't you have told me not to come?"

"I'll take my papers upstairs."

Nathan walked from the kitchen, into the foyer, and up the staircase. He set the papers and books down on his desk. He took deep breaths. The great river of anger that he had once poured into the book—into Mendel's voice especially—had not, he told himself, come from nowhere. Nor had it dried up and disappeared. He sat on the edge of the bed and stared at his desk. He did not want to be with Rachel while she read the chapter. He wondered if she would be able to recognize the changes he had made. To Mendel he had given a few more of his father's sayings—he was pleased to have remembered the story of the grapes and the grape leaves—and some touches borrowed from his reading of Babel: the descriptions of the Cossacks' horses, and of the cutting out of tongues.

He wondered if Rachel would, in the description of the wealthy Jew who will not bow his head, see her father. All the while he was writing the book, when he was a young man, he had feared that his own father would die before he finished. Afterward—after that first moment, when his father saw the dedication, and wept, and they embraced—his father had not talked to him about it. Was that why it meant so much to him, now, that Michael approve? Was that why he was worried about Rachel's reaction? Had he hoped that, by using his father's knowledge and words, he could somehow redeem the man? Perhaps. He heard Rachel call up to him that his tea was ready, but he did not move. Perhaps he would show her the other sections he had rewritten. Perhaps he would tell her that, to test his scheme, he had already sent letters and had replies—from a private collector named Rezak, and from Yeshiva University—asking to see the manuscripts, so that they could appraise them. Perhaps he would tell her that Michael had sent copies of the letters to Gronsky. Perhaps Rachel would notice that he had added to this chapter the line about it being better to love than to be loved.

He was surprised, when he reread the book, to discover that he could still feel what he had once imagined Mendel would have felt. He was surprised at how overpowering the feelings were. Why? He had not asked Michael. He did not really want clinical explanations. And he did not, he knew, really trust Michael's judgment. Michael loved his idea of selling the forged versions to the Russians, but why, Nathan wondered, did he love it so much? Michael's enthusiasm seemed excessive, and it frightened Nathan. Even if the manuscripts fooled the Russians, Nathan did not see how the amount of money raised from their sale could possibly make such a great difference. He looked out the window. Below, in the house next door, the shades were drawn. Nathan thought of Ruth and the children, in Rachel's apartment, and of how happy they had been to see him, how happy they had all been together, after he and Michael had given them the good news.

He sat on the bed again. Ruth! Nathan thought. My beautiful Ruth! He felt her cheek against his own. He heard her voice, talking to him about Ira. Ruth's father and mother were dead. Her grandparents were gone. She had no living aunts or uncles of her own. In all of America, she had two living relatives—one cousin who was a beautician in Delphos, Ohio, and another who owned a bar and grill in Indianapolis—but she had not talked with them or written to them for years. It pained Nathan to think that there was no living member of her family with whom she could spend time, who had known her when she was a child growing up in Indiana. They had talked about it together. Nobody who knew her as a child would ever know her children. *Where did I come from, Uncle Nat?*

"Are you all right?"

Rachel stood just outside the room, her hand on the doorknob. She seemed to be waiting for him to give her permission to enter. "You look very pale."

He smiled, but he did not stand up. He felt drowsy. He wanted to ask Rachel if she had ever read Babel's stories—if she recognized the passages he had borrowed. He wanted to tell her that, even if she did not believe it, there were some passages, almost identical, that he had invented before he had ever read Babel. When Nathan was writing *The Stolen Jew* Babel was already put away in one of Stalin's camps. Before, whenever he answered the phone, Babel would do so in a high-pitched woman's voice. "He's not here. He's gone for a week. I'll take a message." The first words he'd taught his daughter Lida were "Daddy not home." Nathan wished that he could read Babel in Russian. But Michael had been studying hard. Michael could read Russian.

"Are you all right, Nathan?"

He nodded, but he did not move. *Carefully, without splashing himself, the Cossack cut the old Jew's throat.* Nathan wished that the two of them could talk, at length, of Babel's stories, so that he could begin to explain, to her as well as to himself, why it was that he responded to Babel—to the severity and the savagery—as he did to no other author. Nathan could see the butchers carrying the steaming carcasses of dead horses. The Tartars slaughtered five to six hundred a day. They were untrained in the art of butchery. They did not know how to skin the animals properly. The horses, trembling from exhaustion, ate their own droppings. Like de Maupassant, Nathan thought, in Babel's greatest story, crawling around on his hands and knees in the madhouse. *Monsieur de Maupassant va s'animaliser . . .*

"Nachman used to listen at the keyhole," Nathan said. "While I worked."

"Listen?" Rachel asked. "To what?"

Nathan smiled. "I used to talk to myself. That delighted him—to discover that I carried on dialogues with my characters."

"So that you could know what they would do?"

"No," Nathan said. "That's what Nachman thought also. No. I didn't listen to them so that I could copy down what I heard for scenes in my book. It doesn't work that way. I spoke with them in order to find out what they thought about what I was planning to have them do. Or, more often, to get their opinions about what they'd already done—about what I'd already written."

Rachel moved into the room. She smiled at him. "Shall I bring the tea upstairs? It's ready."

"Did you read the chapter?"

"Not yet. I haven't had time. It's only been a few minutes—"

"I lost track. I was daydreaming." He smiled again. "Maybe you shouldn't read it. It's very brutal, if you remember. There was a lot of anger in me then . . ."

"And now?"

"Listen. I was remembering—not when I wrote the chapter I gave you—but later on, when I first wrote the final chapter of the book, in which Mendel kills Noah—when I finished it, I was very upset. When I read the words I'd set down on the page I left the house and I walked up and down Flatbush Avenue for hours, wondering about myself. How much evil did I contain in order to have produced such an evil story?"

"Oh Nathan," she said. "You are a sweet man. Didn't I—"

He stood. "You don't understand," he said quickly. "I'm talking about the chapter with all the blood and with—"

"I know."

He looked at her, trying to understand what it was she knew. "Nachman was very jealous when Poppa took me to *shul* with him in the morning—before Passover—when all the fathers took their first-born sons. A firstborn son is, according to the Torah, entitled to double the portion of inheritance from his father—to twice as much as any brother."

"But two times nothing is still nothing," Rachel said. She smiled. "That's what Nachman used to say. Two times nothing is still nothing."

"Did he?" Nathan did not look toward Rachel. "What does it matter? A firstborn son is also responsible for double the share of his father's debts. His obligations are double. He must—"

"Nathan?"

Nathan stopped and looked at Rachel. The room seemed very long. Rachel seemed very far away. "Yes?"

"Do you still feel some passion for me?"

He nodded. She came closer to him and he did not try to stop her or to move away. He looked toward his desk. He thought of pointing out to her the sentence, in the chapter, of which he was proudest. *God had promised Abraham that one day His Jewish People would be as plentiful as the stars in the heavens and the grains of sand in the sea, yet surely life had shown that it was the bitterness that was forever being held in store for us that was so plentiful.* Nathan nodded again, as if agreeing with his own words. He had written these lines when he was a young man, he wanted to tell her—before he knew how fully he would come to believe in them. He had not yet read Babel. *No iron can stab the heart with such force as a period put at just the right place . . .*

She stood in front of him and he felt numb. He felt neither anger nor desire. She reached up and she touched his cheek with her fingertip. He concentrated on not pulling back, even though he felt as if he might be burned. "Do you want to be near me?" she asked.

He nodded. "Yes," he said. Then, "At times."

She kissed him on the lips, and her lips were very soft. They tasted, slightly, of salt. They were warm. She let her body rest against his, easily; he felt himself growing hard, and he wondered if she noticed. Her eyes were closed. He kept his own eyes open. Suddenly she shuddered, as if she had caught a chill. He drew back.

"I'm sorry," he said. "Rachel—?" He saw them in the hallway of her father's house. She was shivering and laughing. He was laughing with her. They had run all the way from the subway station. They were both drenched. He smelled the wet wool of her expensive suit. He remembered how wonderful it had felt when they kissed, the rain sliding down their faces, so that they had been unable to keep their lips pressed against one another's. It's just like you, he'd said then, to her delight, to tempt me with slippery kisses.

She pressed her head against his chest. She reached up and took his face between her two hands. He was surprised at how soft her skin was. He let her kiss him, and for a brief instant he imagined that he was becoming enraged with her for what she was doing. He imagined himself hurling words down at her with great fury, words that accused her of being deceitful and selfish and cunning and insincere. She looked up at him. "It's all right," she said. "I'm nervous too, Nathan. I'm not always as—well, as assured as I like to seem."

"We could go downstairs," he said.

"Downstairs?"

"It would be warmer there, in my room. There's only a blanket here."

"If you want, but I'm happy here, just as—"

She stopped and he watched her bite down on her lip. She said nothing else. He remembered Nachman's tongue, swollen to twice its size. Was that where the image had come from? Was that why Mendel had said that his tongue was swollen and mute?

My tongue may have been swollen, Nathan, but it was never mute. That was your own invention.

Nathan kept his eyes open. "That night we found you here, I was so scared. Michael was so angry . . ." He touched Rachel's hair, her soft brown curls. He remembered the times he would press down upon his own tongue with his teeth, in order to feel what he had imagined

Nachman felt—but even when he blotted his tongue afterward and examined the pinpoints of blood on the white handkerchief, he could never understand how Nachman was able to do it.

"What if Michael should come home?"

For a moment he thought she was going to laugh at him—at his question—but she did not. "It's too early," she said. "He called this morning. He said he had conferences and that we shouldn't wait for him for supper—"

"All right." Nathan did not want to move. He enjoyed the feeling of her warm body pressed against his own. He was afraid that if he moved, everything would change. He saw sunlight, pouring in through the window of his kitchen in Ein Karem. He saw himself reading in *The Jerusalem Post* about Gail Rubin and Hanoch Tel-Oren. He touched Rachel's eyelids, and ran his index finger over her face, tracing lines that had not been there when she was young. He thought of Esther's scar, in *The Stolen Jew*, of Noah feeling, as he touched it, that he was tracing a journey in sand. He said nothing, and he was glad that she did not speak either, that she did not in any way refer to the times, over forty years before, when they had been together in the room, as they were now. He heard a siren. An ambulance? A police car? He could not tell. The sirens in New York were different from the sirens in Israel. He tried not to think of what things were like outside the house, in the streets. He tried not to think of the filth and the decay. He understood how difficult it would be for Michael to sell the house and move away, forever.

They kissed again. He reminded himself to ask Michael about Lazer Kominsky's age. If Lazer had been approximately the same age as Michael, then he could not have been born after the war, as Michael had said. Michael was thirty-seven years old. He was born in 1941. Outside, the sirens came closer. Nathan closed his eyes. He saw dogs snarling and fighting over garbage. He saw men sleeping in doorways. He saw stores with smashed windows. He saw black women with glazed eyes and platinum-colored hair. He saw Michael's friends, in the schoolyard, setting upon him, with knives. He felt his body tense. He saw Michael soaring toward the basket, through a crowd of black bodies, though at the same time his body lay on the ground, like Ira's, in a pool of blood. It was the gradual deterioration of things that offended him, he decided. That was why he preferred Israel. When Israel was destroyed, it would be destroyed all at once. Israel, surrounded by enemies, would never decay.

Israel would never have a second chance. Israel was allowed only a single mistake. It could not err twice. Israel would die before it would have the opportunity to deteriorate.

RACHEL WAS GONE, TO HER OWN APARTMENT, AND NATHAN WAS, AGAIN, alone in the house. He didn't mind. She had, afterward, said that she had things to do that couldn't wait. He had not asked her what the things were. He did not want to press himself and his feelings upon her too quickly. Nor was he ready, he knew, to let her know, in words, just how wonderful their being together had been for him. He glanced toward the potato bin and he imagined Nachman behind its door, sitting with his knees to his chin, one hand over his mouth, the other across his eyes.

Nathan looked down at the list of items that he and Michael would take with them to Russia. Levi's blue jeans were bringing over 200 rubles a pair on the black market. He and Michael would bring five pairs each, and give them to the refuseniks, who would sell them. They would bring books and records and vitamins and panty hose and cigarette lighters and felt-tip pens and rock-and-roll records and tape recorders and blank cassettes and calculators. They would bring food—matzo and packages of dehydrated orange juice and oxtail bouillon cubes and granola bars. The food would be smuggled in to refuseniks in prisons and labor camps, so that they could maintain their strength. He and Michael would bring books and materials to be used for teaching Hebrew and Jewish history to children. They would each go with two suitcases and come home with one. Nathan would bring the new manuscripts of *The Stolen Jew*. Gronsky had replied at once to Michael's letter. There were buyers waiting. Nathan pressed his eyes closed. It was difficult for him to imagine that writers had actually been murdered because of words that they had set down on pieces of paper.

Nathan looked at the bookcase. Who would kill him for his book? Only Nachman. He would ask Michael if he could take his father's *Siddur* with him to Russia. The book had been printed in Vilna. He imagined Rachel, at the airport, saying good-bye to them. Where was Nachman? Nathan closed his eyes. Nachman let his head rest against Nathan's shoulder. If he parted Nachman's hair, he knew, on top of the skull he would see the long curved scar. He saw Rachel, putting her clothing on the chair, very neatly, setting her shoes under it, side by side.

Well, Nachman said.

Well.

Tell me, Nathan, have you heard the story about the three holes in the ground?

No. Tell me the story about the three holes in the ground.

Well, well, well.

And did you by any chance hear the story about the ghost in the family closet?

No, Nathan, I didn't hear the story about the ghost in the family closet.

Nothing to it.

Nathan saw Nachman smile. In our family we had a lot of closets, but there was never one that was right for me. That was why . . .

Nathan thought of the time he'd tried to write a short story about his Uncle Harry for a high school English class—was it the first real story he'd written?—years before he thought of writing *The Stolen Jew.* Had his Uncle Harry lost the first two joints of his right index finger in an accident in a factory, or had he, as Nathan always believed, cut off the finger himself in order to avoid military service in the Austrian army? When Nathan thought of writing the story for his class, he'd intended to end it with just such a question, and he'd imagined his classmates swarming around him afterward, debating the question, arguing with one another, and demanding that Nathan give them the true answer, so vivid would the story have been.

And yet, not knowing the answer himself, Nathan recalled, he'd been afraid to begin the story. He could hear his uncle talking. He could see how silent and withdrawn his father became in Harry's presence. He could remember how bright his mother's eyes were, when she looked at Harry. He could remember how much he'd hated his uncle for being what his own father was not. He could see his Uncle Harry's hand, pointing at Nathan's father, telling him what he needed to do in order to get ahead in this world. He could remember what the hand had felt like, when Uncle Harry thrust it toward him, to shake. He always expected that the stump itself would be hard and bony, yet it was—it surprised him each time—soft, and his uncle could wiggle it.

The noise in the room confused him. Harry's laughter made him lower his eyes and want to crawl under the table, next to the bookcase. The room was full of relatives—the women knitting, the children sitting on the floor, Harry holding forth with stories of his wealthy clients—and then Harry was telling, once again, the story of how he had outwitted the Austrian officials, of how he had taken nothing for the pain except a large glass of schnapps, of how he had not even fainted.

Now, his father and Harry and all of their brothers and sisters and husbands and wives were dead. All the grown-ups who were in the living room then—all those who had been born in the Old Country—were dead, and Nathan would never know, for certain, how his uncle had lost his finger.

What I thought you were going to say was that I was the ghost in the family closet. You fooled me, Nathan. I thought you were going to talk about how, when I was in the hospital, Momma tried to keep that story in the closet.

The story I found in the seventh room that I want to tell you about is the story of an old writer who is writing seven novels at once in seven different rooms of the house in which he grew up.

It sounds familiar. I like it a lot.

Eventually the characters from one room meet and mingle with the characters from another room, and so on, until they all know each other. When the author commits suicide the characters continue to live with one another and to take care of the house.

Nachman said nothing.

You're not angry with me?

Why should I be angry with you?

For what happened with Rachel.

I thought you meant for your story.

Then you are angry.

You had her first, didn't you? That's what it means to be an older brother. Tolstoy was the youngest of four, so what does that prove? But listen, Nathan, the reason I came to visit you wasn't for envy—the conservation of envy isn't a theory I put much stock in—but to ask if you wanted my secret yet. I had a secret I was saving for you, for your collection, and I thought this might be a good time to give it to you.

One of the books will be called Family Secrets *and another will be called* The Brothers *and another will be called* The Stolen Jew *and another will be called* The Nephew *and another will be called* The Jew in Russia *and another will be called* On a Beach near Herzlia.

You were always good at titles.

I'll call the last story The Seventh Room. *It will be a kind of ghost story, in which the reader gradually comes to understand that the people and stories that inhabit the different rooms of the house are really vying for possession of the writer's soul. In the end . . .*

You didn't say if you wanted my secret yet.

All right. Yes. Give me your secret.

It's about the time you ran away. Remember? I was in the hospital and everybody was worried about you, to do such a thing, and the secret I was thinking of giving you was that when you were a boy and I was a boy and you ran away, I hoped that you would die. I hoped that you would die and that people would then love me more, because of the noble way I endured your loss.

It's a good secret. Only you didn't need to save it for so long.

You're not angry with me?

Why should I be angry with you?

Because it makes you happy to be angry with me. That pleased me, Nathan, when we were boys—that whenever I teased you and stole things from you, you got angry with me. Even when I was in the hospital, after Rachel, you didn't let where I was stop you from being angry with me. You were the only one who felt so free with me. I appreciated it.

You meant "my loss" just before. You said "your loss."

Whatever you say, Nathan. When it comes to words, I defer to you. I always did. Like I used to say, it was always a business doing pleasure with you. You were the firstborn, after all. You were there before me.

And yet I used to think that Poppa loved you more than he loved me. Did you know that? You were a very beautiful child, Nachman. I used to watch you, in Momma's arms, or when Rivka brushed your hair, or playing on street corners, and in Mr. Kobin's candy store . . .

I was beautiful.

I've thought about it a lot, and what I decided is that Poppa loved me for what I could do—for my success—but that he loved you for what you were.

For what I was? But I was lost! I was so lost sometimes, Nathan, in the corridors of my own mind, that I couldn't always find my way back.

Remember how you were always losing the things Momma and Rivka made for you—the wool hats and the scarves and the gloves?

I loved to lose things. That's true.

Sometimes when I would be alone in the house, and you were in the hospital, I would imagine that there was a room inside my brain where all the things you lost were waiting. Like the lost-and-found room at school. And I used to imagine that in the lost-and-found of my mind, you were there too, peering out from under the pile of clothing.

Nathan opened his eyes. The room was cold. He saw Nachman wiping the rosin dust from his violin with a silk cloth. He saw him loosen the hairs on his bow with his thumb and forefinger. Nachman had played for the other patients while they sat quietly on the floor and listened. Nathan looked out the window, eleven stories up, at the park across the street, at a baseball game. Somebody screamed. Somebody else screamed at the first person. Nachman was setting his violin in the velvet-lined case. An aide took it and put it away in the office. Nachman stopped playing. "What do you think, Nathan," he'd asked afterward. "Hath music charms to soothe the savage beast?"

But listen, Nathan, all those years—it's what I've been trying to get you to understand—my life wasn't as bad as you think.

It wasn't so good either.

Who said it was? But maybe—this is what I was thinking—maybe Rachel is only doing what she's doing to get even with me. Has that thought occurred to you?

No.

I'm surprised. It wasn't so easy on her, if you think about it—not her having to put up with my mishegas and my being put away, but—and this is no secret to you—the fact that where they used to put me, I led a very active love life. I was always overextended in my love life. And not only in the hospitals. I told you all about it years ago. You must have forgotten.

I must have forgotten.

Or else you wanted to forget. Ask Michael when he comes home. He's the expert at these things. But like Rachel was saying, I was always a very charming man. Even the last few years, whenever we'd visit Rivka and Leah in Florida, I'd have a terrific time with all the widows. I'd tell them about my life in the hospitals, and they'd marvel at my frankness, my lack of shame. They were very interested. It was a good life, I'd tell them. Out of this world, is the way I'd put it.

Out of this world.

So what else would I say to the women when they'd know my story? I'd say, "I'm crazy about you, darling. I'm mad for you." They'd be a little bit alarmed at first, but pretty soon I'd have them laughing.

You could always make people laugh. I never could. Rachel says you knew how to make her laugh, even in the worst times.

"You drive me out of my mind," I'd say to them. "I'm going berserk over you . . ."

It was a good way to use the life you had, I suppose.

Why throw it away? And if they said back to me that I wasn't being serious enough, I'd ask them why did they think that the language of madness and the language of love were the same? We'd sit and we'd talk. We'd have terrific seminars together. These old Jewish women were hot for education, Nathan, believe me. "Let go," I'd say to them. "Let yourself go nuts over me too."

Enough, Nachman.

To Rachel too. I said the same things to her, that first time she visited me when you went away to work on your book. She took me out on my day off from the hospital. I had a pass. "You make me lose my head," I whispered to her. "You drive me crazy."

Stop.

We can't always make both choices, Nathan. That's the way I look at it. You chose to work on your book and she chose to visit me. You chose to go away for a while and I chose to stay. "I'm possessed," I said to her, and we laughed together. Did I like my unit at the hospital? she asked. Like it? You had to be crazy to want to stay in it, I said, and we laughed some more. She was good to me. She was very kind. Did I dare to hope? "I'm far gone," I told her. "I'm out of my mind, I'm beside myself, I'm . . ."

Enough!

IN A STORE ON FLATBUSH AVENUE NATHAN BOUGHT A BOUQUET OF flowers for Rachel—asters and chrysanthemums. Michael claimed that, after several years of decline, Flatbush Avenue was reviving—that there were interesting new stores owned by Albanians and West Indians and Haitians and Koreans—but Nathan did not see the difference. The sidewalks were crumbling, the streets were littered, the faces were dark. Nathan stood at the corner of Flatbush and Parkside avenues. An old man waited next to him, bent over, carrying a large bundle of newspapers. His neck bulged on the right side, as if, Nathan thought, there were a hand grenade under the skin. He wore an old-fashioned black *yarmulke.* He whispered to Nathan in Yiddish, cursing the black people, asking to be helped across the street. When the light changed, Nathan took the man by the arm and helped him across the street. He stood with him, silently. He imagined for an instant that he and the old man were standing on a revolving movie set; he realized that he was expecting the street to turn suddenly on its axis while he stood still.

The man had his hand out, asking for *tzedaka,* for charity. Nathan looked at the cracked yellow skin of the man's palm. It was as if, he thought, if only they waited together, as motionlessly as possible, the past might reestablish itself before their eyes; it was as if, if only they stood there, without even breathing, near where he and Nachman and Ira and Pauline and Michael had often stood, the old storefronts would return, the black people would become white people, music would fill the air, and they would still be there, in the same spot, two old Jews—like the original Twin Cantors, Nathan thought—their heads slightly forward, their backs somewhat bent, identical expressions on their faces. Then Ruth and Michael would come tap-dancing down the middle of the street, hopping to and from a red trolley car as a chorus of singers and dancers—hundreds of fair-skinned young people—strutted behind, swaying from one side of the avenue to the other . . .

Nathan tucked the bouquet under his arm, took his wallet from his side pocket, and put a dollar bill into the man's hand. The man gave Nathan his blessing. He looked vaguely familiar, and Nathan thought of asking him his name. He thought of asking the man if he had known Nathan's father, Isaac Malkin.

"I call it a neighborhood in transition," the man said to Nathan, in English. "*Zei gezunt.*"

"Yes," Nathan said.

Nathan walked along Parkside Avenue. He thought of telling Nachman about the scene he had seen, in his head, of Ruth and Michael.

I'd say it was more like a neighborhood which has already transished, Nachman said, smiling.

Nathan thought of Tolstoy's grandfather. He had forgotten to tell Nachman about Tolstoy's grandfather. Nachman would have loved the story. Each morning at seven o'clock, on the estate at Yasnaya Polyana, eight serf-musicians, in white blouses, breeches, white stockings, and pumps, would assemble in front of their music stands near an ancient elm. When Tolstoy's grandfather went by in his nightgown, carrying a pitcher of hot water, a little boy would cry out, "He's awake!" Then the serfs would begin to play the opening section of a Haydn symphony. When they were done, they would return to their work—feeding the pigs, spading the garden, knitting stockings, collecting chamber pots, and burning lozenges. *Another Tolstoy* . . .

Nathan crossed Bedford Avenue. Their family doctor—Dr. Abbett—had had his office in a building which was now without windows. Dr. Abbett had always done what their mother asked him to do. He had signed the papers, the first time, committing Nachman to Creedmoor State Hospital. In Dr. Abbett's office, Nachman had unbuttoned his fly and urinated on Dr. Abbett's shoes. Later, in the hospital, the two of them had giggled together, recalling the moment, commenting on the symbolic justice of the act.

A black man, smoking a pipe, said good morning to Nathan. He wore a brown tweed jacket. He was clipping hedges.

"Nice day," the man said.

"Nice day," Nathan replied.

"Those are lovely chrysanthemums and asters," the man said.

"Thank you."

Nathan did not stop. He wondered about Rachel's loneliness during all those months and years that Nachman had been away. He wondered if she had, like Nachman, ever taken lovers. He had been afraid to ask her. They had not spoken Nachman's name. Nor, he realized, had he told her what he wanted to tell her about *kelippot*—about the breaking of the vessels.

He had been surprised at her nervousness—at a shyness in her that seemed new, and that pleased him deeply. *Do you think God will be disappointed in me?* she had asked him, and—too astonished by her question to speak—he had only held her to him more closely.

Nathan passed Michael's schoolyard. He thought of how happy Ira had always been, running out of the house so that he could play ball with Michael. They had been good friends. Nobody was playing basketball now, but dozens of schoolchildren were screaming and running within the fenced-in enclosure. Some of them pressed their noses to the wire diamonds and shouted at Nathan, but even their curses seemed innocent. Nathan smiled at them and walked by. Some of the children were wearing wool hats and mittens. Nathan remembered Michael's blue mittens, the ones Pauline had knitted for him for his third birthday. He remembered going into Manhattan once—they were all going to Radio City Music Hall together for the Christmas show—and watching from behind as Nachman walked with Michael, hand in hand. Michael was wearing a gray checked coat with a black velvet Chesterfield collar. It had been Ira's coat. Nathan had bought the coat for Ira at Browning-King, in downtown Brooklyn, and Ira had outgrown it. They were downstairs at the Prospect Park subway station of the BMT line, waiting for a train. As Nathan watched them walk around a pillar, Michael on the side nearest the tracks, he saw Michael's hand start to slip out of the mitten. Michael was pulling away from Nachman, leaning sideways, and Nathan envisioned Nachman being left with nothing but the small blue mitten in his hand. His heart caught. He recalled the roar of the incoming train, and he realized that he'd stood there, incapable of moving, and had imagined Michael's fall into the well of the subway tracks; he recalled that he had envisioned Michael's upturned face, trusting and puzzled, as the train screeched and then passed over it, making everything black. Then, opening his eyes, Nathan saw that Michael was standing quietly next to Nachman, inside the subway car, the blue mitten enclosed within Nachman's red hand. Rachel was yelling at Nathan to hurry and get on the train. She was holding the door for him. Pauline and Ira were sitting quietly on the yellow caned seats. Nathan saw himself enter the train and, as the train pulled out of the station, he saw his face through a window. Nachman was lifting Michael, so that he could hang on to a subway strap. Michael was laughing. Nathan had frozen. Had anyone noticed?

NATHAN WALKED UP THE STAIRS TO RACHEL'S APARTMENT. HE WAS VERY eager to see her again. He hoped she would like the flowers he had chosen. He smiled. He was done working for the day. They would have time to be alone together. She had been fascinated by the story of *zimzum*. He would sit in her living room and watch her eyes as he told her that some of the rabbis likened the breaking of the vessels, from which all of creation emanated, to a sown field whose seeds could not bear fruit until they had first split open and rotted.

He could see the pieces of blue-and-white china on her kitchen floor. He could see her leaning toward him, wanting to know more about what his father had once taught him, and about what he had read, while in Israel, in books about the Kabbalah. They had no need to feel shame, he would say to her if he had the courage. They had no need. Like the grain that dies in the earth, he would say, so the deeds of man rot in order to bring forth the fruits of redemption.

Nathan thought of the Frankists. They had believed in such doctrines. They had used them to justify the secret rites and wild orgies in which they engaged. They had converted to Christianity. They had defended charges of blood libel, in Lvov, against Jews. They did all these things, they claimed, so as to keep their true faith—the Judaism of Jacob Frank—safe and secret. Their outer garment of Christianity concealed their inner souls of Jewishness. Nathan knew about the Frankists. He could share his knowledge with Rachel. In his last years, Jacob Frank spread the rumor that his daughter Eva was the illegitimate child of the empress Catherine of Russia.

Nathan saw himself in a small living room in Moscow, lecturing to several dozen Jews about their own history. Such a meeting was illegal. Lookouts were posted in the hallways and at windows. Nathan smiled. Concealment was often obligatory. Often in history Jews had been forced to hide themselves for so long that they themselves forgot who they were and why they did what they did. Did not Elijah pass through the world disguised as a poor stranger?

Nathan stopped at the second-floor landing. He unbuttoned his coat. He thought of asking Rachel if she knew what those Jews were named, who, in Spain, still went down to cellars on Friday nights to light candles, though they did not know why they did so, except to say, when asked, that their mothers and grandmothers had done the same.

Marranos, she would say. *Aren't they called Marranos?*

Perhaps, he would reply. *Perhaps.* He would pause. *But I prefer to call them Span-yids.*

He stopped. The door to Rachel's apartment was open. He knocked anyway, his heart beating more quickly. "Rachel?" he called. "Rachel—?"

He gasped. A tall black man in a green leather jacket stepped in front of him. The man's face was pockmarked. He wore rimless glasses and reeked of wine. "What you want?" the man asked.

"Who are you?" Nathan demanded. "Where is Mrs. Malkin?"

"I'm the super," the man said. "Some people here to see the apartment."

Nathan heard voices, from the bedroom. He pushed past the man and walked down the hallway. A short black man, in a tan corduroy suit that was too tight for him, looked at Nathan from the bedroom. A black woman, taller than the man, was examining the closet, which was open. Her hair was streaked with silver. She wore red high-heeled shoes. "You here to rent the place?" the man asked.

Nathan stared. The closet had only a few dresses and blouses hanging in it. The room was filled with boxes and cartons and large cardboard wardrobes, the words BEKINS MOVING AND STORAGE on their sides.

"We seen the place first," the woman said. Nathan turned, to leave. "You don't let nobody push you around, Oliver, you hear? We seen the place first."

In the living room there were no draperies on the windows. Nathan looked out at the red-brick apartment houses across the street. The furniture had been moved into the middle of the room, and cartons and suitcases were piled on the furniture. The oriental rug rested next to the wall, rolled up and tied with twine. The walls were bare of pictures and mirrors. The photos of Michael and Ruth and their children were gone.

He had wanted to see the things that Nachman had left behind. Rachel had promised him that he could look in the closet and in the dresser and in the cartons that Nachman had kept. She had *promised*! Where were those books, from their father, that Nachman had not given to Michael? How would he find them now?

"If you interested, it gone to cost you," the super was saying. "You know what I mean?"

Nathan turned and shoved the man, hard. The man collapsed, as if he were made of air, and fell back against a sofa. A lamp on the sofa seat fell to its side but did not break. The super looked up at Nathan sleepily. "Hey, what you do that for?"

"What's going on?" The short black man had come from the bedroom.

"Get out of here," Nathan said.

"Ain't his place," the super said.

"Call the police," the woman said.

"Get out of here," Nathan said.

"Don't let him push you around, Oliver," the woman said. "You call the police."

"Get out of here," Nathan said.

The black man buttoned his jacket and stepped toward Nathan. "You gone to make me, mister?"

"Get out of here," Nathan said again, but without force. He turned and walked down the corridor, toward the door.

"You gone to make me, mister, huh?" the black man called after him. "You gone to *make* me—?"

NATHAN SAT IN THE DARK ROOM AND LISTENED TO MICHAEL TALK ABOUT the people they would meet in Russia. One was a distinguished cyberneticist who had been waiting for his exit visa for over four years. The man's wife and three children lived in Israel. Another was a woman, a widow, who threatened to immolate herself in Red Square if her son died. She had been granted a visa to Israel, but her only son, nineteen years old, was drafted into the Russian army for seven years. Now she was free to leave, but her son, asking to leave also, had been imprisoned for draft evasion. The Soviet Union was very clever, the woman declared.

They would put an end to her life by imprisoning her son. She would not permit that. She was clever also. If the government wanted to annihilate her, she demanded that they begin with her, not with her son.

Nathan listened to Michael's voice. He had met such people in Israel, at the office in Jerusalem. The stronger and healthier ones rarely stayed. Israel inherited the old and the lame and the sick. Few Russians left their homeland so that their sons and daughters would thereby be free to be killed in the Israeli army. Michael said that it was already arranged: they would meet Nathan's translator Gronsky and they would, he hoped, also meet the brave Sakharov and his wife. Sakharov's mother had requested American sewing needles and knitting needles, which Michael had already purchased. Michael told Nathan that they would, within apartments, often have to communicate by writing on blackboards and magic slates, in case the apartments were under electronic surveillance. Michael had addresses and telephone numbers and lists of goods. He had boxes of medicines he would bring, for heart conditions and other ailments. Nathan did not listen carefully. He did not understand the technical terms for diseases. Michael laughed. His teeth seemed especially white within the circle of his beard. Nathan did not like Michael's beard—he agreed with Rachel about that. He wished Michael would shave it off, so that he would look the way he had always looked. "I'll bring the medicines," Michael said, "but you'll bring the diseases. The medicines will be prescribed for you—for all your ailments, okay?"

"Your mother is already packing, for Florida," Nathan said.

"Good for her."

"I suppose," Nathan said. "I stopped by this afternoon, but she wasn't home. The superintendent was showing people around the apartment. She didn't tell me that she was already packing. I thought she would wait longer."

"Wait?"

Nathan shrugged. "I've enjoyed being with her these last few weeks, you know. Your mother is a very—a very gentle woman. She's been very kind to me."

Michael rolled his eyes. "She's really done a job on you, hasn't she?"

"A what?"

"A very gentle woman," Michael repeated. He came across the room and sat next to Nathan. "You're angry with her, aren't you? I sense that you're very angry with her."

"I don't know," Nathan said. "Maybe."

"What Harvey said that first night—is that what's on your mind?"

"*Gilgul*," Nathan said, staring past Michael, at the bookcase. He nodded. "You were always a good guesser."

"*Gilgul?*" Michael asked.

"The transmigration of souls. The Kabbalists believed that the proof for *gilgul* lay in the commandment concerning a levirate marriage. The brother of the childless man replaces this dead man so that he may merit children in his second *gilgul*."

"But you both had sons."

"Ira is dead."

"Are you all right, Uncle Nat?" Michael put the back of his hand to Nathan's forehead. "I think you have a fever." He turned on a light. "You look awful. The way you did when—"

"She promised me that I could see some of Nachman's things, the way he left them in his drawers, the things he saved—she promised—but they're already packed."

"Or thrown out."

Nathan shrugged. "Life hasn't been easy for her," he said.

"Excessive love is often a reaction formation to feelings of deep hostility," Michael stated.

"Don't be a doctor," Nathan said. He looked away. He could not bear the directness of Michael's gaze. "I don't understand such language."

Michael turned off the light. "Are you still collecting secrets?" he asked.

Nathan tried to smile. "I suppose."

"Okay," Michael said. He sat in front of Nathan, on a brown leather hassock. "Look. You and Rachel are all grown up now, right? So I'm not going to try to tell either of you what to do. My mother is a very gentle woman. She's been very good to you." Michael sighed. His head moved forward slightly. "But she's also a very willful woman, right?"

"I know that."

"She doesn't want me to go to Russia, and if she can get you to stay behind, she figures she might be able to get me to stay behind too."

"She's wrong," Nathan said. "You'd go anyway, without me. I know that. You're very determined."

Michael laughed. "You got it, Uncle Nat. I'm as willful as she is, right?" Nathan tried to understand what Michael wanted from him, why he was looking at him with such intensity. Did Michael suspect what had happened with Rachel years before? Had somebody told him? Did Ruth know? Had Rachel shared the story with Ruth?

"What did Ruth want to tell me about herself and Ira?" Nathan asked.

"That's not my secret," Michael said. He stopped smiling. "You'll have to ask Ruth."

"You said that Lazer Kominsky was your age. How could that be? I thought about it. If he was born before the war, he would have to be much older than you."

"Did I say he was born before the war?"

"You said he was about your age and height."

"He was." Michael pressed his eyes closed, as if forcing himself to remember, and then opened them. "All right. What I said was that his father remarried and that Lazer was born after the war—not before. There were five children born after the war, and he was the only son. He was a few years younger than me, but—remember his life—he looked much older than me, much older than his years. I always thought of him as being older. That's all I meant."

"Does Ruth want you to stay home?" Nathan asked.

"Not really. She accepts the things I have to do—and she feels better now that you're going with me—now that I've promised to sell the house." Michael's face relaxed. "But you're trying to stop me from telling you my secret, aren't you?" He reached out and touched Nathan's hand, and Nathan thought that Michael was thinking of Ruth—that what he was about to tell him he had already told to Ruth. "The way you were just sitting here in the dark with that black look on your face—it reminded me of the way you looked once before, in this room."

"She promised me," Nathan said. "Why did she break her promise? I told her I needed some time. I don't like it when she pushes me. She promised me."

"Let me talk, all right?" Michael leaned back and closed his eyes. "The only other times I ever saw a look like that on your face were when we'd visit my father together. Afterward, in the car, I'd see a look like that on your face, and I used to love it, Uncle Nat—it made me feel that you were so angry you would have murdered people if you thought it would help to get my father out." Michael smiled. "It was a look, I suppose, that I wished I'd seen on his face more often. Because if it had been there . . ."

"You don't have to tell me anything you don't want to," Nathan said.

"Your mother was probably right that first morning, about the secrets—about it only being a joke. I was very upset with Harvey and Rivka—I was angry that Rivka was there. She reminds me too much of Momma."

"I wouldn't tell you anything I didn't want to tell you," Michael said. "In fact, you already know most of the story—about the valentine's card. But—"

Nathan shook his head. "What card?"

"One I bought for Mother when I was in the eighth grade—you don't remember?"

"No."

"It's all right," Michael said. He gestured to the darkened room. "We're in the right room for secrets, don't you think—for remembering?"

"How about forgetting?" Nathan asked. "Are we in the right room for forgetting?"

Michael smiled. "It depends," he said. "But listen. Maybe I told you less back then than I like to think I did. This is what happened." Nathan sat back. He liked the sound of Michael's voice. "I'd saved up my allowance so that I could get my girl friend and my mother expensive cards for Valentine's Day, from a store on Church Avenue. Until then I'd always made the cards, from doilies and ribbons and tinfoil and colored paper. My allowance was only fifty cents a week then and it had taken me over four months to save the dollar and thirty-five cents I needed for each of the cards, but they were worth it. They each had a heart made out of a piece of silk-like material that was raised up by a cushion that had a beautiful scent to it—and inside the lettering of the poem was embossed in gold."

"I never saw the card," Nathan said. "Rachel always showed us the cards you made, but I never saw that one. I'm sure of it."

"So am I," Michael said. His eyes flicked sideways. Nathan wondered what Michael's clinic was like. He wondered if any of his patients were white people. He wondered how Michael could, with words, help people who were so much less intelligent and educated than he was. Were they intimidated by Michael's size? "Okay. I brought the card home and waited until supper and then I gave it to her, and when she looked at it, instead of being delighted, she flung it back in my face." Michael moved closer. His eyes were cold and clear. "She actually threw it at me, Uncle Nat. Do you hear me? 'Anyone can buy a card!' she declared, 'but not every son can make the kinds of beautiful cards that you used to make for me.' Then she left the kitchen.

"I was devastated. My father sat across from me at the table and I remember looking to him for help, for some kind of explanation—but all he did was shrug and say something to me about trying to be more considerate of her feelings." Michael sat back. "Okay. What I'd done wasn't such a terrible thing, he said, but he suggested that I go to her and apologize, that I go to my room and make her the kind of card she wanted."

Nathan nodded. "Nachman always knew how to please her, that's true. He was very good at being considerate of her wishes. He was well trained."

"I went to her room and I apologized and I tried to explain to her about having saved up my money so I could give her the kind of card the richer kids in my class gave their mothers, but she replied by asking me if I thought she wanted me to be like everybody else. She glared at me with such coldness that I got angry too and I let that anger go right back at her—the way I often did in those days. I told her that I'd bought the exact same card for my girl friend and that she'd loved it and had shown it to everybody in our class and that I guessed that meant I was batting five hundred for the day with the women in my life, and that I figured that wasn't such a bad average."

"Why are you telling me all this?" Nathan asked. "I like to listen to you tell stories, Michael, but why are you telling me all this?"

"I'm telling you this because of what you found when you went to her apartment and because of the look I saw on your face when I came home," Michael stated. "All right?"

Nathan nodded. He thought of Michael's voice in Ruth's house, telling them about Lazer Kominsky and about why he was going to Russia. He thought of the enormous cardboard wardrobes in Rachel's bedroom, and of the bed, covered with boxes. Where would Rachel sleep?

"She really let me have it then, but I didn't listen to whatever it was she was saying. I was out the door pretty fast, slamming it as hard as I could, and then stopping for a second—I remember the moment very clearly—cringing for an instant while I waited for the sound of broken glass. It never came. I kept going. I came straight here, to your house, and you made Aunt Pauline and Ira leave the living room when you saw the way I looked. I appreciated that. You made them leave us alone and then you listened to me tell you what happened, and when I was done was when I noticed how dark your face had become. You were sitting just where you are now, and you didn't say anything to me. The more I told you about her reaction, and the more I kept pleading with you to tell me what I could do, the darker your face seemed to become."

Michael smiled and took Nathan's hand in both of his own. "But you took my hand after a while, and you bent over and you kissed my fingertips, and—"

Michael stopped, as if, Nathan thought, he were forcing back tears. "Yes?" Nathan said.

"Do you remember now?"

"I remember. Yes. I think I remember."

"It made all the difference—the way you held my hand." Michael's face was very close to Nathan's. "It was as if, I realize now, you were telling me that I was all right—as if you were denying for me what my mother had, by her actions, been accusing me of. You were telling me that I was a good boy and a loving son and that you understood how much it hurt me to be rejected." Michael sighed. "Forgive the psychological language, if—"

"No," Nathan said. "What you say makes sense. But what's the secret you said you wanted to give me?"

"Ah," Michael said. He let go of Nathan's hand. He touched his beard. "We'll call it a secret, all right? It's something I'd forgotten over the years—even when I was in analysis and I was going over the incident, and feeling again exactly what I'd felt when she threw the card back at me—the extraordinary pain, and then the way I immediately concealed that pain from myself with an equally extraordinary rage—and, more important—when I could feel too that incredible rage I'd felt toward my father—watching him sit there and do nothing to help me, watching him sit there and do nothing to her, watching him sit there and tell me what to do to please her—even when I was remembering all this, what I'd forgotten to remember—the secret I kept even from myself, I suppose —were the things I felt about you."

"Yes," Nathan said. "All right."

"I felt very close to you," Michael said. "You started humming to yourself, while you held on to my hand—the way I remembered Grandpa humming when I was a little boy—and I kept having the feeling that you were remembering everything your life had been like when you'd been growing up in this house, and then I had what seemed to me the strangest feeling of all, though I couldn't articulate it at the time. I kept feeling that what made you and me so much like one another, even though you'd had a brother and two sisters, was that when you were a boy you must have felt, in your deepest feelings, that you were just like me—an only child forever wishing that it wasn't so.

"I had this crazy feeling that we were both orphans somehow, living in an abandoned orphanage together, and when that picture settled into my head I let it stay there, and I let my mind wander wherever it wanted to, the way I imagined you were doing. I let myself feel how much I hated being an only child, and how much I still wished I had a brother, or even a sister, and how much I resented my parents for never having given me one." Michael moved closer to Nathan. "It just never seemed fair to me—not that I had my parents all to myself, but that nobody had ever joined me, as it were, to inherit my crib and my clothes and my baseball glove and my basketball and my toys and my books and my games and the rest. It was as if, without a brother or sister, I was incomplete somehow—as if my parents had never finished making me.

"When I got home later that night, my parents were both asleep, and do you know the first thing I did when I got to my room? I opened *The Stolen Jew* and I read the opening page. *I understand loss.*" Michael took Nathan's hand again. "Do you, Uncle Nat? Did I? Because what I felt was passing between me and you in the silence of this room that night was that sometimes a person could understand loss not just by losing something you loved, the way Tsvi did in the book, but by feeling that you'd never have the thing you loved to lose—"

"You lost Nachman," Nathan said. "You lost your father."

"My father? I lost him years ago," Michael said. "Long before he died. He was never there when I needed him."

"That's what Rachel said about him—about why she loved him—that he was never there when she needed him. She loved his weakness, she told me."

"The way your mother loved your father's weakness?"

"No," Nathan said. "My mother didn't love anything about my father." He smiled mechanically, then spoke again. "I'm sorry, Michael. You're still angry with Nachman, aren't you?"

"No," Michael said. "I don't think I am."

"But with Rachel—you're angry with her for the way she treated him, and for having thrown the card at you?"

"I want to tell you something else," Michael said, without answering Nathan's question. "When I first met Ruth—when we would talk with each other—she reminded me of you. The way she never pushed me to tell her everything about myself, everything I was thinking. She trusted me. She didn't seem to need to know everything about me."

"And now?"

"I think I felt close to you for the same reason—precisely because there was a part of you that I could never see and because there was a part of me you could never see. We both seemed to respect those secret parts. It seemed to draw us closer."

"But I don't think I look at all like Ruth," Nathan said.

Michael smiled. "But do you understand what I'm telling you? When I was with Ruth—when we'd first met and had fallen in love, in France—it was as if I were talking to the sister I'd always wanted and had never had. I felt so easy with her—"

"And when she was your patient—wasn't that when you decided to marry her?"

"No," Michael said. "That was much later. We'd gone our separate ways. I waited until she got well."

"But wasn't that—her getting sick—her way of reaching you? I always thought it was. I always admired her for it—for taking the chance."

"Maybe," Michael said. "But we got past that part."

"Your father proposed to your mother when he was in the hospital."

"Ruth is very unlike my mother." Michael's voice was more insistent. "At the time—sure—it felt good to know that I was helping her—saving her, if you want—but we got past that part. I'd been stupid to let her go. I saw that the second time. Things weren't easy for either of us."

"And now?"

"You asked me that before," Michael said. He flashed a smile that made Nathan uneasy. He spoke slowly and clearly, as if to one of his children. "And now we'll go to Russia, you and me, and I'll do what I have to do, and then everything will be all right."

"If you say so," Nathan said.

"You're skeptical—suspicious."

"I'm not used to the noise—to listening to so many words, to having so many things happen all at once. Things were simpler where I was, Michael. That's all. And I'm afraid sometimes, for you. Maybe we should fly in separate planes, the way Raymond and Leah do. I don't know. I was thinking about it. But if your plane should be the one to crash, how would I feel afterwards? I think of that too."

"How you would feel if you lived and I died?"

"I suppose."

"We don't have to be afraid. We don't have to be afraid of anything, Uncle Nat. Don't you understand? We don't have to be afraid of failure and we don't have to be afraid of women—of strong women—and we don't have to be afraid of madness."

"Is that what you've been learning all these years—?"

"I'm not my father and you're not your brother."

"Was I a good father to Ira, Michael? I wanted to ask you that. Tell me what you think. Was I a good father to Ira?"

"Yes. Of course."

"I was too hard on him, though. When he was a small boy, I used to yell at him a lot because—"

"Yes?"

"I hadn't thought of it before. Because he reminded me of Nachman, I was going to say. Ira was small when he was born. Five pounds. He was ill for a while, the way Pauline always was. He was very beautiful, though—very talented, and I was afraid that . . ." He looked at Michael. "You think I was a good father?"

"Yes. You weren't an *easy* father to have—but you were a good father. Ira was stronger than you gave him credit for. Sure. Whenever my own father would get sick, I used to be happy in part of me because his getting sick meant that I might get a chance to stay with Ira and you for a while. I liked your house more than my own. I didn't even mind the visits to my father, when you were the one who took me."

IN THE KITCHEN, MICHAEL WAS MAKING SUPPER FOR THEM. *MICHAEL wants to be a hero.* Nathan heard Ruth's voice. Why not? He closed his eyes. He remembered how good he had felt, years before, when Michael was in the car with him, his head resting against Nathan's side. He was pleased that Michael, home from Columbia for the winter vacation, had offered to go with him to visit Nachman. Nachman was at a private psychiatric clinic in upstate New York. The sun was just beginning to come up, over the horizon of snow-covered hills. There were no other cars on the highway, and Nathan loved the deserted landscape, the stillness.

On the back seat, wrapped in brown paper, was the package Rachel had prepared: two new sets of underwear, a pair of gray corduroy trousers, *talis* and *tephillin*, cookies that she had baked, a new toothbrush, three packs of Chesterfield cigarettes, and chewing gum. There were also two old copies of *The Stolen Jew*, which Nachman had asked Nathan to bring.

Michael stirred and sat up. "I'll drive," he said, rubbing his eyes.

Nathan pulled to the side of the road, got out, walked around in front of the car, and let Michael slide into the driver's seat. Michael had to adjust the seat, for his long legs. Nathan watched Michael's face, as they drove, hoping to see Michael relax—hoping that Michael might turn sideways and smile at him in the way that, a few minutes before, he had smiled down on Michael. But Michael, his head set slightly forward, his neck and mouth stiff, kept his eyes on the road.

Nathan wished he could say something that would make Michael laugh, something that would make him look the way he had—so peaceful—when he was alseep. "Did I ever tell you about the time Nachman bit Momma—your grandmother—on the lip?"

Michael turned toward Nathan. He smiled brightly. "No kidding?"

"Do you want to hear?"

Michael turned away, his smile gone. "Sure. If you want to tell me."

"It was in a different hospital than the one he's in this time. On Long Island. Creedmoor. I was living in the city with Pauline and Ira—you weren't born yet—and I'd always meet Momma and Poppa in the main lobby. Every Tuesday evening."

It happened, Nathan recalled, in those months before he had decided to make money. It happened not long after *The Stolen Jew* was published. Nathan listened to Michael, in the kitchen, singing to himself. He saw Michael in the schoolyard, ready to kill the black man who had called him a kike. He heard himself telling Michael the story, in the car. He was pleased to know that Michael had enjoyed being with him during those visits.

Sunlight filtered onto the tiled walls, through enormous barred windows. Dr. Teitleman, who was very old and spoke with a heavy German accent, and a man named Mr. Gordon, a student doing his internship, sat next to one another at one end of the long room. "What I want to do," Nathan was saying to them, "is to write my next book about a mental hospital. But before I did I thought I would ask if you thought it might hurt Nachman in any way, because if it would . . ."

Silence.

"What I mean is, it wouldn't be about Nachman, but it would be set in a place something like this, and people might not understand. They might assume . . ."

Silence.

"My basic idea is to write a story about two rabbis, one who's in and one who's out, and of how they change places and nobody knows the difference. That's my basic idea. But before I started, I thought I would ask if you thought it would hurt Nachman in any way . . ."

"How do you feel about your brother's question?" Mr. Gordon asked.

"I like it," Nachman said. "I think it's wonderful."

"The question?" Nathan asked. "Or the idea?"

Nachman laughed. "Very good, Nathan. You're very sharp tonight. Didn't I tell you how smart he was? Didn't I show you his book? When it comes to smart, my big brother is tops, believe me."

"It's a sick idea," their mother said. "What do you think, Isaac?" She turned to her husband. He shrugged. "I'll tell you what I'm thinking, since you asked me," she went on. "I don't see why my son can't wait until Norman is well—why should other people have to know now? Answer me that! Why can't Nathan write a different book if he's so worried about his brother?"

Dr. Teitleman turned to Nachman. "Yes?" he asked.

"I love you, Momma," Nachman said. "I love you so much."

Nachman walked across the room, arms extended. His mother smiled at the doctors, proud to show them that they would now see how her son felt toward her. Nachman bent over, touched her cheek—how handsome he looked to Nathan, the sunlight caressing his young face!—and when he kissed his mother, she screamed. Nachman stood. His mother's lip was bleeding. Nachman was beaming.

Their mother sat there, her hand over her mouth, while Nathan, as horrified as he was pleased, found himself laughing. "I don't understand it at all," their mother was saying, in Yiddish, the blood dripping down her chin. "That's what I mean. I just don't understand it at all—why he does things like this—and I come here so you should explain to me. That's why I come here but all you do is sit and ask how I feel and how Nathan feels and how Norman feels. So why do I come back? Isaac?"

Their father shrugged. "That was a terrible thing he just did," he said to the doctors. He gave his wife his handkerchief. She cursed the doctors. She asked them again why her son did such things.

Nachman smiled. "I'm sorry," he said. "It's just something I've always dreamt of doing and I wanted to be sure not to forget to do it before I left." Nachman waited. Nathan said nothing. "Did I tell you that? That the doctors say I can leave soon? I told them that when I got out I could come into the city and live with you and Pauline, Nathan, because . . ." Nachman stopped. He looked at Nathan. "Can I come live with you,

Nathan? The doctors said they thought it would be a good idea."

"Mr. Malkin?"

"No," Nathan heard himself say. "No. Not now."

"Good," Nachman said.

"I'm sorry. But I just don't think it would be good for either of us to live together again. It would—"

"Listen. You don't have to justify to me, brother," Nachman said. "I understand, believe me. A man like you, what with—"

"No," Nathan said. "The answer is no. If—"

"You're doing the smart thing for once in your life," their mother said to Nathan. She blotted her lip with the handkerchief. "You'd have to have your head examined to let him out now, with the way he's acting." She laughed. "So tell me, if you know so much, why is he here in the first place? Is he alive? Is he dead?" She tapped on the side of her head with her fist. "I bang my head against the wall sometimes, trying to understand, do you hear me? My child is alive—my child is dead! That's what I cry out, but who listens?"

"I'm sorry," Nathan said to Nachman. "I wish—"

Nachman laughed. "And how about me? If you're sorry, how do you think a man in my position feels? Have you thought about that for a while?"

"How do you feel, Nachman?" Mr. Gordon asked. "Tell us."

"Ask him how *he* feels," Nachman replied. "He gave the answer. I was willing to try, wasn't I? Despite everything." He stepped toward his mother. "Don't hurt your head over me, Momma."

"Who am I saving it for?"

Nachman laughed and clapped his hands. "Did you hear, Nathan? Did you hear what she said?" He turned to the doctors. They showed nothing.

"Your brother has his own life to live, Nachman," Dr. Teitleman said.

"That's what they all say. But I don't believe it for a minute—and neither does he."

"Is my child alive? Is my child dead?" their mother asked. "Once he was a beautiful child. He was so good, doctors—he was so talented. And now he's here. What did I do?"

"You were too good to me, Momma," Nachman whispered. He winked at Nathan. "That was your trouble. When you're too good to children they crap all over you."

She sniffed in. "I'm sorry," Nathan said again. "But in the first place,

Pauline and I only have a small two-room apartment, and an eight-month-old baby, and Pauline has been—well—nervous herself lately, since the baby was born. And then too—even if things were different with us, what with my writing and the way Nachman sometimes feels about it, and about me, I just—"

"Could you tell us maybe how you feel about writing this new book?" Mr. Gordon asked. "That might be helpful. That was the question you brought to us today, wasn't it? Perhaps if you could explain."

"I don't know," Nathan said. "It's why I'm asking you. It seemed a simple question when I came here—yes, write it—no, wait awhile. Why can't you answer yes or no?"

"Do you feel you could not write it if Nachman were living with you?"

Their mother took the handkerchief from her lip and showed the spots of blood to the doctors. "I don't understand things. Explain to me. Why does he do such things if he loves me? He was never like this when he was a child. He was a very loving child." She glanced at Nathan. "More than him. That one was always—how do you say?—a cold fish."

"She's right," Nachman said. "That's what Momma always called my big brother. A cold fish."

"I could just as easily write a different book now, if you think that would be best," Nathan offered. "Then after he was well—after he was out of here—then I could write this book. But what I meant was that I thought it would probably be better if when Nachman gets out and sets up his own life he could feel that it hadn't happened because of *me* somehow. So that if he came to live with me, you see . . ."

"He should live at home," their mother said. "They have enough to do, with the baby and with Pauline, she should be well . . ."

"Yes?" Dr. Teitleman asked Nathan. "You feel that you are in need perhaps of our permission to write this book, yes?"

"No," Nathan said quickly. "Look. I was just asking for your opinion, okay? Why can't you just give me your real opinion? Why—"

"You seem to be feeling very angry, Mr. Malkin. You are feeling as if, perhaps, that we have to accuse you of something?"

Nachman's head was on Nathan's lap. "I'd really like to be in your new book," he said, "but I just thought it over and I decided I agree with you about us not living together. I can find a place by myself. Or maybe I could move in with Momma again, or with Rivka and Harvey. You need your privacy for your writing, Nathan. A great man like you! But I understand that. I really do."

"You haven't answered the question, Mr. Malkin. Perhaps if you could try to tell us how you are to feel about what your brother says . . ."

"You don't have to answer their questions," Nachman said. "What do they know, after all. I'm the patient, right? And speaking of patience, how's your lip, Momma darling?"

"I always said it," Nathan heard himself telling the others then, "didn't I? That his bite was worse than his bark—"

He and Nachman laughed together. He stroked Nachman's hair. They embraced. The doctors stared at them, showing nothing.

TWO DAYS LATER, NATHAN RECALLED, HE VISITED NACHMAN AGAIN. Nachman had tried to chew his tongue out. He spoke of spiders that were crawling on his face. When they transferred him to a different hospital, he told the driver that he knew they were taking him to his brother's funeral. That was the first time they put him on a back ward. A building of six hundred patients—D building; D for Deteriorated, a staff member confided—with only one doctor to attend to them. Nathan wrote letters to private clinics, telling them of Nachman's history, of his talent. They thanked him for his moving letters. They gave him their schedules of fees. They wished him luck. They did not have provisions for scholarship patients. Nathan stood beside the iron bed into which Nachman had been tied. Nachman's eyes were closed. His face was bruised. Nathan touched Nachman's skin. Nachman opened his mouth and Nathan saw the swollen tongue. He decided to make money.

Did Michael remember the story? When Michael was in his own clinic—when he had been doing his training at various hospitals—did he think of his father often? Did he somehow hope, by saving others, to save the life his father never had? Or did he, merely, want to avoid having that life for himself? Nathan saw Michael's face, in the car. He remembered that Michael had thanked him afterward, and that Michael's gratitude had puzzled him. Why wasn't Michael angry?

He saw the three of them sitting on Nachman's cot together. Nachman looked terrible—his eyes were almost closed, his face was puffed and splotched, his skin was pasty. Although he was seven years younger than Nathan, Nathan felt as if he were sitting next to a man much older than himself, like the kind of little old Jewish man their father had always sat with in *shul*. Nachman rocked back and forth, shoulders hunched. He asked Michael to tell him about college, and Michael told him that he liked living in the dormitory, that he would be starting on the basketball team, that he thought he would major in biology and be a pre-med.

Nachman patted Michael on the arm, but he said nothing. He untied the package and put the items in his locker. He tried to light a cigarette but his hands trembled too much and Nathan lit it for him. He took the books from Nathan and, without opening them, put them in his locker too. He handed Michael a small black silk purse.

"Here, sonny boy," he said. "Chanukah *gelt.*"

"Thanks."

"The purse was Momma's." Nachman, his eyes now closed, began singing the sentence to himself. "The purse was Momma's, but were we? . . . The purse was Momma's, can't you see . . ."

"You asked me to bring the book," Nathan said. "The book I wrote."

"So who *den*?" Nachman asked, his nose close to Nathan's. "You were the writer, right? And I was the brother. And this is the son. You were the writer, but the purse was still Momma's."

"How are they treating you here?" Nathan asked.

"What a question!" Nachman answered. "You're a terrific travel agent, Nathan, to arrange my itinerary with such foresight. But where's the other book—" he whispered. "The one about the rabbis. I could use a book about rabbis."

"I never wrote that book."

Nachman touched Michael's cheek. "And if I lived with you, where would this boy have slept? You did the right thing, Nathan. You always did the right thing. I wanted you to know I forgot about what you didn't do for me years ago. You'd rather be right than president, right? So you bring presents instead of writing."

Nachman giggled. He put his arm around his son's waist and led him from the room. Michael towered above his father. "Listen," Nachman said. "It's best this way, me living here. You know how I always put it, from way back, so my brother would understand. 'Out of sight,' I said, 'means out of mind.' " He stopped and waited. "Do you get it?" he asked. "Out of sight—out of mind."

He leaned on Michael. Nathan walked behind them. Nachman stopped and introduced Michael to some other patients. His voice was like their father's. He told people that Michael was his *Kaddish'l*—the one who would one day say *Kaddish* for him. A tall man, his hair in curlers, a purple scarf around his wrist, was banging his head against a soda machine. In the lounge, patients sat and watched television. Nachman and Michael joined them. This clinic was costing Nathan two thousand dollars a month. Nachman offered his new pack of cigarettes to the other patients, going to each of them, saying their names, introducing them to Michael, telling them that his brother was there too. "But he's very shy," he heard Nachman say, loud enough for him to hear. "His wealth and his fame have made him very shy."

Nachman let his head rest against Michael's arm. Nathan saw Michael raise his arm—hesitate—and then put it around his father's shoulder, easily and gently. What was he feeling? Nathan turned away. An old man asked him for directions to the Staten Island ferry. Nathan smiled, but said nothing. He was aware of how good he looked—how healthy and prosperous—in his brown business suit. The man cursed Nathan in Yiddish and left. Nathan read the notices on the bulletin board—letters from the director and staff, rules and regulations, therapy schedules, menus.

Nachman touched his arm. "I told him I'm too old to go to college, so he doesn't have to worry that I'd want to move in with him. But tell me something, Nathan—is it true that he wants to be a doctor, that he wants to spend his life talking to crazy people? I appreciate the gesture, I assure you, but . . ."

Nachman started crying then. He walked away from his brother. Nathan walked after him and put his arms around him. Nachman let his head rest against his brother's chest. "Poppa used to give me chocolate bars even though Momma told him not to, did I ever tell you? He gave the aides money so they wouldn't beat me up, in the old days. But we never spoke, Nathan." Nachman looked around and motioned to Michael. Michael came to them. Nachman put his arms around both of them and whispered: "Do you think maybe Poppa was so quiet because his tongue wasn't right? Do you remember when I tried to chew my tongue up, Nathan?" Nathan nodded. "Momma said she was eating herself up because I was sick, so I figured maybe if I did it myself, I could save her the trouble. But listen. Maybe Poppa's tongue wasn't right from the time he licked Momma's feet. What do you think?"

Nathan tried to pull away, but Nachman held on to his arm. "When did he ever do such a thing?" Nathan asked.

Nachman laughed. "You mean you don't remember such a scene and yet you have the nerve to think you can write a book about us? Oh Nathan—sometimes you worry me!" He patted his brother on the arm, then put one arm into Michael's and one into Nathan's and led them along the corridor. "But listen. It wasn't such a big deal, I suppose, but I remembered it one day years ago when I was talking with a nice young woman therapist they gave me in one of the beautiful hospitals you brought me to—like a college campus, Michael—and what I said was that in our home I suppose it was true that our father used to grovel a lot—he was a *mayven* on groveling—and that he used to kiss our mother's feet, and do you know what happened then?"

"What happened then?" Nathan asked.

"I'm glad you asked," Nachman said. "What happened then was that I said the words and I laughed and then I got hit with this very clear picture of Poppa down on his knees on the living-room rug, to show Momma how much he loved her after one of their fights, and he was licking the soles of her shoes and kissing them, and Momma was beaming. It made her very happy." He stopped. "Remembering that scene helped me get out that time. It was what we call, in the trade, a breakthrough. You're sure you don't remember, Nathan?"

Michael shivered. "Just calm down," Nathan said. He led Nachman back to his room and sat him on the cot. Nachman closed his eyes, stuck his hands down, between his thighs, and rocked back and forth, humming to himself. "You know, sometimes I think maybe it would be better if I didn't come so often," Nathan offered. "That maybe it's too hard on you. What I mean is, this is your home now, Nachman. And to receive me here, with Michael . . ." Nathan heard his heart thump. "I mean, I think I know what you must feel, how hard—"

Nachman sat up straight. "*Never!*" he said. "Never! Maybe in your books you can get into other people's heads, Nathan, but not in my head! There are no books there. You never wrote any other books for me. You never loved me as much as Momma wanted you to. You never—"

"You're babbling," Nathan said sharply.

"Drop dead," Nachman replied. He looked up and smiled. He beckoned to Michael, who was standing in the doorway. "Ah," he said. "Now I feel better. I can go home soon. Much better." He looked at Nathan. "Did you see how angry my brother got with me, and for what, I ask you?" He patted the cot, beside him, and Michael sat. "You should try it sometimes, Michael. You shouldn't be afraid. In our family it's a tradition to be angry with your father but not to show it. I know, I know. I put on a little act sometimes, but it really stinks here, if you want the truth. I don't care how much you pay, Nathan. I'm not as crazy as I think I am either. After all, I'm insane, right? That means I'm sane. I'm *in* sane, no?"

Michael laughed.

"In our family we always had a way with words, and your uncle got most of them. But who's counting, right? I'm glad you both came, but you should go before I get too nervous." He giggled. "I don't take my medications," he whispered. "I hide the pills and spit them into the toilet bowl, but don't tell on me. I'll take them from now on." He patted Michael's hand. "When you're in charge, things will be better. They'll stop feeding us poison. They'll listen more, won't they?"

Michael shrugged. "I don't know," he said. "I just started—"

Nachman took Nathan's hand. "So what else did you bring me, darling?"

"Nothing."

"Yourself," Nachman said. "When I say what did you bring me, you're supposed to say you brought me yourself. Haven't you ever been in therapy?"

"I brought you myself," Michael said. "Because I'm in therapy too."

Nachman shook his head. He patted his son's hand. "That's too bad, sonny boy. Your mother should know better. Your uncle too. I mean, I know you want to please me, but I'm sorry to hear it. Listen, Nathan—when you speak to Poppa, you tell him I forgive him, all right?"

"Poppa's dead."

"You'll know how to get in touch with him. I'll leave it to you. Money buys anything." He smiled. "Not to worry, yes? Tell him I said that, the way he always did. Not to worry."

"But I'm not in a hospital," Michael explained. "I'm just seeing this shrink once a week or so, that's all. It's all right. Really. I don't mind. He's a good guy—we get along. He used to play basketball in college too."

Nachman put a finger to his lips, as if to indicate that he would say no more. He clasped his hands upon his lap. He rocked back and forth, and then his eyes began to close and his mouth opened. His jaw stiffened, his arms rose. Michael took his father by the shoulders, and shook him. "Really, Dad—I'm not sick or anything. Don't you understand? I just need to talk to somebody sometimes. I just—"

Nathan pried Michael's fingers from Nachman's shoulders. "Shh," he said softly. "It's okay, Michael. It's just the medications. I've seen it happen before. It's just the medications."

NATHAN HAD TELEPHONED RACHEL'S APARTMENT SEVERAL TIMES, BUT there was still no answer. He sat at the kitchen table, stirring his tea and staring at the potato bin. The house was silent. He walked from the kitchen and, before going back upstairs to continue his work, he peeked into Michael's room. Michael's feet stuck out from under the blankets. He slept on his side, hugging his pillow. Nathan smiled. He remembered the times Michael and Ira would sleep together in the same bed—how happy Ira had been whenever Rachel gave Michael permission to stay overnight. He remembered the times Michael would arrive with his little satchel, to stay for a few weeks, when Nachman was in especially bad shape.

Nathan walked upstairs and sat at his desk. He enjoyed his writing most, he realized, when there was somebody else in the house with him, and when that person was sleeping. But why didn't Rachel answer the phone? It was past midnight. Had she gone to a movie? Was she staying at Ruth's house? Nathan did not want to wake Ruth or the children. He looked at his manuscript. He dipped the little finger of his right hand in his teacup, then pressed the finger against the page, in three spots. He was pleased that he and Michael had talked about the times they had visited Nachman. He was pleased to discover how frightened Michael had been. "From the time I was Bar Mitzvah, I stopped going by myself—or with my mother," Michael said. "I never visited him unless you were there too. Didn't you notice?"

Nathan said that he had never noticed. Had Rachel? When the new chapter was done—when he gave it to her—he would remember to ask.

NOAH'S SONG

Through the window I see that Mr. Brashler waits for me below, on the steps of the hotel. I sit by myself, in the one small hotel room we shared together—here in the middle of this vast new nation, here in the middle of nowhere—adrift from any life I have ever known or dreamt of, and I wonder how it is that my heart can feel so much in so small a space. Mr. Brashler is the man who sold me the coffin three days ago, and prepared Esther's body, and told me he had put the coffin on a train, north for Chicago.

When we first arrived here he surprised me by knowing who I was. He had been to Chicago and had seen posters, he said—NOAH TOPOROFSKY, THE JEWISH PAGANINI. But there were never any posters of my precious Esther, were there? He did not flinch from looking at the scars on the left side of her face, nor did he even gaze curiously at them, at the patterns in reds and violets that ran like the stains in marble, from her temple to her chin.

I gave him my card and I requested a piano. He nodded and the piano was here the next day, sounding as if its case were filled with bottles and wires. It delighted us with its watery tinkle, and, despite Brashler, we were happy during our first days here. In this town, as if to prove her happiness and pride, my Esther chose not to wear the veil that she wore when she would walk the streets of large cities, and that she wore the first time I ever gazed upon her face.

Will I ever forget the moment? We were in the office of my concert manager, Carl Arnstein. Carl told me that she would be accompanying me on my new concert tour, and in that instant in which I looked toward her, in which she lifted her veil so that I might see her fully, my entire life seemed to lie before me, suspended in the dusty air of Carl's office. "When she is on stage, only her right side shows," Carl whispered. Then he went on to give me references and reports, to let me know that he had, of course, already listened to her, and that—again in a whisper—he was reminded of the great touring success of Viotti and Pugnani, in which the beauty of one and the ugliness of the other became so notorious that enormous audiences were lured to the concert halls.

But I was hardly hearing what he told me, for I was inclining my head toward her even while she raised her eyes to mine. She turned her head sharply as I moved toward her, her veil like a spider's web atop her glistening black hair, so that I would see her disfigurement, and when I did it was as if something inside my heart broke. The feeling was so strange and new that it took my breath away, and I moved back at once. She saw my fright, and I feared that she saw also what I could not yet see—that river of feeling that was being released inside me, that torrent of blood that seemed to rush forth to fill my chest.

I had no desire to touch her face, nor did I, to my surprise, fear touching it. But I realized that my hand had, involuntarily, touched my own breast, above my heart, and as I gazed at her I realized too that I was seeing something else: I was watching a little boy who floundered about in a raging sea, and I saw that the boy was me and that the sea was made of blood. His head was bobbing up and down in the foaming red waves, his mouth was open wide in terror . . . and yet I heard no cries. I tried to make the picture disappear by staring at her face even more intensely, and when I did she looked back at me with a directness that astonished me. She seemed to say to me, by her look, that although she believed in me and in my greatness she did not, at the same time, defer to me. She seemed to say that she expected nothing from me except what I had to give, and wanted to give. "I hope we will work well together," she said, and she reached out before I did, to shake my hand. "Let us begin."

What joy it was to work with her! We began with the early Mozart sonatas and went on to Corelli and Beethoven and Tartini and Schubert, and the miracle was that as we practiced and then began to perform we rarely, except for a remark now and then on tempo or phrasing, seemed to need words to express what we were feeling about the music we played. And as we played music that grew deeper and more subtle, so did our feelings toward one another, wordless still, seem to grow deeper and more subtle. Our greatest joy during those early months was to go through all the sonatas of Beethoven or Mozart, or the few that Schubert wrote, beginning with those written when they were young and progressing to those they'd written as they grew older—and as we played it would be, I felt, as if we were young when they were young, as if we were happy when they were happy, as if we suffered when they suffered, as if we approached death when they did.

I began to feel true emotion. I began to turn joyously and freely in a delicate labyrinth of sounds I had but vaguely heard before. I began to give myself up to the music, and to my feelings for it, to hear the wondrous silence between the notes of the Beethoven concerto—the great empty spaces that filled the air between the octave leaps of the opening measures—and the sadness that spoke to my inner ear during the glorious leaps of the final movement. I began to hear, in Mendelssohn's sad sweet melodies, something of what I felt I had seen in my father's eyes when we had lived in Burshtyn. I began to feel the very history of my people in that music: a melancholy song that, no matter its technical complexities, was for me merely the plaintive cry of a lost and homeless boy.

And when I would play the Bach unaccompanied sonatas and partitas, and Esther would sit on the piano bench and listen to me—sitting stiffly at first, and then swaying slightly when I would come to the dancelike rhythms of the partitas—in my heart I felt that I was soaring beyond time, lost in the notes and in the feeling that the music, for all its jaggedness and grandeur and difficulty, was climbing higher and higher, until it moved beyond sound, nearer to silence than any music ever had.

The very simplicity of my feelings overwhelmed me. I would sometimes find myself weeping unashamedly when I was done, exhausted by my performance—by the profound sublimity and the violent contrasts of the music—and also by what I had poured into it; and I would wonder how I had been able to deny, for so many years, that I did truly want to give myself up to music, and through music to others—that I did truly want to love others as I myself desired to be loved.

Like my father before me, I became a lover of second movements. Again and again I played those movements in the great concertos of Beethoven and Bach and Mendelssohn, Viotti and Bruch and Paganini, and even in the lesser concertos of Haydn and Kreutzer and Gade, Veracini and Matteis and Pisendel and Schumann and Lolli. *Grave, adagio, largo, larghetto, lente, sarabande, loure, andante assai, largo ma non tanto* . . . the mere sounds of these words inspired within me feelings for all things slow and deliberate and beautiful, for all things that could return me to myself, and to my father's world. I longed, in truth, to steal my father's childhood, and to be able to feel what he had felt when he had been a young man and had walked unthinkingly through the village we had, on my account, been forced to flee.

Esther would smile, and tease me about the frail excuses I would invent—new suggestions for intonation, new ideas for tempo or phrasing, misgivings about balance—to practice time and again these second movements, for she knew that what I really desired, above all, was to be able to produce and listen to the sweetness and the sadness these movements held for me . . . and to ache all the while to know the difference, forever denied me, between the playing of the music and the listening to the music.

But now she is gone, my faithful, darling Esther, and I am more alone than ever. She was my second chance. I see that clearly now, and my heart calls out to her across the silence—it sings to her as even my precious Guarneri will never sing, for it sings a song that runs so deep it is more silent than silence; it declares to her that I can feel all that she wanted for me—that I can now know that she, having given me this second chance, must have felt, oh so wrongly, that she had no choice but to give herself up forever to God and to Eternity.

Now, even as I imagine myself touching her disfigured face, and even as I hear myself trying to explain to her just how I have come to value the precious gift she gave to me, I also hear her voice, inside me, mocking me for false sentiments, for not knowing, yet again, what it is I truly feel. She understood me too well, my sweet Esther! She understood how the worm of self-contempt has always worked its evil course through my life! She understood how it was that I have always, alas, come to loathe whatever in life I am able to master, or possess.

Now, then, is this small room become an ark, broken and battered, and in it I float safely and freely across the wide, calm oceans. I am isolated and abandoned within a great ring of blue-green water and a new feeling begins to grow within me, filling me with wondrous power. I close my eyes and I dream of her, where she is now, listening to me play as only she believes I can.

The feeling stays with me even when I open my eyes and look around me: peeling *fleur-de-lis* wallpaper, rusted stove, old black upright piano with broken sounding board, tilted brass bed, high smudged windows. Now, in this place, could I play a song for her that would approach perfection! Now could my fingers move as if attached to my very heart! Now, I think, could Paganini himself rise from the grave and envy the miracles I would work in sound. And yet, I think, if the gift is truly within me at last, who will ever know it?

I am only a little boy, far from home. That is what I feel most of all. I am only the little boy of long ago, listening to his father tell him of the gift God has given to him, and of the greatness that he will achieve. I am only a little boy of seven or eight, standing in our two-room home in the village of Burshtyn, taking lessons from an old man who journeys many miles each week to come to our home, and who, when I threaten him by saying I will play no more, weeps real tears. Ah, but I knew my power even then, didn't I, Esther?

I stand on the dirt floor and I practice, again and again, my Kreutzer études—those études I hate passionately—and all the while I practice my father sits beside the stove, on the dairy bench, his head resting on his hand, while his eyes blaze at me with love and with hope, and—I cannot deny it—with the dreams that give me the will to go on. Perhaps, Esther once said to me, if I had not had so great a success at such an early age, my life would have been different. There was, she sensed, something inside me that had, from earliest times, made me despise all things I did well simply because I, and not another, had done them. Perhaps . . .

I am only a little boy, far from home, and I am journeying with my father, my violin on my lap, in his wagon, and with money he has obtained from the elders of the village. We are going to Odessa, there to perform, in a house that seems to me a tsar's palace, for wealthy Jews who dress in silks and strange glasslike shoes, and who speak to one another in a language my father tells me is French. I am ten years old, but I am still small for my age, and my father says that I must admit to being no more than eight. I play two Mozart sonatas for violin and piano—sonatas he wrote when he was not even my age—and I play Corelli's "La Folia," a beautiful adagio with variations that you loved so much, dear Esther, and I play a series of caprices by Locatelli. And then, after I have rested and tasted exotic foods that my father assures me are kosher, and after I have had women with perfumed hair and painted faces press their noses against my cheeks and examine the bones of my fingers, I amaze the gathering by playing, on the G string alone, Paganini's "Variations on the Prayer from Rossini's 'Moses.' "

Afterward I am smothered with kisses and my hands are pressed and fondled passionately, even by the men. The mistress of the house thanks me for my performance, and then, declaring that my father must remain behind, she takes me with her to her bedroom, where she opens a jeweled violin case and shows me a violin such as I have never seen before. It is by a man named Lupot, she says, and on its back are figures of Apollo, Orpheus, Terpsichore, and Amor, and, in French, a gold-lettered inscription which she translates for me: *Young hearts, do not trust perfidious love, but abandon yourself without fear to sweet melody.*

She asks me if I would like to play the instrument. Though it is too large for me, and though I fear that its wood may, at my touch, burn my hands, I set it under my chin and begin to bow the opening measures of Bach's Sonata no. 2, in A minor. She lies on a couch at the other end of the bedroom, one hand upon her forehead, while her other hand is lost in the folds of her silk dress, between her knees. She does not come near me, yet I am terrified. I play faster and faster, and as I do her eyes grow glassy and she moans in such a way that I am fearful she will faint and tumble from her couch. When I stop, she asks me if I would like to keep the violin. I lower my eyes and then she leans back, her mouth opens wide, and she laughs at me.

She places the violin in its case and returns the case to her closet. I am confused and frightened. I feel faint and cannot move, so that, still laughing, she has to take me by the hand to enable me to leave her room. I had not known a violin could make sounds such as those I have just produced, and yet—I think of this all the way home, bundled beside my father in our wagon—in all the world, only she has heard them.

Even in those years, my dear Esther, when I was living in the house in which I was born, and in which I had grown up—even when I was living among Jews who came to my father's house on the Sabbath, for *shaleshudes*, as their parents had come to my grandfather's house—even when I was studying Talmud with our Rebbe, and when I was walking each day in the very streets and fields that my father had known when he too was growing to manhood—even then I felt far from home, as if I lived nowhere.

Although my father glowed with pride, that the village knew of my talents and accomplishments, yet, in my perversity, I placed no special value on the ability that others valued in me. My violin and my power to make it do what I wanted it to do brought me things I craved, of course—difference, isolation, admiration, mastery, sacrifice. Yet I know that I despised my violin as much as my talent; I knew that I always felt that the instrument was essentially, despite the Lupot, only a Jew's instrument: poor and small and cheap and portable—like the lives I saw all around me in our *shtetl*.

During those years when I walked through our village, the admiring and envious eyes of others upon me, what I often longed to be was a trifling thing—I longed to be a boy who would one day become the father of so many sons that, being constantly occupied with providing for them the necessities of life and the natural affection each would need, I would never have had the luxury and time to wonder about what it was I was chosen to make of my life. Such a dream relieved me of my burden. It promised me a life of true freedom, for in such a life, I saw, necessity and desire would be one.

Yet now, in the deep amber curls of my Guarneri's back, it is as if I see the waves of the sea and can look through those waves to the opaline depths in which, becoming lost to something infinitely larger than myself, I wander blindly until I find my home, until I am at peace. I gaze into the curved wood and peer through the irregular stain of varnish and I am drawn down as if to some dim underworld of sound where—as you would wish for me, Esther—I can at last recognize my terrible passion, and surrender to my talent. Oh how tired I am. How tired I am of warring against myself, of denying my true gifts, of wandering in search of nothing, of being bound by the dreams of others, of delighting others with tricks and performances that delight me not at all. How tired I am, without you, my beloved, of life . . .

The eldest of eight children—six years older than I was—Esther had come to this country in order to earn the money to bring her family here, from the village of Ryminov, in Galicia. Like me, she had been their hope, and they believed that her gift for music would one day redeem them and bring them to a new life, to the *goldeneh medina* of America. Before me, she had never known a man, nor thought of marriage. Music had been her life, and she had sacrificed herself to it as her family had sacrificed its life to her. Her abilities were enormous—she could translate an orchestral score into a piano score at sight, or fly through Scarlatti sonatas with ease—and yet I had to agree with her, and with Carl, that though she was an ideal accompanist, she was not, by herself, anything like a great pianist. For too many years, I concluded, she had accompanied others, and whether the desire—always to subjugate herself to others—had been there before the years of doing so had made it her essence, was now a question that, so much time having passed, and habit having become nature, would never be answered.

Feeling so fulfilled by my own flights of discovery, I did not think to find the time or the will to try more insistently to make of her what I was, through her gift, making of myself. When I would touch lightly upon the subject of her own concert career, she would chide me, reminding me laughingly that Maimonides himself declared that a man should not talk overmuch with women, not even with one's own wife, for so long as a man talked overmuch with women, he brought evil upon himself, neglected the study of Torah, and in the end drew Gehenna as his portion. I was the lamp and she the mirror, she said, and she was content to glory in the warmth of my light. She wanted no more from life, she would say, than—as the Americans put it—to play second-fiddle to my fiddle.

And then one morning, in Philadelphia, in the fifth month following our first meeting, when we were practicing in a studio and I was teasing her about her playing—when I was feeling so giddy from the heights I had just reached in playing through the Bach D-minor Partita that in my heart it was as if I were a young boy who could not conceive of ever growing old—I went down on my knees before her and let my head rest upon her lap. "Console me," I said. "I am a naughty boy."

She stroked my hair and neck tenderly, and my giddiness vanished at once. Her body was rigid. I still held my bow, my beloved Tourte, which Carl had given me as a gift after my first concert tour almost twenty years before, and I heard it tapping at the floorboards, my hand had begun trembling so. "Look at me," she said.

I looked. Her left side was turned toward me. She was weeping. I touched her scar, and ran my fingertips around the red and violet undulations, as if tracing a journey in sand. She took my hand and kissed my palm. "You should not be afraid to tell me, but you should also not be beguiled by your own feelings. Because they are so new to you, my dear Noah, aren't they?"

I could not speak at first. I touched her cheek again and felt as if my fingertips were on fire. The pain was exquisite. I let my head rest on her lap once more, and I could feel the warmth of her thighs through the thin cloth of her summer dress. "How long have you known what I was feeling toward you?" I asked.

"It has made me very happy, and I believe it is real," she replied, "but I do not think we can surrender to it. If you feel now like a young boy—you who have known women, you who have seen a wife bear you sons and a daughter, you who have known the world as I never will—can you imagine what I have been feeling? Can you feel how young my heart is—how much younger—after so many years—?"

I threw my arms around her waist, and buried my face in the folds of her dress. But before I could even declare my love to her, other words came to my lips. I could not keep from confessing my feelings to her, as childlike and horrid as they seemed. "I feel somehow as if it is your scar that I love even more than you," I said. "I feel as if it is your suffering I desire to possess, and this desire overwhelms me even as I feel, yet again, a disgust toward myself for such a base and narrow urge. Forgive me, my darling. Please forgive me . . ."

I tried to rise, but with a gentleness that seemed to contain within it boundless strength, she pressed my shoulders so that I could not. I felt myself aroused in my manhood as never before in my life. I desired to do both savage and tender things to her, and I also wanted, I knew, to know her fully—I wanted to lie with her, our bodies as one body, the hot molten flesh of her cheek seared and fused with mine until, unto the marrow of our bones, we would be, one into the other, inseparable.

"There is nothing to forgive," she said. "But I am a Jewish woman and you are a Jewish man, and what God has commanded us—you to your family's honor and me to mine—we may not go against. Our love is strong and true, but it will become weak and vile if we allow ourselves to surrender to it, to our desires . . ."

"Will you deny me then?"

"In loving me, Noah, you are only seeking to atone for the part of yourself you consider unworthy," she went on, as if I had not spoken, as if she had prepared the words beforehand. "I am an ugly and barren woman whose face must be hidden from the world and in whom a man's seed would surely dry up and die. You must give yourself to your wife and children, to the father who has given his life for you, and to the community from which we both come. Here in this new world, my darling, you are the very strength and hope of Zion! Through the genius of men like you our people will persist." She touched my hair. "Without you, I am nothing. But without me, you remain—now more than ever—a beacon light, a . . ."

But her words could not dissuade me. My passion was as deep and intense as hers. I covered her arms and hands with kisses. I wept. I told her that she misjudged the response she had awakened in me. I told her that it would be unjust and unnatural if she did not now share with me the good as well as the evil that had been born with my awakening. "Your love is the Devil's love," I cried to her, "and it infects my soul!"

She covered her face with her hands. "You shame me," she said. "For it is as if I see my own self inside you, luring me on!" Then she uncovered her face, she let her head fall back, and she screamed as if she were being tortured with hot irons. She tore at her hair, and I feared truly that she had lost her senses. Still, my own passion was now become so ravenous that nothing—not even my sympathy for her, nor my fears for myself and what would become of my own life—could restrain me. I rose from my knees and pulled her to her feet, and even while she sobbed and beat her fists against me I pressed my mouth against her chin and then against the left side of her face, expecting my lips to be consumed with fire.

Then the strangest thing of all happened—my tongue began to move of itself, gently and slowly, as if denying the raging body it was part of, and it began to taste the sweetness and coolness of her cheek, to feel the beauty of its ridges and undulations. Her arms were around me at last, and her long fingers—which could move across the piano keys as if, in her words, the keys were a string of pearls—touched me with a great and loving gentleness. Later she told me that her great fear had been that God would be disappointed in her. When she said that I held to her, and I said nothing.

Mr. Brashler sits below, whittling a stick with his knife, and as I look at the back of his shaggy head I tremble with weakness. I feel as if he can, at will, pierce my brain with his mean blue eyes and know the meanest thought that passes through me. When I am near him I grow faint. I try to hold my breath and I avoid looking into his eyes, lest he see my guilt and my humiliation. And though I know exactly why it is that I lend to him such power over me, my knowledge does nothing to weaken that power. The past, which I thought was locked forever within an abandoned room of my mind, the past that I kept hidden even from my dear Esther, has seeped out. Now the door is ajar and foul vapors drift through the house! I am truly lost, nor can I find the energy either to search or to flee. The thought that permeates my being is as hideous as it is ridiculous, yet it is there—as real as her death—and I cannot deny it: whenever I look into Mr. Brashler's vile face it is as if I am seeing the boy, grown to manhood, who was stolen for me so many years ago, in Burshtyn, and sent to serve in my place in the tsar's army for twenty-five years!

I never did tell Esther. For to know that my life and talent were alive because of a low and cowardly act toward another Jew might, if revealed to her, I feared, have killed not only the love she felt for me, but the very goodness this love was giving to me—a goodness that she believed redeemed her own life. But I see too clearly now that I was, in keeping my secret, only repeating the oldest of patterns, whereby in the name of some higher good, yet again did I allow others to sacrifice their lives for mine.

Now, whenever I begin to imagine her face, or to hear again the music that we made together, I see instead Mr. Brashler, on his horse, and he is roaming the Russian steppes and dreaming of the vengeance he would love to take against me. I see him hunting and stealing and torturing. I see him murdering with cold-blooded pleasure, I see him raping innocent women, I see him practicing foul acts upon young Jewish boys. The emptiness of his soul is vaster than the skies and the oceans, and I am lost inside that emptiness.

Can such a man, I wonder, ever have had a father or mother who kissed him or fondled him—can he ever have had a home he cried for when he discovered he could not return to it? I do not even know the name of the boy or the family, in Burshtyn, that suffered for me, and it is many years since I last tried to take that secret from my father. To soothe the guilt he himself felt, he would reply to my questions by retelling the story of Jacob and Esau—by citing to me the rabbis' words that justify Jacob's ways because he is a man of the spirit while Esau is a man of the earth, a hunter whose birthright is not worth to him as much as a dish of pottage. If the Jewish people had been dependent upon the lineage of Esau, we would long ago have perished and disappeared from the face of the earth, my father proclaimed. Just so did Esau despise his birthright and just so did I gain mine, and there was no more to be said.

Mr. Brashler is to me like Esau, like a very bear—massive and dangerous and powerful. Beneath his workclothes, where I cannot see, I imagine that he is covered with thick ringlets of foul-smelling hair. His rough cheek bulges from his putrid tobacco, and there are other odors that rise from his body and remind me of nothing so much as those of many fat pigs, packed together in their own slime for warmth, in winter barns. When I was a boy, I recall, my father took me to see the pigs of the Gentiles, so that I would never be tempted to eat of their flesh.

I had wanted Esther to be buried here, in this small town in Indiana where she and I spent the last weeks of her life together, where we knew happiness. Even when I first felt her cold skin and saw what she had done and knew that she was gone forever, it sustained me for the instant to think of her safely and warmly enclosed below the earth of this village's graveyard. I had believed her when she told me she was ill and had not long to live. It was, she said, the secret she had kept from me, even before my declaration of love to her, and it was because of this illness, she said, that she had allowed herself the pleasures without which her life would have been incomplete.

On the day of her death, only when I opened my case and held my Guarneri did I feel some peace. All things pass. My Guarneri del Gesú alone did not change. When I touched it and gazed upon it I marveled again that, for all the world's progress, no man or place had yet equaled that miracle of wood and glue and sound that was wrought by a few men in Cremona more than a hundred years ago. When I held my Guarneri, the wonder in me was new, like a child's. How, I asked, could such a small and fragile piece of wood, with no markings or stops upon it to tell one where the notes should come from—how could it produce such elaborate worlds of music and feeling?

Now I long to play again, even as I fear that I will find I can play only as I played before I knew Esther. But if I can, or if I cannot, who will ever know the difference? I will hear what I hear in my own heart, but how will I ever know if what I hear will be what others hear? Perhaps, I think, these months with Esther are not at all real. Perhaps these months are not at all the heights I have believed them to be, but merely a ghostlike interlude, a valley that is already, in my mind, disappearing under water.

"Ain't never buried a Jew in our town before," Mr. Brashler said to me, when first I asked him to allow me to lay her to rest here, "and we don't aim to start in now." He spat his tobacco juice at my feet, splattering my shoes. "Doc Lapham tells me she was by way of being in a delicate condition."

"I do not understand," I said.

"That you dipped the stick," he said. "That you put your pole in the hole—that you wet the wick that was tryin' to make another Jewbaby—"

"Forgive me," I said.

He laughed. "Well, she weren't the first and she won't be the last," he said, "but we ain't never had one here in our town yet who took it so hard." He came close to me. "That's a mortal sin, mister," he said, "and we don't take to people who take away what's the Lord's alone to give and to take. We never had a man in these parts let a woman take her life on account of him, and we don't like it much."

I was, may God forgive me, incapable of showing him the anger that began to well up inside me. Nor could I say anything on Esther's behalf. I listened to him tell me how much it would cost to have her body prepared and shipped north to Chicago, to be buried where Jews were buried. I agreed to pay, and I left him. And when, a day later, the money I ordered arrived by Western Union, and I gave it over to him, I knew from his leering snicker, and from the way he told me that things were already well taken care of, that I could not even trust him to do what he had promised. Nor could I find within me the courage to ask for any genuine proof of his act. He gave me a piece of paper, with the amount of money written out, and his signature.

"I didn't charge you for what was inside her," he said, "seein' as we didn't need an extra coffin yet."

Then, at last, for the briefest instant, hearing his voice and looking at the words he had scrawled on the paper—*For One Dead Jew*—I felt as if I could murder, as if I could drive a nail into his heart, as if I could cut his tongue out. He must have seen the rage flicker in my eyes, for he touched me for the very first time, pushing me back against a pillar of the hotel.

"What I figger is that it's best to let you Jews just kill one another off anyways you want, though I ain't beyond bein' pushed to help out if I got to."

He took my right hand in his hands—hands that, though rough and callused, were astonishingly small, like the hands of a man no larger than myself—and he began to stroke my fingers one at a time, as if to apologize to me. "Real soft and fair, ain't they?" he said. "There's lots of things I could think of to do to you, even if you ain't a real man. But they say there ain't a quicker way to let the Devil into your soul than to cohabitate with a Jew!"

He roared with laughter then—letting my hand go—and as quickly as his laughter began, it ceased. He spoke again and told me that he and his friends in town had been debating the question, during the previous weeks when Esther and I were playing together, as to whether I made the sounds all by myself, or whether I had the Devil's assistance. He said he had sat below our window by himself one night, and listened carefully, and had decided that he had heard at least two violins playing at the same time, and maybe a third. He took my hand and inspected my fingers again. "They seem real enough," he said. Still, unable in his mind to solve the mystery of the extra violins, he sulked, like a spurned child, and for an instant I almost felt tender toward him, I almost wanted to explain . . .

"But let me ask you somethin' else," he said then. "Is it really true, what I hear—that you people bury yours standin' up?"

I could not reply. I left him and I walked in the graveyard. I wondered if, a year hence, there would be a grave and a stone somewhere in Chicago in front of which somebody might be reciting the *Kaddish* for Esther. I thought of asking Carl to write to her family—I could tell him the story she had first given to me, of her illness. But then I imagined a house in her village like the one in my own, into which I was born, and I imagined the faces of her parents, receiving the news. I wanted to weep for her, I wanted to tear at my hair, to rend my clothes—yet I could do none of these things.

I stood there looking out at rows of headstones, some sunk below the ground so that the names of the dead were already gone, and I felt again a feeling I thought, in my foolishness, I had lost, one that I had expressed to Esther when first I had begun to reveal myself to her: that my life was not merely a mistake, but that it was somehow already over. I had done all I would ever do, and yet I had not done and never would do what I had most wanted to.

I had erred terribly, and I thought of myself once more as if I were at sea, on a vessel bound for nowhere. I thought of myself as if I were shipwrecked on strange African shores, and I saw myself walking along beaches of clear sand, playing Bach sonatas for naked black natives, charming them so as to save my life. And in my heart, imagining myself in this way, I loathed my self-pity as much as I loathed the feebleness of my imagination.

I was not surprised then—nor was I angry or sad—when I returned to my room at dusk and found that Mr. Brashler had been there during my absence. On the bed the violin case was open, and my Guarneri was in pieces on the floor—the top and back pried off, the neck split open, the bass bar and sounding post torn out and sawed through, the varnish scraped mercilessly from the wood.

If you have no grave, my sweet Esther, that is all right. Nobody knows where the graves of Mozart or Antonio Stradivari are. Nor does anybody truly know just what did fill the empty years of Paganini's life—those years from which the great legends have been born. Was it really because, caged in a prison for having killed an unfaithful mistress, he had only the G string left on his violin, that he learned to play it so magically? It comforts me now, in my perversity, to think of him near the end of his life—unable to play his violin anymore, unable even to use his voice—limping through the streets of Paris with Berlioz, the great friend who had never even heard him play, and having to converse by writing down his words upon the pages of a notebook. What cruel pleasure it gives me, though for an instant only, to think of confiding in Mr. Brashler that, when the real Paganini died, the bishop of Nice denied him extreme unction and a Church funeral because he claimed that Paganini had had dealings with the Devil.

But you would, I know, chide me for such thoughts, Esther. You would chide me, yet again, for misusing the gift you gave me—for being so harsh with myself. You would chide me with great gentleness for not being willing to accept and hold on to those feelings that, though you may have given me access to them, yet, you would claim, are truly mine. You understood this part of me too—this fear—and wished, more than anything, that I might someday be as strong without you as with you. And yet—do I fail us both? —it remains the one thing I fear most of all that I am incapable of being.

I do try to listen to you, my darling Esther—I do try to listen to your voice as it sings to me from within my heart . . . And so, without you and without my violin, I must now take leave of this town and begin my life again, trying to find—even, perhaps, within the bosom of the family that has been and is still mine—the boy who never knew that he could dream of becoming anything other than what he had been until he knew you.

8

RACHEL WAS GONE. BUT WHY? NATHAN WALKED TO THE POST OFFICE AND mailed her the manila envelope containing his story. Rachel would not return. Her apartment was rented, her possessions were in a moving van, on a highway somewhere between Brooklyn and West Palm Beach. She would live where Leah and Rivka lived, in Century Village, a retirement community of fifteen thousand senior citizens, mostly New York Jews. Another ghetto, Nathan thought. For Jews, it seemed, the travel arrangements were made at birth: from the *shtetls* to the ghettos to the concentration camps; from the Lower East Side to Brooklyn to the senior-citizen cities of Florida. The journey was ever the same.

Nathan waited for the bus. He would visit Michael at his office. He would surprise him. In less than a week the two of them would be in Moscow together. Still, before he left, he wanted Rachel to have his story. He had felt close to her while he was writing. He had wanted her to know what he felt for her. He had wanted her to know how wrong she had been to leave—to abandon him.

He sat near the back of the bus and looked out the window. He felt so much when he was with Rachel, and yet he was able to share so little. Why? The fullness of his feelings—the tenderness, the easy access he had to memories and desires long forgotten—astounded him, and though he sensed that Rachel bore equal love toward him, once they began talking the words themselves seemed always to be barriers between them—

assaults somehow upon his feelings—and their conversations seemed, often, to deteriorate into games and tests, into poses and maneuvers. What did she want from him? For him to talk more about himself and Nachman and their childhood? He had told her about *zimzum.* He had told her about *kelippot.* Now he was giving her "Noah's Song." If she looked at the original, in the book, she would see that the passages he had added were all passages that spoke of how he felt toward her, of how—at times—she had been able to make him feel again those feelings and desires that he had forgotten he possessed. He did truly desire to love others as he himself desired to be loved. But how? When he wrote now it was as if his fingers were, like Noah's, attached to his heart, but when he stopped writing—when he was with her—what was it that made it so difficult to say to her the simple things that Noah said to Esther? He wanted to be able to hear her voice.

"You're so possessive of your childhood, of your loss," she'd said to him, "that you've built a wall around it that allows you never to give it up, but that keeps *you* locked in."

Maybe, he thought. Maybe. He looked around him, at the other passengers. He was the only white person on the bus. An enormous black woman, carrying two shopping bags on each arm, her left leg swollen with elephantiasis, limped toward a seat. She smiled at Nathan with yellow teeth. Nathan showed nothing.

What if, receiving his story, Rachel should be so moved by it that she would offer to return? What if she should offer to wait for him until he came back from Russia? What if she asked him, again, not to go? Was that what he was waiting for—for her to take the initiative? Perhaps. Although Rachel was pleased that he was writing again, she remained unenthused about his scheme to trick the Russians. Nathan smiled. He saw how cunningly his own feelings worked to deceive him, for if she took the initiative, he saw, that would be enough to make him want to resist her, wouldn't it? That would be enough to make him want to strengthen those walls around his feelings that would keep her out. *It is the fear in men's hearts that builds up walls against the light.* Nathan nodded to himself, acknowledging the truth of his father's words.

The bus moved on, along Flatbush Avenue, past Parkside. Nathan remembered holding Ira's hand when they would step down from the trolley car, at the corner of Flatbush Avenue and Empire Boulevard, and would walk toward Ebbets Field, to see a baseball game together. Ira had loved sports. He had once tried to show Nathan, with diagrams and formulas, how a curve ball curved. He had been better than Michael at memorizing rosters and batting averages. Nathan chided himself for not having shared such things with him more. They had gone to few games. Nachman had taken Michael more frequently. Sports had never, since childhood, interested Nathan. He had always found it hard to take an interest in the exploits of men who were younger than himself. He had snapped at Ira whenever Ira asked him his opinion of the newest Dodger player. He had commanded Ira to pay more attention to the front pages of the newspaper, to the news-of-the-world. He had been wrong. What could one do about the news-of-the-world? Nathan saw himself in his kitchen in Ein Karem, reading in *The Jerusalem Post* about Gail Rubin, and about Hanoch Tel-Oren. He saw himself looking at the headline, in the *New York Post*, about Ira's death, and returning the paper to Rivka without reading further. They had, Rivka said, spelled Ira's name incorrectly. And why was the story on page twenty-six instead of in the front section?

Nathan looked out the bus window, at the trees that lined both sides of the street. He had written most of "Noah's Song" before he had ever known Rachel, and this fact surprised him. He remembered what Michael had said to him, that one sometimes understood loss not by losing something precious, but by not having the thing you loved to lose. Had he, then, understood the love between Noah and Esther so well precisely because he had not yet, at the time, truly loved a woman? Could desire make a thing more real, in the imagination, than it could ever be in reality? Nathan closed his eyes. *Some memories are realities, and are better than anything that can ever happen to one again.* He thought of the time he'd gone to a baseball game at Ebbets Field, with Nachman and their father. His father understood nothing about the game and Nachman was proud to be able to explain it all to him. His father met one of his *landsleit* at the game and that man had his son with him also. Nathan could see the two fathers, in the grandstands behind the first-base dugout, looking out at the emerald green grass of the playing field and laughing together about being Americans who took their sons to baseball games. How often had he seen his father laugh? Nathan and Nachman had great fun teasing them—telling them that the bases were pillows and that the players beat each other with the bats and that the man in the black suit was the undertaker.

The bus passed the Empire Boulevard entrance to the Botanic Garden. Nathan recalled walking in the Garden in the spring, with Nachman and

Rachel. Nachman was gathering an armful of cherry blossoms—he was giving them out to all the women they passed. Now, Nathan knew, Ebbets Field was gone. In the Botanic Garden policemen patrolled on motor scooters. They chained trees to the ground, to protect them from vandals. The bus stopped at Grand Army Plaza. Nathan looked right, at the entrance to the library. He imagined Nachman standing on the steps, in front of the wide iron doors, holding soup greens and carrots in his hands. All that Nathan had learned, about Cossacks and Russia and the violin, he had taken from books. When he read "Noah's Song" to Nachman, in their room, Nachman had been delighted. Nachman had offered no corrections, though surely he had been aware of the errors Nathan had made.

The bus pulled away from the curb. To the left was the entrance to Prospect Park, for cars. The bus moved in a curve, passing a giant arch that was a memorial to the dead of past wars. Rewriting the book sometimes confused Nathan. Sometimes while he wrote, and wondered if what he was changing he was changing for the very first time, he heard his mother's voice, screaming. *My child is alive, my child is dead . . . My child is alive, my child is dead.* He wondered if Michael or Rachel or Ruth could explain to him what the relations were, exactly, between his book and his life. Whose scars were on Esther's face? Whose dead child was in her womb? Why was Noah so terrified of Mr. Brashler? What were the sources of his tenderness? . . . *My book is alive, my book is dead,* Nathan thought. *My book is alive, my book is dead.*

The black people on the bus seemed very quiet and polite. In the post office, all the workers had been black or Spanish. Nathan imagined that some of the people on the bus were Michael's patients, that they were traveling to Michael's clinic. Rachel had, at the airport, told him again that she was still worried about Michael. Despite what Nathan had done, she worried more about Michael than about Nathan. Why, she wanted to know, had Michael mentioned to her, several times, that in America psychiatrists had the highest suicide rate?

Outside, the street seemed suddenly narrow. There were no trees. Storefronts were boarded up. Once these streets had been beautiful; along them had been the homes and stores of those Jews who were wealthier than his own family. Nathan had tried to reassure Rachel—to tell her that Michael was fine, that he would, in Moscow, prevent Michael from doing anything rash, that he would protect him—but she had not seemed to be listening to him. The bus stopped suddenly, so that Nathan was thrown forward. He held on to a metal pole, to keep from falling. A child wailed. Horns blared. The bus driver opened his window and cursed at a taxi driver. Nathan had asked Michael to write to Gronsky and ask Gronsky if, during their stay, it would be possible to meet Nadezhda Mandelstam.

The bus stopped again. The rear doors opened. The woman with elephantiasis limped down the steps. The bus driver waved to her. Next to Nathan a woman was reading a newspaper in which there was a photo of a dead baby that had been found rotting in the locker of a junior high school. *Why do you think you ought to be happy?* Nathan watched the woman with elephantiasis walk along the street. When Mandelstam was gone and Nadezhda was left alone, she was, she had written, sustained by the memory of those words—*Why do you think you ought to be happy?*—and by a passage from the life of the archpriest Avaakum, in which his exhausted wife asks him, "How much farther must we go?" "Until the very grave, woman," he replies. Whereupon the wife got to her feet and walked on.

But Rachel had said to Nathan that they could be happy together. Each time she was with him she had said that they could be happy together, that they should give themselves a chance—a second chance. Was it possible? The bus passed Atlantic Avenue. The downtown section seemed even more garish and filthy than Nathan had imagined it would be. He got off the bus near the Nevins Street subway stop, across from the Brooklyn Fox Theatre. A black man with what appeared to be Vaseline smeared over his closed eyes stood at the corner and strummed a guitar. There was a hand-painted sign and a tin cup beside him. Nathan did not read the sign. He crossed the street. Pieces of greasy waxed paper swirled about his feet. Rock-and-roll music blared from the loudspeaker of a store. Slashes of red and black paint advertised sale prices for radios and tape recorders and cameras.

Nathan had no desire to look at what he saw around him. He bent his head against the wind, and walked. He passed stores that sold fried pigs' tails and egg rolls. He passed newspaper vendors and men selling watches and women's jewelry and women's wigs and windup toys. He passed clothing stores and restaurants and drugstores. Across the street, where the Brooklyn Paramount had once been, Long Island University was now located. A group of students, their books against their chests, laughed at an old woman who stood in the middle of the street shouting obscenities. She wore a lamb's wool vest over a flowered red-and-yellow dress. She shook her fist at the students. Red lipstick was smeared around her mouth and chin.

Nathan entered Michael's building and walked up the stairs. DOWNSTATE MENTAL HEALTH CLINIC, MICHAEL MALKIN, M.D., DIRECTOR. Nathan opened the door. In the waiting room there were about fifteen people. Nathan tried not to look at them. He thought of the surprise —the gift he had brought for Michael. He told the receptionist who he was. She said that Michael was seeing a patient, but that she would tell him that his uncle was waiting. Nathan sat. He picked up a copy of *The New Yorker*. Next to him a teen-age Puerto Rican girl, her hair in braids, sat with her mouth open, her eyes closed, her arms bent at the elbows. Nathan looked at the photographs in *The New Yorker*, of diamonds and brandy bottles and leather boots and golden beaches. He looked at photos of elegant and beautiful women, draped in furs. I. J. Fox. He remembered the store and the sign. His mother had bought her fur coat there. Persian lamb. She had sold his father's silver spice box and *kiddush* cup, and with the money she had gone out and bought her fur coat, second-hand.

Nathan sniffed in, as if to inhale the pungent fragrance of the spices. Each Saturday evening one breathed in this fragrance from the tiny door on the side of the box, so that one might, for the coming week, preserve the sweetness of the Sabbath. After his father was dead, and Nathan had begun his collection, the first item he purchased was a nineteenth-century spice box, from Poland. Silver, with filigree work around the edges and tiny bells that tinkled, it was shaped in the form of a tower with a pointed roof. Pauline had loved it. Ira had loved it. He had sold it, with all his other Judaica, to a Chassidic Jew on West Forty-seventh Street. Why should he have chosen it and saved it from among all the other items?

On a brown leather chair a mother was changing her child's diaper. The telephone was ringing. A woman was scraping her nail polish off, flicking the delicate red curls of paint into an ashtray. There were doors that led from the room and they had the names of doctors and social workers on them.

"Hey man, don't you say nothin' 'bout my mother."

Nathan turned.

"I didn't say nothin' 'bout your fuckin' mother."

The first man rose. "There you go, talkin' 'bout my mother again." He reached into his pocket. Another man grabbed him. Nathan imagined knives and blood. The second man, a black man with powerful arms, was an aide, dressed in white. "Hey man, didn't you hear him? Didn't you hear him talkin' 'bout my mother?"

The aide forced the man into his seat and spoke to him quietly. The man's voice soothed Nathan. He thought of Lazer Kominsky, and he realized that Lazer Kominsky had sat in the room where he was now, waiting for Michael. *What exists in God, unfolds in man.* Nathan heard his father's voice. Words and letters had magical powers. The *Sefirot*, from which all of creation came, were themselves letters and numbers. All the real beings in the three levels of the cosmos—in the world, in time, in man's body—came into existence through the interconnection of the twenty-two letters that God had engraved upon the primal air. But if his father had believed so little in the Kabbalists, why had he spoken of them to Nathan so often?

Poppa's books. What good did all of Poppa's books and words ever do for Nachman? his mother asked. When Nachman was well, he had, like their father, been an honored man in the synagogue. He had been happy in *shul*. He had had friends there. He had often led the morning *minyan* in prayers. Michael had gone to *shul* with his father each Saturday, during the years Nachman was at home. Nachman had been proud when Michael was the president of the youth group, when Michael was the star of the synagogue's basketball team. In the mornings, Nathan knew, Michael had watched Nachman put on his *talis* and *tephillin*. Michael had gone to Hebrew School and had learned about the history of the Jews. He had, returning home, been beaten up several times by gangs of blacks and Catholics. Nathan could understand why Michael felt so deeply about going to Russia, to help Jews. But why did he feel so much for all the black and brown strangers who came to his clinic?

Nathan thought of the Arabs, in Ein Karem. He saw them in Jerusalem, begging. The sight had always angered him. When students at Hebrew University marched in favor of giving the Arabs a homeland, on the West Bank, he had been furious. He had wanted to break through the police lines and smash the placards. He had wanted to wring the necks of the young Jews. Didn't they know who they were? Didn't they know that they were Jews too, despite the freedom of their lives? Israel was surrounded by twenty-one Arab nations. Let those nations give homes to their own kind. Let Jews take care of Jews. They could save the world later.

"Mr. Malkin?"

Nathan stood. He followed the receptionist through a door and along a corridor. An attractive young woman, in white blouse and blue pants suit, emerged from an office and smiled at Nathan. She carried a clipboard. She spoke with kindness to a middle-aged Puerto Rican woman. The receptionist knocked on Michael's door. Nathan entered. Michael stood and came around his desk. Nathan shook Michael's hand. He looked around the room, surprised at how pleasant it was: there were curtains and diplomas and books and photos of Ruth and the children, and of Rachel and Nachman. In the bookcase were several trophies.

"Outside," Nathan said. "In the waiting room. It reminded me of visiting Nachman—of hospitals."

Michael shook his head. "It's not a hospital—that's the place we're trying to keep them from, right?"

"The way we couldn't keep Nachman? Is that what you're trying to tell me?"

"I'm not trying to tell you anything."

Nathan shrugged. He looked up at Michael, and when Michael smiled he felt as if Michael were urging him to speak, to tell him things. But Nathan did not know what kinds of things Michael wanted him to talk about. Michael's face looked very relaxed. He seemed happy in his office. "Do you remember the time you came to visit me, to show me a copy of *The Corsican Brothers*?"

"The Classic Comic?"

"Yes."

"It was my favorite," Michael said. "I loved to sit on your living-room rug and read it. Mother always used to make me do something else if she caught me reading comic books."

Nathan nodded. "I've changed my mind," he said. "It's why I'm here."

"Yes?"

"What I've decided is that instead of collecting secrets, I want to give some away, all right? The picture of you bringing the comic book—that was part of what made me think of what I wanted you to have, before anybody else." He looked down. "Also Rachel's leaving."

Michael picked up his telephone. He told the receptionist to hold all his calls. Then he stood and locked the door. He pulled a chair close to the chair Nathan was sitting in. "That's been upsetting you, hasn't it?"

"I was thinking that maybe the reason she went to Florida was because she wanted to get away from me—because she was afraid I still wanted her secret."

"I doubt it," Michael said. "My mother's not afraid of much."

"Maybe I was joking that first morning, like Rachel said," Nathan said. "But after she left I changed my mind and I decided that instead of collecting secrets, maybe I should give them away."

"Is that a joke too?"

"I'm not sure."

"You've seemed different since she left—less confident, less—" Michael searched for words. "I don't know." He laughed. "There's something softer about you now, more vulnerable—in fact, the way you came in before, almost meekly, not at all like the Uncle Nat I know, you reminded me a lot of my father." He paused. "Do you know what I mean?"

"I used to think that Nachman and I were like the Corsican brothers," Nathan said. "That we were somehow joined invisibly the way Siamese twins are, but that where we were joined, instead of in the foot, was in the heart."

Michael smiled. "Maybe the reason I loved it so much, especially when I'd read about one of them being in pain or in danger and the other feeling it, even though he was hundreds of miles away, was because I wished so much that I could have had a brother. We were—"

"I want to tell you about the happiest moment of my life," Nathan said. He thought, also, of telling Michael that he had mailed the story to Rachel, but he was afraid that Michael would ask him why, that Michael might disapprove. "That's why I'm here. I want you to know. I used to think that the happiest moment of my life was when I first saw Nachman in the bedroom, at Momma's breast after he was born, but I decided that he was right about my envy—about even the ordinary jealousy I must have felt in that moment." Nathan leaned back. "The happiest moment of my life, I decided instead, was the time Poppa and I went with Nachman to see Mr. Langenauer about Nachman's violin playing, when Nachman was only five years old."

"He never told me," Michael said. "He never told me much about his childhood—in fact, he never really told me much about anything that happened before his first breakdown."

"Momma had bought a piano for Rivka—it was sold years ago, before you were born—and what I used to love most was when Nachman would tiptoe into the living room and, just like Rivka's teacher, whenever Rivka would hit a wrong note, Nachman would leap up onto the piano bench and slap her hands." Nathan smiled. "Well. You know about how talented your father was. I'll give credit where credit is due. Even Rivka always talked lovingly of his talents when he was a child, about how he could go to the piano and play any melody he heard—from *shul*, from what Rivka was learning, from what Poppa sang with the men on *Shabbos*—and he could play with both hands. 'Maybe he's another Paderewski,' Momma said, but in this Poppa defied her. He wanted Nachman's gifts to come from him, I think. He understood how hard it would be for Nachman to fulfill any dream Momma had for him."

Michael nodded, as if agreeing with Nathan. Nathan thought of Noah and Esther, the first time they met. He saw them playing together, smiling at one another. *You must know everything!* his mother screamed at him. "So instead of giving Nachman lessons at the piano," Nathan continued, "one day Poppa brought home a tiny violin for him. I'd never seen Poppa's eyes sparkle the way they did when he unwrapped the brown wrapping paper, and then the newspaper. He opened the black leather case and handed the tiny instrument to Nachman. Nachman's eyes sparkled as much as Poppa's. Nachman took the instrument, and plucked it, and looked into its openings, and held it to him as if it were a doll. At night he took it out of its case and wrapped it in a little blanket and slept with it. Did you know that?"

"No."

"Momma was furious—we already had a piano and a piano teacher who could have started to teach Nachman too when his feet were longer, she said, and she yelled at Poppa for spending the money on the violin and on the extra teacher. The teacher, Mr. Itzkoff, was only a poor musician himself, a young violinist who spent his life giving lessons to boys and girls without Nachman's gift, and he must have charged pennies. But Momma always held it against Poppa. When Nachman held his violin in bed at night, it was always as if, I thought, he were afraid Momma would come in the middle of the night to snatch it away from him."

"The way gypsies stole children?" Michael offered.

"The way gypsies stole children," Nathan said. He felt himself stiffen slightly, at Michael's interruption. He saw Brashler, examining Noah's fingers, and peering into the violin. "But one day the music teacher waited until it was dark, when Poppa came home, to have a talk with him, and the next day the three of us—Nachman, Poppa, and I—were traveling across Brooklyn Bridge together on the streetcar, all the way uptown, near where the Metropolitan Museum of Art is. Nachman was still five years old and I was twelve. We both wore our best knickers. Mr. Langenauer was the director of a musical conservatory whose name I cannot recall. He lived in a beautiful town house on Fifth Avenue, and a servant came to the door to let us in. Poppa whispered to me that Mr. Langenauer was Jewish, and this surprised me—I'd never known Jews could live in houses like his." Nathan stopped. "Your mother lived in a house like that when I first knew her." Michael nodded, but said nothing. "We waited in a room that had an enormous piano, and Mr. Langenauer played notes for Nachman and he had to name the notes. Then he asked Nachman to take out his violin and he tested him some more. He would play a melody on the piano and he would ask Nachman to repeat it on the violin. He asked Nachman to play the same melody in a different key.

"And all the while Poppa and I sat, our hats on our heads, on silk-covered chairs, Mr. Langenauer showed no reaction at all. He had a pointed white beard and piercing gray eyes and was very Germanic. Even when he spoke in English I could hardly understand what he said. But Nachman did. He was thrilled, he was unafraid, he was smiling, he was lost in the musical games, and he was eager to please. He was so eager to please, Michael! So eager!"

"Yes." Michael's eyes were soft. He seemed very happy.

"Mr. Langenauer set up a music stand for Nachman and put music on it, and then the two of them played together—a movement from an early Mozart sonata Nachman had never heard before, in which the violin is really playing the accompaniment for the piano at first—and only when that was done did Mr. Langenauer react. Then the ice in his gray eyes melted, the pursed lips became soft and full, and the severe Germanic teacher vanished—Mr. Langenauer lifted Nachman up by both arms and kissed him on both cheeks. '*Wunderkind!*' he exclaimed. He set Nachman down gently, and left the room—all this without talking to Poppa—and he came back a few seconds later with a long bar of chocolate, which he presented to Nachman.

" 'This boy may become a very fine musician,' he said to Poppa. 'He certainly has the talent for it. Let him hear some good singing, whenever he can, but do not force music upon him. When the time comes for serious study, bring him to me, and I shall be glad to supervise his artistic education.'

"That was the happiest moment of my life," Nathan said. "Seeing Nachman and Poppa look at each other with such happiness. They embraced, there in Mr. Langenauer's music room, and Poppa was crying too. Mr. Langenauer did not smile again, though. As for me, I felt very left out, yet I felt very happy. Nachman put his violin away carefully, and opened his chocolate bar, and he came to me and gave me half. He was a very generous boy, even then. He carried the chocolate bar and I carried his violin, when we left. Poppa kept thanking Mr. Langenauer, but not in any servile way. It was the proudest moment of his life, I think."

"I wish he'd told me—"

"Shh," Nathan said. "You shouldn't interrupt. Mr. Langenauer said to Poppa to bring Nachman back to him in two years' time. But tell me what you think, Michael—was God jealous of our happiness? Fifteen months after our wonderful journey, Mr. Langenauer died. Poppa showed the article in the newspaper to us, and then he cried. In the article it said that Mr. Langenauer had been the foremost pupil in America of the great Joseph Joachim, who had been a violinist and head of a conservatory in Berlin. I remember that. Joachim had trained Rubinstein also, when Rubinstein was a little boy. Momma was herself. She said that she didn't wish this Langenauer dead, but that she had never understood how Poppa expected to *shlep* Nachman to Manhattan every week for lessons. He had trouble enough *shlepping* himself to and from work each morning.

"Some disappointments are too great for some people to bear, aren't they, Michael? That's what I decided. There are strong people and there are weak people, and some disappointments are too great for some people to bear." He looked at Michael. Michael's eyes seemed glazed. "If it had been a few years earlier—before Nachman was born, before Momma became so bitter—Poppa might have been strong enough to—" Nathan stopped. "What's the use, Michael? Everything changed after that. Everything went sour. Nachman kept playing, and Momma even got him a teacher—Momma, not Poppa—but it was never the same."

"I'm sorry," Michael said.

"Why should you be sorry?" Nathan asked. "I must have been very angry with Poppa. But who could have known it then? Later, when we'd visit Nachman in the hospital and he would sit there like a lump and do nothing to stop Momma, I wanted to kill him sometimes. I wanted to lift him and smash him against walls. I yelled at Momma, but I must have been just as angry with Poppa." Nathan shrugged. "Who could have known? He was who he was the way I was who I was and Nachman was who he was. And even if Mr. Langenauer had lived, who knows if Nachman's life would have been different?"

"Or yours?"

"Or mine," Nathan said. He stood. "You must have things to do. I saw people waiting . . ."

"I'm glad you gave me the story."

"Don't mention it. What could I do with it anyway, after all these years? And it may not look it, but remembering Poppa and Nachman back then made me very happy again for a moment—not the way I once was, of course—but it did make me happy to share it with you."

"And you wouldn't mind—later on—if I told the story to Ruth, or to the children?"

"No," Nathan said. "It's your secret now. You do what you want with it."

Nathan went to the door and tried to leave, but the door was stuck. Michael opened it. Nathan realized that he was hoping that Michael would say something about all that he was feeling toward him, but Michael said nothing. He smiled. Then, as Nathan walked through the doorway, Michael caught Nathan's arm and bent down and kissed Nathan on the cheek. Michael's eyes were moist, and when his lips moved away Nathan realized that he was feeling exactly the way he felt when he was a little boy and he would wait at the front door for his father to come home from work, so that his father would be able to bend down and kiss him, before he got to anyone else.

NATHAN WALKED TO ATLANTIC AVENUE, TO THE LONG ISLAND RAIL ROAD station. Next to the ticket window, on the floor, a man with stumps for legs was propped up inside an old tire. The man's face was covered with tiny boils. In front of him was a black cap, filled with coins. The man whimpered and pulled at Nathan's trousers, begging for money. Nathan wanted to kick the man. "Let go," he said. He paid for his ticket and walked away. On the train he found a seat next to a window and closed his eyes. He saw flames. The house was burning, and his manuscripts were floating into the air like charred feathers. Were all the memories that Michael longed for burning also? Before Nachman was born, their father had loved to sit Nathan on his knee and tell him stories. Nathan tried to imagine his father as a young man—younger than Michael was now—walking through the streets of Burshtyn, the admiring eyes of the young men and women of the village upon him. His father had been a carrier-of-heavy-loads. His father had been a brilliant scholar. He listened to his father tell him the story of Rabbi Hanina ben Tradyon.

Rabbi Hanina had been a great hero to Nathan when he was a boy—greater than Akiba or Bar Kochba. Rabbi Hanina had chosen to teach Torah in public places, despite the Romans' decree forbidding such a practice. He stood in the marketplace, with a Sefer Torah in his arms, and he taught those Jews brave enough to listen. One day the Romans captured him and they wrapped him in the scroll itself—in the very Torah—and piled branches upon him, and lit the branches. They placed wet wool over his heart so that he would not die quickly. Then, while the flames leapt up and consumed him, Rabbi Hanina told his friends and disciples, who were watching—weeping in their helplessness and shame and grief—of what he saw. "The parchment is burning," he called out to them. "But the letters—the letters are flying free!"

IT WAS ALREADY DARK WHEN NATHAN'S TRAIN ARRIVED IN ROSLYN. HE took a taxi to Ruth's house. She seemed happy to see him. She kissed him on the cheek.

"I brought you a gift," he said.

She put a finger to her lips. "Shh," she said. "I just put the children to sleep. Come—"

She took his hand and he followed her to the family room. "Who's there?" Miriam asked. She stood on the landing above them, in her pajamas.

"Hello, darling," Nathan said.

"Hi Uncle Nat," Miriam said. She smiled. "Mommy said you might be visiting us. I waited up—"

Nathan looked at Ruth. "Michael called before," Ruth explained. "He told me that you'd visited him. He told me that he thought you might visit me next."

"Can you tuck me in, Mommy?"

Nathan walked upstairs with Ruth. He kissed Miriam good night. He looked into Eli's and Aaron's rooms. They were fast asleep. He thought of Tolstoy, sitting in his grandmother's room and listening to the blind storyteller. He walked downstairs and waited. He heard his father's voice. *There is no wealth without children.* Ruth came down a few minutes later. "She hasn't been sleeping well," Ruth said. They sat in the family room together. "She's scared about Michael going to Russia. She's still upset about seeing her grandfather buried. Last night when I went in to cover her, before I went to sleep, she woke up and told me she's been having a nightmare—from a horror show she saw at a friend's house, about people lost in space. She was afraid to go back to sleep." Ruth stood. "Do you want a drink? I need one."

"No," Nathan said.

"Have you had supper?"

"I'm not hungry."

Ruth poured herself a glass of bourbon, and sat again. "She asked me if she and her brothers would be orphans after Michael left. I told her that they wouldn't. I told her that I was sad too about Michael's leaving, and then she said—get this—that sometimes she thought it would be nice to be an orphan. I asked her if she'd ever met or read about any orphans, and she replied that Sleeping Beauty and Snow White were orphans, weren't they?"

Nathan smiled. "What I decided to do," he said, "instead of collecting secrets, is to give them away. I already gave Michael his. I came to give you yours. It's why I'm here."

"Follow me," she said. "You look pale. I'll fix you something."

Nathan followed Ruth to the kitchen. Her voice was hard, her manner more tense than usual. She lit a cigarette.

"But Miriam knows we'll be back soon—in two weeks—doesn't she? And that Michael will come home then, to be with you."

Ruth laughed. "Will he?"

"He said so—don't you remember?"

"And you believe him?"

She opened the refrigerator and took out a plastic container. She poured its contents—stew—into a pot. "Why shouldn't I?"

"Oh Uncle Nat," she said. "Don't you know that Michael has no plans to return? Don't you see that?"

"No," Nathan said.

"I thought Rachel had talked to you," she said. She shrugged. "She said she would talk to you about Michael before she left." Ruth turned and faced him. She brushed her hair from her forehead. "Look, maybe it doesn't show to you, but his father's death has had its effect on him. It's—"

"Nachman was his father," Nathan said. "I know that. But I visited Michael at his office. I go to *shul* with him every morning, for *Kaddish*. He plays basketball in the schoolyard, on weekends. He seems very happy—very much in control of things."

"Full of stories, too, isn't he?"

"He likes stories," Nathan agreed. "In the evenings he likes me to tell him stories about what things were like when Nachman and I were growing up together . . ."

"Sure," Ruth said. She stubbed out her cigarette in the sink. She bit her lip, then nodded, as if she had reached a decision. "I'll give you your secret then, all right? Since you came for it."

"But I didn't," Nathan said. "I told you before—what I decided to do was to—"

She waved a hand at him. She stirred the food in the pot, then turned back to Nathan. "It comes to the same thing, doesn't it? And who knows, Uncle Nat—maybe Michael will infect you too so that you won't come back either—and then what would I do with all the stories *I've* been saving . . ."

"You seem upset," Nathan said. "You seem very upset with Michael."

"And why in hell shouldn't I be!" she shouted. "Why shouldn't I be! He's a goddamn fool. Don't you see that? Him and his clinic and his precious schoolyard and his precious house. Don't you see how easy it is for him there, Uncle Nat? Don't you even see how much easier your coming back has made things for him?"

"No. I don't understand."

"Sit," Ruth commanded. Nathan sat. She gave him a bowl of stew and a glass of grape juice. "There are no women to bother Michael in his schoolyard. There are no children and no wife to bother him in his home. In his clinic there are only sick people who are grateful to him. He's very good at helping people he doesn't know, don't you see that? He doesn't have to worry about pleasing and displeasing people whose judgment really—"

"You're wrong," Nathan said. He tried to concentrate, but he felt very weak. "You're wrong. I know that. What about Lazer Kominsky? What about—?"

"You believe that story?" Ruth asked.

"Yes."

Ruth sat. Her face softened. "Michael has an extraordinary imagination, doesn't he?"

"You don't believe the story?" Nathan asked.

"Like you, when you were young—like his father—Michael loves to make up stories. And sometimes he comes to believe in them so much that he can't tell the difference between what happened and—"

"Sometimes when I write now, I can't tell the difference," Nathan offered. "Sometimes I can't tell if I'm inventing something for the first time or not. It happens."

"Michael can live in his schoolyard," Ruth said. "He can live in Russia. He can live in France. He can live in Brooklyn. He can live in your old house. He can live in a mental hospital, if he has to, or in Israel too, I suppose, if that idea occurs to him. He can live anywhere but in his own home, with his own family."

"Why?"

"Let me give you your secret, all right?" Ruth smiled, but bitterly. "You went into Aaron's room before, didn't you?"

"He looked very sweet. He was sleeping with a stuffed animal."

"It bothered you, didn't it, when Ira died, that he had never married—that he had no children."

Nathan set his spoon down. "I don't understand."

"Just listen," Ruth said sharply. She swallowed the rest of her drink. Her eyes watered. "Who does Aaron remind you of, Uncle Nat?"

"I've only seen him a few times. I don't—"

"*Who does he remind you of?*"

Nathan shrugged. "Myself," he said. "The first time I saw him, upstairs, behind all the books and furniture, with the water guns in his hands, he reminded me of me, when I was a boy."

"Who else?" Ruth demanded.

"I don't know," Nathan said. "Ira maybe. He looks a little like—" Nathan stopped. His hand moved to his chest. He felt as if something were burning him there. He needed air.

"There's your secret," Ruth said. She stood. "Ira did not die childless."

Nathan pressed his eyes closed. When he opened them, Ruth was gone. He felt very dizzy. Why had she said such a thing to him, he wondered. *There is no wealth without children.* He looked around at the brightly lit kitchen. He looked at the deep purple of the grape juice. He wanted to get up, to follow her, to find out if what had just happened had really happened, but he could not move. *Am I real and will death really come?* At the end, when Mandelstam was in prison, he was told that someone in one of the death cells in Lefortovo had scratched the line, from one of his poems, on the wall. The news made Mandelstam happy for a few days.

RUTH'S EYES WERE RED. SHE HAD BEEN CRYING. "I'M SORRY," SHE SAID. "It's just—" Nathan sat next to her. He lifted his arm—hesitated—and then put it around Ruth's shoulders. She leaned against him and wept. "I'm sorry if I hurt you," she said, "but it just scares me so goddamned much about Michael, Uncle Nat, don't you see? Sometimes he acts as if he can put the whole world on his back and walk off with it, but he's really just a scared little boy, and I love him. I still love him, goddamnit." She rubbed her eyes against Nathan's arm. "I'm sorry, but—"

"It's all right," Nathan said.

"That was why, with Ira," she said. "I just had to have some way of reaching Michael, of getting through that smile of his, of getting through that—" She broke off. "I don't know. I'm sorry if I hurt you. I'm sorry I said anything, but in less than a week he'll be gone and then what will I do? What am I saving anything for?"

"I'm not angry with you," Nathan said. "There's nothing to be sorry for."

"You're not?"

"I don't think so," he said. "Mostly I'm numb, if you want the truth. Mostly I'm wondering why they're all dead—Ira and Nachman and Pauline and the others."

"The others?"

"Gail Rubin, Imri—"

"Who are they?"

Nathan began to tell Ruth about Gail Rubin and about the family of Hanoch Tel-Oren. She dried her eyes. He told her about what he'd read in the newspapers. He told her about going to the nature sanctuary and about finding the telegram waiting for him when he returned. He told her that he did not think he would have come back had he received the telegram in time for him to have been at Nachman's funeral. He told her that he was pleased not to have been there. That was the secret he had come to give her. Before he left for Russia with Michael, he wanted her to know about Gail Rubin.

"When I read about her, she reminded me of you," Nathan said. "I never saw her picture, but when I imagined her lying on the beach, I thought of you."

"Dead?"

"Dead."

Ruth touched his hand. "It's all right," she said. "Actually, it's better than all right. It means you love me, doesn't it?"

"Yes," Nathan said. Ruth's directness did not bother him.

"And you will do everything you can to see that Michael comes home, won't you?"

"Does he know about Ira—about you and Ira—?"

She shook her head sideways. "No," she said. "At least not officially, right? He's always suspicious, of course, and sometimes I like to get a rise out of him by hinting at things, but no—I never actually told him. I was always too afraid of what the news might do to him. And now . . ."

"And now?"

"Do you think he has to know, Uncle Nat? Couldn't it be our secret?" She breathed out. Her cheeks were red and streaked from her tears. "I thought I was drawn to Ira's weakness—his loneliness—but I was wrong. Not about why I was drawn to him—I did want somebody I could give to, somebody I could take care of and be kind to, someone who needed me—but Ira wasn't at all weak. He knew what he wanted in life and, mostly, he got it."

"He had dreams. He wanted to make great discoveries."

"He might have. His work was going well. He believed that his best years were still ahead of him. He called himself a late bloomer."

"He did—really?"

"You seem surprised."

"I thought he was depressed during that time. I thought he was depressed because of his age—because he had passed that age when great scientists usually made their breakthroughs."

Ruth smiled. "I changed that," she said. "Wasn't that good of me? His confidence came back, before the end. He was very hopeful." She smiled. Nathan thought of Einstein, who felt, wherever he lived, that he was a stranger. Einstein was a lonely man who avoided intimacy. "I came to like him a lot, Uncle Nat. It was very confusing for me, but I came to like Ira a lot. I don't think he would have done the kind of thing he did—in the subway—if he hadn't been optimistic. He was willing to take chances. I worked on him the way I never had to work on Michael. Ira was willing to take risks. He was willing to give of himself. He had worlds inside him that I never suspected were there, at first . . ."

"What would you have done if he hadn't died when he did?"

She patted his hand. "You ask all the right questions, don't you?" She shrugged. "I don't know."

"You don't know."

"He saved me, I suppose. I was very upset when he died—how can I even talk about it?—but I was relieved too. I knew it, even at the time. And when you left the country—that helped also. There were no reminders. When you showed up at Rachel's apartment, I was angry. It would have been fine with me if I'd never seen you again."

Nathan did not ask her if she still felt the same way. He imagined that, in Florida, Rivka and Leah were introducing Rachel to men who had lost their wives. He had never told Ira about himself and Rachel. Had that been Ira's way—his letting Ruth tempt him—of getting even on Nathan's behalf for what Michael's father had done to his own father—Nachman's taking Rachel as his bride—so many years before? As soon as the question was there, Nathan chided himself for the perversity of his mind.

"You're not angry with me—for telling you?" Ruth asked again.

"I'm not angry with you," Nathan said.

WHILE NATHAN WORKED IN THE UPSTAIRS ROOM, TYPING HIS MANUSCRIPT, he thought of the downstairs rooms as being the cellar of the house. He imagined that his mother and father and sisters and brother were all still living there, in underground rooms. He thought of the Marranos, the Frankists. The *Sefirot* emanated in succession, one from the other, as if, the Kabbalists suggested, one candle were being lit from another. Thus God was diminished in no way. The worlds which preceded our world and were destroyed were like the sparks that scatter and die away when the forger strikes the iron with his hammer. But the remnants of these destroyed worlds never entirely disappeared. The *shechina* of God—His spirit—was itself, like the people of Israel, perpetually in exile, waiting until the end of time, for redemption. If there were, in fact, genuine correspondences between these theories and what modern scientists had discovered, did this prove that, long before telescopes and electron microscopes and interstellar satellites, God had implanted within the mind of man knowledge of His universe? Nathan wondered what Ira would think. He wondered if any of Ira's colleagues were continuing his researches.

Nathan walked down the stairs and was surprised, on the ground floor, to see sunlight shining in through the windows. He was surprised that there were no stone walls, no candles lit. In his dreams, though—he wondered what Michael would make of it—there were never cellars anymore. There were never windowless rooms. The first act of God, according to the theory of *zimzum*, was not one of revelation and emanation, but of concealment and withdrawal. Creation was possible only through the entry of God into Himself.

Their suitcases were lined up in the foyer, next to the front door. Their plane would leave in a few hours. Nathan had several more pages to type for the manuscript of *The Stolen Jew*. He thought of Tsvi's choice, in saving Noah, of how awful and true it had always seemed to him. He thought of his own choice, of his decision to go with Michael, despite what Rachel had asked him.

Michael would be home soon, from the schoolyard. Michael would shower and dress. They would finish their packing. They would eat supper together, they would close up the house, and then they would take a taxicab to the airport. Would Ruth and the children be there? Nathan did not think so.

Nathan felt very close to Ruth. He was glad that he had told her about Gail Rubin. He looked at Michael's bookcase. He thought of Ira's office, at Columbia. He imagined himself in front of Ira's grave, on Long Island. Ruth was at his side, and in his mind he was telling Ira that everything was all right, that he knew about Ruth and about Aaron. But Ira had not lived to see Aaron born. Ira had never known. Ruth had said that Michael's story was not true. Was hers? Ruth had been an actress. What could Nathan believe? Ruth still loved Michael as much—more—than she ever had. Nathan would never be able to share his memory and knowledge with Ira. *God created the world because He loved stories* . . .

Ruth had spoken with Nathan about how good she and Ira had been for one another, about how she and Ira were able to talk hour after hour about what their lives had been like before they'd known one another. Inevitably, Ruth said, they would wind up talking mostly—as she had with Michael, in their early years together—of how lucky they had been to have found one another. Having been only children was part of it, they would tell one another—Ruth the sister/brother Ira had always desired and never had; Ira the brother/sister she had never had. And now?

In the kitchen, Nathan put the kettle on to boil. Then he telephoned to Florida, to Leah's apartment, where, he knew, Rachel would be staying until the apartment she was buying was ready.

"Hello?"

"It's Nathan. I'm glad you answered, Leah."

"Wait," Leah said. "Rachel and Rivka are here too. They'll want to talk with you, to say good-bye—"

"Don't leave," Nathan said. "I have something I want to say to you."

"What?"

Nathan could hear the fear in Leah's voice. Poor Leah. Was she still afraid that he wanted her to talk about the time the man in the black greatcoat came and they laid her on the kitchen table, with Momma holding her head? It was no secret, really; Rivka and Harvey knew, though Nathan did not think that they had ever told Raymond or Nachman or Leah's two children. Maybe, Nathan thought, whenever he imagined Tsvi thinking of what it was like to see his grandfather's body being prepared by the *Chevra Kedisha*, he had really been remembering Leah. When Nathan heard the screams, he had come to the kitchen door to see, but the door was locked. Behind it his mother was cursing Leah in Yiddish, calling her dirt and filth. But Momma was fair, Nathan thought. She yelled at the man also, for what he charged, for being who he was, and Nathan had no doubt but that his mother ended up paying less than she had contracted for. His own business skills, Nathan told himself, had not come from nowhere.

"You always tried to be very good, didn't you," Nathan said. "To make up for not being the favorite."

"I don't understand what you want," Leah said. "Let me get the others—"

"When Rivka and Harvey were married and were living upstairs, I remember that you went out and picked flowers and put them on their pillow the first night, and then hid in the closet to see their reaction."

"I'd forgotten."

"You were always my favorite sister," Nathan said.

"Stop," Leah said. "There shouldn't be favorites in a family. You must want to speak with Rachel. She's so worried, Nathan—about Michael and about you. About Ruth and the children. She hasn't been sleeping well—"

"You were always more loving to me than Rivka was," Nathan said. Leah had looked for love wherever she could find it, since she had not found it in her mother or her sister.

"Don't talk this way."

"I decided not to collect the family secrets."

"*What?*"

"I decided that instead, before I leave, I would give my own away."

"I never understand you, Nathan. Sometimes you're worse than Nachman ever was, with your ideas."

"When I wrote *The Stolen Jew*, I used to think of your face whenever I would write about Esther."

"Is that the secret?"

"No."

"You don't have to give me one just because you don't want one from me anymore."

"I never thought you had a bad secret," Nathan said. "That first day at Rachel's, I was very upset, I was angry with Rivka for being there, I was only trying to scare people."

"Are you sure?"

"What I wanted you to know—the secret I saved especially for you—is something I know you always worried about. I wanted you to know that I didn't push Nachman off the fire escape. He was already falling when I was waking up."

"You're not fooling with me, Nathan—you're not going to turn around and tell me the opposite tomorrow, or the next day?"

"Tomorrow I'll be in Moscow."

"You're really going then? It's not just another one of your games? When I first heard your voice, I thought that maybe you'd changed your mind, that—"

"Now let me talk with Rivka."

"What you told me makes me—" She was unable to continue. Nathan heard her put the phone down. He went to the stove and poured the boiling water into his cup. He turned off the gas. He dipped his tea bag into the hot water. Pauline had, when he first met her, reminded him of Leah. She had been very loving, very undemanding. In all their years together she had rarely complained—except, of course, about how hard he worked. She had, like Leah, always been concerned about how hard he worked. She had urged him to rest more.

"Nathan? Where are you—?"

"I'm here," Nathan said.

"Leah said you wanted to say good-bye to me," Rivka said, "and then I pick up the phone and there's no answer. I was worried."

"I didn't mean to give you such pleasure," Nathan said.

"You're not funny," Rivka said. "So tell me what you want."

Nathan could see Rivka, turning around in front of her bedroom mirror, wearing their mother's Persian lamb coat. Rivka wore it when she went out on her dates with Harvey. Uncle Harry had arranged her first meeting with Harvey. Harry had set Harvey up in business. "I called to tell you that I've decided not to collect the family secrets."

"I don't want to hear."

"Instead, I've decided to give my own away, one to each of you. I wanted—"

Rivka laughed at him. "When people give away nothing they always want something," she said. "I agree completely with Harvey about you, Nathan. Your imagination is still your disease. What Nachman didn't—"

"You sound like Momma," Nathan said. He smiled. "Poppa was right about you. Poppa couldn't always tell the difference between things, but he was right about you, Rivka. He worshiped Momma, but he never liked you much. He preferred Leah. When you were together once, he asked me how it was that two such different women could have come from the same womb."

"It's the same old Nathan, isn't it?" Rivka said. "If you really loved me you wouldn't talk to me this way."

"I could love you if you were dead."

Rivka hung up. Nathan looked at the potato bin. The door was open. Nachman was smiling at him. It was a line, Nathan knew, that Nachman would have liked to use. Nathan sat at the table and sipped his tea. Well, he thought. He had lost his chance to have pried from Rivka whatever secret she might have been hiding. But it had been worth it. He felt relieved. He had not really known what secret he would have given to her.

The telephone rang. Nathan answered it. "Hello," he said.

"What did you say to Rivka?" Rachel asked. "She's very upset."

"I gave her her secret," Nathan said. "I told her that I didn't need or want anything from her ever again."

Rachel said nothing. Nathan imagined her smiling at him. "How *are* you, Nathan?"

"I'm all right."

"I miss you."

"I miss you too," Nathan said. "Also, I told her that I didn't love her, the way I didn't love Momma."

"Is that true?"

"No."

"Nathan?"

"Yes?"

"I'm glad you called. I was hoping you would call before you left."

"I was very angry with you for a while."

"You don't sound angry."

"I'm frightened now. That's why I sound this way."

"But you're still going?"

"I'm still going."

"And you'll come back?"

"I'll come back."

"Then tell me what this nonsense is about secrets—Leah said you're not collecting them anymore, that—"

"It doesn't matter," Nathan said. "I think you were right the first time, that I was only joking. But the second time I don't think I'm joking. I decided to give myself another chance. I decided to give away some secrets, and here is what I wanted you to know."

"Yes?"

He breathed in. "I wanted you to know that I don't really want to go to Russia with Michael."

"Is that all?" Rachel said. "But I knew that already. I—"

"Then why didn't you say anything?"

"Because if I had said something, you would have done the opposite."

Nathan looked for Nachman's face, but he couldn't find it. "It feels strange, talking to you on the phone across such a distance. I wish I could see you. I wish you were near."

"Yes."

"All right," Nathan said. "I called to say something else."

"I was hoping—"

"Don't!" Nathan said. "Don't tell me you know everything that I'm already thinking—"

"But I'm not," Rachel sighed. "I'm only—"

Nathan saw Rachel, as she had been when she was younger, and she was standing in her own kitchen, throwing the valentine's card back at Michael. Nachman sat at the table, slumped over, smiling. Like Poppa, Nathan thought. The cold rage in Rachel's eyes made her seem especially desirable to Nathan. He saw her in the bedroom, looking in the mirror on her vanity table while Michael tried to explain himself. He saw her on horseback, in her black velvet riding cap. He saw her visiting Nachman in the hospital. She looked very beautiful, very much in control of things. She looked, he realized, something like his own mother, before

Nachman was born, and before her left eyelid began to droop. He wanted to melt Rachel's coldness, to get past her rage, to break down her terrible will. "We'll only be gone for thirteen days," Nathan said. "It's a thirteen-day tour, and—"

"And what?"

"And I was going to ask you if you thought you could wait for me. That's what I wanted to ask you."

"And are you? Are you asking me that?"

Nathan swallowed. "All right," he said. "Have it your way this time, Rachel. Yes, I'm asking you if you'll wait for me. I'll come down to visit with you as soon as we return. Will you wait then?"

"Of course I'll wait," she said. Her voice was warm again—easy and gentle. "Didn't you know I would?"

"Good," Nathan said. "But don't tell the others."

She laughed. "I won't." Then she whispered, "You're very sweet. Have a safe trip, my darling. I liked the story you sent. Very much. Did I tell you that?"

"No."

"And take good care of Michael. Come home—both of you. I'm not worried now. I'll be waiting."

NATHAN FINISHED TYPING HIS MANUSCRIPT AND HE PUT IT WITH THE other sections. He had now rewritten virtually all the major sections of the book—all but the final chapter. He put the manuscript in his suitcase, but he kept out the chapter he had just rewritten—"Kehilla" —to give to Michael for reading on the airplane. He wondered if Michael would remember the original well enough to notice the changes. Michael had never known Harry. When he had created Mirsky, the head of the Kehilla, Nathan had thought of his Uncle Harry, making his father beg. Nobody had ever asked, though, if Mirsky had been modeled upon Harry, and now that he had, in the new version, given Mirsky a hand with four fingers, there was nobody alive—except, perhaps, for Rivka and Leah—to remember Harry, to make the connection.

Harry had died of a heart attack at the age of fifty-six. He had smoked too many Cuban cigars. While Nathan's Aunt Zlata was still in mourning, Nathan had bought Harry's business from her. *I bought it for a song.* He had bought the business at a price that would have horrified Harry.

He would have turned over in his grave, as the saying goes.

He was too big. Harry was too fat to turn over. There was no room in his coffin.

It would have made Poppa happy. That you got even. You're very good about getting even. But what was the song, Nathan? I don't remember any song.

Bitterness. That was the song.

Ah, bitterness! Your favorite song, wasn't it? Also, I wanted to tell you that I liked what you said to Rivka. Thank you, Nathan. It felt as if you were saying it for me too.

Did you come for your secret?

Did you think I'd let myself be left out?

No.

And you're not afraid to give away so much, Nathan?

I'm not afraid.

I'm surprised. Most people think that if they give away too much, they'll get emptied out. I used to think that way, remember? I used to think that if I lost my sickness—if I ever found somebody to give it to, like you, for instance—

Or Michael.

Or Michael—I used to think that if I gave it all away, that there'd be nothing of me left. That I'd be empty.

You were wrong. Don't you remember the riddle? What's the one thing that the more you give it away, the richer you become?

I give up, Nathan. What's the one thing that the more you give it away the richer you become?

Love.

Was that from Poppa? Was that one of his stories?

No. It was from me. I just made it up.

You always had a way with words, Nathan. Didn't I say so? Remember the time I was operated on—for my lung—and you came to visit me? Didn't I say it then?

You said it then.

So give me my secret. Michael will be home soon and I wouldn't want him to find me here, visiting you. He might get jealous. He might want me to tell him about what happened with Ira and his wife, and think of what that news would do to him on the very eve of his departure.

Nathan stared at the bookcase. He thought of his father's *Siddur*, packed in the suitcase between rock-and-roll records and blue jeans.

How would he explain all the blue jeans and records and calculators and panty hose to the customs officials if they opened his bag? Michael had told him not to worry. The percentages were with them. Nathan had three copies of the Russian edition of his novel to show the officials. In Russia, writers were honored. Yes, Nathan thought. In Russia, writers were honored. Nowhere else on earth were so many writers murdered for their writing. Nathan saw Marina Tsvetayeva, with the rope around her neck. Her husband, she discovered, had been executed, her daughter sent to a concentration camp. She had returned from Paris to be with them. They evacuated her to the town of Elabuga where, in August 1941, she hanged herself. Nathan looked at the ceiling. He remembered coming in one time and finding a rope there, on the light fixture. Nachman was under it, stepping down from a chair. "Were you trying to hang yourself?" Nathan had asked. "I was trying to hang myself," Nachman replied, giving Nathan the line from the old joke, "except that when I tightened the rope around my neck, I couldn't breathe."

I think I blamed myself because you had no life.

Do you know what, Nathan?

What?

I don't believe you anymore. So try to give me another secret.

When you first got sick and they took you away, all dressed up in Rivka's clothes, I was glad.

Ah. That's better. That's much better, Nathan! You're on the right track now. That's a much better secret, even though I knew that one also.

It was a relief to me that you were locked up. And also, it made people start to worry about me too, because they knew how close you and I were. I got some of your attention.

I felt exactly the same.

I was tired of being proud of all the crazy things you did.

And of the way people would ask me why I couldn't be more like you.

That also.

Do you remember the time I tried to strangle you?

If you'd really wanted to kill me you would have used a knife. I said so to the doctors.

At least I tried to keep things in the family. You have to give me credit for that. If I'd wanted to I could just as easily have gone out on the street and tried to murder a stranger.

You didn't want to.

You always won, didn't you, Nathan? Even when I was trying to murder you, you stopped me with your bare hands. Somehow my craziness gave you more adrenaline than it gave me. So I ask you—did that make sense?

What made sense? Nothing made sense in those days, Nachman. Except at work. I was good at making money. The more I worked, the more money I made. I could count on that.

Before you go, though, darling, you shouldn't forget to ask Michael about my good lung. Ask him if they found another black spot, all right? It might explain things for you. It might make things easier.

I hear Michael coming.

Have a good trip, Nathan. And don't worry about me while you're gone. I'll be fine. I'll keep an eye on things. If buyers should come, I'll tell them to wait.

Nachman?

Good-bye, Nathan. Good-bye and good luck. Shalom! Do svidanya!

Nathan heard the door close. He heard Michael call to him. He opened his eyes. He saw Michael smiling. He saw white bandages.

"Are you all right, darling?"

"Darling?" Michael asked.

"I was dozing," Nathan said. He stared at Michael's arm, which was in a white plaster cast, the cast held up by a sling.

Michael sat on the couch. His cheeks, above his dark beard, were scratched and dirty. "I'm okay. Sure. What do you think?"

"But are you all right?"

"I'm all right, I'm all right," Michael said, irritably. "But with this damned thing on me, I'll need you to help me get washed—"

"What happened?"

"I broke my arm, that's what happened. Can't you see?"

"Nobody broke it for you?"

"Nobody broke it for me. I hit it against the backboard, that's all. I—" He winced. "Oh damn. Look. We're late. Help me get washed and changed. Then let's move, okay? We can't be late."

The phone rang. "I'll get it," Nathan said.

"*No!*" Michael grabbed Nathan's arm with his good hand. "Just leave it alone. There's no time, can't you tell? The plane leaves at ten-fifteen and we still have—"

Nathan pulled away. "Everything's packed," he said. The phone kept ringing. "It might be Ruth," Nathan offered. "Maybe something's happened to one of the children—"

"No!" Michael said. "Just leave it. I said we don't have time."

Nathan followed Michael to his bedroom. Michael sat. His neck and ears were red. Nathan untied the laces to Michael's sneakers, and pulled the sneakers off. Then he pulled off Michael's socks. Michael lay back on the bed, his good arm across his eyes. Were his ears ringing?

"Did you find another spot on Nachman's lung?" Nathan asked. "I meant to ask."

Michael sat up. "No," he said. "I didn't. I'm not a lung man."

"Did anyone?"

"I didn't ask," Michael said. "There was no autopsy. Here—" He lifted his arms, so that Nathan could help him pull off his sweatshirt.

Nathan pulled the sweatshirt, and then the T-shirt. He was surprised, so close to Michael, at how broad Michael was around the chest. Rachel's father had been a large man. Michael slipped out of his pants and walked to the bathroom. He bent his head sideways and took the sling off. He put a plastic bag over the cast. He took off his underpants and got into the shower. "You'll have to help me dry myself."

Nathan waited while Michael showered. When Michael stepped out, he seemed relaxed again. He said that he felt better. He said that he was sorry if he'd been short with Nathan, but that he was angry with himself for having had such a stupid accident. It had not even happened to him in a game. It had happened afterward, when his friends had placed a dime on top of the backboard. When he had been in college Michael had been able, with a running start, to leap up and snatch a dime from the top of the backboard. His friends in the schoolyard had taunted him, telling him he was an old man now, that he had lost his touch, that white boys couldn't jump the way black boys could. Michael had taken a running start, but at the last second, just as he began his leap, he had, feeling the heaviness in his legs, and knowing he would not reach high enough for the dime, hesitated briefly. His forearm had crashed against the metal backboard. He had fallen to the ground in pain. His friends had taken him to the hospital. It was, fortunately, only a simple fracture of the ulna. It would heal in about four weeks.

Michael dressed, with Nathan's aid. The phone rang again. Neither of them answered it. Michael went to the cellar and turned off the heat and the hot water and the gas. He set up timers, upstairs and downstairs, so that while they were gone lights would show and radios would play. He went into each room, stayed for a few seconds, and then went into the next. In Russia, Nathan knew, it was a custom, when saying good-bye, for two people to sit side by side and not to say anything for a few seconds, but simply to think of one another. Michael telephoned for a taxi.

"Let's go," he said.

They carried their suitcases to the porch, and waited, without talking. They heard radios playing Spanish music. They heard a bottle crash to the sidewalk. Across the street, in a doorway, Nathan saw a teen-age boy and girl kissing. The boy had his hands under the girl's sweater. The taxi came. They walked to it and placed their luggage in the trunk. On the way to the airport, Michael slept, his head against Nathan's shoulder.

Ruth was not waiting for them at the airport. There were one hundred and eighty other people on the AAA tour, Michael told him. Some of them were also carrying in materials for Jews, but Michael did not know who these people were. Michael was his ebullient self again, introducing himself to others, sharing information about the exchange rate and the black market, asking questions about where people were from and what they were looking forward to seeing. He introduced Nathan to each man and woman he himself met. He told the others that Nathan was his uncle and an author whose book had been translated into Russian. He told people that his own father—Nathan's brother—had died recently, and this elicited expressions of sympathy. "My father always dreamt of going back to Russia, to see where his father was born," Michael said. "So now I suppose I'm doing it for him."

Michael seemed very sincere, Nathan saw. That was the trouble, though, wasn't it. A man could not, truly, *seem* to be sincere. Nathan watched their luggage go through flaps of rubber, and disappear. He and Michael walked through the security check. Nathan said nothing. He felt very weak and nervous. A security guard opened Nathan's shoulder bag. The guard checked Michael's shoulder bag and returned his camera to him. "Are you all right?" Michael whispered to Nathan. "You look pale."

"I'm frightened," Nathan said. "I'm very frightened. I don't think I want to go."

Michael pressed Nathan's arm firmly with his good hand. "Are you thinking of the last trip you made?" he asked.

"No," Nathan said. "I wasn't thinking of that trip. I had to wait a long time at Ben-Gurion Airport. It was very different then."

"Then what are you worried about?"

"I don't know," Nathan said. "I'm just frightened of going where we're going."

"Everything will be all right," Michael said. "You'll see." He laughed, and raised his right arm slightly. "Just like me to do something stupid at a time like this, but, like the guys said to me, I won't need my jump shot in Russia."

"You make too many jokes," Nathan said. "You're just like your father."

"Am I?"

Michael was smiling. He let go of Nathan's arm. They walked through a tunnel and found themselves on the Aeroflot plane. Soft music was playing. *I bought Harry's business for a song.* Michael winked at the blonde stewardess. She smiled back and spoke to him. Nathan thought of Ruth, and of Ruth's red eyes. He thought of Aaron and Eli, asleep in their rooms. He thought of Nachman, the hospital sheets pulled to his chin. *Good-bye and good luck.*

"How did I get here?" Nathan asked.

"Shh," Michael said. He nudged Nathan gently, urging him down the aisle. "We'll have lots of time to talk and to think. It's a long trip. The tour leaves us lots of free time. No patients, no cooking, no shopping, no going to *shul*, no trips to Long Island, no schoolyard. We'll have lots of time."

They found their seats. Nathan took the envelope from his shoulder bag. "Here's the chapter I finished this morning. I thought you might want to read it during the flight."

"Sure thing," Michael said, but he did not look at the envelope or open it to see what was inside. He smiled at the passengers going by. He joked with them and shook hands with them, using his left hand. He explained that he had injured his right arm playing basketball. He was a doctor, he told them, and what he learned from his fellow doctors when he went to the hospital was that a thirty-seven-year-old doctor should not be playing three-man basketball with teen-agers.

Michael sat beside Nathan. Nathan reached across and locked Michael's seat belt for him. "Wanted that dime too," Michael said.

Nathan closed his eyes. He listened to the sound of the airplane's jets, warming up. He listened to the soft music. He listened to the Americans, all around him now, chattering to one another. Why, he wondered, were they so happy to be going to such an awful country? He saw Nachman, smiling and waving. Why was Nachman so happy? Nachman was lying in his bed, under the white sheets. Nathan was still visiting him, in the hospital. Under the sheets, Nachman's chest was bandaged.

NATHAN WALKED THROUGH THE DOOR AND NACHMAN SMILED AT HIM. "You look good," he said.

"I'm glad you noticed." Nachman lowered his eyes. "I'm having an affair."

"Really?" Nathan asked, and he gave Nachman the line Nachman was waiting for. "So tell me—who's catering?"

Nachman laughed. "Do you remember the time all the patients ganged up on you when you came through the door, and kept yelling their questions and hanging on to you because I'd told them you were the new rabbi?" Nachman looked down. "You haven't asked me how I am."

"How are you?"

"Don't ask," Nachman said. "But tell me, since you're so smart, Nathan—where is the yet? Is it near the lungs?"

"I'm not a doctor," Nathan said. "Your son is the doctor."

"Help!" Nachman cried. "My son the doctor is drowning!" He beckoned to Nathan with his index finger, to come closer. He spoke softly. "That was another operation. To find the yet. I heard the nurses talking. They operated on the woman who was shot and the bullet is in her yet."

Nathan came closer to Nachman's bed. He tried to smile. "They took out your lung," he said.

"I have another one," Nachman said. "But listen. Before they operated—when they found the black spot—I told them that what they were seeing was only Momma's left eye, which had been there for many, many years. But they didn't believe me. I told them I learned that from all the other hospitals and doctors—they could ask my son. My son's a psychiatrist. I told them that the psychiatrists taught me that we often look at ourselves, from inside, with the accusatory eye of a judging parent. But they wouldn't listen to me. They took out the lung anyway."

"You shouldn't talk so much," Nathan said. "You must be tired."

"It's no easy thing to lose a lung," Nachman said. "I agree. I must be tired." He put a finger to his lips. "Shh," he said. "Close the door." Nathan closed the door. "I wanted you to know that you shouldn't worry about me being here and having lost my lung. Do you know why?"

"Why?"

"It's something I couldn't tell the doctors, but I wanted you to know before anybody else, because I'm sure you must have been worried about the black spot and what happened when they took it out, yes?" Nathan nodded. Nachman sat up, leaning on his elbows. His face was radiant.

"This is what I've been waiting for you to come so I could tell you. It's a secret I saved for you. Guess what happened to it."

"I give up," Nathan said. "What happened to it?"

"I'm glad you asked," Nachman said. "Momma was too clever for them, Nathan—that's what happened. She was too clever for anyone, like always. That eye that always looked at me from my lung—she let it slip down into my heart." He grinned broadly. "It's really where it always belonged, don't you think?"

"Enough," Nathan said. "Please. No more jokes."

"It's no joke," Nachman said, and he lay down again. He sighed. "It's a very tiring experience, to have your chest opened up, I can tell you that. The way I look at it, though, it was a treasure chest, but I got to keep the treasure."

"You should rest," Nathan said. "I just wanted to see how you were."

Nachman sat up. "Don't go. Please?"

"What will you do when you get out? I already told Rachel that I don't think you should go back to work. I can take care of things."

"You were always good at taking care of things. But I'll go back to work."

"You shouldn't be on your feet all day."

"So that I won't be on your mind? You don't have to worry. How could I be in two places at once?"

"I wish it sounded funny, Nachman."

"You didn't have such a terrific life either, brother," Nachman said. "Did I ask you to buy me the music store? Did I ask you to visit me today? My hospital was always bigger than your office or your factories. And, when it comes down to it, what do you think you have to give me that's so valuable? Answer me that. I could have been just as sick in state hospitals, the way I was the first time. Rachel's watching the store, in case you were worried. I know, I know—the neighborhood's changing, but the *schvartzes* love music even more than the Jews. They're not so terrific with the fiddle, but—"

"You're babbling," Nathan said. "You're—"

"You won't be able to get me angry," Nachman said. "If you think you're so smart to work me up so that I'll let my anger out at you—the envy and the rest of it that you and my brilliant son talk about together—I have some good news for you. You don't fool me. I don't know how to get angry. I only know how to get mad."

Nathan stood, to leave. "I'll see you tomorrow," he said.

"Also, you shouldn't forget what Poppa taught us about the miser —and in Yiddish a miser is called a cheap lung, remember?"

"I remember."

"A miser who used to look through his window to see the whole world, but when he became rich and covered one side of his window with silver, he only saw himself. Do you see, Nathan?"

"I'll see you tomorrow," Nathan said.

Nachman closed his eyes. He slumped back on his pillow. Nathan was surprised to see tears on his brother's cheeks. He waited, without moving. Nachman's body heaved up and down, under the sheets. "I'm sorry for being so mean to you," Nachman said. His voice sounded very normal. "But I really can't help myself when the words come onto my tongue. It's always been like that, Nathan—that I can't stop myself from doing things—even if you've always believed differently."

"It's all right," Nathan said.

"Do you think I liked my life?"

"You have Michael and Rachel. You have Ruth and Miriam now."

Nachman's eyes were wide open, above the white sheet. "But do you think I *like* my life—?"

"No."

Nachman nodded. He smiled and spread his arms. "Come—" Nathan stepped forward and embraced his brother. He kissed him on the cheek and felt Nachman's warm tears. So many years, he thought.

"But answer me this," Nachman said. "The truth, please, this time, and I'll never ask you anything else, all right?"

"All right." Nachman let him go.

"If you love somebody very much, and you know something you have to say to them will hurt them very much, is it all right to lie to them instead?"

Nathan nodded. "I think so," he said. "I think it's all right to lie to the people you love."

"Then it's true that I really love you!" Nachman declared, bursting into a smile.

THREE

SECRETS

9

NATHAN OPENED HIS EYES. THE ROAR OF THE PLANE'S ENGINES HAD diminished, and the pilot was speaking about the altitude and the weather, about their projected course and their estimated time of arrival. Nathan thought of Rachel, walking along the oceanfront in Palm Beach, arm in arm with Leah and Rivka.

"Here," Michael said. He placed a yellow sheet of paper on Nathan's lap. It was a newsletter on Soviet Jewry. "Read this and then destroy it. Tear it up and put it in your ashtray."

Michael's voice sounded different—sober suddenly. "Why?" Nathan asked.

"So that you won't think—from the way I've been acting with others—that I've forgotten why we're here."

Nathan took the sheet of paper and read about things he had read about when he was in Israel. He read about the murder of Yiddish culture. On August 12, 1952, Stalin had had twenty-six of the leading Yiddish critics, dramatists, novelists, and poets executed. Until then Yiddish had been the major language of Russia's three and a half million Jews. Before that night, the secret police, in January 1948, had murdered the great actor-manager of the Moscow Yiddish Theater, Solomon Mikhoels, while he was on a visit to Minsk. Less than a year later, on Christmas eve, the secret police arrested the Party's own man among Yiddish writers, Itsik Feffer, who was never heard from again. Others disappeared, usually in the middle of the night. Nusinov and Bergelson and Kvitko and Belenky. Mikhail Golodny was killed in the street by a state car. Of those who were murdered, the names of the most prominent writers were known. Thousands of others disappeared with them.

Later, during Khrushchev's reign, the story was told. The entire Jewish intelligentsia had, under Stalin, been given a secret trial. They had been charged with creating a bourgeois nationalist plot to transform the Crimea into a Jewish state that would serve as the base for an American invasion of the Soviet Union. Had Stalin actually believed the story? Who would ever know? The arrests and disappearances continued. On August 12, 1952, he ordered the twenty-six remaining major Yiddish writers arrested and shot.

Stalin had, in his madness, been logical. The existence of a nationality in the Soviet Union, a nationality whose historic roots were elsewhere, was intolerable to him. Forcible assimilation could best be achieved by cutting the nationality off from its history, culture, traditions, and language. Jewish schools, newspapers, publishing houses, theaters, and other institutions were abolished, and workers in them were sent to camps. To ensure that no revival would occur, the very source of culture—the creative and the knowledgeable leaders—were murdered.

Nathan read on, his ears filled with soft violin music and the voices of American tourists. He was angry with Rachel for being in Florida with Leah and Rivka—he was angry with himself for imagining her walking with them. In *Hope Against Hope*, the yellow sheet noted, Nadezhda Mandelstam told of what happened in the Kursk region, which had been famous for its nightingales. Nathan knew the story. The nightingales always learned to sing from certain older birds that were especially gifted. But the best songsters among these older birds were caught and put into cages and sold in the marketplace, at bird auctions. Then the young birds had no way of learning anymore. Thus, the famous Kursk school of nightingales was destroyed.

Nathan looked toward Michael. Michael had the envelope in his lap, the manuscript on top of the envelope. In the dim half-light of the darkened cabin, his eyes were bright and steady. His jaw was set firmly. He breathed in and out steadily, calmly, and he seemed as beautiful and determined and enraged as Nathan had ever seen him.

KEHILLA

"Where are we going, Poppa?"

My son, Noah, is bundled close to me in the cart, for warmth. "Nowhere," I answer him.

"But we can't be going nowhere if our horse is moving in front of us," he laughs. "You always say that to me—that we're going nowhere, when—"

"You sleep awhile," I say, and I kiss my fingertips and press them upon his eyelids. "Just sleep, *totela*. You worked so hard today—you played so beautifully."

Our horse Tsitsik splashes through ice-covered puddles, his hooves making their thin surfaces crackle. We are in the poor Jewish quarter now, and Noah looks down. He does not like to look at the houses of the poor Jews, at the beggars and children who, even now, when it is nighttime, come out and crowd around us and follow us, hoping we will have scraps of food for them. "Please tell me where we are going," he says again. "Please?"

"All right," I say, and I find a way to tell him the truth without telling him the truth. I tell him I must see a friend, but that I have promised my friend never to reveal who he is.

"Is your friend in danger?" Noah asks.

"Yes."

Noah sits up straight. "Then what if the police should see us visiting him? What if they should report us to the Kehilla? What if—?"

"Shh," I say to him, and I stroke his brow gently. "Shh. Not to worry," I say. "Yes, the police and the Kehilla are mighty and ever to be feared—the Kehilla more so than the police, alas—but it is very late and very dark, and your poppa is a careful man. If anybody should stop us, I will be full of stories, believe me."

"You're always full of stories, Poppa!" he says, and he snuggles next to me again, pulling the blanket to his chin. I look to see that his precious fingers are covered. "Nobody can tell stories the way you can—"

"When a poor man gets to eat a chicken—" I begin.

"—then one of them is sick," Noah finishes, sharing our joke.

"When it's time to send for the Angel of Death—" I say.

"—be sure to send a lazy man."

"Love is sweet," I say, "but tastes best with bread."

Noah laughs. "I like being alone with you, Poppa," he says. "In the middle of nowhere." He tugs on my arm and pleads with me for stories.

"All right," I say. "All right." I close my eyes for a moment, and then begin. "My father, Zanvel the book peddler, once told me of Reb Nachman of Bratislav—the Good-bye Rebbe he was called. Did I ever tell you about him?"

"Would you, Poppa? Please . . . ?"

I flick the reins and our horse and cart move slowly up the muddy road. "Reb Nachman was a widower," I begin, "and when he had, at last, given his youngest daughter away in marriage, he decided that he would leave Russia and journey to the land of Israel, to die there. And so he began saying his good-byes. He went from village to village, even to Burshtyn, my father told me, and in each village, when he would say good-bye to his old friends, and to new ones, they would ask things of him and he would accept donations. He was invited for dinner, he was given bags of food for his journey, he received money, he had his clothes mended, he had a place to sleep each night. In return, he promised to send earth from the land of Israel, to say a prayer at the grave of Rabbi Meir the miracle worker, to contact lost relatives, to chant at the Wailing Wall."

"And then—did he leave Russia and go to the land of Israel to die?" Noah asks, but even as his voice rises I see that his eyelids drop down, and I feel his body sag against my own.

"Reb Nachman wound up saying his good-byes for many years." I laugh and draw him closer to me. "This way of making a living by saying good-bye was regarded by Jews in those days as a perfectly respectable one . . ."

I tuck the blanket around Noah's legs. Our horse moves on, and I see that Noah is already fast asleep, and that I need tell him no more stories. I stroke his forehead and sing to myself, softly. I think of my grandfather and his friends, singing and laughing in our house one *Shabbos* afternoon during *shaleshudes,* while I sit on my father's lap—my happiest time—and I hear them talk about how delighted the good Tsar Alexander was to discover that his Jews called Napoleon *Napol Tippol*—the phrase from the Book of Esther—which, the tsar was told, meant "thou shalt surely fall."

Yet even in that peaceful moment far from home—even while we make our way out of Odessa, across frozen fields and ice-covered roads, even while I reach across and feel Noah's smooth brow beneath my gloved hand and find myself smiling because I see that he is, by his insistence and questioning, truly his father's son—even in that instant a weight falls suddenly upon my heart and I want to curse the Creator of the Universe for ever having let me be born into the world! For it is my very pride in my son that makes me fear—how prophetically!—that such an inheritance from me, such a desire to know the truth and to bring that truth to others, may yet prove to be not his blessing, but his curse.

Such fears I hide from him, even as I hide from him other thoughts and hopes and deeds—even as I hide from him the nature of our destination, and the contents of the small package delivered to me there. Later, while he sleeps, I hide the package behind me in the cart, inside an old violin whose back I have previously, for this purpose, removed. I am on my knees, burying the violin beneath bundles of candles and rags and books, when he stirs beside me and smiles up at me. "Are we home?" he asks, and he falls back to sleep before I can answer him.

When I was a small boy I wanted to be, it is true, not a book peddler like my father, but the writer of the books he sold. I dreamed of seeing him go from village to village, selling, along with the *Devotions of Sarah Bas Tovim*, the *Tsena Urena*, the *Kitzur Sheloh*, the *Kol Ba*, *The Shining Candelabrum*, *The Book of the Angel Raziel*, *The Chastening Rod* (which thrilled me most of all books, with its wondrous visions of the punishments awaiting us in Gehenna if we sinned greatly in this world), and along with the novels of Menasseh ben Porat and the great Abraham Mapu, books by his own son, Tsvi ben Zanvel Chaim! I longed for the day when he would set out from Burshtyn, his cart laden with copies of my first book, and I longed more for the day when he would return, his cart empty, his eyes shining with happiness and pride.

Like my father, I considered myself one of the *maskilim*—a follower of the enlightened writers of the Haskala movement—of Moses Mendelssohn and Joseph Perl and Isaac Baer Levinsohn. I wanted to be, not a despised *zhid*, but that great thing, a Man-and-a-Jew. And so I imagined that I would write tales that would inspire all those who read them to lift their bent backs and raise their downcast eyes and to become men at last—men who would walk through the streets of Russia and ride through its forests and journey across its countryside with their heads held high—men who would, in their new freedom, neither forsake their love of Torah, nor be slaves unto it.

I imagined learned men and wise Rebbes discussing my stories—stories about an enlightened young man from a small *shtetl* in the Pale, Nachman ben Tsvi, who, at great personal risk, journeys through Russia and Poland and into Germany in order to study in the new modern schools of Mendelssohn, where he becomes a great scholar and leader, after which he returns to Mother Russia, there to set up schools for the Jews. Eventually, by his wisdom and his strength, his gentleness and his courage, he becomes to the tsar as Joseph had been to the pharaoh—the second-in-command of the entire nation—and his Jews, free at last from ignorance and poverty, and from the two-edged sword that hung above them (the dreadful ukases of the tsar, and the backward rigidity of the Orthodox), thrive and prosper both as men and as Jews.

Too long had we crawled like the worms and vermin and lice and forked-tongued serpents the Gentiles believed we were! Too long had we accepted their views of ourselves! Too long had we hewn to superstitious ways of dress and vulgar modes of speech, hiding within our kaftans and our Yiddish! Too long had we avoided learning the foreign languages and new sciences of which the world was being made! We could not, my stories would teach the Jewish people, be a light unto the nations if we hid ourselves in the dark caves that were our ghettos and *shtetls.*

Often I would sit beside my father and dream such dreams, and while I listened to the steady clop of our horse's hooves and the squeaking of the cart's axle beneath us, I would imagine how those who today were ground into the mud by the wheel of oppression would, upon the morrow, when the wheel turned half-circle, be on top breathing free air! I would imagine how my stories would come to be known by every Jew in the Pale of Settlement, and how these Jews would come to bless me and call me their Savior. Then my father's eyes would shine with pride and he would recall those long rides we had taken together, and he would muse to himself: *To think—my child, in his silences, was drinking of wells that could bring forth such a glorious new life! To think—he seemed only a boy, and he was only a boy, yet within his small body there was growing a story and an idea that would change the world!*

Yet I never became that writer, or anything like him. I may have dreamt of salvation, but I was capable only of destruction. When our small hut was silent and I was but a few days old and my parents were asleep and I gurgled happily in my bed, Lilith must surely have been there, creeping into my dreams and corrupting me. My story is not, then, as I claimed earlier; the story of my loss, but of the pride that created and sustained that loss. I have, you see, only one story to tell, and have ever had one story to tell. Which story is the same one, no matter what disguises I put upon it, and which story is, such is my endless vanity, merely the story of my own worthless life.

There was, on the east wall of our home, next to the embroidered Mizrach, with its exotic landscape and its fabulous beasts, a small illustration in color, like those my father sold, of Abraham and Isaac. Isaac's face does not show in the picture. His neck is bared and his head bent and he is on his knees in front of a bundle of brambles, upon which he is to burn. Abraham stands over him, his knife raised, and in his frightened eyes, which I stared at for more hours than I could ever count, I used to see, may God forgive me, my own father's eyes when he would stare down at me sometimes as I feigned sleep. I would trick him by letting my eyelids rise enough to see him through the lashes, yet not enough so that he could know I was awake.

What pleasure it gave me to see the suffering in his eyes! To see the puzzlement! Isaac, I would often imagine, must—his face hidden from me—have been smiling into the brambles just as I was smiling inside my head. For he would have known that though his moment of death would last but an instant, yet would his father's anguish continue until the end of time.

Though we often talked and sometimes laughed together on our journeys, my father knew there was a part of me I kept secret from him, and he must have feared that in that secret part of me lay great danger. Though there were times when I yearned suddenly to bring peace to him—to throw my arms around his neck and tell him all that I was thinking and feeling, all that I understood about the hardships of his life and the vexations of his heart —yet something kept me silent. Whom God would sorely vex, he endows with abundant sense. In that, my father and I were like one another.

Often he would tell me that he had chosen the picture of Abraham and Isaac because it showed what man was like without God, while at the same time it also showed what man was like when he believed in God. It showed man as he was when he was about to lose everything, yet did not lose his faith in God. It showed what a valley of blood and tears this world would be without God's mercy. And it also demonstrated the trust that men could place in one another—for the beauty of the story, he said, was that such a moment could have occurred, in which a man was willing to sacrifice his most dearly beloved, and yet—after God had intervened and spared the two of them—they could live on together, more loving than ever.

But I did not believe him. I believed, instead, that he meant to frighten me with his own fears. He must have had dreams once also, I knew, dreams that were dead inside him, and I believed that he wished to lay these dead dreams to rest inside *my* soul, hoping thus to give himself some measure of peace.

I had lived, remember, and my brother had died, and whenever my father looked at me I knew that he was imagining his other son, grown to young manhood. Who can tell? Perhaps when I was remembering my mother slapping my brother at night, so that Lilith would not steal into his soul, I was really remembering the time Lilith stole into mine, and the blows I myself, when I was certain everybody else was asleep, had laid upon my brother's face.

Who shall live and who shall die? On Yom Kippur, our Day of Atonement, God inscribes us all in the Book of Life for the coming year, whether for joy or sorrow, for wealth or poverty, for good health or ill, for life or for death. But in my book He must have written, Thou shalt destroy and yet live to see thy destruction, to delight in it even as you burn in it. For if you think that I was only acting in the manner of all young brothers—jealous and fearful of losing my father's love and my mother's attentions—you would be wrong. There is, in the universe, an Evil Impulse and a Good Impulse that make war inside man for possession of his soul, and only the Holy One knows why it is that sometimes the Good wins out and sometimes the Evil.

Where, then, dear reader, was I journeying to that night, so many years ago, with my son, Noah—my darling Noah, dead now before his time. I was journeying to the village of Zaitsev, there to receive from my beloved friend, Reb Mordechai, copies of my poems—printed by him at great danger to his life—poems written to protest the evil and hypocrisy of the Kehilla. These poems I would place in the pockets of their coats, which coats hung outside the meeting room in the *Volost,* our town hall, while they met to find new ways to restrict us and to tax us and to enrich themselves. These poems I would, in the middle of the night, post upon the door of our *shul,* and the walls of the *cheder,* and the windows of the shops in our marketplace, and on the trees that surrounded our village.

There were at the time, by a decree of the government dating from October 27, 1836, only two Hebrew printing presses that were allowed to operate in all of Russia, these in the cities of Vilna and Zhitomir. And who dared to give these presses any words or poems or tales or books that were critical of the Chassidim or the Kehillim or—unthinkable thought—the evil Tsar Nicholas himself? For thirty years, only two Hebrew printing presses allowed to operate in all of Russia! Can you imagine that, my readers here in America—can you remember when it was so? Can you remember—or do you believe that when the Children of Israel went forth from Egypt, you were not there with them? Have your parents erased from your memory their old lives with your new lives? Have they made you forget already what happened only yesterday when we, the People of the Book, were denied our very life's blood—that freedom which to us is second to none? Who speaks of milk and honey when there is no water . . .

And do you also forget, you who may be as old as I am and who have made the same journey across the ocean, do you forget to tell your children the most shameful fact of all—that although the tsar himself may have issued the decree, yet it was Jews who enacted and enforced that decree! And in just such a way, alas, did Jews enact and enforce that decree of which my story is made—the dreaded cantonist *gzeyra* which sent Jewish boys into the tsar's army for twenty-five years' service! Yes—*it was Jews who sent other Jews, in chains, to serve Nicholas, and it was Jews who profited from doing so!* It was Jews with money and power who, by refusing to resist and to protest, enriched their own lives—and who maintained their positions of power by refusing to look away, or to ignore, or to succor, or to forgive, when we poor Jews risked our lives to do what they should have been doing. May they live forever with pearls around their necks and stones upon their hearts!

Rich or poor, strong or weak—how well I know—to be a Jew is no easy thing. True, there were members of the Kehilla who were good men—who saved young Jews, who disobeyed the tsar's edicts, who sometimes ransomed young lives with their worldly possessions. There were Jews who were merciful, yes—who sent twelve-year-old Jewish boys to the army instead of eighteen-year-olds, for the eighteen-year-olds already had wives and children! There were Jews who were merciful, yes—who sent off the poor and the weak and the ill, many of them no more than eight or nine years old, knowing that more than half these boys would die before they ever reached their destinations! There were Jews who were merciful, yes—who sent off the dull and the ignorant and the maimed, thereby hoping to save the sages of the future.

Evil choices! Foul reason! Despicable self-love! How can it ever be good that one man preys upon another for his own survival? And how much more loathsome when a man does so in the name of the community, in the name of some Higher Good? But these holy men of the Kehilla claimed that if they did not choose, the tsar and his soldiers and his police and his government agents would, and that that would be infinitely more horrible for us all. Better for Jews to choose Jews, they said. Perhaps. Who can know? But the answer to the question—what should a Jew do in such a situation—had long ago been given us by the great Maimonides, and I had printed this up also, to the great anger of the Kehilla, and had posted it and spread it where I could:

FELLOW JEWS! AWAKE AND LISTEN AND HEAR!

EYES HAVE THEY BUT THEY SEE NOT! EARS HAVE THEY BUT THEY HEAR NOT!

Here is what the great Moses Maimonides, physician and philosopher and author of A GUIDE TO THE PERPLEXED, ruled more than five centuries ago, in THE FUNDAMENTALS OF TORAH.

"IF THE PAGANS SHOULD TELL THE JEWS, 'GIVE US ONE OF YOURS AND WE SHALL KILL HIM, OTHERWISE WE SHALL KILL ALL OF YOU,' WE SHOULD ALL BE KILLED AND NOT A SINGLE JEWISH SOUL SHALL BE DELIVERED."

This is what your trusted friend ADON YID FREI reminds you of, oh exalted members of the Kehilla, and humble people of THE JEWISH COMMUNITY.

My friends! Weep, ye daughters of Zion, and remember! Only remember!

ADON YID FREI, A Free Jew ✡

Ah, what a noble thought lay in Maimonides' ruling—and what noble and good men would be needed to carry it out! Were there ever such men? And how many? How easy it was for me to judge before I myself had to choose. I was, in truth, like the man of whom it is said, He will never fall because he is already lying down. For only a few nights after I had posted these words . . . But come. Come and visit with me in my home. Come and enter just as that other visitor entered, and listen to what we said to one another, and you will see what a brave man I was when I too was trapped.

I am sitting at the kitchen table, on the meat bench, reading in the *Pirkay Avos*. Our candelabrum—the Sun of our home—is lit, so that I may see. Leah is at the stove, rendering goose fat into cracklings and humming to herself as we listen to Noah, behind the wood partition which divides our house in two, practicing his violin. This, for me, is happiness—to be drinking in the sounds and fragrances and signs of knowledge and family and music. As the rabbis say, Who is the wealthy man?—he who is content with his portion in life.

But then there is a knock at the door and I answer it. It is Mirsky—Avrahom Dov Mirsky—my wife's cousin, the head of the Kehilla of Burshtyn, and I know at once, from his broad smile and his outstretched hand, that he means to do me harm. His hand is before me, and I stare at it—at the four fingers, at the stub of a middle finger that seems especially hideous to me tonight—but I take this hand with my own and I invite him in and Leah kisses him and asks of his wife and daughters and says how honored she is to receive him. She offers him tea and honey cake. He takes off his *streimel*—his fur-trimmed hat—and puts on a black *yarmulke*.

"Ah—goose cracklings, am I right?" he says. "How I adore the odors of frying goose fat and onions! They remind me of my childhood, Leah . . ."

"What you adore, Avrahom," I say, "is that such odors are in our kitchen and not yours. What you adore is the distance, in wealth and importance, that you have traveled since you were a child and your family was poor like ours."

Mirsky smiles. "Your love for me is touching," he says.

Leah tells her cousin that I am not myself of late, that I am worried for my friends and for the sons of my friends, because of the *gzeyra*. Five boys will be chosen this week. Mirsky tells her that he enjoys my small barbs. Without my words, he says, his life would be dull. Like *arbus* without pepper. Leah says she will get Noah, but Mirsky puts a hand on her arm and a finger to his lips. "Like the music of the angels!" he whispers. "Let me listen. Only let me listen!" Mirsky tells us of the honor our son brings to Burshtyn. When Mirsky goes to Odessa on business, he tells us, they say to him, "Mirsky of Burshtyn? Ah, but is that not where the boy with the golden fingers who can make a violin sing like the sweetest human voice—is that not where he comes from also?" And he tells us how proud he is to call Noah family.

I say nothing, but I hate him more than ever—for being able to partake in this way of the gifts that my son gives to the world, for being able to make what is mine his. Leah returns to the stove and stirs the goose fat. From a ring that hangs from the ceiling she takes an iron pan, in which she kindles dry sticks, to give us more light. Mirsky sips his tea and sighs. In the silence, Noah's music seems louder and more insistent.

For years Mirsky has been selling liquor to the peasants through his numerous Jewish agents. This year, he tells us, he is also investing in clothing mills that manufacture hats and gloves. He has no reason to hide from us the dangers involved. Now that the tsar has expelled to the interior of the country all Jews who live within fifty *versts* of the frontier, to prevent smuggling, his profits dwindle quickly. Those who continue to smuggle goods for him demand higher fees, the authorities demand more in bribes, the tax collector squeezes him dry, and the landlords to whose serfs he sells his goods demand higher and higher sums of money. And what does he get in return? Heartache and ingratitude! The peasants hate him because he has stopped supplying them their liquor, and they hate him because he has ceased to grant credit, and they hate him because his prices are so high, and they hate him because he is a Jew.

"In truth, *chaver,*" he says, placing a hand upon my sleeve, "I am like a poor grain of wheat being squeezed between the millstones of the aristocracy and the peasants. Everything is taken from me and my life is always in danger. Do you understand?"

"I understand," I say.

"And then, when I return to my village, which I call home, what do I find? That those to whom I have given the fruits of my hard life, those to whom I dedicate myself—my family and my fellow Jews—I find that they too are rising up against me. Do you understand?"

I say nothing. Leah does not move. Mirsky leans forward so that his nose almost touches mine. "Ah, Tsvi—sometimes I think you are the only one in our whole village who can understand what my life is like. Do you know why?"

"Tell me," I say.

"Because your life too is full of danger." He draws back and smiles. "Tsvi, Tsvi—my brother, my friend—are you afraid of me?"

"No."

He nods. "Well, you are right. You need not be afraid of me. I would do anything to save a member of my family from harm." He leans forward again and whispers, so that Leah cannot hear. "But you are in danger, Tsvi—and not only you, but—why I am here—your son, Noah, is in danger!"

I must struggle to hold the raging words from rolling off my tongue. "I do not understand," I say. "I am only a poor book peddler. I am—"

"Ts-ts-ts-ts . . ." he says, and his voice is playful. "With me you will make a joke, yes?" He glances at Leah, then bends toward me and whispers again. "Your son's life is in grave danger," he says. "I have warned you." Then his voice rises, so she can hear what he says. "How I envy you, Tsvi, to have a son! I, who have three daughters—may they marry scholars and live to have sons themselves—I envy you the pride you take in your beloved son. Ah, what it would be to lose such a son, I, having none, can imagine."

He wipes his mouth with a lace handkerchief that he takes from the sleeve of his caftan, and turns to Leah. "Another glass tea, Leah darling," he says. "And then I have some business to discuss with Tsvi."

Leah brings him tea, and leaves. Mirsky drinks. "Men like us—" he says "—men who are not afraid of the world, *chaver,* men who are not afraid to risk great dangers if what they seek to gain is worthy of these dangers—we can understand one another." I lower my eyes, and he speaks with kindness. "Ah, Tsvi, my cousin—do not flatter me with your silence, but let me hear what is in your heart and then I will tell you what is in mine, for my greatest desire—my reason for visiting with you alone—is to help you save your son."

"Tell me," I say.

Mirsky looks around, as if to others. "He speaks, my friends, did you hear? He speaks—and he asks me to tell him of the dread paper which I hold in my pocket. You are my witnesses before God. He speaks. 'Tell me,' he says."

I rise and grip the soft fur of his collar. "Tell me!" I demand. "Tell me and be done with it. Only tell me!"

"Shh," he says, and he takes my hands gently and removes them. I stare at his misshapen hand. I imagine him as a boy, standing in his father's slaughterhouse and holding the bleeding stump in the air. He has a proud smile on his face. While others scream and shout and scurry about, he smiles and endures the pain. I recall the accounts of his bravery. *He is not human!* the men cried. *He is not a boy!* . . . "Not to scare Leah and the child. I told you before—there is no danger. I am your friend, am I not? What befalls all Jews will befall each Jew! Would I let harm come to my cousin Leah? Would I let the milk she gave to Noah—who gives to me such *nachas*—would I let it curdle and have been given in vain? You do not know me, Tsvi Toporofsky. I am not an evil man."

"You have what you want in life, Avrahom," I say. "You should be content. Now tell me. Only tell me. And then—"

"Here," he says, and he takes a paper from his pocket. "You are a scribe and a book peddler, Tsvi. You read books I would not dream of reading, do you not?" He laughs at his joke. "You and your beloved *maskilim*—your scholars of this so-called Enlightenment! You and your dreams of free and modern men! You read, do you not? Then read this."

"To read is to know," I say, looking away. "I will not read. You will not be the one to force me to be the one who—"

"Who what—?" He waits. Beneath the stove, the chickens squawk and then are silent. "Ah—" Mirsky says. "Now I am understanding what you fear. But look, Tsvi—this is not what you think it is. This is something I bring you to read that is dear to your heart. It is only a poem."

"It is only a poem," I say.

I raise my eyes and take the paper from his hand. It is not what I had feared, but it is just as bad. It is the paper I have posted on the door of his house the night before. He asks me to read the poem to him, but I refuse. "See, my friends?" he says, gesturing to the empty room. "See how grown men are frightened of reading mere words from a piece of paper? I am criticized and hated and reviled behind my back—but when it comes to doing, I am the only one with the courage to—" He breaks off. "Ach! But why should I sing my own praises, when in our midst is a poet who does me honor?" He laughs. "Please read to me, my cousin. You are a peddler of books and poems, are you not? Do not you followers of the Haskala—you enlightened members of the community—do not you read novels and poems along with your Talmud? Read! Please. Read and tell me what you think."

"I do not think about such things, Avrahom. Here in Burshtyn, you in your generosity, you do such thinking for all of us."

"Read!" he commands.

I look at the paper, and I read the familiar words, silently.

THE WOLF OF BURSHTYN

There was once a wolf unlike the others
For he preyed upon his brothers
(He preyed on others, it is true
But most of all he preyed on Jew!)
The leader of his pack, this beast
Took all from them for his own feast.
He killed young cubs to glut his lust.
There were no wolves who gave him trust!
And yet the wolves were sore afraid
To kill this wolf who suffering made.
They could not commit an evil deed—
To do so went against their creed.
But a wise old wolf among them said,
"He is a wolf, it may be true,
Still, there is this that we can do.
We can refuse to him to give
The honor and food that let him live."
And that is the beginning! Oh my Jews!
WE ARE SAVED IF WE REFUSE!

ADON YID FREI, A Free Jew ✡

I hand the paper back to him, but I say nothing. "I am no scholar of poetry," Mirsky says, "but the work of King Solomon or Judah Halevi this is not." He laughs. "Listen, Tsvi—do you think I am offended by what you say in this poem?"

"I already knew that nothing could offend you, Avrahom."

"I know that I am the one who saves Jews," he continues, ignoring my remark. "I know that I am the one—and not you—who sees to it that we get enough food in the winter, and that our best students do not go off to die in the far reaches of Siberia. Do you think I am offended by what you say? By what you say, never!" He goes to the stove, crumples my poem, and sets it on fire in the iron pan. He returns. "But I am hurt that you should want to hurt me, your wife's cousin. That is what offends me, and what I would wish changed. I would like you to soften your heart toward me, Tsvi, do you understand? That is all I ask."

"Never," I whisper.

He inclines his head toward me and cups his hand around his ear. "Tell me what I hear?"

"Never," I repeat. "Punish me as you wish—you have the power, if you can prove that I am the author of this verse—but do not ask me to love you. That I cannot give."

"Ah, but you underestimate your own heart," he replies. "Look at me, a man you despise—did I want you to marry my darling Leah? I said never also, remember? But have I not come to accept you, even while you have come to reject me? There we have a true poem, my friend—a poem of how God can work to soften our hearts and incline us toward loving-kindness, as the rabbis teach."

"Never," I say again.

"You may notice that I am not even angry," he says. "Because why? I will tell you why, my great wise man. Because you are the evil man in our village, that is why. Because you are opening gates which you do not know how to close!" He stands and speaks with great bubbling sounds, like a crown rabbi, appointed to rule according to the law of man. "I am not the ignorant man you believe me to be," he proclaims. "Unlike you I read in books with which I disagree, and I can tell you that I have read more than the poems and complaints of one Adon Yid Frei. I have read those afflicted with your disease, my friend—a disease of Enlightenment! I have read your Mendelssohn and your Porat and your Mapu. And do you know what I think of them?" He spits on the floor, and grinds the spit into the earth with his boot. "That is what I think of them. They want us to be men, they say—yet they want us to give up our caftans and our *streimels* and our very *mamma-loshen*—our beloved Yiddish! They are the wolves, my friend—

they are the wolves, coming into our village when the rivers are frozen, to steal our life's blood. They want us to read the word of God, the Holy Torah, in German and in Russian and in other languages! They want us to study what others study—science and mathematics! They want—" He stops. "Pheh on all that. Tell me, Tsvi, when we were all present at Sinai, did God speak to Moses in German? Answer me that, my modern scholar! Answer me that—"

I say nothing. "Your silence is your grave," he says. "But why do I even tell you these things which I know that you know, just as your *luftmensch* of a father knew them before you. Hah! Maybe he was such a free and strong man that he was the one who gave you to suck at his breast—and so, in this way, passed on his beliefs to you." He enjoys his vulgar joke. It is ever the same, I think. God loves the poor, but he helps the rich. Mirsky comes to me and breathes upon me. I feel faint. "They would see us abandon everything, my friend, don't you see? Our candy with our Aleph-Beth, and then our Yiddish and our caftans and our sidelocks and our fringed undergarments . . . and soon our Sabbath! Soon—"

"Never!" I shout. *"Never!* How you change things! How you distort to suit your own foul ends. That is what you *wish* to believe, Avrahom—to soothe your evil conscience. That is—"

"And our Sabbath!" Mirsky continues, pounding the table with his fist, inspired by my reply. From the other side of the wall I hear Leah burst into tears. "You will see. Because why do I say this and know this? Because think about it. They want nothing less than what the evil tsar—and I will call him that too, to your face, and I will fear nothing!—what Nicholas the First, the second Haman!—wants from us. Think about it. He too would like us to abandon our caftans and our Yiddish and our *shtetls*. He too would like us to learn Russian and to send our children to his Russian schools and—"

"For different reasons," I object. "For different reasons."

"He takes our young boys into the army so that they will abandon their ancient heritage, does he not? Do we not all weep when we think of what happened at Kazan—when Nicholas himself was promised a mass baptism of Jewish soldiers, and saw instead three hundred of our own young men throw themselves into the Volga and drown? Do you forget already, my friend?" He shakes a finger at me. "We do not forget, and we weep, all of us who are not afflicted with your disease. A disease of Enlightenment!"

"I weep also," I say softly. "And I remember Zion." Why should I hold my tongue any longer? "But you and your friends know only how to kiss the hem of the tsar's garments," I declare. "You prey upon our love of Torah to keep us poor, while to enrich yourselves you bow down to idols! You could refuse, Avrahom," I say. "Don't you see? You could refuse! If all of you refused to do the tsar's work for him, then—"

"Then what?" he says, and he laughs. "Ah, Tsvi, how little you understand of the world's ways, of the power that rules us all. Even now, when your only son may be . . ." He shakes his head. "How little you understand."

"Then I am blessed, Avrahom, to be living in such ignorance."

He clicks at me with his tongue. "The tsar takes our sons into the army so that they will abandon their ancient heritage, does he not? He offers them money if they convert to his Christianity, does he not? What you do not want to see, my friend, is that the tsar is afraid of men like me." He glares at me, prouder than ever. "There is the joke on you! The tsar is afraid of me because of who I am and what I do. Do you hear me? Because of what I *do*! As they say, my brave *maskil*, if you cannot bite you should not show your teeth."

"And as my father said," I reply, "if the rich could hire others to die for them, the poor could earn a good living."

"You are a very clever fool, Tsvi. Very clever and very foolish." He laughs at me. "But I am a Jew and I am a man—and you are the worm and the coward! The tsar wants to destroy the Kehilla, just as you do—but you cannot and he cannot. For his government needs the money and the wisdom of Jews like myself. If he destroys the Kehilla, how will he get the taxes we have kept from him? How will he get the loans from foreign nations—from our Jewish brothers in Jewish banks—that he so desperately needs? Answer me that."

I say nothing. What good are words? Mirsky uses his power over the tsar so that through him the tsar may use it over us. Mirsky sits, his eyes triumphant. "Oh, your books are full of rational schemes, Tsvi, and of logical arguments—but one does not change a way of life that is in our blood with theories and logic. A Jew is a Jew—and to tempt a Jew by telling him he can be a man like any other is to be more cruel than I could ever be. Men like you want only what the government wants. To convert us and assimilate us and destroy us. Hah! Do you think that if you begin to dress like a *goy*, the tsar will accept you as if you were a man?"

He laughs until the tears are rolling down his cheeks. "What a rich joke that is!" he cries. Then his mood changes and his tears are of a different kind. He pounds his chest with his fist, as if he is in *shul* on Yom Kippur.

"Do you think my heart does not break in two when I must tear a young boy from his mother's breast? Do you think I am made of stone? But if I did not do it, *they* would come and do it—they would take away our very best and wisest. Do you think I do not know that I come as a thief to families and that they despise me even as you do? But let me be despised, I say. History and God will be my Judge!"

He holds his hands aloft, in front of the candelabrum's flames. "Yes, these hands are full of Jewish blood, just as your wolf's mouth is full of the blood and flesh of his own kind—but in my heart I know that someday the Jewish people will bless me! Men like you know only how to set down clever words—and not even so clever. Ah, how you love to condemn men like me, not being in my place! You think and you write and you whine and you scurry about in the darkness, laying schemes and plans—but you are incapable of *acting*, my dear King Solomon. That is the difference."

"Sometimes," I say, "it is better not to act. It is better to refuse."

He is whispering again, his face close to mine. "You are cowards, all of you. You are cowards who hide behind words and theories and false names. When I issue decrees, Tsvi, my name is upon them, in the name of the community. I am the one who must answer to the people, and to the government, and to the Holy One, Blessed Be His Name." He sits and takes from his pocket another piece of paper. "Now then will we see if your words are real, or if they are like the wind that passes over us, without even stirring the grass. Now then will I prove to you your weakness and the truth of all that I have been saying. Now then will you have to bear in your heart all that I must bear every day of my life—all that you despise me for."

I know what the paper is, and I tremble. I pray unto the Lord to grant me strength and to save me from my own iniquity. I reach for the paper, and Mirsky pulls it back. "But first, Tsvi, before I give this into your hands," he says, "and before I ask Leah and Noah to witness what we say to one another, I beg you to give yourself a chance for life. Do you hear me? I beg you. In my heart, I am on my knees before you, asking you to think of others before you think of yourself. Let bygones be bygones, is what I say. I love you, Tsvi, my cousin, did you know that? I love you like a brother, more so for your enmity against me. For you have made me question what I do and you have made me find the answer I have given to you. You are, you see, the one who has come to bless my life."

"May God forgive me."

He closes his eyes and hums to himself, and in my mind's eye I see myself as a boy, running to the prayer house on a fast day, carrying the little bundle of food that my mother has given me, and I remember listening to our fathers singing and chanting and arguing, while I share the food in that bundle, the bread and herrings and onions, with Mirsky.

"We were boys together," I say.

He puts his arm around me, even as he begins to put the piece of paper back into his pocket. His eyes are moist. "Listen to me, Tsvi. I have power. I can arrange anything. Let me be your friend, all right? There is no need for you to read this second piece of paper. As they say, a wise man hears one word and understands two. There is no need for you to read this second piece of paper . . . *if* you can soften your heart toward me. *Rachmanos*, Tvsi. *Rachmanos*. Let us forgive one another for the hurts we have brought to one another. Let us be one family again."

"What do you wish of me?" I ask.

"Only a small thing," he says. "A small thing. So small . . . and yet to me so valuable. But when we lose the most precious pearl we search for it with a poor candle, do we not?" He smiles. "I ask only this, Tsvi, for it hurts me as only family can hurt family when they quarrel and withhold their love—I ask only that you give me your solemn promise that this Adon Yid Frei will cease his child's play. I ask only this, and—"

"Never," I say, but quietly, and I draw back, startled, even before he pulls away from me, as if I am the one who is stunned by the word which has come from my mouth, as if that word has struck me.

"What do I hear?" he asks.

"Never!" comes the word again, and with that one word my fate and the fate of my child and the fate of my children's children is sealed forever, until the end of time and the coming of the Messiah.

But Mirsky is not even angry. "It is not so much that I ask," he says, his eyes closed, "yet you are not enough of a man to give it. You sin greatly, my friend, to put yourself above the needs of your family—to put the thoughts of your small mind above the health of the community. Your disease makes my heart heavy."

He shakes his head from side to side, and then he opens his eyes and smiles at me, happier than I have ever before seen him. "Then we will have to see what kind of man you truly are," he says, and he calls for Leah and Noah to come into the room. I cannot speak. I take them to me and hold them in my arms, but I am not strong enough to give them the comfort they will need. Leah is crying, her face against my chest. Mirsky withdraws the paper from his pocket once more. "My darling Leah, my precious Noah, I must be the one to tell you that I have been unable to prevent what had to be." He unfolds the paper and reads: " 'For offenses against the Jewish community of Burshtyn, and by the power given the Kehilla to draft at any time by verdict any Jew who is guilty of irregularity in the payment of taxes, or of vagrancy, or of any offense not tolerated in the community, I, Avrahom Dov Mirsky, leader of the Kehilla, in the name of the Kehilla, order that Tsvi Toporofsky, the book peddler, give up on the third day of Kislev next, his only son, Noah, for service in the Army of the Most Supreme and Exalted Tsar Nicholas I, Ruler of Russia and of—' "

The cry that breaks from Leah's chest is so terrible I fear she will send herself straight to the grave. I try to hold her, but she thrashes about like a wounded lamb. Mirsky reaches toward her. "My darling cousin," he pleads. "Do not despair and grieve before the day is over, for I have a plan! Please—please listen to me! Listen to your loving cousin! All is not lost! Your Noah may yet be spared! Do you hear what I say?"

"Tell us," I say, but I dare not look into my son's eyes.

Leah has left me and is on her knees before her cousin, her face upon his lap, her tears flowing freely into his coat. "Ah, how you misunderstand me," Mirsky says, as if pitying me. He strokes my wife's face and looks at me. "Do you think I would come here to tear my cousin's only son from her bosom? I am not an evil man, Tsvi. But you will see. Perhaps it is better that you refused my wish, for now you will come to understand just what my life is like." He reaches toward us with his right hand. The stump, where his middle finger once was, seems to glow. "Come to me, Noah," he says. "Come to your Uncle Avrahom and let me tell you how you may yet be saved."

Noah presses closer to me and I hold him. "Tell us," I say. "Only tell us."

"The son is like the father, I see," Mirsky says. "So be it. But I pray that he may be spared his father's foolishness." Mirsky looks at Noah. "Do you think the Kehilla wishes to take our best young men and send them into misery and death? Your father knows as well as I how hard we have worked to save only sons such as you, to save—"

"Do not believe him," I say to Noah. "He who has the whip in hand uses it," I declare, "and never stops to think that his own back was beaten just yesterday, and with the same weapon! I spit on you, Mirsky!"

"Ah Tsvi," he says, smiling. "You would not speak to me that way if you loved me."

"I could love you if you were dead," I say. His smile broadens, as if he is pleased to see that I have not lost my tongue. "A fat belly and a fat wallet protect you from memory—from your own and from the memory borne by others!"

"See how your father misunderstands me still," Mirsky says. "How he will say anything to protect his wounded pride—how he will sacrifice anything, even at the final moment, to preserve his madness and his foolishness." He laughs and turns his eyes to Noah. "As my father used to say—a fool can grow without rain. Your father is the fool, my child—it is he who has visited the evil I bring into your home upon his own head, by the writing of Adon Yid Frei. But come. Come to me, my son—come to me, Noah. Come and give your Uncle Avrahom a kiss. Come, my child—"

Noah does not move. He looks up at me. "Poppa?" he asks. "Will I be able to take my violin with me into the army?" And at this—hearing his sweet and awful question—Leah shrieks again and begins to tear at her hair.

"But I have come to *save* your son!" Mirsky cries, pulling at her hands, trying to restrain her. "Listen to my words. I have come to save your son. If you believe your cousin would come to you with only bad news, you do not know him. Here. I will prove it. Here—!"

From his coat he pulls out a small sack, which he casts upon the table. Money spills from it. Leah stares. "Tell us," I say.

"Tell you what? There is nothing to tell. That is my gift to you," Mirsky says. "I know you are poor, and so I give to you this money. It is my gift to you, Tsvi, and I ask nothing in return. See then how you misjudge me! A gift!"

"Tell us more," I say.

"A gift which you may keep—or return. The choice is yours."

I pick up the sack and the coins which have spilled from it, and I start to return them to Mirsky, but he raises his hand to stop me. "Ah, but if you give the gift back to me I will use it to save your son. Do you see? There is your choice! There is my plan! For the money that you now give to me I can pay to have another boy—one not so gifted as your Noah, one from a family without a relative such as me—sent in his place. That power I have."

"You are an evil man," I say.

He smiles at me. "And you are better?" he asks.

Leah turns to me, her eyes wild with fear. Noah hugs me tightly, about the waist, and he looks past Mirsky, to the east wall. He says nothing, yet I feel by the pressure of his small precious hands upon my own that he has chosen to put his faith in me, that he will abide by any decision I make.

But how can I give up my only son, condemned for the sins of the father?

I think for a brief moment of bowing my head and begging Mirsky's forgiveness, of telling him that Adon Yid Frei will be forever silent. But there is no need. The deed is already done. I will never have to beg. I will never have to go down upon my knees. *Never!* The Kehilla has acted. Adon Yid Frei is dead already. And even if Mirsky takes back the dread *gzeyra* he will still have to send another boy in Noah's place, as he has planned to do from the beginning.

"You are the true coward," I say. "You are the one who cannot bear the truth. Yes, Avrahom, you must make difficult choices—evil choices—but I see now that all you have wanted is that the act, for this one time, be by *my* hand. All you have wanted is for me to choose—to seem to choose."

"To *seem* to choose?" He laughs again. "How you play with words, Tsvi. Don't you see that sometimes, no matter what we do or how we choose, we cannot remain innocent? Don't you see that sometimes, and especially for Jews, all choices are evil choices?"

I place the sack of money in Mirsky's hands. Leah falls upon me, wetting my face with kisses. She is on her knees, kissing Mirsky's hands, and then she and Noah are clasped together, weeping. I sit and feel nothing at all.

Mirsky tells me that I have, at last, done the right thing. I have acted as all fathers would act. I am not so different from other men. I will be able to understand him better now—what the anguish of his life is—and we will become like brothers. I ask him to leave my home. Leah is showering blessings upon the three of us. Mirsky is making Noah get his violin, and while Noah plays for us, Mirsky reminds us of what the rabbis say, that the man who takes from the world a single life is like the man who has murdered all men until the end of time. But I have saved a life, and now Mirsky promises me that he will have the *khappers* choose a strong young Jew who will be able to survive. He gives me his word. And to spare us all, he will never reveal to us, of the new group he must send from our village, the name of the boy or the family. This burden he will take upon his own head, for us. He caresses Leah and tells her how she can see now that he never would have come to our house with only the evil order. He would never be a man to open gates that he could not close.

"You are the one who uses words with cleverness, Avrahom," I say. "I pray that the Lord may visit upon you the evil that you visit upon others."

"No!" Leah cries. "Please, Tsvi—"

"You are right, that the act is by my hand now. You are right that sometimes all choices are evil choices," I say. I move closer to him. "But someday we Jews will not live like slaves."

He moves to the door. "And when that day comes, my friend, I will be Moses and you—with your words—you will be Aaron, yes?" He opens the door. He smiles. "And then we will lead our people to the promised land, yes?"

"Someday we will be free," I say. "Someday we will live like men."

"On the day upon which, as they say, the whole world will be Jewish, yes?" He walks out, into the night. "Ah Tsvi, what a rich joke that is. What a rich joke . . ."

He laughs in my face, and neither Leah nor Noah can understand the meaning of his laughter. So many Hamans, I think, but only one Purim. I hear his laughter in the darkness. I can no longer see him. My decision, I know, is already made. I will journey to Odessa and I will make the arrangements for us to leave Burshtyn. By morning the whole village will know of what happened between us this night, and of my decision. If I cannot get the money from Odessa, from wealthy Jews who wish to further Noah's career, then I will turn to Mirsky and he will, for the rejoicing of his foul heart, give me the money and help to make the arrangements. We will go to America. I know this even before I close the door.

This, then, is how, in a brief instant, I lost everything. A trap had been set for me by an evil man, it is true, but the trap that was locked inside me, that would not allow me, even when I knew my son's life was in danger, to bury my pride and let me be, for an instant, humble and human—as distasteful as this was to me—ah, but that trap was the deadly one, and snared inside it I never escaped. I loved my pride as if it were my child.

I was in this, I have often thought, like a mother with a small child, one among many, which child has an incurable illness that enfeebles it, yet does not kill it. And so the mother travels from town to town and from doctor to doctor and from Rebbe to Rebbe, hoping that her child, who can neither walk nor talk nor think nor eat like other children, may yet be visited by a miracle.

How swiftly the mother grows old, loving her child and caring for it and worrying over it, though the child cannot respond to her. *My child is alive, my child is dead!* the mother cries out. *My child is alive, my child is dead!* And neither the fact of her other children, nor the prayers from the Rebbes, nor the love from her family, can ever comfort her. Only when her sick child is at last buried in the ground and she can, as is the custom, rend her garments and tear her hair, does her soul find a portion of peace in this world. Only then, broken and spent, can she accept the love and comfort of those near to her, of those from whom she has wanted, for all these years, to hide.

Just so is it with me. The child born into the world from my seed is dead, and I can live with that loss. But the evil and misshapen force inside me that caused his death and that caused me to survive after him—ah, but that is the demon I have been afraid most of all to lose. That is the sick child—the Evil Impulse—I have given a home to within my bosom. And, having given it a home there, I have come to believe that, just as I once gave life to it, so it now gives life to me.

Who can know? Perhaps if I had chosen otherwise—if I had had the strength not to be less proud, but to be more proud—perhaps if I had followed my pride to the end of its road and had not weakened and allowed Mirsky to save my Noah with his money, perhaps . . .

But see how I dissemble still. How I am incapable of changing the evil and self-serving nature that was ever mine. How I seek, even now, to believe that it was the goodness in my love for my son that was the true source of my act. Perhaps if I had defied Mirsky, as I urged others to, and had allowed my son to be punished for my offense, they would all be alive today—my Noah, his family, and their murderer—the boy Mendel, whose name I know now, and who for more than twenty-five years nurtured in his heart a dream brighter and more passionate than any I ever possessed—a dream of vengeance that sustained him and enabled him to survive, until, free at last from his bondage, he could follow us to America . . . Perhaps. But if I had been a man capable of giving up his only son for the offense I had committed against Mirsky, then I ask you what . . .

◇ 10 ◇

NATHAN STOOD IN RED SQUARE AND WATCHED THE OLD WOMEN WATER down the cobblestones. The women wore white aprons and black boots. They used twig brooms. They emptied the urns that were implanted in the sidewalks. Nathan could see the clock on the Spassky Tower, above the Kremlin walls. It was ten minutes past midnight. He looked beyond the old women, to the serrated spirals and onion domes of Saint Basil's Cathedral. The air was fresh and clear. The night was beautiful. Where was Michael?

Nathan turned. In Florida, at this hour, he knew, Rachel would be eating her breakfast with Leah and Raymond. On Long Island, Ruth would be getting Miriam and Aaron ready for school. Nathan stared at the squadrons of old women. He marveled at their energy. He felt very cold. He imagined that Nachman was standing beside him, watching.

Did I ever tell you the story of the two old men who sell religious medals in front of the Catholic church in Brooklyn?

I'm listening.

One of them looks a little like you, Nathan. Very handsome and successful-looking—a little bit shaygetz—and he says good morning to all the people as they come out of church and he wishes them a good week and he hopes all their prayers are answered.

His medals sell.

Of course. And the other man is more like me—he has sad Jewish eyes and he doesn't dress so well and he mutters in Yiddish and when people pass him by without buying, he curses them with the evil eye.

So that the beautiful goyim begin to know him and to curse back at him each Sunday morning when they come from church—and they take to buying from the handsome old Jew, is that what you were going to tell me?

Exactly. And one of the goyim is especially angry with the dirty old Jew, and every Sunday he gives him a lecture on why he remains poor and unsuccessful by pointing to the other Jew, across the square, whose business is flourishing. But the old Jew spits and curses the Catholic. *And the* Catholic *man stalks away and buys a dozen medals from the nice old Jew. He calls the other Jew crazy.*

And then, a few minutes after he leaves, when all the people are gone and the street is very quiet, the dirty old Jew turns to the handsome old Jew and he says—

—Nu, Moishe, so now they're *going to tell* us *how to make a living?*

The crowd laughed. "Come," Gronsky said, touching Nathan's arm. "We can walk now. It's the right time, I believe."

"But Michael—" Nathan said.

Gronsky pointed to their right. "Later," he said. Michael stood next to Sonya, their Intourist guide. Sonya had short blonde hair, cut in bangs straight across her forehead. She was in her mid-twenties. Her arm was hooked inside Michael's arm and she was leaning against him. Michael had organized this sightseeing expedition. He had been the one to rouse the other Americans from their rooms, so that they could come and watch the old women working at midnight. "Come," Gronsky said again. "It's time."

Michael's bearded head towered above those of the other tourists. He wore a fur hat he had bought in a Beryozka store. He was smiling and pointing to one of the old women. Sonya took his camera. Michael snatched a broom from the old woman and began sweeping the street. The Americans laughed. The old woman wagged a finger at Michael. He bent down and spoke to her in Russian. She laughed. He kissed her cheek. She beamed. Sonya took a photograph of the old woman dusting Michael's coat with her broom.

Nathan turned away. He felt very tired, very weak. He did not understand what was happening, or why he was there. He wished that Rachel were with him. "All right," he said. "I'll come."

They began to walk away from the others. "There are some people who have been most eager to meet you," Gronsky said softly.

"Yes," Nathan said.

"I would have arranged things sooner, but it seemed safer this way—safer for you, my good friend—if we waited until you had only a few days left. In case there were—well—complications, let us say. The KGB was most interested in you during your first few days here. I can tell you that much."

"Yes," Nathan said.

"Not for your book, which, thanks in good part to my own efforts, they admire, and not for your nephew, whom they are considering in his own right, but for your work in Israel, with the United Israel Appeal."

Nathan thought of the Arab beggars in the streets of Jerusalem, their heads covered with white *keffiyehs* that were held down by colored cords. He saw himself at Lod Airport, sitting and waiting for a plane to take him to New York. Nathan enjoyed the sound of Gronsky's thin, nasal voice. Gronsky spoke with a marked British accent. He never spoke ungrammatically. His mannerisms—his clipped way of talking, the affected way he lit and smoked his cigarettes, his nervous laugh—all seemed very British to Nathan, very practiced, as if Gronsky had trained himself by watching old English movies.

He walked with Gronsky toward the Moscow River. In the floodlit square, the old women worked on relentlessly. Nathan saw his mother, on her knees, scrubbing the kitchen floor. He saw his father yelling at him, for not helping his mother. Did he think only of himself? His mother smiled. Nachman got down on all fours, and began scrubbing. The brightly painted domes of Saint Basil's were now above them, but Nathan did not look up. Napoleon had considered the cathedral a monstrosity and had wanted it destroyed. He had stabled his horses in its chapels. Ivan the Terrible, who had had the cathedral built to commemorate the conquest of Kazan, had, when the building was completed, put out the eyes of the architect Barma, so that Barma would never be able to duplicate his creation. Or so, Sonya said, the legend went. Nathan thought of Tolstoy's blind storyteller, talking in Russian to Tolstoy's grandmother. Nathan saw himself in bed, reading to Nachman. He saw Nachman smiling happily.

Everything Nathan had been, was, and was to become, had somehow been caught up in the one small book he had written over forty years before, when he was a young man. How could it be, he wondered. He walked with Gronsky, from the square and toward the Moskvoretsky Bridge. He looked down at the river and imagined that he could see his father's books floating there. Gronsky stopped and looked back. Gronsky's right sleeve, where there was no arm, was tucked into his coat pocket. He had lost his arm during the siege of Leningrad. Gronsky pointed to the round platform of white stone, in front of Saint Basil's. Did Nathan know that it was from this platform that the tsar's edicts—including the cantonist *gzeyra* of Nathan's tale—had been issued? Nathan nodded. On their first day in Moscow Sonya had told them about the platform. It was called the Place of the Skull. Upon it men and women had been hung and beheaded and whipped to death and scalded with boiling water. Traitors had had hot molten lead poured down their throats.

Nathan stared at the empty sleeve of Gronsky's jacket, rippling in the wind. He saw his own father, on his knees, in their living room. Nathan's mother sat on the couch, beaming with happiness, while Nathan's father licked the soles of her shoes to show his sons how much he loved her. She laughed. Her left eye was wide open. Had it really happened? Nathan walked close to Gronsky. They walked along the Naberezhnaya—the embankment of the Moscow River. The streets were dark now, the buildings close together. To the left, a block away, towering into the black sky, was the Rossiya, the world's largest hotel, a massive jumble of stone and glass where, on the sixth floor, Nathan and Michael shared a room. Nathan imagined that he was walking beside Nachman. *It really happened*, Nachman told him. *Poppa kissed Momma's feet and we watched*. Nathan tried to imagine Ira, in bed with Ruth. He tried to feel what Ira might have felt, to be loved by such a beautiful woman—to be loved by his cousin's wife.

Well, Nachman said. At least they kept it in the family.

On 25 October Street, Nathan and Gronsky passed the building that Nathan had entered the day before, the home of the first printing press in the Soviet Union. Nathan felt himself being lifted up in his father's arms. He saw the pages, in the building in New York, skimming off the press, over the long line of small blue flames that dried the black ink.

"In Burshtyn," Nathan said, "my father was a learned and honored man. He was a carrier-of-heavy-loads. But in America . . ."

Gronsky nodded. "In America everything went wrong, didn't it? It's one of the strange ironies that pleased the authorities, when I pointed it out to them—in your work, as well as in Singer's—that for all its great freedoms America is always seen, in your fiction, as a land of loss and death. In America everything always goes wrong. Why?"

They were in the Kitai-Gorod, the old trader's city. The Chinese City,

Sonya had called it. Moscow was even quieter now than it was during the day. Moscow was a remarkably clean and quiet city. What the government ordered was done. Cars rarely honked. Sirens did not wail. No airplanes flew overhead. There were no factories in the city's center. The government forbade the use of oil as a heating fuel. The air was clean. Gronsky put his good arm inside Nathan's. He talked to Nathan of *The Stolen Jew*. He told Nathan that he had enjoyed very much reading the earlier drafts to the book. He believed he could persuade his publishing house to print an annotated edition of this earlier version, for which he would supply the notes.

"And, as promised, my friend, I will have the translation into English ready for you soon—before your departure certainly—of my introduction to the Soviet edition."

"Yes," Nathan said.

"It's much more difficult, though, to translate into English," Gronsky said. "I hadn't tried it since my university days. I had forgotten just how difficult until now. But I see very clearly, once again, why we translators have always translated *into* our native tongues."

Nathan tried to imagine that his father was holding the Russian edition of *The Stolen Jew* in his hands. Would he have read it and have spoken with Nathan of it afterward if the book had been in Russian? Or in Yiddish? The streets were very still. Nathan heard no sounds except those of their shoes, on the sidewalk. He thought of the empty house in Brooklyn, of how silent the rooms were. He thought of his typewriter, on towels, while Nachman and Leah and Rivka and his mother and father slept below. He looked to either side, at the peeling walls, the elaborately carved stone ornaments above the doorways. He thought of his life in Ein Karem. Ein Karem had been small and beautiful. Moscow was immense and ugly, yet in it, he realized, he felt very much as he remembered himself feeling when he had lived in Ein Karem.

Nathan heard footsteps behind them. "Come," Gronsky said. "Michael has created the necessary diversion. He has his assignment, you see. It's all been worked out very carefully. It was best not to inform you. Michael will see that groups of Americans go to the dollar bars, after they leave Red Square, so that you will not be the only one to return home late." Gronsky laughed. "Americans like to sit in our squares at two in the morning without the fear of being mugged. It's a story they can take back with them to the States, you see—of how safe our streets are. Ah yes. In the Soviet Union the streets are very safe."

Nathan did not smile. Nothing surprised him. He felt as if all that was happening to him had happened before. He had been right not to want to come to Russia. He had learned nothing from being there. He visited the museums and the mausoleums and the parks. He ate in the restaurants and hotels and cafés. He listened to the tourists and the guides. He went with Michael and Gronsky to meet Jews and to exchange merchandise and lists. Everything was arranged. His days were full. He felt little. He was, once again, he told himself, a stranger in a strange land. He walked the streets and he rode the buses and the taxis and the trains. He sat on benches in the botanic gardens and he shopped in the stores and he visited the homes of dead writers, and he was, all the while, comforted, as he had been in Ein Karem, by the sounds of a foreign tongue—by the endless hum of words he did not understand.

He thought of Gail Rubin, walking along the beach at dawn. He thought of Rachel, and of the wonderful softness of her skin—of being held by her. Was she right? Could they still, after all that had happened, be happy together? He did not want to think of her in her new apartment in Florida. He did not want to believe that she had, by moving there so swiftly, betrayed him again. He heard her voice, on his first night in New York, telling him that he had wanted to be comforted and held by his mother too. He saw the pieces of the broken dish on the linoleum. "I want to go home," Nathan said.

Gronsky smiled. "So do we, my friend," he said. "So do we."

"I don't understand."

"Ah, my good friend Nathan. This is how I like to put it," Gronsky said. He licked his lips. "We are really Israeli citizens who are, as it were, temporarily stranded in the Soviet Union. Don't you see?"

Nathan nodded. He walked with Gronsky along a narrow street where the housefronts were all painted yellow. "Are we really in Russia?" Nathan asked.

"And is Gronsky really Gronsky?" Gronsky replied. He laughed softly. "We are in Russia," Gronsky stated. "I would say that we are definitely in Russia."

Nathan breathed in. He wondered: could God have withdrawn into Himself in order to make room for the Soviet Union? He saw his father in the red easy chair, reading. His father was smiling. "Yes," Nathan said.

"In a nation of informers," Gronsky said, "it is often difficult to know how to determine what is and is not real." He touched Nathan's hand. "Before the war, within one week's time, on two entire floors of my apartment building, I became the only person left. In those days we sat in our rooms and we listened for the sound of the elevator. It was how we passed the time. In two and one half weeks' time—it was most strange—more than three-quarters of my entire building, all my neighbors, disappeared."

"But you did not."

"I did not." Gronsky smiled in a way that made Nathan want to pull away from him. "But I am only a translator, my friend, don't you see? You should not forget that. I was never a man to take large chances. Why did I survive? Who can tell, my friend. They let me survive, perhaps, so that they could plague me with life. I am a bit like Tsvi in that, don't you think? They took away everything except my life. They took away my wife. They took away my neighbors. They took away my friends. They took away, for a while, my job. They took away my mother and my father. They took away my two sisters and their husbands. They took away my son Yuli, whom they sentenced to a term of ten years without the right of correspondence."

"Ten years without the right of correspondence?"

"That meant, in those days, that he was shot."

"I'm sorry."

"I suppose my punishment was life itself," Gronsky said. His voice was light, almost cheerful. "Without explanation. Is Gronsky really Gronsky? Who can tell, my friend. The state gives and the state takes away, and we wait." Gronsky pressed closer to Nathan. "Still, even though I am alive and the others are dead, I hope you will let me be your friend, Nathan. I think I can be a good friend to you. Please?"

"Yes," Nathan said. "You can be my friend. I consider you my friend."

Nathan tried to smile, but his lip trembled. He thought of a story Michael had told him, one night during their last week together in Brooklyn, about an American professor in Moscow who wanted to meet Nadezhda Mandelstam. The professor met first with Jewish refuseniks who arranged things. He was taken to Nadezhda's apartment, where he met other dissidents. He was led into Nadezhda's room. She spoke bitterly and eloquently of her life. She recited her husband's poetry for him. She asked the professor to help, to commit himself to the cause, to smuggle out manuscripts. Her criticisms of Soviet life were acid and deeply felt. And the entire episode, Michael explained, had been staged by the KGB in order to test the professor, and to entrap him. It was a stunning performance that, had the professor not recognized one of the dissidents—an aging actor whom he had known years before in Hollywood—would have succeeded. Was Gronsky really Gronsky?

"There were many errors of fact in my novel," Nathan offered. He saw Rachel smiling at him, in the writing room upstairs. She patted the bed, for him to come and sit beside her. Her eyes were rimmed in red. "I was very young when I wrote it. But you never mention the errors."

"Ah," Gronsky said. "But your Russia is a Russia of the imagination, is it not?"

"My Russia is a Russia of the imagination."

Nathan thought, for a brief instant, of telling Gronsky the truth—that the drafts he had given him were not really the original drafts, but had been composed within the past few months. Thus, he would explain, he had, in his rewrites, been forced to leave the errors uncorrected. How could he have had his facts right in the early drafts and not in the final version?

"I wanted to tell you something about the manuscripts I gave you," Nathan said.

"There!" Gronsky exclaimed. "There! See how peaceful it looks."

They were in Dzerzhinsky Square. Nine roads converged upon the traffic circle, in whose center was a monument to Felix Dzerzhinsky, the man who had been, in Stalin's time, the sword of the revolution, the head of the dread Cheka. Beyond the statue, on the rise of a low hill, sat a mustard-yellow building. In the building the lights were, as always, lit. There were neat white curtains in each window. At the turn of the century, Nathan knew, the building had been an insurance office. Now, as in Stalin's time, it was the headquarters for the secret police.

"The Lubyanka," Nathan said. "I've been here before."

"I thought, before we go where we are going, that you should, perhaps, gaze upon it for a few minutes. You know, of course, what goes on inside."

"I know what goes on inside," Nathan said.

"It is rarely used for foreigners," Gronsky said. He forced a smile. "Or so I am told. Exceptions are sometimes made, but mostly the right to be a guest of the Lubyanka is restricted to Soviet citizens."

A single green taxi drove around the monument, slowly. Was Gronsky trying to scare him? Nathan tried to recall details, from *Hope Against Hope*, of life inside the Lubyanka. He saw, instead, Nachman, in the tiled hospital room, bending toward their mother and biting her lip. He saw a dark stain on his father's trousers, at the crotch. He tried to imagine

Mandelstam facing his accusers. But he could see nothing except the prim white curtains and the dim yellow light and Nachman's insane and triumphant smile.

"They interviewed Mandelstam here," Nathan said. "About his poem."

"Yes," Gronsky said. "I have seen the room."

An old woman, weeping, her head in her hands, had been shown the mutilated and blood-soaked head of a prisoner and had been told that the prisoner was her son. They wanted some small piece of information. Was it actually her son? She had not been able to tell. There is no need, Nadezhda had written, to sing as we fall into the grave, or to face the gas chambers with courage. The fear that went with the writing of verse had nothing in common with the fear that one experienced in the presence of the secret police. Screaming was a proper response to the fear of violence and destruction.

"Come," Gronsky said. "We do not want to be late. But first—first I want to take you somewhere else, just in case . . ."

He led Nathan from the square, along dark cobblestoned streets. Gronsky talked of Mandelstam's courage, which was mixed in equal parts, he said, of bravery and foolishness. He recited Mandelstam's poem, in Russian and in English—the poem that Mandelstam had recited to a group of friends one evening, the famous poem about Stalin the mountaineer, his fingers fat as grubs, about Stalin the murderer and peasant-slayer, the words falling from his lips like ten-pound weights. Mandelstam had been very brave, Gronsky stated, but he had been more suicidal than was necessary.

Nathan wondered about himself: would he have survived had he been sent to one of the camps? Had he lived in Russia, would he have spent his life writing stories and books? In Russia, poets were valued. Would he have continued to write books had he thought he might be imprisoned and murdered for writing them? He saw Nachman standing outside his door, smiling and playing sweetly on his violin, a Kreutzer étude. Was death, then, the muse he had longed for all along? Perhaps.

So many Jewish boys wanting to be writers, Nathan thought. In Russia. In America. Babel and Mandelstam and Pasternak—perhaps the three greatest Russian writers of the century—were Jews. America's two living Nobel Prize–winners, Singer and Bellow, were Jews. Nathan imagined Bellow's mother, getting the news that her son had won the Nobel Prize for literature. She telephoned. She wondered if she could at last call him *Doctor* Bellow. She was overwhelmed with joy and pride, but she wondered also—this in a whisper—if it would really hurt him if he finished his Ph.D. Who knew what life could bring? So many Jewish boys wanting to be novelists, Nathan thought, when the novelist in America was only the poor *melamed* in disguise. One who cannot even tie a cat's tail, his father had taught him, became a *melamed*. To share a wealth of knowledge is a beautiful thing; to sell a meager stock of it is unworthy.

"I'm very cold," Nathan said. "I never imagined that it would be this cold in Moscow."

Gronsky pressed his good arm more tightly against Nathan's. Nathan heard footsteps. Nathan longed to see moons like those in Babel's stories—moons that were green, like lizards. Gronsky stopped, glanced behind, then drew Nathan with him, into the corridor of a building. The corridor smelled heavily of cabbage and mildew. "Here," Gronsky said. "On the second floor—the door that is painted a dull shade of purple—there is where I live. If you should ever need me, you must come here. If I am not at home, my dear friend Kogan, with whom I share my apartment, will know where to find me. All right?"

"All right," Nathan said. Gronsky went out into the street. Nathan wondered why Gronsky was telling him these things. He tried to recall what Ruth had said to him about Michael being able to live anywhere but with his own family. All was silent. He wondered if he was really there, in the hallway, by himself. He wished very much that he could have asked Ira if he was really there. There were things that existed and acted, Ira had once said, that had never been seen.

"Come," Gronsky said, through the open doorway. "As you say in your country, the coast is clear." Nathan stepped out into the street. The air was damp. The cold penetrated to his bones. "Observe the landmarks," Gronsky pointed. "We have been walking in a circle, my friend. There, again, is the Spassky Tower, and there is the Moskvoretsky Bridge."

They walked quickly. Nathan saw a flag fluttering from one of the Kremlin towers. Nathan heard Ira's voice, pointing to the flagpole in Ebbets Field, in front of the center-field bleachers. Was it the flag that moved, or was it the wind? Nathan said that it was the wind. Ira shook his head. It's neither, he said. It's your mind. Nathan nodded to himself. Einstein had said that the only real time existed in the observer, who carried with him his own time and space. But Einstein had never been in Moscow. "Where we are going," Gronsky was saying, "people may ask favors of you, but remember that you are not obliged to do what anyone asks of you. Especially Cherniak. If he asks for your manuscripts, refuse him."

"Alexander Cherniak?" Nathan asked. "But I thought he was in prison."

"Alexander Cherniak is not in prison, and neither is he waiting for us," Gronsky said. "Alexander Cherniak is a patient in one of our fine psychiatric institutions. Tonight I speak of his brother, Lev Cherniak. Lev will be waiting for us, if he is well enough. He too has been a guest of our prisons and hospitals. He too, like his more famous brother, waits for his exit visa, to go to the land of Israel." Gronsky closed one eye. "Or so he says. In these times, my good friend Nathan, it is difficult to know whom one can trust. Do you see?"

Nathan shivered. He wished suddenly that, just before her moment of death, he had had the courage to lean down and to whisper into his mother's ear that he had thought about it for many years, and had conferred with many doctors, and that what they had all decided was that she was to blame for Nachman's life, for his illness. That was the gift he wanted to give her for her journey. A going-away present. "No," Nathan said. He looked around. He wondered where Michael was. He wondered if Michael missed his three children. He saw Michael in Red Square, laughing with the other Americans. He saw Michael on the basketball court, soaring gracefully above outstretched black arms. Nathan's teeth ached, from the cold. What worried him about Michael, he realized, was that, ever since their arrival in Moscow, Michael had taken few real chances, had done nothing rash. Michael had given away the blue jeans and the calculators and the medicines and the panty hose and the books and the vitamins to Jews, for sale on the black market. Michael had taken messages and lists, to bring back to America. He had talked with Soviet Jews about Israel and he had listened to the stories they told him—of imprisonment and exile and separation and loss—stories that, in America, would have moved him to rage and to tears, and yet Michael had done nothing rash. He had been cheerful. He had seemed relaxed. He had shown no anger. "No," Nathan repeated. "I don't see."

"But surely the author of *The Stolen Jew* need not be reminded that sometimes Jews prey upon Jews. It is an old tradition with us, is it not?" Gronsky laughed. "You will see from my introduction—and you will come to forgive me, I hope—that your book is welcomed by Soviet officials not only as a great anti-tsarist tract, but also as one that is anti-Zionist. The ironies are most rich. In their eyes, you are truly an enlightened Jew, my friend."

"Michael said that you wrote to him and explained. I wasn't surprised."

"It was what, of course, I had to say to get the book published," Gronsky explained. "You do not condemn me then, I hope. I have been hoping that you do not."

"Why should I condemn you?"

"Even the great Mandelstam, in order to save his life, was, later on, willing to write an ode to Stalin."

"Yes," Nathan said.

"And others—Akhmatova, Pasternak—they too did what they had to do. They did what they had to do." Gronsky's voice was suddenly passionate. "Man's first duty is to live, is it not? *Is it not—?*" Gronsky stopped. "Are you still cold?"

"I'm very cold," Nathan said. "I don't think I can hear everything you are saying."

"Come then. I hear no footsteps. Our circle is nearly complete. Our ruse has worked." Nathan saw lights ahead of them. He thought of Tolstoy, on one of his many pilgrimages, trudging along a country road with hundreds of others, disguised as a peasant. Tolstoy's feet were bleeding. Disguised as peasants too, his servants walked behind him, among the muzhiks. At night, in the loft of a barn, when Tolstoy was disturbed by the snoring of an aged muzhik, the servants forced the muzhik to leave and to sleep elsewhere. Nathan looked up. He heard voices. *Another Tolstoy,* he thought. He shivered again. *A cold fish.*

"There," Gronsky said, pointing to the entrance of the Hotel Gogol. "We will be able to talk freely there."

They entered the hotel. The lobby, carpeted in olive green, was dimly lit. It smelled of onions and stale cigarette smoke. There were no people sitting in the chairs. There was no clerk behind the counter. Nathan followed Gronsky up a steep wooden staircase and entered the café. What were they preparing him for? The room was warm. Against the far wall four people sat at a round wooden table. The other tables in the room were empty. Nathan blinked. His eyes watered.

"Come—"

Nathan followed. A tall young man rose. The man was terribly thin, his cheeks were gray, his eyes were wild. He stood as if he had been ordered to attention. He wore a blue wool sailor's hat, pulled down on one side of his head. He looked very familiar to Nathan.

"Hi, Uncle Nat."

Nathan looked down. Michael smiled up at him. Michael sat with his back to the wall. Sonya was next to him, her hand on his. Nathan stared. Michael withdrew his hand. Gronsky bowed his head slightly. The thin young man, still standing, bowed elaborately from the waist.

"Nathan Malkin, author of *The Stolen Jew*?"

Nathan nodded. "Yes," he said. "I suppose."

Michael was smiling very broadly. Why? His cheeks were flushed. His right arm, in its cast, rested on the table, next to his fur cap. Sonya whispered to him, in his left ear. Nathan thought of asking him why he had left his walkie-talkie home. The thin young man grabbed Nathan's right hand and pressed his lips against Nathan's knuckles. Nathan was too numb, too stunned, to pull his hand back. He wished that he were at home, that he had never agreed to come, that he had never left Israel. The man's lips were warm. "I am deeply honored," he said. "I have waited for this day."

"Lev Cherniak," Gronsky said. "And may I also present to you my good friend Boris Lipavsky."

Another man, short and stocky, stood and put his hand forward. "I believe we have already met," he said. His English accent was almost flawless. The tips of his index and middle fingers were missing. "At Igor Rabinov's house. You were with Michael."

"Yes," Nathan said. Lipavsky was a playwright. He was writing adaptations for the stage, of Babel's stories. He wanted, he said, to prepare a stage version of *The Stolen Jew*, and was awaiting permission from the Writers' Union. Lipavsky wanted to go to Israel—to apply for a visa—but his father would not leave, and Lipavsky would not abandon his father. Nathan had met the father. The man was in his mid-eighties. He sat in a wheelchair and muttered to himself. He had lived through the Russo-Japanese War and the First World War and the revolution and the civil war that followed the revolution. He had lived through the Second World War and he had survived the concentration camp at Sobibor. He had lived through the pogroms and the purges and the camps and the famines. He saw no reason to emigrate to a nation that was forever at war. He preferred to wait and to die where he was born, in the Soviet Union.

Nathan had been drawn to the man. He had wanted to touch him, to caress the man's thin white hair, his withered hands.

Cherniak's nostrils flared. His long narrow face, his wild wide-set eyes, his thin hooked nose—Nathan concentrated, then nodded, making the connection: Cherniak looked very much like a friend of Nachman's, Sidney Forbush, who had lived most of his adult life at Creedmoor State Hospital. When he was well, Sidney had been a diamond cutter. The other patients had called him the Birdman, and whenever they did Sidney would grin and flap his arms. Cherniak spoke, as if reciting from memory: "I believe *The Stolen Jew* to be a great and prophetic parable, written many years ago, yet coming true into our own time. Excuse me. In your great story, Nathan Malkin, you have to see the evil and choice that marks our condition and forever, under tsar and soviet. I am grateful to you. Excuse me please. I kiss your hand."

Cherniak grabbed Nathan's hand and kissed it. Then he bowed from the waist, and sat. He looked down at once, as if ashamed. He drank quickly, from a small glass. His body sagged; he seemed exhausted. Sonya put a hand on his arm. She spoke to him in Russian. She rose and went to the counter at the end of the room.

"My friend Lev is sometimes, shall we say, extravagant," Gronsky said. "But he has a good heart. He has a good heart."

Nathan sat. "I thought you were with the Americans," he said to Michael.

"I was. But now I'm here."

"Why?"

Michael smiled. "Not to worry, okay?" he said. "I know what I'm doing. I minimize all risks."

"I don't understand anything," Nathan said.

"Good," Michael said. "Then you won't have anything to fear."

Lipavsky smiled. "There is always something to fear," he said.

Sonya returned to the table. She set a meat pie in front of Cherniak. She set a glass of tea in front of Nathan. "Would you like some bread?" she asked.

"No thank you," Nathan said. He drank and warmed his hands on the glass. He stared at Cherniak. Cherniak ate rapidly, as if he had not had food for days. Michael and Gronsky spoke with one another, about the prospects for Alexander Cherniak's release. Cherniak's fate was of great concern to Soviet Jews. Cherniak had edited an underground newspaper, for refuseniks. He was accused by the state of conspiracy to hijack an airplane that would have taken Jews to Israel. Cherniak had been tortured. He had appeared in court, at his trial, robed in *yarmulke, talis,* and *tephillin.* To all questions and accusations, he had had but a single reply: "Hear O Israel the Lord our God, the Lord is One!" Now, because of reactions from the outside world, they had transferred him to a psychiatric hospital.

Nathan sipped his tea. He saw his mother, in the kitchen, talking to Nachman on the telephone. Nachman was feeling much better. The doctors said that he might be able to come home in a week. Nathan and his mother would be surprised, when they saw him, at how good he looked. Nathan's mother was smiling. There were tears in her eyes. *And listen, Norman,* she said. *Listen, darling. I'll see you on Sunday, all right? There's only one thing.* Nathan saw himself smiling. *Don't disappoint me, all right? Don't disappoint me.* Nathan saw his own face go pale, his fingers tighten into fists. He saw himself turn away. *You know what I mean.* His mother hung up. Her face was radiant. Nathan stared at the iron door of the potato bin. He said nothing.

Nathan looked up, afraid that the others might see the expression on his face—afraid that they might ask him questions. But nobody was looking at him. Michael was telling Gronsky that he had persuaded two more Americans to bring back messages and manuscripts in their luggage. He laughed. He told Nathan that he had practiced more general medicine since their arrival in the Soviet Union than he had since his internship ten years before. He felt as if he were a doctor in a children's summer camp. And each time he examined a tourist's throat or eyes or ears or chest, or took a blood pressure, or bandaged an ankle, or looked at a bruise, he exacted a favor.

"You Americans are very generous," Lipavsky said. His left eye did not seem to focus, and Nathan realized that it was a glass eye. Lipavsky's skin was jaundiced, as if stained with nicotine. He laughed. "In the camps it is believed that for every year you spend there, you will, upon arriving in America, receive one year's pension. It is believed that those who are incarcerated for more than ten years, upon arriving in America, are given pensions for life."

Gronsky laughed. "If I were a writer, I would use such a detail." He shrugged. "But I am only a translator."

Cherniak wiped his mouth with his sleeve. He stood. He reached into an inside pocket of his jacket and withdrew a penknife. Sonya grabbed his arm. She tried to force him to sit. Cherniak's eyes widened. Michael pulled Sonya's arm from Cherniak's. "Let him be," Michael said. Cherniak leaned across the table and jabbed the blade's silver point toward Nathan. His wild eyes focused for a second upon Nathan's mouth. He smiled and Nathan could see his chipped yellow teeth, the gaps where there were no teeth, the gold fillings. The inside of his mouth was the mouth of a very old man. Nathan did not move. Was Cherniak really Cherniak? Did he really have a brother whose bravery was known throughout the world? Cherniak grabbed the lapels of Nathan's jacket. His hand moved deftly, like that of a skilled butcher. Nathan heard Sonya gasp. He felt something tear, near his chest.

He looked down. He did not expect to see blood. He heard Michael laughing. Lipavsky was blowing through his lips, in admiration. Gronsky sighed. Cherniak's hand was next to Nathan's chest, inside the lining of Nathan's jacket. Cherniak withdrew his hand and in his fist he held a thin packet of American money.

"Did I to scare you?" Cherniak asked. He smiled happily, like a child. "Michael give to me the permission. Excuse me."

"I'll take the money," Gronsky said. His hand was open.

"I didn't know. All this time I didn't know." Nathan tried to smile. He touched his jacket. "I decided to make money," he said.

Nobody asked him what he meant. They looked at Gronsky, who held the bills in the palm of his hand and rippled them with his thumb, expertly, like a bank teller. "Eighteen," he stated. "Eighteen twenty-dollar bills. Three hundred and sixty dollars."

"Maybe twenty-five hundred rubles on the black market," Lipavsky said. He smiled. Nathan did not like the man. He did not trust him. "Maybe more. Perhaps enough for one exit visa to Israel. It depends."

"But why eighteen?" Sonya asked. "Why not twenty?"

Cherniak banged on the table with his fist. "I know the answer," he exclaimed. "Eighteen is the magic number. Eighteen is *Chai*. Eighteen is life. You give to us life!"

"Shh," Sonya said. Her hand was on Cherniak's arm. "Shh . . ."

"Let him be," Michael said. He smiled.

"Excuse me," Cherniak said. "Now you will to permit me to celebrate the occasion." From below the table he lifted a wooden bucket, covered with a napkin. He pulled off the napkin, revealing a bottle of champagne in ice. He showed the label on the bottle to the others. They murmured their approval. "I have not many chances," Cherniak said. "So I will to ask you my question. Excuse me, but Gronsky writes that we see in *The*

Stolen Jew the evil of capitalism and the oppression of mankind. The Kehilla is to be like unto the corporate state. Mirsky is to be like unto the capitalist without value except profit. Tsvi and Noah are the emblems of the proletariat. There is no choice." He leaned forward, his nose close to Nathan's face. "Do *you* agree, Nathan Malkin?"

Michael laughed. Gronsky spoke to Cherniak in Russian, sharply. Cherniak became angry with Gronsky. He scowled and sat. "I hope you will to honor me with your reply," he said.

"He distorts," Gronsky said. "But you will see. What I say, actually, is that the book lends itself to a traditional Marxist interpretation, but I go on to say that, of course, the issues are more complex. That is the beauty of—"

Cherniak banged on the table. "Leave him to answer with his own mind," he said. "I have but one chance. After this night, no more. I repeat—do you agree?"

Nathan looked into Cherniak's face. He thought of Nachman, holding *The Stolen Jew* against his chest and introducing him to other patients —to social workers, to aides, to doctors—showing them all Nathan's photo on the back of the book. *My brother read it to me before it was even a book.* "I didn't think of it that way—about capitalism—when I was writing," Nathan said to Cherniak. "I'm sorry."

Cherniak beamed. "Did I not to tell you?" he said. He spoke rapidly to Lipavsky in Russian, intentionally ignoring Gronsky. Lipavsky translated. He said that Cherniak excused himself, but he wondered if Nathan knew of his brother, the great Alexander Cherniak, who was at this moment receiving insulin shock treatments in a Soviet psychiatric prison, who was at this moment having the cells of his brain burned away. Nathan nodded. Cherniak smiled. Cherniak excused himself again, but he wondered what Nathan thought of Cherniak's own interpretation of the book. Cherniak believed that the book was nothing less than a study in the guilt that binds brother to brother—a reenactment of all the great biblical stories that told of brothers: Cain and Abel, Isaac and Ishmael, Jacob and Esau, Joseph and his brothers. The book was anti-tsarist, it was true, but, Cherniak claimed, despite Gronsky's introduction, the book had no genuine political value. It had what Cherniak called private value. It had been passed secretly from Jew to Jew before Gronsky's official translation because it was a cry from deep within the Jewish experience—a cry for a kind of freedom, personal and collective, that Jews had rarely, in history, known.

Cherniak stood and lifted the bottle of champagne. "In the warmest of Soviet hearts," he declared, "there is always a cold spot for the Jew, yes?" Cherniak's cheeks were now glowing. He said that he understood the book in a way Gronsky never would because Cherniak knew how much he himself had loved and hated his own brother, Alexander Cherniak, who was a strong man. Lev was weak. He admitted it. The self-hating worm that gnawed from within, he declared, was more powerful than the sword that smote from above. Mirsky was, then, merely an alter ego, a projection of Tsvi's evil self. Guilt and envy were more powerful than the edicts of tsars. Tsvi feared most of all the strength of his own desires and dreams. He feared to surpass his father, whom he secretly despised. He feared to spurn his mother, whom he secretly loathed. He feared to surpass his son, whom he secretly envied. Thus, he made his son—his own potential in flesh—the victim of his thwarted and poisoned desires. He was right to despise his own vanity. Nathan was right to have portrayed a world in which there was, at the end, neither love nor hope nor redemption. What hope, in the long age of history, could there ever be for Jews? The chosen people? Cherniak laughed. Chosen for suffering! he declared. The only hope and goodness in life lay in man's ability to record the truth of how horrible life was, and Nathan Malkin—like the author of the Bible itself—had performed that act of goodness.

But now Cherniak wondered: if Nathan was so bitter when he was a young man, what, in his later years, did he feel? Had the bitterness been made more profound, or had it been replaced by something else? It was fitting, Cherniak declared, that a man who had written such a book should never write another. The life, most appropriately, had come to embody the art. Death and silence, he declared, were the only true redeemers.

Cherniak sat. He looked up and smiled boyishly, the bottle of champagne pressed to his chest like a toy. He spoke to Nathan in English. "Am I to making sense to you?" he asked. "I think of your book as to be about characters living on islands of no choice. Like our own Russian fable, in which the hero is to come on his white horse to a road that forks in two and must to decide and no matter onto which road he chose, he is to die. Excuse me. Do you like me?"

"What?" Nathan asked.

"I am sorry." Cherniak touched Michael's good arm. "Your nephew Michael is like the great man we are to follow if he will lead. Can I tell? Is there yet hope? Your nephew is reminding me much of my brother." He turned to Lipavsky. "If my brother were to grow a beard, would he not to look like Michael?"

"There is a slight resemblance," Lipavsky said. "Yes—I suppose you could say that. Alexander is quite tall."

"But even now, as in your great tale, there is this," Cherniak said. "There is that Jews remain free today in the Soviet Union when others do not and that is why we are hated so well. Excuse me." He closed his eyes. "In all of the Soviet Union it is Jews alone who have, of any nationality, the chance to leave. Not Ukrainians. Not Georgians. Not Russians. Only Jews." He slapped his palm against the table and laughed. "Are the anti-Semites not right to believe that it is Jews who are to be in charge of the KGB? Why is it we can leave, but none others? The answer, my sir, is told in the chapter called 'Kehilla.' For does not Tsvi to leave and Mirsky to remain behind? Am I not free and my brother imprisoned? And are we not all likened to prisoners who believe they are to be free because to them the right is given to choose their warden?"

"Tolstoy," Lipavsky said, leaning toward Gronsky. "He is quoting from Tolstoy."

Cherniak raised one finger in the air. He recited in Russian. "Chekhov," he said when he finished.

" 'Lice consume grass,' " Lipavsky translated, " 'rust consumes iron, and lies consume the soul. Lord have mercy on us sinners!' Very familiar."

"Does he not?" Cherniak asked. "Are we here?" He raised the bottle of champagne. "Now we are to drink to our great meeting in the custom of my countrymen. Excuse me, Nathan Malkin. I will show to you the way we Georgians are to drink our champagne."

Cherniak withdrew another and larger knife from his inside jacket pocket. "The blade must to be heavy," he said. With his left hand he held the bottle around the label. He pointed it toward the wall. He tested the blade on the hair of his left arm. He raised the knife. He shouted in Russian, and then he brought the blade down sharply on the bottle's neck. The bottle cracked and foamed. He poured the bubbling champagne into glasses. He held the bottle up for Nathan to see. It was sliced smoothly across the neck at a sharp angle. He bent down and picked up the cork, which had hit the wall and fallen to the floor. The cork was still lodged within the bottle's top. "Drink!" Cherniak ordered, proudly raising his own glass. "Drink! It is like fire and ice when it is to emerge this way! *Mir i Druzhba!*"

Nathan drank. His nose tingled, his eyes watered. Cherniak sat. He whispered to Sonya. Sonya smiled. "He asks if perhaps you have a manuscript from *The Stolen Jew* that you could give to him. He says he will treasure it. He says that he will not be offended if you refuse him. Do you like him? He is ashamed to ask of you this great favor, but he has only this one chance."

Nathan glanced at Gronsky. Gronsky showed nothing. "I'm sorry," Nathan said. "No."

Cherniak looked down at the table. Were there tears in his eyes? Had Nathan been right to do what Gronsky asked him to do? Michael put a hand on Cherniak's arm. Nathan watched Lipavsky touch his lip with the stubs of his missing fingers. He saw his Uncle Harry laughing at his father. He saw Mirsky, howling in the darkness as he walked from Tsvi's home, and he remembered, briefly, how much he had, while writing, hated Mirsky. He remembered how weak and angry he had felt when the doctors would not tell him if he should or should not write his book about the two rabbis. Cherniak was grinning at Nathan in a way that made Nathan feel slightly ill. Michael's eyes were bright. "Listen, Uncle Nat," he said. "What I told him was what I didn't want you to know until now. I didn't want you to worry, okay? I told him that they granted me permission to visit his brother and to tour the wards. Professional courtesy." He gestured to Gronsky. "They'll let me see what they want me to see, sure, but that's all right too. Their so-called psychiatric hospitals have received such a bad press worldwide that they must figure things couldn't be worse. Who knows?" Michael shrugged. "Gronsky arranged it all. I sent him reports and brochures and papers. He told them I run a place for blacks and Puerto Ricans and poor people—a regular proletarian clinic, right?"

"Correct," Gronsky said. "Who knows why some live and some die, yes? It was considered a great favor to Nadezhda to inform her, definitively, of her husband's death. Most of us never knew such things for years." He stood. He seemed very impatient suddenly. "It is late, my friends. We should leave separately. The Americans first."

Lipavsky and Cherniak shook Nathan's hand. Cherniak said nothing. His hand was frail and cold. Gronsky walked downstairs with Nathan and Michael. Sonya walked with them. "You were right to refuse him," Gronsky said, patting Nathan on the back. "I admire you for that. He's an extraordinary fellow, really, but he simply can't be trusted. When he was given money previously by you Americans, to be used for refuseniks, he spent it all on manuscripts, you see. Tsvetayeva, Babel, Mandelstam, Bergelson, Gumilev—he specializes in manuscripts by writers who were killed by Stalin, it seems. An interesting hobby, wouldn't you say?"

"But I'm alive," Nathan said.

"Ah, but not as a writer," Gronsky replied quickly. "Not as a writer." Nathan's heart fell. "If you will forgive me for saying so." Gronsky smiled warmly. "Although I could not, of course, say so in print, I did agree with Lev's theory about your life having imitated your art. The passages where Tsvi talks of having only one story to tell are very much to the point, and—but there is no time, my friend." Gronsky extended his good hand. Nathan shook it. Gronsky lifted his right sleeve from its pocket. He showed Nathan the twenty-dollar bills, where the empty sleeve had been. He pursed his lips, then placed the sleeve inside the pocket again. "You have given us—shall we say—a hand, yes?"

Nathan did not smile. He looked at Michael. Michael had his arm around Sonya. "You should not be seen with me at this hour," she said to him. She stood on tiptoes and kissed Michael on the cheek. Her eyes were closed. Her cheeks were rouged. She drew Michael down, by the back of his head, and spoke to him softly, in his ear. Nathan recalled sitting with Ruth, her head against his shoulder. He wished that Ira were still alive. He wished he could laugh with Ira about how Nachman would hold his breath when they played *zim̀zum* together. Ira would have understood a man such as Mandelstam. *Am I real and will death really come?*

"Nobody knows exactly what Lev does with his manuscripts," Gronsky said. "Nobody has ever seen them, once he's purchased them."

"Come," Michael said. "I'm ready—"

"In the thirties, many of our best writers kept themselves from starving by selling their manuscripts," Gronsky said. "Often they would even invent variations and false early drafts merely so that they would have more manuscripts to sell." He laughed. He bowed his head slightly. "We are a people who love literature, you see. We love the written word."

Gronsky opened the door. Nathan stepped from the lobby into the street. Michael was beside him. Nathan felt chilled at once. "Do you know the way home?" Nathan asked.

"I know the way home," Michael said.

They walked without talking, Michael's arm around Nathan's shoulder. Nathan thought of Nachman, in the cold ground of Long Island, his black-and-white *talis* wrapped around his shoulders. He recalled a joke that he had heard at the agency, in Jerusalem, about the eighty-eight-year-old man who showed up each day at the Bureau of Emigration, and waited in line to see if his exit visa to Israel had been granted. Each day the old man was refused. Each day he returned. Finally, one of the officials, irritated at saying no so often, spoke to him and told him that if he came back in ten years he would have a definite answer for him. "Come back in ten years." The old Jew nodded. "In the morning or the afternoon?" he asked. Nathan saw Nachman smile. Nachman liked the joke.

"Michael! Wait!"

Nathan turned. Sonya ran toward them. She held Michael's fur hat. He took it. They kissed, on the lips. Nathan looked away. A second later he heard Sonya running from them, in the direction of the hotel. Nathan walked. He let Michael's arm rest on his shoulder. He would not give Michael the secret Ruth had given him, about Ira and Aaron. He counted. He had already given secrets away to Michael and to Ruth and to Nachman and to Rachel and to Leah and to Rivka. He would, then, he decided, give the seventh secret to himself. Why should he trouble anyone else with his gifts? "Ah," Michael said, looking back. "The things one has to do sometimes, right, Uncle Nat? The sacrifices one makes in this life, to save Jews."

◇ 11 ◇

NATHAN AND MICHAEL WALKED FROM THE HOTEL. WHEN THEY WERE several blocks away, Michael hailed a taxicab for them. He gave the driver a pack of Chesterfield cigarettes and spoke to him in Russian. Nathan looked down at the tattered cloth seat. The first time he and Michael had entered a taxi, eleven days before, in order to deliver some of their merchandise, there had been a blood-covered screwdriver on the seat. Michael had gotten out, smiled, and closed the taxi door. "No thanks, pal," he'd said. "I get the hint. *Do svidanya,* right? *Poka!*"

Now there was nothing on the seat beside them. The taxi moved rapidly through the streets, making its way past the outer ring of the city's center to a section of old apartment buildings. The taxi stopped. Michael paid. He and Nathan waited until the taxi had driven away, and then they walked several blocks. In the failing light, women were sweeping the streets. Children were kicking balls back and forth. Nathan felt tired and cold.

They entered an apartment building and walked up three flights of stairs. The corridors were dark and narrow, and smelled, vaguely, of disinfectant. Paint was peeling from the walls. Nathan thought of Rachel's building, on Linden Boulevard. He thought of the boy who had tried to steal his suitcase. He remembered the pleasure he had taken from slamming the suitcase against the boy's head. A door opened and Nathan saw light and faces. "*Shalom!*"

Michael entered and Nathan followed. The apartment seemed to overflow with people. There was hardly room to move. Nathan heard names—Grossman, Katz, Losovsky, Vladimir, Schweitzer, Tufeld, Yelena, Kupietzky, Vera, Fishman, Halpern—and he felt his hands being touched. The apartment was brightly lit. On the walls were framed photographs of Israel: the Wailing Wall, Yad Vashem, orange groves in the Negev, Masada. Someone took Nathan's coat and laid it with others, on a large piece of white paper, in a corner. Someone took his arm and led him from the narrow corridor into a small living room.

In the middle of the living room a long table was set, for the Sabbath meal. Nathan gasped. He stared at the white tablecloth, the silver candlesticks, the braided *challah*. His heart was pounding. He looked around. "*Shalom*," somebody said. "We are so happy you could come to be with us." Nathan saw the faces of children now. "*Shalom!*" they shouted to him. "*Shalom! Shalom! Shalom!*"

Nathan was afraid that he was going to cry. He took a deep breath. He tried to remove, from inside his head, the picture of his own home, when he was a child, on Friday night. He tried not to think of his father, raising the silver *kiddush* cup and chanting the blessing over wine. He tried not to see his father—on the first *Shabbos* after Nachman was hospitalized—breaking down in the middle of the blessing and weeping for his lost son. What had his father felt, through all the years that followed?

The sound of words—in Russian and Hebrew and English—rolled past Nathan's ears and filled the room. He saw two people he recognized, from the AAA tour. They moved toward him. They introduced themselves as Jack and Sylvia Stein. They smiled and shook Nathan's hand.

"It's good to see you here," Mr. Stein said. "My wife and I come from Philadelphia. I understand you're a collector."

"Not anymore," Nathan said.

Mrs. Stein smiled. "Good *Shabbos*," she said. "I wanted you to know that I read your book. I liked it very much."

"When I was a kid I collected stamps," Mr. Stein said. "And seashells. Those were my hobbies, you could say."

"Isn't this wonderful?" Mrs. Stein said.

Nathan stared at the table—at the silver *kiddush* cup and the wineglasses and the flowered plates and the gleaming silverware. So many years, he thought. So many years. He took deep breaths. He felt a book being thrust into his hands. It was the Russian edition of *The Stolen Jew*.

He smiled. Somebody put a pen in his right hand and asked him to autograph the book. He nodded. He opened the book and, under the Cyrillic letters, he signed. Everybody applauded.

At the other end of the room, Michael held a small child in his arms, and the child was touching the ceiling and laughing. Other children were begging to be lifted up. Michael wore a *yarmulke*. Another book was put into Nathan's hand, with a slip of paper upon which was written the owner's name. Nathan inscribed the book. He perspired. The table was set for at least twenty people. In the middle of the table was a vase, with red and yellow tulips. A child brought a book, to show Nathan. It was a book for learning Hebrew. The child spoke to Nathan in Hebrew. He told Nathan that his name was Yakov Losofsky and that he was ten years old and that he hoped to be Bar Mitzvah at the Wailing Wall.

Nathan touched the boy's forehead. He told him that he spoke Hebrew very well. The boy blushed. The boy's father shook Nathan's hand. His grip was powerful. "I have been refused two times, but I think the next time they will not refuse me. From now until the Olympics they will let more of us out. What do you think?"

The room was quiet. They waited for Nathan's answer. "I hope so," he said.

"We hope so too," the man said, and the entire room laughed. "But give us your true answer, please."

"When I worked in Jerusalem, at the United Israel Appeal—" Nathan offered "—they said the same thing. They expect immigration to rise until 1980."

"And after—" The man gestured with the side of his index finger, across his throat.

"We're so glad we can help," Mrs. Stein said to Nathan. "They know so little. They have so much hope."

"It's not such a risk, for Americans," Mr. Stein said. "The KGB knows what we do. What they don't want us to do they'll let us know. But I feel that we're very privileged and we should do everything we can. A Jew is a Jew. My whole family just about was killed in the camps." His eyes watered. "We got out in '34. My father's brothers made fun of him, for leaving, but he got the last laugh, I suppose. My father was a great man."

A woman was showing Nathan a scrapbook that contained Jewish New Year's cards, sent to her from America. She showed him the cards that had come to her from people in Brooklyn, and she asked Nathan if he knew any of them. He did not. She showed Mr. and Mrs. Stein the cards that had come from Philadelphia. They knew several of the families. Then the woman turned the page and showed them the card she had received from Mr. and Mrs. Stein, only two years before. Again, there was applause.

"I think children should have hobbies when they're young," Mr. Stein said. "Did you have any hobbies?"

"My hobby was surviving," Nathan said.

Mr. Stein laughed. "I think I get what you mean," he said.

Nathan thought of correcting him, of telling him that he did not know what he had meant, but he said nothing. Michael was waving his arms, for quiet. "*Sheket!*" he shouted. "*Sheket!*"

"*Sheket bevakasha!*" the children chanted in unison. "*Sheket bevakasha!*"

Michael spoke in Russian and in English. He told them all how proud and happy he was to be with them. Before they began the Sabbath meal, though, he asked if at least nine men could join with him—a *minyan*—for the evening prayers, so that he could say *Kaddish* for his father, who had died five and a half months before.

Most of the women left the room. The children stayed at the edges. While the men shuckled back and forth and chanted the prayers, sharing the few *Siddurim*, the children stared and giggled. Michael led the group in the prayers. He wore a blue-and-white fringed *talis* across his broad shoulders. His voice was strong and clear. When he recited the *Kaddish* the room was silent. When he finished, he turned and smiled. The other men shook his hand. Nachman was his father, Nathan thought. But neither of them—neither he nor Michael—had had their fathers' lives. Neither of them had failed, and it hurt Nathan, despite the years, to realize that by not having the life his father had had, he had fulfilled the dream his mother had dreamt for him. *You must know everything.*

The women came back into the room, carrying dishes and pots. Nathan sat where they told him to sit, at one end of the table. A young woman lit the *Shabbos* candles, then covered her eyes and recited the blessing. "Good *Shabbos*!" everybody said when she uncovered her eyes. "Good *Shabbos*!" Michael put the silver *kiddush* cup into Nathan's hand. "They have asked if you would recite the *Kiddush*."

Nathan lifted the cup of wine. He thought of his mother and the mothers of his friends. These Russian and Polish women who carried the world on their backs—they beat down their husbands so that they could raise up their sons. Why? He saw Nachman, in the far doorway. Nachman shrugged. He didn't know the answer either. Nachman smiled and pointed to the *kiddush* cup. Nathan's chest hurt. He cleared his throat and began to chant the blessing. The faces of the Russian Jews, watching him, seemed so eager and happy. Why? Most of them had never seen their fathers chant the blessing that their grandfathers had chanted. Nor had they seen their mothers bless the candles, as their grandmothers had. Mrs. Stein was right. They were Jews, yet they knew so little. Nathan sang the words, in Hebrew, that told of how God had chosen the Jewish people from among all other nations, and had sanctified them through His commandments. In love had He given the Jewish people His Sabbath, for rest, and for gladness, and for rejoicing. In love had He given the Jewish people the Sabbath, to commemorate the liberation from the land of Egypt.

Nathan drank the wine, which was homemade, yellow instead of purple. It was very sweet. Others raised their glasses and drank. Nathan sat. He did not want to embarrass them by leaving the table to wash his hands. Instead, he touched his fingers to the wooden table, under the cloth, as he had seen his father do. But why did the rabbis consider the touching of wood a substitute for the ritual washing of hands? He drew the blade of his knife across the lace napkin that covered the *challah,* and recited the blessing, thanking God, Who brought forth bread from the earth. He removed the napkin. He set the knife down and tore off a piece of the golden *challah,* the way his own father had always done. He sprinkled salt on it and ate. He remembered, from the airplane, the tale of the caged nightingales. The faces he looked into, into whose mouths the pieces of *challah* he tore and distributed were now being placed, had been cut off from their own heritage. They were all, with respect to the customs of Judaism, like schoolchildren. In America, his Aunt Zlata had always sprinkled salt into her tea, to remind her, she said, of the tears of the *goless*—the Diaspora.

The meal began with gefilte fish. Michael and the Steins praised the cooks. The table was full of talk and of argument. Nathan ate. He did his best to answer the questions that were put to him. Someone wanted to know if Nathan thought that Israel should give up the West Bank and recognize the PLO, and they were delighted when he said that he did not believe one should ever talk with the murderers of women and children. Israel, they claimed, should never compromise. Israel could not afford the luxury of momentary weakness. They asked Nathan what he thought of Jewish-American writers such as Salinger and Mailer, Malamud and Bellow. They praised Nabokov—a favorite—and told Nathan proudly that Nabokov's wife Véra was Jewish. They asked Nathan if he had read Bulgakov's *A Dog's Heart*, which he had not. Someone left the table and returned, to show him the manuscript, duplicated in purple ink.

Nathan's plate was taken away and another put in front of him. Had Nathan received any royalties for his book? Nathan said that Gronsky had introduced him to a member of the Writers' Union who had given him a chit, for royalties. Nathan had used the chit at the Detsky Mir, to buy gifts for Michael's children. He had also used it at the Moscow House of Books, where he had bought some art books for Michael's wife and mother. And—he whispered—he had also let Gronsky help him spend some of it, in a store whose name he did not know. He hoped those purchases had reached their destination.

At the other end of the table Michael was arguing with a man about Freud. The man was laughing about Theodor Herzl's ties to his mother. Herzl, he said, was, after Freud, the greatest Momma's boy of all time. Herzl had, throughout the years of his greatest success—all through his marriage—gone home to his mother's house each day for lunch. Did that not explain the origins of Zionism? the man asked, and everybody laughed.

Nathan listened to people talk of Scharansky and Sakharov and Guberman and Cherniak. He heard them talk of other prisoners of conscience, and of their physical and mental states. He was told that the petitions and congressional hearings in the United States were a great help, even if American Jews did not believe it. The Soviet government was very sensitive to international criticism. Had Nathan read the *Gulag*? Did he know what had gone on under Stalin, in the camps? Was he shocked? Nathan had read the *Gulag*, he replied. He knew what had gone on under Stalin. He was not shocked. He thought of Gail Rubin, lying on the beach. He thought of the article about her in *The Jerusalem Post*. The revelations in the *Gulag* had not taxed his understanding of life. Five thousand years of Jewish history was, a man declared, the best preparation for twentieth-century life in the Soviet Union. Nathan did not laugh.

Michael was saying that, with respect to great Jewish men and their mothers, he himself had come up with a revision of Freud's theory: a man who had been the acknowledged favorite of a doting mother did not go through life with the feeling of a conqueror—he went through life with the feeling that he must *become* a conqueror. Nathan leaned forward, to be closer to Michael. Others nodded, in agreement. These men went through life, Michael said, trying to conquer the world so that they could at last come and lay that world at their mothers' feet and thereby win their love. But could they ever fully win it? someone asked. Michael shook his head and smiled. No, he said. Of course not. Such women were pathologically insatiable. Their extraordinary narcissism, which gave to them their great ambition and strength, lived by destroying and degrading others.

Nathan looked at snapshots that somebody was showing him, of Jews in concentration camps. Poppa's books, he thought. Where are Poppa's books? He stared at platters of roast chicken and boiled potatoes and fresh broccoli. There were plates filled with beets and chick-peas and herring and noodle pudding. The women argued with the men, about Irina Kupietzky, who threatened to immolate herself in Red Square if her son died in the Soviet army. They spoke of Ida Nudel, alone in exile, and of her vow of silence. They asked Nathan if he had ever met Golda Meir or Teddy Kollek or Moshe Dayan. They asked him to write to Senator Jackson to see what the senator could do to help the Jews of Kharkov erect a monument to the victims of the Holocaust. They told Nathan that what they needed most of all, besides money, were schoolbooks for their children. The Soviet police, only two weeks before, had raided one of their apartments and destroyed all their teaching materials—books and tapes and posters and maps. When they went to the police and complained that there had been a robbery, the police replied that no robbery had taken place since nothing of value had been taken.

Mr. Stein asked if they shouldn't speak more quietly. Might not the apartment be bugged? They laughed. The KGB would learn nothing new from their Sabbath meal. And anyway, one man joked, the Sabbath was a day of rest, was it not? They were conducting no business. They were only talking and arguing about imaginary situations; they were like the rabbis of old. The man's wit, translated for Nathan, was praised. In any event, a woman said to Nathan, Sakharov himself—the father of the Soviet H-bomb, the great and brave dissident—believed that the KGB now practiced surveillance from great distances, with the use of laser beams. There was no hope of secrecy. Nathan listened to tales of Jews who had lost their jobs in the universities. Sakharov himself had no work. His second wife was a Jew. The situation was as bad as it had ever been under Stalin. Nathan was given statistics. Whereas, in 1963, Jews numbered 84 out of 410 graduates of Moscow University's faculty of mathematics, since 1970 only 2 to 4 Jews a year were admitted. And in the divisions of applied mathematics—the Institute of Electronics and the Institute of Transportation—things were even worse. They now accepted no Jews at all.

Nathan listened to the familiar tales. As soon as a Jew applied for an exit visa, to go to Israel, he or she was fired. They were then out of work, subject to charges of parasitism. If the government chose to bring such charges, they faced prison, camp, or exile. A man was refused an exit visa because his military service, completed fourteen years before, put him in possession of classified military information. Nathan looked at photos of another man's wife and three children, who were living in Chicago. The family had taken the chance that he too might someday be granted his visa. He had been waiting for four years. Had Nathan ever been to Chicago? Could he telephone them when he returned?

How could the author of *The Stolen Jew* not know how deeply anti-Semitism resided in Soviet soil? A woman showed Nathan a recent example that she had brought with her—to use for his next book, she said. It was a print of a prize-winning painting from a national art exhibition—two military boots inscribed with swastika and a Star of David. She translated the caption "Two boots that endanger our world."

Nathan listened to them talk of Jews who were shills for the government. The chief Moscow rabbi was a shill. Had Nathan met him? The *shamas* of the Leningrad *shul* was a shill. They were like the crown rabbis, appointed by the tsar. What need had the KGB for bugging apartments when there were always, even in the very room in which Nathan now sat and ate, human beings with a price, human beings who could be intimidated or bought? The room was suddenly silent. Nathan swallowed. Did Nathan know, a woman asked, that the only spontaneous torchlit parades ever held in Stockholm for Nobel Prize recipients were for Martin Luther King and Andrei Sakharov? Had Nathan met Sakharov?

Nathan had not. Sakharov could not receive or make international calls. His letters were opened and destroyed. He was allowed to keep his phone so that the KGB could, regularly, telephone him to warn that he would be assassinated. Nathan thought of talking with Sakharov about *zimzum* and *kelippot*. He thought of sharing with him the fact that his son, Ira, had been a physicist too. Scharansky was in danger of going blind, someone said, unless the Soviet officials allowed adequate medical care. Could Michael speak to the authorities when he saw them? Perhaps Michael would be allowed to visit Scharansky, in Chistopol. Perhaps, in return, he could promise to write a favorable article about conditions in the hospitals.

They drank tea and ate brown sugar cookies and sponge cake. Michael told jokes, about immigrants coming to America. His laughter sounded like Nachman's laughter. Nathan led them all in the prayers following the meal. The men and children sang lustily, banging on the table with their palms. Under the table, a child tugged at Nathan's leg. Nathan smiled. He hoped the child would try to tie his shoelaces together.

"It's so *froelich*!" Mrs. Stein said to Nathan. "It reminds me of my own home, from when I was a child. We had a large family. Did you come from a large family?"

Nathan said that he had two sisters and one brother. His brother was dead. His sisters were alive. Michael translated a request, for Nathan. Could he sing one of the songs his father had sung, from when he was a child? It might be a song that had originally come from Russia. Inside his jacket, Nathan was perspiring. He dipped his fingertips in the cup of cold water that had been passed around, for the ritual cleansing of hands after the meal. Michael smiled at him—Michael's face was glowing with pleasure and innocence. Nathan saw Michael sitting at his feet, in the living room in Brooklyn, with Ruth. Michael began to hum a melody. He said that it was one his own father—Nathan's brother—had often sung. He said that his father had been a fiddler, that his father had been a great prodigy like those Russians—Heifetz and Elman and the others —who had come to Leopold Auer in their velvet suits. One person at the table had heard of Leopold Auer. He had read of him in Babel's great story, "The Awakening." Nathan could see Mr. Langenauer lifting Nachman in the air. *Wunderkind!* Michael began to sing. Nathan closed his eyes. He felt warmth begin to flood his chest. He saw his father, smashing dishes in the sink. *What is it you want from me?* Nathan relented. Why should he resist? What could anyone ever do to him that had not already been done? What could they take away? Of what could they accuse him? It was all right, he decided, if these Jews—these strangers—wanted things from him. It was all right. He began to sing, in Yiddish, and he was surprised that he could remember the words. *Az de rebbe shluf . . . az de rebbe shluf . . . shluffen alle chassidim . . .* He began to sing and to let his body sway from side to side, the way his father's had, and soon the others were humming with him, singing the words and clapping their hands.

One man rose and pulled another man with him. The first man took a handkerchief from his pocket. Others joined them. Nathan continued to sing. He clapped his hands. He heard Michael's voice, above the others. Nathan let his cheek rest against his palm. He opened his eyes. The Russian Jews, in their ordinary clothes, were dancing in a long line around the table, their children with them, squeezing between chairs, their arms raised high, handkerchiefs held aloft between outstretched fingers, and they seemed very happy, very free.

Later, when Nathan was sitting in a chair, telling the others some of the stories his father had told him when he was a boy, and telling them also about the letters that his father had saved—the letters that had been, of course, the inspiration for *The Stolen Jew*—Michael came and sat next to him. "Isn't this what it's all about, Uncle Nat?" Michael whispered in his ear. He gestured to the room. "Wasn't it worth the journey to see this—to bring such a gift?"

TOWARD MORNING, NATHAN AWOKE. HE WANTED TO SPEAK WITH MICHAEL, to tell him all that he was feeling about these Russian Jews. How could it be, he wondered, that such an awful nation had produced such extraordinary people? How could it be that, after decade upon decade of oppression and torture and murder, so many great writers had survived and had created? Nathan nodded. He saw an immense forest, as if from the window of a plane. It was devastated, wasted. They were nearing Moscow. Most of the trees lay on the forest floor, charred and rotting. But here and there a single broad-based tree arose, almost to the plane's belly. Nathan turned "Michael—?" he whispered. If only Death had stood by his half-open door, years before, he knew, he might have continued to write. If he had thought each day might be his last . . . *You were very sweet,* he said to Nachman, *but Death would have been a better muse.* "Michael—?"

There was no answer. Nathan got out of bed. Michael's bed was empty. Nathan walked to the door and opened it. He looked down the long hallway. At the far end, next to the television set, the *dezhurnaya* —their floor lady—slept. Nathan closed the door. He got back into his bed, which rose along the middle like a loaf of freshly baked bread. He smiled, remembering how he and Michael had been tipsy together on the way home, how they had sung *zmirot* in the elevator, their arms around one another. He rubbed his hands together for warmth, and then looked at his hand, at his outstretched palm. He saw the little old man there, smiling up at him, happy to have spent *Shabbos* eve with Nathan and Michael and their new friends.

Then you're not sorry you came, Nathan, are you?

No. Not yet.

I didn't expect you to bring me with you, if you want the truth, and I hope you won't mind, but as long as I was coming this far, I decided to bring some friends with me. They've been wanting to talk to you. They've been waiting. It's a sort of surprise we've been saving for you.

I like surprises. I'm glad you're here.

But first tell me, is it true what I hear? That you've decided never to write again?

It's true.

Then I can give you your surprise. Close your eyes, all right? Open your mouth and close your eyes and I'll give you something to make you wise.

Nathan closed his eyes. He opened his mouth. He could still taste the homemade yellow wine. He left his hand outstretched, above the covers, in darkness. Where was Michael? Babel had been in a factory and had seen what he called the most terrible thing of all—young women tearing the covers from books, to prepare them for pulping. The destruction of books went on day after day. And what if it's only the beginning? Babel asked. Still, Nathan smiled. *Remembrance makes possible redemption, forgetfulness prolongs the exile.* His hosts had recited the words to him just before he left. Michael had translated. The women had kissed Nathan on both cheeks. The men had kissed him on the lips. They had blessed him.

All right. You can open your eyes now.

Nathan opened his eyes and he saw them there, staring at him.

Hello Nathan, Tsvi said. It's been a long time.

Hello Nathan, Noah said. I've been thinking about you.

Nathan put his hand to his chest. Noah's voice seemed so young, so gentle!

Hello, Mendel said. You've been on my mind. I've been saving some things I wanted to say to you before you went home.

Nathan could hardly breathe. He was frightened. Where is Esther? he asked. Is she all right?

Here I am, she said. I was standing behind Noah. You were very worried about me, weren't you?

Nathan nodded. He listened to the sound of his heart. He saw the Russian children, twirling their handkerchiefs and giggling. Such innocence! Why was Michael gone?

That was sweet of you. She turned to Noah. Didn't I tell you there was still a great sweetness in him?

I didn't disagree, Noah said. He looked at Nathan. I brought my violin. If there's something special you'd like to hear . . .

Shh, Tsvi said to them. Let me be in charge. Don't forget—the story was mine. The rest of you only spoke through me.

Through Nathan, Noah said, correcting his father.

But we agreed that I would be the one to speak for all of us, Tsvi said. I suffered the most loss, didn't I?

See how he bullies us! Mendel said. And yet you made me the villain. Why?

I only wish there were some others I could make music with, Noah said. Besides Esther. I've always held that against you, Nathan, that you made me such a virtuoso that I could never play in chamber groups or orchestras. You wouldn't believe how I wait here sometimes, longing to play in a trio, or a quartet, or . . .

It's very, you should pardon the phrase, dis-concerting for him, Mendel said.

Noah laughed. Mendel! he exclaimed.

I didn't know you had a sense of humor, Nathan said to Mendel. He wanted to smile. He tried to imagine that the Jews he had met that evening were in his room, standing in a circle around his bed, and smiling at the scene. Would it make them happy? Tolstoy had once put on a play at Yasnaya Polyana, for his muzhiks, whom he declared the best judges of art. They had laughed in all the wrong places. They had not understood a word.

It came to me very late in life.

Shh, Tsvi said again, while the others laughed. Please. Why won't you let me tell him what we agreed we came here that I should tell him? Why—?

My father understands loss, Noah whispered.

See how they mock me, Tsvi said. See what they do to me. And after all I went through for them.

Look! Esther said, pointing at Nathan. He's smiling! We've made him smile.

Then the journey was worth it, Mendel said.

I agree, Noah said.

Tsvi cleared his throat. What we wanted to do was to thank you, he said. That's why we came. We wanted to thank you for not writing the last chapter of the book again. That was the seventh secret, wasn't it? The one you saved for yourself? We wanted to thank you for stopping before the end.

It's true, Mendel said. I'm very grateful. I didn't want to make that journey ever again, from Russia to America. I didn't want to follow Noah on his tour, spying on him, remembering, storing up my hatred.

And we needed the time to rest, Noah said. That also. It's given us the chance to get to know one another—to learn to live together.

For after you're gone, Esther said. Forgive my bluntness, darling, but that's what we mean. The way you wished it, Nathan.

In my time, Mendel said, after a pogrom we would dig up the earth so that the blood would be buried with the bodies.

I thought I was doing the right thing, Nathan said, to decide to stop writing. I really thought so. I didn't want to hurt anyone ever again, the way Momma always said I hurt Nachman.

See? Mendel says. See how he distorts our words? We speak of him not rewriting the last chapter of one book, and he talks about not writing all his books.

But there is something we would like to know about before we leave, Esther said. We'd like to know where we all come from, if you could tell us. We'd like to know what you felt when you first gave us life.

Don't speak for me, Mendel said. I know enough already.

I agree, Noah said. It's better not to know some things. You don't have to know everything. The important thing is that I'm glad you didn't kill me again. I'm glad I didn't have to go down on my knees and tell Mendel that I understood the rage in his heart. I'm glad I didn't have to feel again what my death would make my father feel.

And Mendel wasn't even satisfied, Esther said. That was cruel of you, Nathan.

I'm sorry, Nathan said to Mendel. He concentrated and remembered what he had felt years before. That was a surprise to me, that when I got to the end of the book, and after all the years that you'd dreamt of your revenge, that the taking of it did not satisfy you. I hadn't thought, before, about what you might feel. I only realized it in the moment in which you had your knife raised above Noah. Then I saw your face. It was very puzzled, very innocent.

You make me laugh, Tsvi said. You can call a face like his innocent? He murdered my son, didn't he? And when he was in Siberia, he did worse things, which I won't go into.

I was young, Nathan said, quietly. He saw Nachman nod his head, urging him to continue. He saw Rachel, holding the telephone to her ear, and telling him that she would wait for him. According to the old Russian proverb, Gronsky had said to him, to go through life was not as difficult as crossing a field. Nathan stared into the cold room. Why did Michael wait until their last day to visit Cherniak? Why had Gronsky shown Nathan where he lived?

Don't hold back, Esther said. Not now. There's no time.

He saw Rachel nod her head, in agreement.

I was really very young when I wrote the book, Nathan said. Yes. But the answer to your question, Esther, is that I can remember you all running around inside my head as if I were going mad—and yet, in the moment in which I actually gave you shape on the page, I was never calmer, never less mad. I loved you. That's true. I loved having your voices inside my head. Momma would mock me and say that if I kept up my scribbling I'd wind up in a hospital with Nachman. But letting your voices live inside my head helped shut out all the other voices. When I was lost in my words—when I was listening to you love and hate one another, when you were scheming and dreaming and hoping and making choices—then I *was free. It was nicest at night sometimes—the way it is now—when everybody else in the house was asleep and I would get an idea and go upstairs to my room and put my typewriter on a stack of towels, to muffle the sounds, and I would work.*

If he steals stories from his own books, what does that make him? Mendel asked.

I give up, Noah. What does that make him?

A second-story man, Mendel said.

And answer me this—what writer's house of fiction had the strongest structure? Noah asked.

James Joist? Mendel replied.

They laughed. Tsvi shushed them and told them to stop their nonsense. Also, he said, we wanted you to know that we all think you did the right thing to come to the Soviet Union.

Speak for yourself, Noah said. I thought he should go to Florida and marry his brother's widow. Why should she wait? I thought he should be among people with whom he shares feelings and a history. What will he find here that he can't find in his own heart?

Esther stood beside Noah. I agree with what Noah says, she told Nathan.

Mendel leaned toward Nathan. And I agree with Tsvi, he declared. I think you should stay here and be arrested for espionage and get to visit the Lubyanka. I think that you've walked right into the trap they set for you and it makes my heart glad. Who do you think you are—Lord of the Universe? Ha! I always said so, that you were playing God with us, that you had no work you loved, once you'd made us. You made us and then you rested.

Mendel! Esther said. Must you? She turned to Nathan. When he's away from you—when he's resting with us—he's really very sweet and kind, Nathan. He forgives you then. Don't you forgive him then, Mendel?

Mendel sighed. She's right. I do forgive you. But what I'm worrying about is this—once you're gone, what will happen to us?

The house in Brooklyn will be empty, Nathan said. Michael will go to live with Ruth. I'll go to Florida, or back to Israel. You can live there, where Nachman and I grew up. Nobody will bother you.

You should stop running away from life, Nathan, Esther said. That's what we're all trying to say, don't you see? I disagree with Tsvi, about coming here. I know what they do to Jews here. Look at what happened to each of us, when we ran away from Burshtyn. You should learn from your own stories.

He'll never change, Mendel said. Michael is right. He'll take every journey except the journey into himself.

But maybe he thinks he can feel things here that he can't feel there, Tsvi said. Has that thought occurred to you? We can't know everything in his head. Don't forget—we came from him. He didn't come from us.

Not true, Esther said. If we hadn't come into his head, he would have been a very different man. We gave him whatever joy he had in life.

I disagree, Noah said. And I think he should stay here and write more stories, not one of which will bring him joy. I think he should write about Nachman's violin and about the broken dishes and about the fire escape and about his father's books and about making money and about Nachman's hospitals and about his dead son.

Don't be an idiot, Mendel said. What would that do for him now? Why should you think—?

Please, Nathan said quietly. Please don't fight. Please? It hurts me.

Fight? Tsvi said. Who's fighting? It's the way we talk to each other.

When you fight it makes me hear what it was I did wrong—why my life was such a mistake. Can I tell you now, as long as you're here?

They were silent.

You'll listen to me then? Because it seems very simple, but for me it helps to explain so much.

I believe I can speak for us all when I say that we are listening very attentively to your words, Tsvi said. I believe—

Shh, Esther said. Let him speak.

I didn't love you enough, Nathan said.

They were silent, and then Mendel laughed. That's all? *he said. That's your big secret?*

If I'd loved you more—without being afraid—and made you differently, you wouldn't be asking such a question of me. That's the difference. I loved my delight in creating you more than I ever loved you. That's what I think.

Nonsense, Mendel said. Knowing you, who could ever—?

I never loved you the way I wanted to. Yet once I'd made you, I didn't know how to set you free, really—how to let go. If Nachman—

He means that he didn't love himself enough, Esther said. But I think he's changing the way things actually were, with his memory. What I like to believe is that until Nachman got sick again and he decided to make money—to use his own life to set Nachman free—he really loved us with all his heart.

It's very Jewish, Tsvi said, to believe that anything you do or anything you are can be taken away from you at any moment. It's why people are afraid to give to each other. You shouldn't be ashamed of such a feeling.

Especially, Esther added, when you did try so hard with Nachman.

And failed, Noah declared. The truth is that as strong as Nachman thought Nathan was, he just wasn't strong enough to take the chance to set us free. He tried to free Nachman because he was afraid that, inside, he was like his brother. No separation. That was his problem. That's the way I see it. He was afraid he was like his father, and so he acted in a way that he hoped would keep others from mocking him. Michael is right about that too. He identified with his mother's strength—and yet he despised her. So that—

Enough, Esther said. Let Michael explain these things.

All right, Noah said. But the truth is that he only kept us alive for his own purposes. He could have set us free easily enough if he had simply gone on and written other books. Then he wouldn't have needed us so much.

But if he could have written other books, Tsvi began, and then he looked around, very puzzled, not knowing how to complete his sentence.

You were never larger than my bitterness, Nathan said. Didn't you see how unemotional I was when Ira was buried, when Nachman died, when—

Tears aren't everything, Esther said. I read all of Hope Against Hope *and I never cried.*

It's all very simple, if you ask me, Mendel said. Instead of letting others judge him and accuse him, he judged himself. Whenever he wanted to feel bad, he just listened to the voices inside himself. Lots of people live the way he did. The problem is that if he could only have stopped being so harsh with himself, he would have been easier with us. That's what's so sad. That's my point.

I think we've gone far enough, Tsvi said. The rest is up to him. Good-bye, Nathan.

I won't see you again?

No, Tsvi said, and he smiled at Nathan for the first time. Now that we know for certain that you won't write the last chapter of your book ever again, we can rest in peace. We're free.

That's all we really came to tell you, Esther said.

I disagree, Mendel said. If he really wanted to set us free, he would have let Mirsky come and say good-bye also. But he didn't, which proves that he still wants to hold on to certain feelings.

He's still a collector, Noah said. He still likes to collect pictures and keep them inside his head, if you've noticed. Like the one of his father kissing his mother's shoes.

That was quite a feat, Mendel said.

It was a habit he could never lick, Noah said.

They clapped their hands in delight. Not to worry, Tsvi said. They're just overtired. They get like this whenever they're overtired. They begin to talk to each other the way you and Nachman often talked.

You never had Nachman's talent, Noah said. His voice reeked of bitterness. You never knew what it was like to know so much so young. Your talent came to you when you were a grown man. It's very different for a musician. We hear so much when we know so little.

Don't cry, Esther said, comforting him, and pulling him to her bosom. You'll only upset me now, at the end.

Sometimes he thinks he's *Nachman, Mendel whispered to Nathan. It's why he gets so weak and so angry sometimes. It's why he . . .*

It's time, Tsvi announced.

Poka, Mendel said.

Do svidanya, Noah said.

We love you very much, Esther said. Don't be so hard on yourself. Try.

Good-bye, Nachman said. Good-bye and good luck. What else can I say? Give my love to Rachel. Take good care of my son, all right? I love you, Nathan. I love you just—

Nachman was weeping and smiling at the same time. Nachman! Please don't go. Please—?

What I was going to say, Nathan, was that I love you just—just like a brother. Good-bye, darling.

Nathan started to smile. He reached for them with his hand, but they were gone, and the little old man who lived inside Nathan's chest, like a child, in a room slightly below and to the left of his heart, was gone with them. Nathan closed his eyes and nodded. He heard footsteps outside the door. They must have sensed that Michael was coming back. Well, Nathan said to himself. It was something, after all, to have thought of conjuring up such a man, to have imagined and felt all the things he imagined, to have had them say all the things they'd said to one another, to have brought them with him, across the ocean, to Russia. Not many men could have done it.

Would they have spoken with each other this way had they not made the long journey? Who would ever know. Nathan lay down under the blankets. He did not want Michael to think that he had been waiting up for him—that he had been spying. The door opened. Nathan closed his eyes. He tried to listen to Esther's voice—so like Rachel's—telling him to be gentle with himself. He heard Nachman trying to calm him down. Nachman was gone, forever. The door opened. Nathan's mind drifted, free. Nathan and Nachman were at Ebbets Field, and Nachman had spent the first three innings telling Nathan not to worry about Nachman's running away. He had come with Nathan, he said, in the hopes that he would see Pete Reiser try to knock himself out again by crashing into the center-field wall. Nathan heard Michael moving, behind him. Nachman knew that the Dodgers had padded the wall since the first time Reiser crashed into it and injured himself, but Nachman's good friends were always able to do anything they wanted to themselves, even in padded cells, if they wanted to badly enough. Desire was everything, Nachman said. Then he made jokes about how fitting it was that the Dodgers, who played their games less than a mile from their house—with Babe Herman catching balls with his head and Casey Stengel letting birds nest under his cap and Van Lingle Mungo being as daffy as his name—had always been the craziest team in baseball. The Dodgers beat the Giants 8 to 5, and Nathan took Nachman back to the hospital at night, and Nachman was in wonderful spirits. At the fence he bet Nathan that he could tell him the score of the next day's game before it began. Nathan told him that he accepted the bet. Nothing to nothing, Nachman said, smiling happily. That's the score of the game before it begins. Then he climbed the fence. Nathan held his hat, and tossed it over, after him.

◇ 12 ◇

NATHAN AND MICHAEL ATE BREAKFAST IN THE HOTEL'S MAIN DINING room, and then returned to their own room and packed their suitcases. It was five minutes after nine. Their plane would leave at 3:30 from Sheremetyevo Airport. Michael's appointment at the hospital was scheduled for 10:00. Their AAA chartered bus was scheduled to leave the hotel at 12:45. Why had Michael arranged things with so little leeway?

Michael asked Nathan to come into the bathroom. Nathan entered the bathroom. Michael handed Nathan a saw-edged knife and asked him to begin cutting into the cast where Michael had drawn a line and had already begun carving. Michael let his arm rest on the rim of the bathtub. "I don't have the control with my left hand that I thought I would," Michael said.

"But why?"

"Because I'm tired of it," Michael said. His eyes flicked sideways, toward the window. He seemed very nervous suddenly.

"Is it time? It's not even two weeks—"

"It's time. I'm the doctor, right?"

Nathan began to saw at the plaster cast. "Make the line as even as you can. I may need to put the cast back on."

Nathan bore down. He watched the white powder drift into the bathtub, like fine snow. "No snowflake ever falls in the wrong place. Do you agree?"

"Do I *what*—?"

"Ira once told me that. Did he ever tell you?"

"No."

"You seem very upset," Nathan said. "Very nervous."

"Why not?" Michael said. "I lost a lot of sleep last night. I'm leaving good friends behind. Who wants to visit one of their fucking hospitals?"

"You lost sleep?"

"You were up," Michael said. "Don't play games with me now, okay? I heard your voice before I came into the room. I could tell from the way you were breathing." He sighed. He looked at the thin opening in the plaster cast. Below, his skin was pale and withered.

"Yes," Nathan said. "I was up. I was talking with your father. I told you that before, didn't I? That sometimes I imagine we still talk with each other."

"Sure," Michael said. "It's easy to talk with him now that he's gone, isn't it? But you should have talked with him more when he was alive. It might have helped."

"I'm sorry."

"Sure," Michael said. He winced. Nathan looked down and saw blood under the cast, on Michael's forearm. "Keep cutting, okay?" he ordered. "It's just a nick."

"I always thought your father was happier the less he had to do with me. I always thought my presence reminded him of his own failures."

"Failures?" Michael laughed. "He produced me, didn't he? He had Rachel, didn't he? He *chose* the moment of his death, didn't he?" Michael shook his head. His eyes were bloodshot—simmering with rage. "Oh you're a good man, all right, Uncle Nat, but you never understood my father, and how much he needed your love." He smiled, bitterly. "Can you imagine how much you would have hated him had he not been ill, had he turned out to be more of a worldly success than you? Did you ever think of that? Did you? *Did* you?"

Michael grabbed the knife from Nathan. "I'm sorry you're so upset," Nathan said. "I used to get angry this way too, whenever I had to leave on a trip."

"So did Freud." Michael chopped at the cast in short hard strokes. The last bit of connecting plaster gave way. He wriggled his wrist and forearm. The cast came off. "Good," he said. The skin on his forearm was a strange shade of unnatural pink. Nathan saw bluish folds. Michael rubbed his arm with his left hand. "Ouch!" He closed his eyes, in pain.

"Too soon. You were right." He slipped the cast back on. He gave Nathan a roll of adhesive tape, and Nathan taped the opening closed. Then Michael put his arm back into its sling.

Neither of them spoke. They put on their coats and went downstairs. Michael hailed a taxi and gave the driver instructions in Russian. He stared out the window, away from Nathan. Nathan tried to think of something he could say to him that might make him less angry, but he could not. He had thought, on the plane ride that had brought them to Moscow, that, together in the strange city, their life might come to seem larger than it was in Brooklyn. He had thought during the evenings in which Michael had told him tales of Soviet Jews—of their suffering and bravery—that he and Michael might, in aiding these Jews, draw close to one another, closer than Nathan had ever dared imagine they could. He looked out his window, at the dull red-brick buildings, the solemn statues, the leafless trees, the shoppers in their dark cloth coats. Now, at the end of their brief sojourn, and despite the night before—the beautiful Sabbath meal—Nathan felt mostly that, in Moscow, his life was smaller than it had ever been.

He wished suddenly that Michael could have been there in the hotel room with him, that Michael could have heard what the others—Nachman and Tsvi and Noah and Mendel and Esther—had said to him. He reached over, impulsively, and touched Michael's good hand. "I *am* glad I came with you," he said. "I *am* glad we were here together. Despite everything."

Michael turned and faced Nathan. His eyes were moist. "Sure," he said, softly. "Me too, Uncle Nat."

"I feel as if we've been nowhere," Nathan said. "It all seems so unreal, and yet—"

"It's real enough," Michael said. "Believe me." He sighed. "And I'm sorry I yelled before, about my father. Okay? You did the best you could. It wasn't easy for you, either."

"Then you forgive me?"

"There's nothing to forgive. But listen—" He licked his lips. "If anything should go wrong while I'm in there, don't worry, okay?"

"What could go wrong?"

"Just listen." Michael grabbed Nathan's arm and held it tightly. "You've read all the right books, haven't you? Even your own." He smiled. "I heard you say so last night. You—" Michael's eyes seemed to glaze over. "Did I ever tell you that I used to imagine you were twins?"

"Yes, but—"

"Shh," Michael said. "There's not much time, okay?—and I have some things to say. I didn't rehearse this. But sometimes, when I was playing ball in the schoolyard, I used to imagine that I was twins too. I'd sit with my back against the fence between games, sipping a Coke and talking with my friends about the Dodgers or the Knicks or our team at Erasmus, and I'd be imagining that there was another Michael waiting for me at home—a kid brother who looked just like me, a kid brother I'd been wanting to have ever since I could remember, and do you know what I'd imagine then?"

"No."

"I'd imagine that he'd be doing badly in school and that he'd be stealing money from my dresser drawer and that he'd tease me and taunt me for being popular and a good athlete and having pretty girl friends, and that I'd be lecturing to him and screaming at him to try to straighten him out in time, so that he wouldn't—"

The taxi stopped. "We're here," Nathan said. "I think we're here."

Michael paid the driver. He gave him an extra pack of cigarettes. "He'll be back for us," Michael said.

The hospital, an enormous structure of dull orange brick, was set back from the street behind a black iron fence. The windows were barred. Nathan followed Michael through the gate and into the building's lobby. Nathan saw Gronsky standing there talking with two well-dressed middle-aged men. Gronsky waved and smiled. The other men smiled also.

Michael held on to Nathan's arm. "Listen, Uncle Nat. The Russians knew it, didn't they?—that it was best, in these situations, to have no ties. They always knew that—"

"I don't understand." Nathan's heart was pounding so loudly that he could hardly hear Michael's voice. "What are you trying to tell me, Michael?"

"You should know as well as anyone," Michael said. "Ruth and the kids are on their own—they've been on their own for almost a year. They'll manage. Everything's arranged. Sweet Aaron! My lovely Miriam!" He smiled. He was, Nathan saw, forcing back tears. "And my mother has you now. You have her."

Michael bent down and kissed Nathan on the cheek, quickly. "I love you, Uncle Nat. You've changed a lot, did I remember to tell you that? Since you came home from Israel, you've changed so much. I'm very happy for you."

"But why—" Nathan looked up at Michael and recalled, at once, how handsome Michael had looked when he had found Nathan in the upstairs room. How long had it been?

"Take care—" Michael turned and walked to Gronsky. They shook hands. Michael shook hands with the officials. He waved to Nathan. The officials opened folders and Michael looked at whatever papers were inside the folders. He laughed. He seemed very much at his ease. Nathan stepped backward. The lobby smelled vaguely of ammonia. Nathan saw no patients. He saw no visitors. Gronsky came and drew Nathan with him to a wooden bench.

"What's going on?" Nathan asked. "Please tell me."

"Shh. They've agreed to let Michael see Alexander alone," Gronsky said, and he smiled happily. "Along with several other patients. It's been arranged. Don't ask me why they're relenting, but—everybody owes somebody a favor, right?—they're allowing it. So long as he takes no tape recorder or notebook into the room with him, they've decided to let them be alone for a while so that Michael can come to his own conclusions about Alexander's state of mind. I think they have actually convinced themselves that Alexander Cherniak is truly deranged." Gronsky laughed easily. His hand trembled as he drew in on a cigarette. "Who else but a deranged man would want to leave this wonderful nation, yes? Who else but a deranged man would flaunt the authorities, in court, the way Alexander did—and thereby endanger so many others whom he claimed to love, yes?"

"Is he too, then, more suicidal than necessary?" Nathan asked.

"Ah my good friend—you remembered my words, didn't you?" Gronsky stood. He shook Nathan's hand. "You will wait for Michael here. It shouldn't take more than an hour. They know about your airplane. The schedule is close, but they are most efficient here, I can assure you. They are—shall we say—*terribly* efficient."

"You're leaving me, then?"

"It's best," Gronsky said. "Believe me."

Nathan felt as if he were out of breath. "*Kominsky!*" he declared, standing and holding on to Gronsky's good arm. His eyes were burning. "Lazer Kominsky! Kominsky—!"

"Shh," Gronsky said. "Kominsky? I don't—"

"Have you heard of him?" Nathan squeezed Gronsky's arm. "Tell me! Answer me that."

"Lazer Kominsky," Gronsky repeated. "No," he said, easily. "Kominsky is a common enough Jewish name here. Lazer Kominsky. No. Should I have heard of him?"

"I don't know." Nathan sat, suddenly exhausted. He felt dizzy. "I don't understand anything." He looked up. "Please don't go. I don't want to be left here alone."

"Memories of your brother?" Gronsky asked, patting Nathan's shoulder. "Michael has told me of your brother's sad history. His father, yes? The other night, when Lev was talking about—"

"My brother is dead," Nathan stated. "I was not thinking of my brother. I'm worried about Michael." Nathan stared across the tiled waiting room. "You said that I could trust you, that I should consider you my friend."

"I am your good friend," Gronsky said with feeling. "And that is why I must leave you. Everything will be all right. Trust us, Nathan. Your nephew is a brave and cunning young man. Most shrewd. We all admire him greatly. And your influence upon his life—upon what he is—has been considerable." Gronsky pried Nathan's fingers from his arm, one at a time. "Your book has shaped his life, really. You should, as the old Jews used to say, *shep* great *nachas* from him, from how you have been a teacher to him. He admires you the way we all dream that our sons might one day admire us. That is no small thing."

"*Something's wrong!*" Nathan cried out. "Something's wrong. Something's wrong."

"Shh," Gronsky said. He pushed Nathan down onto the bench with force. "Shh. Nothing is wrong. Everything is arranged. There is no danger. You must wait here, alone. Should you show that anything is amiss, then, my friend, there might really—"

Gronsky stopped. He bowed his head in farewell. "*Shalom*, my friend," he said. "*L'hitraot!*"

Nathan stayed where he was, on the bench in the deserted lobby. He closed his eyes. He saw nothing. He waited.

WHEN NATHAN OPENED HIS EYES HE SAW THAT GRONSKY WAS THERE again, at the far end of the room, talking to a group of officials. Lipavsky was with them. They were all laughing. The iron door opened. Nathan saw what appeared to be Michael's head, above the others. Gronsky pointed to his watch. Michael nodded and began to walk with long strides across the room. He raised his arm, in its white cast, gesturing to Nathan. Nathan stood. He exhaled in relief. He smiled. He looked at his own watch. It was ten minutes to eleven. How long had he been sitting there, dozing? Michael was only a few steps away. He turned and waved to the others. Gronsky called to him to hurry, so that he would not miss his plane.

Nathan looked up into Michael's face, and he gasped. The face was not Michael's! "Not to show," the man whispered quickly. "It is to hurry up."

The man took Nathan by the arm and led him from the building. The taxicab that had brought them to the hospital was there, waiting. The man shoved Nathan into the back seat, and then got in after him. The man was almost as tall as Michael. He wore Michael's shirt and tie and jacket and pants. He had a beard like Michael's. He had dark curly black hair like Michael's. He wore no glasses. He had Michael's cast on his right arm, Michael's sling around his shoulder.

"No," Nathan said. "You have no right. You—"

The man dug his nails into the back of Nathan's hand. The taxi moved away from the black gates of the hospital. The man put a finger to his lips and pointed to the driver. "Too late," he said. "Must to protect both."

Nathan mouthed the man's name soundlessly: "Alexander Cherniak?"

The man nodded. "Yes," he said. Then he let his head fall backward. He closed his eyes. Nathan seethed with anger. He wanted to do something—to throw the man from the taxi, to scream, to wake himself from what was surely a nightmare. But he knew at once that there was nothing he could do. He stared out the window. At the corner, in a crowd of shoppers, he saw a tall young man who looked like Lev Cherniak. The man was smiling in a very normal way. Nathan thought of the story Michael had told him, of the false Nadezhda.

Michael was crazier than his father had ever been, Nathan decided. How could he believe that, in the Soviet Union, he could get away with such an insane scheme? The authorities would stop them before they arrived at their hotel. They would stop them in the bus. They would stop them when they walked from the bus to the airport. Nathan looked at Cherniak's face. Cherniak was fast asleep. His chest wheezed. Outside, in Mayakovsky Square, the taxi drivers stood in the cold, stamping their feet and swinging their arms back and forth, to keep warm. Nathan was angry with himself for not having seen the signs, for not having recognized the many clues Michael and Gronsky had left for him. Ruth had been right about the story Michael had told them that night. Surely Cherniak and Kominsky were the same man and surely Michael had known all along what the purpose of their trip was. Had Cherniak's father been saved from the Nazi death camps by being sent to the Siberian labor camps? Nathan did not bother to ask. He was, he decided, no longer interested in irony. Cherniak's skin, like Lipavsky's, was a sickly shade of yellow, like the nicotine stains on the fingers of heavy smokers. Their passport photos were in color. Surely the authorities would notice the difference. What if Cherniak were asked questions? What if the other tourists noticed and began asking questions?

Nathan closed his eyes. He saw Rachel, sitting on her horse and leaning down. He saw her smile. He saw her lift her black velvet riding cap and tuck her leather whip into the saddle. What would he say to her? Or—could it be possible?—had Rachel known and approved? Was that what she had meant when she had given him, on the phone, her reasons for not encouraging him to go? Nathan looked out the window. The sky above Moscow was steel gray. Would it snow? Would their departure be delayed? Cherniak was snoring lightly. There was spittle at the corner of his lip. Nathan saw blue-black crows, pecking at the ground. His most peaceful moments in Moscow had been at the botanic gardens. He had thought of Rachel there. Had they given Cherniak shock treatments, and how many? Nathan saw Nachman lying in bed, after the insulin shock treatments he had received. Where was the piece of rubber they had made him bite down upon? Or was that only for electric shock therapy? Nathan trembled. He wanted to tell the driver to go back to the hospital, but he knew he would not. He looked out at the sky. He saw snowflakes falling. He imagined Michael floating down toward earth, suspended by a giant billowing silk parachute.

They had all said that Michael was crazy, even then, hadn't they? Yet they had loved him. Michael had, in his summer camp, parachuted down onto the camp's baseball field, holding leaflets in his hand, leaflets that announced the start of Color War, when the two hundred campers would be divided into two teams that would vie, for four days, in a series of games and athletic contests. Michael had been a counselor that year. Ruth had not been with him. He had not met Ruth yet, though Ruth knew the story. Michael was trying to prove that he wasn't his father, she'd said once. Trying to prove that he wasn't his father helped him to succeed. Michael had never put on a parachute before that day. Rachel had been beside herself with worry. Nachman had been in the hospital at the time. Ira had, like everybody else—like all the young people—admired Michael even more. There was nobody like him—nobody else who would take the chances he took. But for what?

The taxi stopped. Cherniak awoke at once. He stared into Nathan's eyes. "All right," Nathan said. "I'll do my best."

Nathan offered to pay the driver, but the man pushed back Nathan's hand. He had already been paid. "Good luck to you, my good friends," the driver said, speaking the words with difficulty. He smiled. His teeth were capped with gold crowns. "*Shalom* to you."

The taxi drove off. In the lobby, many of the tourists were already gathering, with their suitcases. Nathan led Cherniak to a staircase, at the side of the newspaper kiosk. They walked up the six flights. Their floor lady nodded to them and gave them the key. She did not seem to notice anything. Nathan unlocked the door. His mind was moving very quickly.

"You stay here," he said.

Cherniak nodded. He sat on the edge of the bed. His back was very straight. He smiled. "So far, so good, right?"

Nathan blinked. "We'll see," he said. He demonstrated his wishes, at the door, to be sure that Cherniak would understand. "Lock the door behind me. Answer nobody. Do not open."

Cherniak nodded. Nathan took the elevator down. He found Sonya. She smiled at him. He told her that Michael was not feeling well. He told her that—despite Michael's profession—like a child, he still became carsick whenever he went on long voyages. Could she tell the proper people that Michael preferred not to take the bus to the airport? Could she see that there was a taxi waiting for them in about forty-five minutes? Sonya nodded. She smiled, as if she shared Nathan's sense of Michael's sweet vulnerability. She showed in no way that she knew what was happening.

Nathan walked across the small park that surrounded the hotel. It was snowing now, lightly, steadily. When he was a block away from the hotel, he began to run. *Gronsky!* he thought. *Gronsky!* People stopped and stared at him. He did not care. He looked up toward the Spassky Tower, to determine where he was. He saw the Moskvoretsky Bridge. He ran quickly, along the narrow streets. The air, in his chest, felt cold and good. He found Gronsky's building and opened the door. The odors were foul. The staircase was dark. Nathan stopped and breathed in deeply. He tried to make sense of things. Surely Gronsky had shown him where he lived so that, now, Nathan would know where to come. He started up the stairs. His left arm ached slightly. His chest hurt, from the cold. But what could Gronsky do? What did he want from Gronsky? Had they involved Michael merely to strengthen their case against Cherniak?

He found the purple door and knocked. He heard footsteps. An old man opened the door, partially, and peered out from behind it. "*Da?*"

"Gronsky!" Nathan said.

The old man spoke in Russian. "Where is Gronsky?" Nathan demanded. The old man's eyes suddenly blazed with alarm. He began to close the door. Nathan shoved back. The old man muttered in Russian for Nathan to go away. "Gronsky!" Nathan cried, and he pushed with all his might. The door flew open. The old man began to back away. "Gronsky not here," he said in English. "Not here. Go away."

"Kogan?" Nathan asked.

The man nodded. "Not here. Go away. Plane."

All the available space in the room was filled with books and manuscripts. They were piled everywhere—on tables, in chairs, along the walls. There was no floor space upon which to walk. Kogan backed up. He looked around, as if ashamed of the room. He shrugged. To one side, beside a kerosene stove, was a narrow bed. Next to it, on the floor, were the rumpled blankets and sheets of what must have been the other bed. There were no doors leading from the room. Dishes and glasses were stacked on the floor, next to a green plastic basin. The room reeked of rotting food and of what Nathan decided was printer's ink. "Go away," Kogan said. He talked rapidly in Russian. He pulled his bathrobe tightly to him. How old was he? Had he been in the camps? Had Gronsky ever been in the camps?

"He said to come," Nathan said. "He told me to come."

"Go away now. Yes." Nathan thought the man was going to cry. He seemed very frightened. His forearm was raised up, as if to cover his face from blows, and Nathan realized that, as he approached the man, stepping on magazines and scraps of paper, he held his own right hand in the air. He looked at it. The fist was clenched. The old man's mouth opened wide. He had no teeth. He begged Nathan, in Yiddish, to leave, to go away. "Plane," he said.

Nathan wanted to be closer to the old man. He wanted to lift him up and slam him against the wall until the man's bones came away from his flesh. "Gronsky!" Nathan shouted again. "Where is Gronsky?"

Kogan sat. He rummaged among papers. He found a box and lifted it, toward Nathan. Nathan grabbed it. "Kogan find, yes?" Nathan looked inside and saw the manuscript of *The Stolen Jew*. He threw it at Kogan. The papers fluttered about. Kogan began to whimper. Nathan turned. He started down the staircase, his right hand against the wall so that he would not fall. Above him he heard Kogan, on the landing. "Mischa Gronsky is a good man!" Kogan called after Nathan, in a voice whose strength surprised him. "He is a good man, do you hear? He is a good man. He is a good man . . ."

When Nathan arrived back at the Hotel Rossiya, the buses were already there, parked in front of the main entrance. Some of the Americans called to him, telling him to hurry. He saw Sonya. She pointed to a taxicab, fifty feet in front of the buses. He nodded. He went upstairs. Cherniak was there, where he had left him, sitting on the edge of the bed. His eyes were very tired, very dark. "Come," Nathan said. "It's time."

He went to the window. He beckoned to Cherniak. Cherniak came and stood beside him. Nathan pointed to the buses, and then to the taxicab. Nathan spoke very slowly. "We will go in the taxi. Do not speak to anyone until we are on the airplane and the airplane is no longer—" Nathan searched for words that he thought Cherniak would understand.

Cherniak touched Nathan's arm. "Maybe," he said, mouthing his words, "maybe will work. Michael say to tell you not to worry, yes? Excuse me. I do not understand. He say also, nothing adventure nothing to gain."

Nathan saw the exhaust fumes from one of the three buses. The first bus pulled away. "Nothing ventured, nothing gained," Nathan said. "An old American saying."

"Not Jewish?"

"Not Jewish," Nathan said. "Come."

WHEN THEIR TAXI ARRIVED AT THE AIRPORT, THE SKY WAS ALREADY BLACK. The snow fell more heavily. "Many flights," Cherniak said. "Best time." Nathan and Cherniak entered the terminal and walked. Nathan nodded. He saw hundreds of tourists, talking and laughing and saying good-byes. He tried to see Rachel, to imagine the softness of her skin, the sweetness of her smile. Who would be waiting for them in New York? Cherniak held his passport and his customs declaration in his hand. Nathan took out his own, from his inside jacket pocket. He stared at the tourists who walked in front of them. He saw Soviet soldiers, in long gray coats with red epaulets on their shoulders. They looked so young! Their cheeks were so pink! Cherniak pointed to a window, and he and Nathan changed their excess rubles back into dollars. They weighed their suitcases. All around them people were embracing one another. Were there any Soviet citizens embracing Americans? Nathan looked for the Steins, for familiar faces. He saw none. The green-hatted border police let them pass. Nathan and Cherniak walked up a staircase to the departure lounge. Tourists moved slowly through five separate lines of customs officials. Cherniak chose the third line, in the middle, where the customs officials waited patiently. There were no Americans in front of them. Nathan wondered if they would check his suitcase, to see if he still had the jeans and tapes and books that he had declared two weeks before. His heart beat heavily. Inside his jacket, his shirt stuck to his back. Their bags passed through the X-ray machine. Nathan braced himself for a confrontation. He walked steadily. The customs officer took his declaration, looked at it briefly, smiled, and slapped it down on the metal stake.

Nathan stopped. He breathed more easily. He heard Cherniak's voice. "Hi," Cherniak said. Nathan remembered Michael saying, when they entered Russia, that customs officials knew that Americans always said something or smiled whenever they were confronted by authorities —police or bureaucrats or customs officials. Cherniak had been well briefed. Nathan looked back. He saw a crowd of officers. He saw them examining Cherniak's passport. He saw Cherniak's face, above the others. Cherniak stared ahead proudly. Cherniak inclined his head toward Nathan, as if urging Nathan to move forward. Nathan could not move. He saw policemen coming down the aisle toward them. They spoke with the customs officers. They moved very deliberately. They spoke to Cherniak. Cherniak stared down at them. He said nothing. His face seemed to glow slightly. He turned away and walked in the opposite direction, back toward the departure lounge, with the police. Other men and women were still passing through customs. Had any of them noticed?

Nathan felt, to his surprise, relieved. He had been right. The scheme was too impossible, too naïve. "Are you all right?" One of the American women, from the tour, was speaking to him.

"I'm out of breath," Nathan said.

"Where did they take your nephew?"

"They want to check his luggage more carefully," Nathan said.

"These Russians!" the woman said, and she laughed.

These Russians, Nathan thought. He saw a man running toward him. Nathan's eyes would not focus. Everything was blurred. The man was arguing with the officials. Then they were all laughing together. The man showed them a book and the officials let him pass. They seemed to be warning him, but good-naturedly. The man approached Nathan. It was Gronsky.

His smile was broader and more hideous than ever. He clapped Nathan on the shoulder, as if he were an old friend. He was acting, Nathan knew, for the benefit of the customs officers. "Everything will be all right, my friend," he said through his smile. "You will see. I promise. Everything will be all right for Michael. He will be the victim of a plot. He brought a hypodermic and drugs. At this minute he is fast asleep, in Cherniak's bed. He is happy. He does not know yet."

Nathan said nothing. He wondered why Gronsky was talking to him, why Gronsky was bothering to tell him such things. Gronsky leaned forward, still smiling, as if to embrace Nathan. Nathan's hand shot out, and the flat of his palm struck Gronsky's chest. "No!" Nathan said. "*Never!*" The rage rose in him like venom. He breathed in rapidly, through his nostrils. He glared at Gronsky, murderously.

"We had to try," Gronsky said. "It was Michael's idea in the first place, and we thought it was worth a try. We thought there was a chance that it might succeed. Really. We thought there was a good chance it could succeed. Do you believe me? Do you believe me, Nathan?"

Nathan turned and walked. He did not look back. At the door to the airplane, a customs officer stopped him and asked him, politely, if he could examine the contents of Nathan's shoulder bag. Nathan gave the man his bag. The man looked inside. He took out an envelope that Nathan did not recognize, and opened it. On the first sheet of paper were typed the words *The Stolen Jew*, and Nathan's name. The officer looked at Nathan, questioningly. Nathan reached into the shoulder bag and brought out a copy of the Russian edition, which he knew would be there. He showed the book to the officer and showed the officer his name. The officer looked at the book and at the manuscript and at Nathan's passport. Then he smiled, with what seemed to Nathan to be genuine happiness, and carefully slipped the manuscript pages back into the envelope. He said that he was honored to have met a true American author. He said that he had read books by William Saroyan and Jack London and Mark Twain and Mayne Reid. Did Nathan know William Saroyan, who was still alive? Nathan said that he did not. The officer bowed his head slightly. He wished Nathan a good journey.

Nathan found a seat on the plane. He heard music and chattering. His shirt was drenched. He saw the shards, of the blue-and-white dish, on Rachel's floor. He tried not to hear Gronsky's voice. Promises, he thought. And more promises. Like broken dishes. He sat and closed his eyes. A woman noticed that he was sitting by himself. She asked him where Michael was. Nathan smiled easily. Michael had decided to stay awhile longer, Nathan said, as a guest of the Soviet government. He was investigating their psychiatric hospitals, for a study he was working on.

The woman nodded, as if impressed. Nathan gave the same answer to all the others who asked him about Michael.

FOUR

HOME

◇ 13 ◇

Nathan did not want to go to Florida. He did not want to look at palm trees or swimming pools or condominiums or retired Jews. He had been to Florida once, seven years before, to visit Rivka and Harvey. He had stayed with them after Pauline's death, in their two-bedroom apartment in Century Village. He had slept on their screened-in patio. He had walked with them across the village's lawns. He had sat with them and listened to them talk with their friends.

Nathan stared into the darkness of the airplane. He listened to the drone of the jet engines. Beside him, to his left, Mr. and Mrs. Stein slept. Nathan did not know what time it was. Their airplane had been grounded for thirteen hours in Helsinki, and all the tourists had complained to one another, proudly, of their fatigue. Nathan did not feel at all tired; he felt, in fact, exceptionally alert. It was as if he could not imagine ever falling asleep again. He could see paddleboats and sailboats drifting around a lake. The lake, man-made, was in Century Village. It surrounded an island on which the village's clubhouse sat. The clubhouse was an enormous two-story colonial-style building that serviced the needs of the village's fifteen thousand senior citizens. The golden years, Nathan thought. He saw the trams lined up, side by side, in front of the clubhouse. He could hear Rivka blabbering to him about how marvelous Century Village was, how busy people kept themselves, without jobs and without children. Sewing clubs, musical groups, Talmud classes, folk dancing, *Mah-Jongg*, canasta, chess, yoga, theater groups, exercise clubs, Hadassah, golf . . . the list was endless. In Century Village, Rivka had said to him, every day is Sunday. The golden years.

Still, Nathan had decided, if Rachel were there, he would go to her. He would walk with her through the village's streets and across its footbridges, and they would sit together on its benches and stare at the identical two-story houses—at the tile roofs, the louvered windows, the lawns; at the flowering plants, the ducks, the canals—and they would talk with one another. They would visit with Leah and Raymond and Rivka and Harvey. They would watch the long lines of senior citizens, on their oversize tricycles, their safety flags fluttering in the breeze, and they would speculate about Michael's fate. In Century Village, Harvey had said, keeping in shape is a way of life. What, Nathan wondered, could such a sentence mean? He thought of Mandelstam, in the loft of his concentration camp, wild-eyed, reciting his poems to criminals by candlelight. Keeping in shape is a way of life.

When Nathan thought of Century Village, it seemed to him, in prospect, more awful than Moscow. Nathan thought of Cherniak, walking away, between the policemen. He thought of Lipavsky's father, in his wheelchair. He thought of the others, dancing around the table. Perhaps there would be a Russian Jewish family in Century Village, brought there by the village's synagogue. Perhaps he and Rachel would become friends with them. A Russian Jewish family in America would be living examples of what the life of the Jew—the wandering Jew of fact and of legend—had been like the world over, for most of recorded history. Strangers in a strange land. American Jews, privileged and sheltered, knew little of what this life had been like. It was their rare and good fortune to have been brought to the shores of the United States, or to have been born there, and to be living in what Nathan knew was one of the Golden Ages of Judaism. To be an American Jew during the fourth quarter of the twentieth century was to be free, as a Jew and as a citizen, as few Jews had ever been.

Why, then, Nathan wondered, did Century Village exist? Had God withdrawn into Himself to make room for Century Village? Why were all these thousands of old Jews living in a clean and modern walled city, cut off from their children and their grandchildren, cut off from the places in which they had been born and had lived for most of their lives? Nathan sniffed in. He knew the answers, of course. He knew that Century Village was better than apartments with triple locks, in decaying cities. Still, he wondered why there had been no alternatives. He knew that if he journeyed to Florida, he would, as he had seven years before, find the smiling faces of these old Jews unbearable. He thought of their tanned and wrinkled faces, their painted hair, their red lips and brightly colored clothing, their loud voices, and he cringed.

He opened the envelope and looked once again at the manuscript. He had read it in the airport lounge during the stopover in Helsinki. It was not, of course, his own manuscript, but was, instead, the story of a Soviet Jew—told in first-person, as a memoir—who had survived Soviet concentration camps. It was the story of a Jew who could recall each detail of each day in each camp, and yet could not recall the simple, and terrible, details of his childhood, of his life before the camps. Was the story Alexander Cherniak's memoir?—or was it an invention? Nathan could not tell. There were five tissue-thin pages inserted within the manuscript, written in Russian. Nathan would deliver the manuscript, with these pages, to the National Conference on Soviet Jewry. Michael had not succeeded in getting Alexander Cherniak out of the Soviet Union, but perhaps Nathan had succeeded in bringing with him Cherniak's story, a story that would now belong to all people. Perhaps the five pages contained information that would free many Cherniaks. Nathan saw Michael telling him and Ruth the story of Lazer Kominsky. He wanted to laugh, but did not.

He recalled the time Nachman had asked him to take a bag of laundry home for him, from the hospital. Nathan had brought the bag home, and had not looked at it for two days. Then he had emptied it. At the bottom, with the underwear and socks, was Nachman's straitjacket. Nathan had smiled. The message was clear: If Nachman was sending his straitjacket home, then he himself was sure to follow. Nachman had come home two weeks later. But Cherniak would not follow. Of that Nathan was certain.

Nathan wondered if Alexander Cherniak really had a brother. He had meant to ask him, but there had not been enough time, and he had, at the airport, been too nervous to remember. Was Michael's arm really broken? How much had Sonya been told? Had Michael and Gronsky known all along that their scheme would not work—had it all been, merely, a diversionary tactic that was part of some larger scheme? Surely Michael and Gronsky and Cherniak and the others had not gone through all their efforts merely to ensure the smuggling out of the manuscript Nathan held in front of him. How had Michael known the outlines of

Cherniak's story before he left America? Did Gronsky really have buyers for Nathan's manuscripts? Had the authorities allowed the exchange merely to have more evidence against Cherniak? Nathan believed that he would never know the answers to his questions, and the truth, he realized, was that this did not displease him. Was Gronsky really Gronsky? Did it matter?

Nathan looked out the window and saw nothing. His own manuscripts were still in Gronsky's apartment, full of the same errors the book had contained forty years before. Then, only reviewers in Yiddish newspapers and Jewish periodicals had mentioned them. They had been generous to Nathan—they had assumed that he had altered facts, not out of carelessness or ignorance, but because he was free to do so, because he was writing fiction, not history. But why had they been so kind to him, so gentle? Whom had he really fooled? They had not even named all the book's errors; they had never suggested to the world that its author was a fraud.

Publish or perish. Even while Nachman was locked inside a hospital, behind an iron door, Nathan's book was being praised, his errors were being ignored or discounted. Had the world turned upon him then, and accused him of profiting because he lied and schemed and cared as little for others as he did for the truth, would he have survived? If only Gronsky were right, he thought. If only Nathan's Russia had been, fully, a Russia of the imagination. He closed his eyes. The list of errors was there, inside the darkness. There were no real pogroms in Russia, as Jews came to know them, between the years 1650 and 1881. The Kehilla was abolished by Nicholas the First in 1844, yet Mendel was snatched by the *khappers* in 1852. The dates concerning Haskala authors such as Abraham Mapu and Isaac Baer Levinsohn and Menassah ben Porat were incorrect. Mapu was born in 1808, so that Tsvi could not have read his books when Tsvi was a child. Porat had not written the kinds of books Tsvi claimed he did. Levinsohn was not even a novelist. Gordon's famous *Awake My People* was written in 1863, yet Tsvi quoted him in 1852. The Jews were banished from Moscow in 1891, not in 1881. There were never midnight expulsions from Kiev. Noah's career was implausible—few Jews played the violin until the very end of the century, and few if any violinists until Ysaye, the Belgian, employed vibrato. Why had Nachman never corrected him?

And where in his book—this book that others claimed to love—were the names of trees and the passages of seasons and a feeling for what the villages and landscape truly looked like? *To share a wealth of knowledge is a beautiful thing; to sell a meager stock of it is unworthy.* The truth, Nathan now saw, was that he knew more about coats and buttons and interlinings and money than he knew about Russia. The truth was that he still wished he could know all the things that were in his father's books. The truth was that he still envied his father his knowledge the way he envied Nachman his flights of fantasy and his ability to become lost in his music, to find some peace there. If he were granted another lifetime, he thought, he would wish to spend it in learning Russian and Yiddish and Hebrew, in reading all his father's books, in reading the great multivolume histories and studies by Graetz and Dubnow and Baron and Wolfson.

Mrs. Stein stirred. Her hand moved to the armrest, next to Nathan's elbow. Nathan thought of Rachel's hand, on the belt of her bathrobe. He thought of the passage, in the manuscript he was bringing home with him, in which, in Kolyma, the Jew chops off his frozen toes in order to prevent gangrene. He saw his mother, smiling at him. He saw his father, asking his mother's forgiveness. He saw himself, standing in the doorway and holding Nachman's hand. The two boys watched while their father tried to show their mother just how much he loved her. Momma and Poppa had fought. Now they would make up. Nathan's father began kissing Nathan's mother, on the neck and then the cheeks. Nathan's mother's body grew rigid, her face turned to stone. When his father kissed her on the lips, she stared ahead and did not move.

What Nathan was feeling, he realized, was that writers such as Baron and Wolfson could have spent entire lives trying, so very slowly, to find out what truly happened for no other reason than because that was what they truly wanted to do. They loved their work, Nathan thought, in a way that he himself had never loved anything. His mother had loved him for what he could do, early on—for his talents, his success—but she had loved Nachman for what he was. Nathan nodded. He was right to have said so to Nachman. He knew that much with certainty. Baron and Wolfson and Dubnow and Graetz—the knowledge these men possessed existed in their books, but when they were dead, where, Nathan wondered, would one ever find the knowledge that enabled them to write those books? Nathan tried to imagine Nachman—he tried to see Nachman's glistening eyes, his sweet smile. He wanted to have a conversation with Nachman. He wanted Nachman to look at him, again, with awe and with love and with trust. Nathan could not see Nachman. He could not hear his voice. He wanted Nachman to look at him—just once more—the way he did on all those nights when, on their bed in their room, they would sit together, cross-legged, facing each other, and Nathan would read to Nachman the chapter of *The Stolen Jew* he had just finished writing.

Everyone else in the house would be asleep. What happens next? Nachman would always ask eagerly when Nathan was done. It wasn't fair, Nachman would say, that you know what will happen tomorrow, and that I have to wait. But I don't know, Nathan would tell him. That's what makes it so beautiful for me also. I don't know. Well, Nathan thought. Nachman was dead. Nachman was dead. There was still music in the world—the same music Nachman had played—but the knowledge of that music, the knowledge that rested in Nachman's fingers, that had died with him.

What did it mean, then, to truly know something? He wished that Michael were beside him, to help answer the question. He wished that his father were beside him. He wished that Ira were there. Hadn't he known, though, what Noah and Tsvi and Mirsky and Esther felt? Hadn't he known what he felt when he listened to Nachman play? Hadn't he known how much he felt when he saw his father's books in the rain, or when he saw Nachman in Mr. Langenauer's arms? Hadn't he known that Michael should not have gone to Russia? He closed his eyes. His questions hardly comforted him. Michael was in Moscow. Cherniak was in Moscow. Rachel was in Florida. Ruth and the children were on Long Island. And he was on a Russian plane, somewhere over the Atlantic Ocean, with 180 sleeping Americans. He knew little, and he understood less. He wanted to be home, with somebody to take care of him and to comfort him and to answer all his questions. He wanted to be able to rest. He had no secrets left, though. What, then, when he saw Rachel and Ruth, would he have to give to them? What would he have to give to them, he wondered, other than the story of what had actually happened. Would they want more?

NATHAN PASSED THROUGH CUSTOMS AND WALKED TOWARD THE PASSENGER terminal. He would go to Florida. He would stay at Kennedy Airport and get a plane for Florida. There was no reason to visit the house in Brooklyn, or to stay on in New York. He would go to Florida and tell

Rachel what had happened, and they could send for Ruth and the children. Nathan sensed that Ruth would not be surprised.

Mr. and Mrs. Stein shook Nathan's hand. Mrs. Stein handed Nathan a piece of paper with their address and phone number in Philadelphia. They told Nathan that their trip had been a great success. They had delivered their goods. They had brought back messages. They had made arrangements for the dates and times at which certain telephone calls would be made. They told Nathan to give their regards to Michael, when Michael returned. They walked away.

Other passengers shook Nathan's hand. Why were they all so happy? Leah and Raymond might be pleased, he thought; he and Michael had, at least, not returned in the same plane. Nathan carried his suitcase and shoulder bag and walked into the passenger terminal. He saw bright lights and smiling faces. He was in America. He saw crowds of Americans behind the roped-off area, laughing and waving and shouting. He saw couples embracing. He wondered which passengers were carrying back items for Michael. He wondered if they knew what to do with the items. He wondered what day it was. He wondered how many hours it had been since he had left Moscow, and whether Michael was still asleep. What were they doing with Cherniak?

"Nathan!"

Nathan stopped. He saw Rachel standing in front of him. She opened her arms and Nathan set down his suitcase and shoulder bag and stepped forward. He held her to him, as tightly as he could, and he realized, an instant later, that he had not tried to stop himself from crying. He let the tears roll down his cheeks. Rachel's warm skin was against his own. *Michael,* he thought. *My sweet nephew Michael!* He knew that Rachel knew.

He saw Ruth, holding Eli in her arms. Miriam and Aaron stood next to her, holding one another's hands. Ruth held Miriam's hand. Nathan nodded. Ruth let the children go. Nathan moved back from Rachel and bent down. Miriam and Aaron threw their arms around his neck. "Uncle Nat came home!" they cried. "Uncle Nat came home! Uncle Nat came home!"

Nathan looked up. Ruth rocked the baby in her arms and shook her head sideways. Nathan understood. He was not to say anything to the children about Michael. They all walked together, from the terminal. Nathan saw the headlights of cars and buses and taxis. He heard the sounds of horns and sirens and planes. Ruth gave Eli to Nathan, to hold while she went for the car. Rachel talked to Nathan easily, telling him that he looked good, but tired, and asking him about the flight home. Miriam and Aaron asked him questions about Russia. Aaron asked him if he had been in the cockpit with the pilots. They told him that they were angry with their father for deciding to stay in Russia longer, but that their mother had warned them that he might do something like that. Still, Aaron said, Michael had promised them that when he returned he was going to come home again, to live with them, and Aaron smiled proudly when he declared to Nathan that his father never made promises he couldn't keep.

Ruth drove up and they got into the car. Nathan sat in the front seat, with Eli. Eli slept on Nathan's lap. Nathan touched the baby's cheek. Ruth told Nathan that Eli had a slight fever—that was why his cheeks were so warm and flushed. They drove from the airport, and onto the parkway. In the back seat, Rachel talked with the children. She said that she would stay with them a while longer, and this pleased them. They called her Grandma. They asked Nathan how long he would stay with them. "I don't know," he said. They asked him if he could stay with them forever, and Rachel laughed.

When they arrived home, Ruth put the children to bed. Nathan went in to each of them and tucked them in and kissed them good night. Aaron showed Nathan his walkie-talkie, which he kept under his pillow. He said that he had talked with his father a few hours before, all the way to Russia. "Really?" Nathan asked. Aaron grinned, shook his head sideways, and told Nathan that he was only teasing.

Nathan went downstairs and sat in the family room with Ruth and Rachel. They told Nathan that they had received a telephone call five hours before, from Washington, giving them the basic story and telling them that Michael was being detained. Nathan said that his plane had been held over for thirteen hours in Helsinki. He said that he had an important manuscript to deliver to the National Conference on Soviet Jewry. There were several pages in Russian script that Nathan believed contained important secrets. Secrets? Rachel and Ruth looked at each other. Nathan leaned back, into the cushions of the couch. He told them that he had not slept at all since he had left Moscow. He did not know how many hours that amounted to. He asked them if they wanted the whole story, of what had happened to Michael. They said that they did, but that there would be time in the morning. They knew the essentials. It was late. Nathan needed to sleep. They all needed to sleep.

"It's a mess," Ruth said. "That's what they said. But they're optimistic. Whatever *that* means."

"We were both very upset," Rachel said. "But not surprised."

"Yes," Nathan said.

Ruth bent down and kissed Nathan on the cheek. "I'm glad you're home," she said. She stood. "Michael got his wish, though, right? He's a hero now."

"I don't know," Nathan said.

"Ruth," Rachel chided. "Not now. Please—"

"I am entitled to some small measure of bitterness, don't you think?"

"Please," Rachel said. "Later."

Ruth sighed. She glared at Nathan. "Did you give him my secret—to keep him company while he—"

"No," Nathan said quickly. He wanted to stand, to put his arms around Ruth. "I'm sorry. No."

"Too bad." She forced a smile. "If the secret police want to drive him crazy, that bit of news would be sure to do the trick."

"We're all tired," Rachel said. "I think we should talk more in the morning, after the children are gone to school. We'll know more then. They said they would call first thing in the morning."

"It will be early evening in Moscow," Nathan said. He smiled at the two of them. "I brought presents for the children. Can I give them their presents in the morning?"

"Sure," Ruth said.

"And for the two of you," Nathan said. "They had royalties saved for me, from my books. I used their money."

Rachel laughed. "Even in Russia he's a good businessman," she said. "Nachman would have approved."

Nathan gazed at Rachel. Was she teasing him, or mocking him? He couldn't tell. "I'll leave you two," Ruth said. "But my suggestion is that you get some sleep too. The next few weeks may be very hard on us all. We don't need to be physically exhausted too. They said that they would try to keep it out of the papers, that they thought the Russians wanted to keep this from getting international publicity—it was, in their words, one of our strongest cards. I know Michael, though, and my opinion is that they won't succeed." She smiled mechanically. "But let's decide not to worry about Michael, okay? How about us letting him worry about us for a change? Can we agree to that?"

"Go to sleep, Ruth," Rachel said. "I'll show Nathan where his room is."

"Michael always comes out on top," Ruth said. "He's very tough. He's a real survivor, Uncle Nat. Just like you."

Rachel stood and walked to Ruth. She tried to put her arms around her, but Ruth pulled away, and when she did Nathan became frightened. "Don't go!" he said. "Please don't go. I want to tell you what happened."

But Ruth was gone. Rachel spoke to Nathan and Nathan followed her to the guest bedroom. He carried his suitcase and shoulder bag. His bed was made, the covers turned back. Rachel kissed him good night, on the cheek, and said that she would see him in the morning. She hoped he slept well. He held on to her hand, but she pulled away from him easily. "In the morning," she said.

NATHAN HEARD THE SOUND OF DISHES. WERE THE CHILDREN ALREADY UP? He wanted them to have their presents before they left for school. He slipped into his bathrobe and walked downstairs, to the kitchen. Rachel was alone. She turned. She gasped. "Oh—" she said, her hand at her mouth. "You surprised me—"

"I didn't know what time it was."

"You've only been sleeping for an hour," Rachel said. She breathed out. "Less."

"And you?"

"I couldn't sleep. I'm making some tea—would you like some?"

Nathan nodded. He sat down at the kitchen table. "Is Ruth still angry?" he asked.

"She'll be all right," Rachel said. She pulled the belt of her robe to her, more tightly. Nathan stared. He remembered the softness of Rachel's pale skin, and all that he had felt. He remembered his anger, when Harvey had joked of his obligations toward Rachel. Nathan heard his father's voice. *Only the dead are free of Torah and commandments.* His mother and his father were dead. His brother was dead. His wife and son were dead. He looked out, at the endless horizon of headstones. There seemed to be nobody standing between him and his own grave. Rachel smiled down at him as she poured boiling water into a cup. She wore no makeup, and the lines around her eyes seemed wonderfully soft. He felt drowsy and numb, the way he had felt when he awoke in the upstairs room in Brooklyn to find Rachel and Michael looking down at him. Hello death, he wanted to say. How are you?

"She's right about it being a mess, but she's also right about Michael. Think of how much worse things would be if Michael had succeeded."

"*What?*" Nathan asked. Then he heard her words. "Yes," he said. He looked up at Rachel. "Do you know what she meant, about the secret she gave to me? I don't think she meant for—"

"I know," Rachel said.

"You know."

"I know about Ira and Aaron."

Nathan nodded. He lifted the cup to warm his hands. He saw Lev Cherniak, smiling broadly. *Do you like me?* "When I was a boy," Nathan said. "I used to wonder why it was my mother never left my father. My Uncle Harry had friends—bachelors, widowers—he used to bring to the house, and Momma always seemed more happy and beautiful when they were there. Her eyelid didn't sag so much. She had been a beautiful woman when she married Poppa. But what I used to wonder about —even in those days—was why she remained so true to Poppa, why in all the years she never—"

"Maybe," Rachel said, leaning toward Nathan, "it was because she knew that she could never find anyone else to degrade the way she degraded your father."

Nathan felt his heart lurch. "What?" he asked. Then he nodded. "Yes," he said. "Yes."

Rachel sat across from him. "I saved Nachman's things for you," she said. "The things he kept in his dresser. I saved them and I brought them back with me. I'm sorry I didn't show them to you in Brooklyn, but you never asked, after the first time."

"Yes," Nathan said.

"There's an old newspaper clipping, with your picture, from when your book was first published. There are some books, from your father. There's a bag of marbles. There's his extra set of *tephillin*. He saved some of your letters, and also some old letters written in Yiddish . . ."

Nathan heard the sound of Rachel's voice, but he could not hear her words. He knew that there was no point in waiting any longer. He felt very frightened, but that was all right, he decided. Nadezhda was correct. Only people beyond hope were beyond fear. Nathan looked at Rachel, and he tried to see her exactly as she was. He stopped himself from summoning up, in his mind, pictures and voices. He stopped himself from making jokes. Rachel looked very beautiful to him. She did not look at all young. The softness of her hair and her skin made Nathan feel weak. Where was Michael? Why had Rachel thrown the valentine's card back in his face?

Nathan looked at his teacup. "You don't have to break any dishes," he said.

"I don't understand," Rachel said, and her face seemed to grow larger as it moved toward him. "I don't understand," she said again, but Nathan sensed, from the way she was smiling, that she did.

Below the table, his knees were actually trembling, he realized. He felt like a very young and nervous boy. He shuddered. The four words had been in his head for weeks, he knew. For years. "Will you marry me?" he asked.

"Yes, Nathan," she said. "Yes."

ABOUT THE AUTHOR

Jay Neugeboren is the author of four highly praised novels, Big Man, Listen Ruben Fontanez, Sam's Legacy, An Orphan's Tale; *a collection of prizewinning stories,* Corky's Brother; *and a memoir,* Parentheses: An Autobiographical Journey. *He is also the editor of Martha Foley's memoir,* The Story of STORY Magazine. *His stories and articles have appeared in* The Atlantic Monthly, Esquire, Sport, TriQuarterly, Ploughshares, Commentary, The American Scholar, Parents' Magazine, Mademoiselle, *and other periodicals, and have been reprinted in several dozen anthologies. He is forty-two years old. He lives in North Hadley, Massachusetts, with his wife, the painter Betsey Neugeboren, and their three children.*